On the Barbary Coast

Alaric Bond

ISBN Paperback: 978-1-943404-40-7
ISBN E-book: 978-1-943404-39-1

Published by Old Salt Press. Old Salt Press, LLC is based in Jersey City, New Jersey with an affiliate in New Zealand. For more information about Old Salt Press titles go to www.oldsaltpress.com

* * *

Thanks to Kitty, Tessa, Joan, Rick, Antoine, Fred, Chris, Philip, Ken, Seymour, Linda, George, R&L and Bob as well as Keith, the archivist at Fort Amherst (www.fortamherst.com).

For Linda and Bob

Other novels by Alaric Bond

The Fighting Sail series
His Majesty's Ship
The Jackass Frigate
True Colours
Cut and Run
The Patriot's Fate
The Torrid Zone
The Scent of Corruption
HMS Prometheus
The Blackstrap Station
Honour Bound
Sealed Orders
Sea Trials
Lone Escort
The Seeds of War

and

Turn a Blind Eye
The Guinea Boat

The Coastal Forces series
Hellfire Corner

Contents

On the Barbary Coast

Part One

Chapter One

There had been no sight of land for several days, they had finally left Nova Scotia and King was glad to have done so. Glad also not to be lumbered with a bunch of merchants to nursemaid home; a convoy was being formed when *Tenacious* swept out of Halifax harbour, but his Commander-in-Chief had felt pity and sanctioned a solo passage. For there were more than enough reasons for him to wish for a speedy return home.

The first was sufficient in itself; his frigate had been on the North American Station for over four years with the last two spent fighting a particularly drawn-out and frustrating campaign. Time, weather and enemy action had worn *Tenacious* down and, though there were numerous patch-up jobs in the Halifax yard, she was now in need of a major overhaul. Once they made England the frigate would be taken in hand and was unlikely to see open water again for at least a year. Or possibly never, King supposed; his country was waging war on either side of the Atlantic, but both were steadily drawing to a close and soon there would be less need for warships of any description. *Tenacious* could even be making her final passage; this might be the last time she took an active part in hostilities, and King suspected the same could be said for him.

And he was not sorry. Much of his adult life had been spent fighting one nation or another and, in the twenty years or so since King first boarded a British Navy warship, there had been many changes. The most obvious of these was the loss of his left arm. The limb was removed after a wound became infected and, though many thought him quick to accommodate the loss, rarely a moment passed when he did not consider it. This was not the full extent of his injuries though, and the others were more subtle.

Yet despite this, and the fact that spring was still to arrive, making bad weather especially likely, his thoughts were not on himself, his ship or the end of either war; there were far more pressing matters to concern him. The letter had been waiting when *Tenacious* returned from their final patrol. It was one of five sent from his companion, Aimée, and the latest in date so was opened first.

This was a habit developed after his family left the American Station and returned to England the year before. He would skim through the most recent to check all was well, then enjoy the others at his leisure. But this time there were no gentle ramblings about their daughter's first words or young Robert's new tooth; both children were seriously ill.

Dread struck him in a cold wave. Immediately he opened her letter from the week before and read it with shaking hands. But there was nothing of note: their son had been helping Jed the gardener with early planting and Muffy was starting to walk and finally enjoying solid food. No mention of heightened temperatures, rashes, or any other symptoms of what was likely to be measles.

He then returned to the latest letter and read it again; in the space of seven days a good deal had happened and Aimée's shaky writing said as much as the message it conveyed. Robert was struck down first, although he seemed to be fighting the disease off, their daughter was the most affected. King remembered willing further information from the creased paper before taking it down to where Bob Manning would be reading his own post in the frigate's sick bay.

And the surgeon was reassuring – or at least he had tried to be. Manning also knew of the outbreak, a letter having arrived from Kate, his wife. And there was comfort in knowing the woman,

2

an experienced midwife, intended visiting Aimée to help care for the children. That was over a month ago; by now both should have made a full recovery – or so Manning presumed. Yet despite his friend's assurance, King could not dismiss another possible outcome.

The noise of flapping canvas caught his attention, breaking into his thoughts and awakening the seaman's brain that never stayed dormant for long. The wind, which had been agreeably on their quarter for some while, was shifting; it had backed by less than a point, although that was sufficient to slow them if adjustments were not made. He waited for several tortuous seconds yet there was no action. Summers, their third lieutenant, had the watch and King glared at the back of his head, only relaxing when a muttered command finally sent hands to the braces and order, along with the ship's full potential, was restored.

King then switched his attention to the sails, gleaming slightly in the gathering dusk, and wondered perhaps if the royals, struck a few hours before, could be replaced. Eventually he saw sense and decided not; the wind remained as strong and *Tenacious* was hardly in the best of shape. And, while he was thinking more rationally, King realised it was unfair to transfer his frustration onto Summers; the lad must be almost as keen to raise England as he was. After four years on station, the same could be said about most aboard *Tenacious,* and Summers would order an increase in canvas as soon as it was feasible.

They had been making good time so far; if luck stayed with them, England should be in sight by the end of the month although a full-blown storm could just as easily move their homecoming well into March. King's attention returned to the young lieutenant standing motionless next to the binnacle. Michael Summers first sailed with him as a raw volunteer many years before; since then, the pair had gone through much together and it was good to note he was steadily becoming the competent officer King always predicted. Yet even he had been showing signs of weariness, although Summers might have another reason.

King had agreed to the lad's new bride accompanying them home in a moment of soft heartedness, and long before receiving his own devastating news. And she turned out to be one of several; after a four-year deployment it was no surprise to discover a number of hands had struck up long-term relationships; five so-called wives had already been discovered secreted in the dark confines of the frigate's lower deck. In Summers' case the woman – who was in truth a widow and nine years older than her husband – was causing few problems yet that did not stop King wishing her gone. Even on what should be a simple run home he preferred his officers to think of nothing other than their duties and any female in the gunroom was a distraction.

The bell sounded three times. Being a dogwatch, those below should soon emerge and Summers, along with most on the quarterdeck, would retire. As could King; a captain stood no watches and might come and go as he pleased. Indeed, on such a trip many would spend their time below allowing others, doubtless equally competent, control of the ship. But King had been on deck since before the start of the previous watch and had every intention of remaining long into the night. His presence might not add a knot to their speed or a yard to their progress although, if there was a chance it would, he must take it.

"Deck there!"

The call came from the masthead and all on the quarterdeck tensed.

"There's sail to the nor-east; looks to be several; a fleet mebee..."

Summers glanced across to his captain and King gave a reassuring nod. "That will be Patterson's convoy," he told him. "We sighted them leaving on making Halifax."

"I remember, sir."

The merchants were shepherded by a handful of warships. Had *Tenacious* arrived a day or so earlier she would have been forced to join those escorts and, with a sudden stab of horror, King realised they still might.

"Take us to starboard, Mr Summers," he ordered. "I want us heading south without delay."

The lieutenant hesitated for no more than a second before seeing the frigate on a southerly course. King pursed his lips; with the wind now more on the beam they were travelling more slowly and in the wrong direction although, paradoxically, that was necessary if he wanted to make a quick passage. For some while the ship continued through the dark seas, and then King noticed Manton mounting the quarterdeck ladder. The sailing master had probably been summoned by the sudden change of heading. He

4

touched his hat to Summers, then approached his captain and saluted more formally.

"We spotted what appears to be Patterson's ships," King explained.

"And believe they might invite us to join them?" Manton had a knowing twinkle in his grey-blue eyes.

Few convoys carried sufficient escorts, so a stray frigate would be looked upon as manna from heaven. King could not tell if *Tenacious* had been spotted; if so, he might receive a mild reprimand for taking such evasive action. The prospect did not bother him greatly, however, and was surely preferable to spending the rest of the journey bound to a bunch of sluggish merchants.

"Indeed, Master. And I am eager for a fast passage."

"What of the convoy?" Summers' hail to the masthead broke into their conversation and both officers awaited an answer.

"Losing them quick, so we are," the lookout replied. "Be over the 'orizon in no time. Though there's sommat else."

Dusk was falling fast now and fresh sightings were likely to be speculative, yet the seaman's tone was reassuringly positive.

"Sail to the west – right in the sun an' with the wind on 'er tail!"

King resisted the temptation to look; the light was fast disappearing for those on deck.

"What do you make of it?" The sailing master's voice.

"'Ard to say for certain. There're tops'ls an' a for'ard t'gallant, though I'd gauge her to be a tiddler."

"Masts?" Manton again.

"Heading right for us, but I'd say no more'n two. Mebee a brig or the likes; she's closin' fast so must be goin' a rare old pace."

Despite the gloom, King and the sailing master exchanged glances.

"A drop out from the convoy do you think, sir?"

"It's possible, though why, when she is moving so?"

"Maybe they needed repair," the older man mused. "Or p'raps she's a runner?"

Private ships that could show a good turn of speed or were exceptionally well armed might be granted licence to make a crossing separately.

"Again unlikely; the next convoy was due to leave in a

5

matter of days; it would take some urgent business to make any master opt for an independent course even this late in the war."

"In that case, I suppose there is only one other option, sir," Manton said.

"Indeed," King agreed. "She must be an American raider."

* * *

Below, in the gunroom that served as *Tenacious'* wardroom, her off-duty senior officers were at rest. At the head of the dining table Cooper, the frigate's first lieutenant, was deeply engrossed in yet another book while further down, Heather, the purser, and Woodward, their second officer, had joined the two marine lieutenants to make a four at cards. Manning, the surgeon, sat at the foot and was also reading while Woods, a naval chaplain who had sought passage to England, was dozing by the pantry entrance in the only upholstered chair. Apart from the slap of cards and an occasional grunt from the players, there was an amicable silence that suited all, including the only woman present.

She was in her middle thirties and attractive in a motherly way, with tightly curled hair and a comfortable figure. She also sat at the dining table, in what had become her customary spot: between the surgeon and the card players but not too close to either. For Suzie Summers did not socialise easily and, when her husband was elsewhere, kept very much to herself.

This was not through any distinction felt or imposed upon her; she simply did not belong in such an environment and the differences went far beyond her gender. Most significantly, Suzie Summers was the only one present currently living with a spouse and the only one with the misfortune to have lost one in the past.

She had married her first husband and moved to New Brunswick ten years before and, with the little love they shared soon fading, it was then that she put on the weight. So, when he died, Suzie had only been mildly sorry. It was a selfish sadness, though; there could be little else for someone who had turned out a liar, a bully and a cheat. But, until a fellow hunter mistook him for a caribou, Suzie was only moderately unhappy: with his passing things became considerably worse.

When her scant allowance stopped and other bills,

together with far older unknown debts, appeared, she had little choice other than to return to her parents, still thankfully living in Halifax. For a while she was safe, if forcibly contrite – her mother had never cared for her choice of husband and delighted in repeating the fact. Then a group of unofficial debt collectors caught her scent and made everything just that little bit more horrible.

Michael Summers came to the rescue. She met the young lieutenant by chance when an errant hackney carriage sent her sprawling into the dirt of George Street: something that turned out to be the kindest of favours. And Summers changed everything. After a failed marriage, widowhood and several months of living with her mother, his sunny disposition, quiet competence and youthful energy attracted her more than any syrup pudding.

And there was no confrontation with the debt collectors one sight of a Navy uniform in attendance being enough to send them scurrying, and Suzie felt herself blossom under such protection. Within five months, a period which – due to Michael's duty – amounted to ten days in each other's company, the pair became engaged and were married before Christmas. And now they were heading to England, a strange and daunting prospect for one whose previous move from Nova Scotia had ended so disastrously. England remained Michael's home, however, so she was determined to make it hers. And with the prospect of peace in Europe, she was equally keen for him to say goodbye to the sea and remain with her. His prize money was considerable and would set them up in a small business, or they could simply enjoy a few years of leisure while she accustomed herself to life in a different world.

A different world and with a man who genuinely cared for her, one who would never stray, never betray and give nothing other than support; such fortune rarely fell upon a woman past her thirtieth year. In time they would become established; a retired naval officer and his lady which was more than she ever expected and, as Suzie freely admitted, more than she probably deserved.

A clatter from outside made them all look up, then the door flew open and a windswept midshipman blew in.

"Beggin' your pardon, gentlemen – madam," he said, snatching off his hat, "there's somethin' about on deck. Masthead's reported a sightin' and Captain's callin' for Mr Cooper an' Mr Woodward's attendance."

7

Instantly the calm was shattered and, even after those called had departed, an air of tension remained. Though not with Suzie, she returned to her needlework without a second thought. Michael was already on deck, and Michael could make anything right.

* * *

The more King considered the matter the more convinced he became; the sighting must have been trailing the convoy. And now they were deeper into the Atlantic, far away from support though close enough to the American coast to see a capture safely home, this was the ideal time to snap one of the merchants up. Patterson's force was limited to two frigates and a handful of smaller stuff with a stately, yet almost useless, liner as his flag. Well handled, a small warship could cause true havoc amongst the sixty or so traders and, in an agreeably murky night, should easily bag a prize.

King stared back over the taffrail; the darkness was complete now, even their masthead had lost the sun and he only held the vaguest idea of the convoy's position, let alone the tiny vessel preparing to prey on it. However, *Tenacious* lay between them both and, while she remained so, there was every chance of diverting an attack.

The new watch had been called; James Woodward, the frigate's new second lieutenant, now had the deck although both Manton and Summers remained. And Jack Cooper was with them also, standing alongside, silent but attentive, like any good first officer. King turned to him.

"I believe her to be a raider," he said. "And feel we should take a hand."

"You wish to intercept, sir?"

It had long been accepted that, once their captain initiated conversation, it was acceptable to reply – only uncalled for comments raised King's ire.

He nodded. "Should our friend turn out to be a Jonathan it would not look well that we let him pass."

It was one thing to avoid supplementing a convoy's escort force, quite another to do nothing and expose it to certain danger.

8

"Though she might not be an American," Cooper suggested. "And the night is dark, it may be hard to check, especially as she is likely to have the heels of us."

King considered this; there was nothing he would have liked more than to ignore the sighting; with the convoy now invisible, they might resume their previous course and continue to make for England, home and Aimée. But he had been a fighting officer for much of his life, and the thought of a potential enemy within reach was simply too hard to resist.

"I am aware of that, Jack, yet feel we should try. Prepare to take us about, Mr Manton." He paused to clear his throat. Then added, "And clear for action if you please."

* * *

Captain King's tone had been soft, although the task would be anything but, and Cooper immediately quit the quarterdeck to supervise. At the start of the commission, when he was her second officer, turning *Tenacious* into a true ship of war had been a complex business that could be positively dangerous; more than a few bruises, bumps and scrapes were caused even during daylight exercise. Yet despite the dark, and her worn condition, there was little wrong with the frigate's current crew. The past four years had seen them sent to quarters countless times and then often into the heat of action. And just because *Tenacious* was homeward bound, with most aboard her soon to quit the sea for good, their duties remained ingrained, and Cooper knew they could be trusted.

The galley fire – at that point in the day little more than ashes and embers – was dumped over the side, preventer stays and additional slings were rigged aloft and the temporary bulkheads that gave a modicum of privacy, heartlessly broken down. So practised were they that all was carried out with just the occasional shout, the rumble of feet or a squeal of gun trucks to break the silence and having night now fully upon them only added spice to their work.

And some appeared unusually keen; when *Tenacious* left Halifax the inference had been her war, and theirs, would soon be over. Recent land victories had finally punctured the bubble of Napoleon's invincibility, and a conflict that began more than twenty years before finally looked like ending. Then there was the American War, the one they had more recently been fighting; a piecemeal conflict that often meant firing on men who, if not brothers, shared the same language. That was also coming to a close; the Johnathan's initial success in single-ship duels had been short lived and what remained of their navy was now heavily blockaded leaving only privateers to pose any form of maritime threat. For most on *Tenacious'* lower deck this would mean the end of their time at sea, a life that was likely to have been inflicted upon them although, even for the most reluctant, one they had come to accept. Some might actually view the prospect of living ashore, and in a world free from strife, with caution so it would come as a relief to find that, once more and possibly for the last time, they were to be put to the test.

Cooper also accepted it may be *Tenacious'* last battle but was far more circumspect. This was in no way due to a reluctance to fight, however. He was an experienced officer; in addition to seeing a deal of naval action, he had also fought his way home from a French gaol. And their current opponent appeared little more than a brig: *Tenacious,* with her batteries of eighteen- and thirty-six-pounders, would handle her with ease. What worried him most was his captain.

He knew Tom King of old and felt they were as close as was possible, considering their differences in rank. Certainly, an understanding had built up between them. And he could be both moody and unpredictable while his approach to commanding a ship was at the least unique. There could be no doubting his skill as a captain, though; impulsive or not, Cooper and his fellow officers held nothing other than respect for the man while the lower deck regarded him with a mixture of admiration and reverence. It was only that damned letter that had brought on such a change.

The news was terrible, of course, so any first officer would anticipate the worst from his captain. And in King's case he expected it to bring on an excess of referred energy; perhaps sudden and strict regimes of exercise for the crew or the ship regularly pressed beyond her normal boundaries. In his rush to be home it would have been no surprise to see a dangerous excess of canvas ordered, or other foolish risks inappropriate in a vessel in need of repair. But Cooper was wrong; instead, the man had retreated into himself which was every bit as troubling.

Since leaving harbour King had barely left the quarterdeck, and though he often sailed the ship to the limit he did not overstep it. Yet, now that the smallest of threats had appeared, he was beginning to display a particular form of recklessness that could be equally dangerous.

Tackling a raider in the dark might be a trifling matter, especially when the enemy in question would be inferior in strength, but there was still doubt as to the vessel's identity. Rather than the privateer King supposed, she might as easily have been a Dane, a Spaniard or even British. There was a myriad of reasons why such craft could be so placed and travelling as fast, yet King seemed convinced of only one, and it didn't help that Manton had encouraged him so.

With darkness and the disparity in speed, there would be little chance to discuss the matter; *Tenacious* must shoot first and identify later. To Cooper's mind peace and an honourable retirement was finally in sight, and he was reluctant to take chances. It would only need one well-placed broadside to account for such a vessel and probably a good many of her people; were she then discovered to be a neutral – or worse – it would be an unfortunate end to all their careers.

* * *

Tenacious had turned and was coming back on a more northerly course with the wind comfortably over her larboard quarter. There was no moon, nor would there be for several hours, and only feeble light from a handful of stars although the sea itself gave a phosphorus glow bright enough to reflect in her canvas.

"Little point in darkening ship," Woodward, the second officer, grumbled noticing this. "Americans'll see us a mile off."

"If she is an American," Summers said.

"Captain seems to think so." Woodward's voice was low as the great man stood close by.

Summers shrugged. "In that case she must be."

Woodward glanced up to the masts as if doing so might encourage their lookouts, then turned back to his friend and was about to speak when a call finally came from above.

"Deck there, I have her!"

A bunch of hands in the waist began to babble excitedly. "Silence!" the master at arms grunted.

"Where away?" Woodward this time.

"Off our larboard bow and coming up fast." It was Vernon, who had been sent aloft to supplement their duty lookout.

"Will we catch her?" the captain demanded from further aft.

"I'd say so, sir," the midshipman replied.

Woodward's eyes returned to Summers; the pair were almost the same age and only a marginally earlier commission marked Woodward as the senior man. "Won't make a deal of difference either way," he murmured. "The old girl's carrying all the canvas she can handle."

Summers was not so sure but held his peace. Woodward had only joined the ship a week before her last patrol; he had still to fully experience their captain's occasional bouts of enthusiasm.

"Mr Woodward, I'd be obliged if you would take up your station with the great guns."

King's voice came from close behind; he must have crept up on them and the shock, mixed with guilt, made both lieutenants jump. With a final glance to Summers, Woodward stole silently away.

"Looks like we'll be seeing action after all, Michael," King said when he had gone.

"Yes, sir," Summers agreed.

"We should be able to make her out at any time," Cooper said, joining them.

The three officers peered out into the night; it was just as dark and, with *Tenacious* travelling at speed, hard to focus on one specific area. Yet if Vernon had her in sight, and she was as fast as he claimed, their prey should be closing on them.

"There she is!" Summers exclaimed, pointing further to the west than his seniors had been searching. Cooper grabbed at the deck glass, focussed, and then passed it over to Summers with a grunt.

"You'd better look," he snorted. "Younger eyes and all that..."

Summers took the telescope, and all waited while he studied.

"She's a Baltimore Clipper," he said at last, and there was a distinct sigh from King. An American-built craft made his guess more likely, although still not certain – plenty such vessels had been captured in the past two years and some were regularly used for crossings.

"And making a fair speed in the current wind," Summers continued. "I'd say close to ten knots, maybe more."

The last cast had shown *Tenacious* to be travelling at a little under six. There were currents to be taken into consideration of course, and the wind might change but, yes, they should be able to head the sighting off. Only one question remained, was she an American?

* * *

James Woodward joined *Tenacious* less than three months before and was yet to see action, let alone fire his guns in anger. More than that, in his previous posting – his first as a commissioned officer – he was the junior lieutenant in a line-of-battleship, a position that attracted far more mundane duties. However, as *Tenacious'* second officer, he had overall responsibility for her main armament; the long eighteens that provided the frigate's rate and formed a major part of her broadside, as well as the heavier, shorter range, carronades further aft. Even the two six-pound chasers mounted forward fell under his control. Which was all well and good although, in contrast to many about him, Woodward had limited experience with ships' artillery.

And he could have wished for better conditions on his debut – a night engagement with a small, fast-moving target, was hardly ideal. But Woodward was a conscientious officer who had studied this new discipline and now considered himself reasonably informed – in the theory at least. He had also exercised the men well. During his short time aboard there had been numerous drills and, despite these being as much for his benefit as the hands', he still felt confident of putting up a reasonable show.

There would be little honour to be earned of course; Baltimore Clippers were known for their speed and manoeuvrability. *Tenacious* could hardly stay within range for

13

long; he would have minutes, possibly less, to disable his opponent.

And it must be done neatly: stop her with the least possible fuss. With such disparity in power, the clipper would be easy to destroy, though doing so would hardly make him popular. A sound prize with her cargo intact and suitable for sale was what everyone wanted and must bring the greatest return. Yet equally he could not let her escape, for that would be shameful indeed.

"Guns are currently loaded with round," Daniels, the gunnery midshipman informed him when Woodward took up his station in the waist. "Shall I order them to be drawn and reloaded with bar?"

Woodward shook his head. "No, they may remain as they are."

Despite the darkness, he could not miss the look of disapproval on the young man's face. Midshipman Daniels was an unpleasant fellow who never tired of reminding everyone of his good connections. With an established father and high-ranking relatives infesting both forces, the lad was destined for greater things. And – just as disconcerting to Woodward – he was also more experienced with the great guns, something that would normally have made him the ideal junior but in Daniels' case did not.

"Round shot will have the better reach," Woodward added, "and I have no wish to draw them now, not when we will be in action shortly."

"Maybe after the first broadside?" Daniels persisted. "Reload with bar?"

"You will call me sir," Woodward hissed, and the midshipman had the grace to look abashed.

"Beg pardon, sir," he said, yet this was mere lip service; whatever the actual difference in their ranks, Daniels plainly considered himself superior.

Which in some ways, he was – or soon would be. There was bound to be an examination board on their return to England; Daniels would be up before it and likely to sail through. Once a lieutenant, they would be of equal rank, the only advantage being Woodward's slightly earlier commission date, although that would disappear once the cove was promoted to commander. Which, if he had anything like the support supposed, was extremely likely.

14

Woodward found the thought of having Daniels as his senior officer highly distasteful, especially as he had the knack of often being right.

And this was a case in point; bar shot was certainly more effective against an enemy's rigging but had a shorter reach so would prove useless if this remained a long-range engagement. The chances of *Tenacious* closing to the extent that bar was called for were small, yet they remained.

Fear of the enemy escaping still hung about the young lieutenant; such a thing would be embarrassing, and doubly so if his choice of shot were to blame. Should that happen, Daniels would doubtless inform everyone his advice had been ignored.

"No," he repeated firmly. "We shall continue with round."

"Very good, sir," Daniels replied, ever the dutiful deputy. "As long as you're sure..."

* * *

Now the clipper was in clear sight from the deck; she lay off their larboard bow and somewhat less than a mile away. Meanwhile, *Tenacious* was closing rapidly; King sensed if he handled her correctly they would get in at least one broadside before the tiny craft was swallowed by the night.

"Stubborn little blighter," Cooper said, then, realising he had spoken out of turn, looked away as if to defuse any comment. However, his captain was in an unusually affable mood.

"She is determined to make for the convoy," he agreed.

"Yes, sir. Though she would not know it to be there."

King turned sharply.

"What do you mean, Mr Cooper?"

The first officer flustered for a moment. "When initially spotted, Patterson's ships were only just in sight," he said, "so they would have been invisible to our friend."

"But an American would know of the convoy."

"Of their existence, perhaps, not that they were so close." Once more Cooper appeared to be regretting having started the conversation. "And the chase is holding her course; she has not tried to avoid us."

"Avoid us?"

15

"We may not be certain of her nationality, though she will have little doubt of ours."

"They declined to answer our private signal," King pointed out. "And are showing no ensign."

"No, sir, but she is a tiddler and may be poorly manned. Such mistakes might be down to the inexperience of the officer of the watch."

"What are you saying, Jack?"

Cooper swallowed. "I mean the clipper's captain appears confident we will do them no harm, sir."

"So, you still don't believe her to be an American?"

"No, sir."

King searched for the truth in Cooper's words. Any vessel that came within the reach of a warship at night was taking a risk, although this one did seem confident of not being fired upon. Without an ensign, the principle means of identification was her performance, and that suggested a friend or at least one from a neutral country. He considered the craft again; she was cutting through the waves, a thing of beauty yet desperately frail. *Tenacious'* broadside could turn her to dust in an instant. And there would be no time to stop to ask questions; slowing would guarantee her escape and King had no intention of allowing that. Patterson's convoy was a large one, a determined raider would find it with ease and cause mayhem.

"Perhaps we might chance a shot across her bows, sir?" Cooper was being greatly daring.

"No," King snapped. "There is not time; I think her American." He turned to the sailing master. "Be ready to take us to starboard, Mr Manton." Then, in a bellow, "Prepare the larboard battery, Mr Woodward – I want that tophamper down!"

Chapter Two

"She's turning!"

But King had seen the signs before Manton's warning. The clipper's canvas fluttered as her helm was put across, then, almost in an instant, she was steering a more northerly course to prevent *Tenacious* from crossing her bows. The move meant the annoying little craft could even rake his own ship in time, should King permit such an indignity. Cooper may be right, the other captain might just be bold, or foolish; certainly he was risking much on his vessel's speed and agility. Yet rather than clear up any confusion, the recent change of course simply added to it – was this the move of an enemy avoiding action, or simply the prudence of a friend? King still sensed the former and his instincts rarely failed him. And then he lost patience; there was a lot on his mind, he had no room for fools pretending to be raiders. The time had come to end this nonsense.

"Port the helm – take her five points to starboard!"

Then, as the sleek vessel crept into his guns' arc of fire, he bellowed again.

"As your weapons bear, Mr Woodward!"

It would be long-range though still under a mile and strange if at least one important hit were not made on that fragile tophamper. Which was all they needed, he told himself; carry away a spar or two, maybe even down a mast and she would be theirs.

All on the quarterdeck waited, the only noise was the hum of wind in the lines and a muttering of gun captains as they targeted their weapons. Then *Tenacious* completed the turn and, with a spluttering broadside, she spoke.

There was scant chance of following the shot in such conditions and, as the barrage would have been aimed high, no telltail splashes revealed how well it was laid. For a moment all in the British frigate hung in expectation. And then the terrible truth began to dawn; the enemy's rigging was undamaged.

King stepped forward to the break of the quarterdeck and

stared down. His larboard gunners were already hard at work reloading their pieces while Woodward and his midshipman seemed inordinately enthralled in their efforts. A voice from behind made him turn.

"Target is turning to stay with us, sir."

It was Cooper. The first officer had followed him and was looking out to larboard where the clipper was now broadside on and keeping pace. Or maybe not, maybe she was gaining, which was to be expected considering her rig and size. Yet there remained a chance, a faint one perhaps, that *Tenacious* might be allowed another try.

King was about to reply when something else caught his attention. A faint prick of red issued briefly from the clipper's side and then seemed to run along her hull: the blighter was firing back!

Such a craft was unlikely to be carrying anything heavier than six-pounders yet the hands still gave a murmur of derision when no shot struck. And in King's case the relief was greater, for now there could be no doubt they were truly facing an enemy.

Cooper was saying something else, although King was too engrossed to listen. Woodward's men were still more than a minute away from having their guns ready, but it would take far longer to manoeuvre and allow their unused starboard battery into play. Besides, it seemed unlikely the clipper would simply hold her course and so it proved.

Again, she turned and, again, turned quickly; in little more than the blink of an eye, the clipper was heading north once more and presenting her stern. King measured the distance in his mind; now it would be long range indeed, especially as he still intended to merely wing the beast. He glanced down; one gun captain was raising his hand and two more quickly followed. And there was Woodward: the man had moved between two cannon and hitched himself onto the bulwark for a better view. And then *Tenacious* spoke again.

This time King thought he caught sight of a shot, though it may have been an illusion. But there was no doubting the broadside was better laid. The clipper's foreroyal split into ribbons and, almost simultaneously, her main topgallant mast began to fall.

"Bring her back to larboard!"

18

King's words must have been anticipated as Manton was already issuing orders and soon *Tenacious* was on the same heading as her wounded prey. The clipper was in a sorry state, tangled remains from the upper main hung in a muddle of wood, line and canvas; only the foretopsail and course were drawing fully, and her speed had been drastically reduced, yet still she was gamely trying for escape.

Tenacious settled quickly and started to gain; before long King would be able to pick away with his bow chasers. It remained a small target, however, and, if the Americans made good their repairs, there was still every chance the clipper would evade them. And then the unimaginable happened. Even as he watched, his opponent began to turn with the wind once more. In no time she was broadside on as *Tenacious* bore down and, when the frigate was approaching point-blank range, the clipper delivered a second broadside on her bows.

* * *

In the waist, Woodward was close to despair; there could never be a more public demonstration of his incompetence. *Tenacious'* long-reach eighteen-pounders formed a significant part of her broadside yet, with two attempts, he had failed miserably. When faced with the smallest of opponents, the best he could do was to tear a sail and knock away a single spar.

"Shouldn't we have reloaded with bar?" It was Daniels, the ever-present doubter, and despite his annoyance Woodward felt a twinge of guilt. With the range diminishing, bar was indeed becoming the logical option, although when he looked to his teams, he knew it was too late. Both shot and charge had been rammed home, all they need do was prime then haul back and the weapons would be ready to train.

"No," he said with as much assurance as he could muster. "We shall stay with round."

At that moment there was a double snap as *Tenacious'* twin chasers were despatched; the third lieutenant was firing off their light, forward-facing guns.

"Go for'ard to Mr Summers," Woodward ordered, grateful for the hint.

"Beg pardon?"

"I said go for'ard," he repeated. "Mr Summers will doubtless appreciate your advice."

The midshipman paused and for a moment Woodward thought he might disobey. But Daniels knew his limitations and stole sullenly away.

Left on his own, Woodward was little happier. *Tenacious* continued to head straight for the enemy; already she had endured one broadside from the impudent little craft with most shots striking home. One of Summers' gunners had been carried screaming below while the boatswain and his team were working to rig new lines. Woodward did not know the full extent of *Tenacious'* injuries, although it was possible a damned clipper had inflicted more mischief than his frigate's mighty long guns.

The gun captains were signalling their pieces ready, but the target was forward and beyond their arc of fire. He glanced up and aft to the quarterdeck and noted Captain King and the first lieutenant were no longer in sight; they must have retreated to the binnacle after being disappointed by his performance.

"Very well, stand down," he said, and the men around him relaxed. *Tenacious* was bound to take the clipper; anything else was inconceivable. Though it seemed the captain was no longer relying on Woodward's cannon for assistance. His chance had come and been wasted.

* * *

There was the distant rattle of another broadside from the clipper and King swore as the shots dug deep into his ship's tender prow. He had no idea why the American was stringing matters out so, but it was costing them much in time and materiel, not to mention the risk to his people. Less than a cable now separated them so it must surely end soon, then he might discover why his opponent was so determined to fight.

"Bring her to starboard and heave to," he said, and Manton ordered the wheel across; *Tenacious* speeded up momentarily, then slowed as her main was backed. King stared out at the insignificant little vessel that had proved so annoying. Now facing a frigate's broadside and at close to point-blank range, she must surely strike, although King still had his doubts. There was a suitable pause to allow the threat to sink in, then Woodward, in the waist, released another barrage.

And it did more damage than any so far. As if swept by a mighty broom, the clipper's tophamper was wiped away. Though not all the shots were aimed high, whether by chance, or mischievous design, some fell lower.

The vessel bucked and wallowed under such punishment while her hull appeared to crumble with the impact of at least three eighteen-pound balls. And then, when she finally began to settle, there was silence.

"Enemy has struck, sir," Cooper advised after a pause.

"So I understand," King replied softly. "You may secure her."

* * *

It was less than twenty minutes later when the small group was led into King's quarters. *Tenacious'* hands were yet to fully restore their ship, only the forward bulkhead had been replaced. The eighteen-pound long guns that shared the captain's accommodation were still cleared for action and there was a strong smell of burnt powder and sweat in the air.

"Bring chairs," King commanded on realising at least two of his American visitors were civilians and one a woman. Then he turned to the balding man who wore something approaching a uniform.

"You had better tell me who you are," he snapped. "And exactly why you behaved so."

"I think it is us that deserves an explanation." It was one of the civilians, probably a passenger; the elderly man's voice was calm and even, while his tone suggested this was nothing more than a neighbourly dispute, rather than a case of unnecessary slaughter.

"I have nothing to explain to you or anyone else," King grunted before turning back to the clipper's captain.

"Except why you chose to wreck my vessel," the seaman replied, and there was a brief stand-off.

"And you are?" King demanded.

"Jeremiah Adams, Master of the *Gladiator*."

"Where from and where bound?"

"We were one and a half weeks out of Boston carrying a cargo of willow hoops and fence posts – that is until we had the misfortune to run across one of King George's warships."

"You are well armed for a merchant," King said as two stewards appeared bringing dining chairs from their place of safety below.

"I also carry a letter of marque," the American agreed. "It allows me access to heavier weapons, which are mounted for my own protection."

King waited.

"I have no wish to prey upon your shipping if that's what you're thinkin'." Adams continued, "Though accept there will be Englishmen stupid enough to see any vessel as a potential pirate."

"You have not fully answered my question; where were you bound?"

"The North African Coast – I think you'll agree that is no place to approach without being suitably prepared."

"And were these people aware of the dangers?" King briefly regarded the older man and what might be his daughter who had seated themselves.

"They were my passengers and the reason we were sailing so," Adams spoke coldly. "Perhaps you would prefer to interrogate them?"

"I'm speaking to you," King snapped. Both he and Adams were ignoring the empty chairs. "And still do not see why you were so heavily armed."

"I am an American, so no passage is without risk, and few destinations safe," the master replied. "I carry weapons in case I am attacked. They were used tonight because you chose to fire upon me. And did so first, as I recall."

"We were the superior ship: you should have struck. By replying you caused unnecessary death."

Adams drew breath. "Captain, I'll remind you that men died aboard my ship; if anyone is guilty of needless killing, it is you."

King supposed the man might have a point. He had still to speak with Woodward yet already knew there would have been no direct order for those low shots, which were far more likely to have

22

been caused by the vagaries of smooth bore cannon. But if the Americans had seen sense there would have been little reason for them to fire at all. "I repeat, you should have heaved to when we came in sight," he said.

"Heave to?" Adams questioned. "Because you fly the union flag? Dear God, is there no end to an Englishman's gall!" On blaspheming, the man flashed a worried glance to the seated civilians whom he plainly held in some regard. But King could not have cared less.

"Because we were the superior ship," he countered, eyes fixed on Adams. "There is a convoy in the vicinity, as well you know, and I believe your intention was to raid it."

"I know nothing of any convoy," the American declared. "And neither does it interest me. My goal was to deliver these good people to their destination, then make what trade I could before returning to my own country."

"Is that so?" King rocked back on his heels. "Need I remind you, we are at war? Capturing a single British merchant would have made you a rich man."

"I have already said, I know nothing of a convoy." Adams' words rang true, but King was not so easily put off.

"A ship like yours played hell in St George's Channel no more than a year ago," he said.

Adams shook his head. "Why should I rob a merchant when I am one myself?" Now he switched his attention to the seated man and for the first time King properly turned in that direction.

He was tall and dressed plainly – almost determinedly so – with black coat and britches, coarse white stockings and shirt. The latter was of the cheapest cloth yet surprisingly well cut. The man himself might have been sixty with deep chocolate-brown eyes and wearing a round hat that topped a full head of long grey hair.

"I should introduce Caleb Palmer," Adams muttered. "He and his daughter had chartered my vessel. Delivering them was my main concern as they will doubtless confirm."

"Mr Palmer," King nodded.

"Caleb Palmer will do, I'll have no truck with titles." The older man stood and, after consideration, offered his hand. His voice had a soft yet strangely compelling tone. "And this is my daughter Hannah. We hail from Nantucket Island and what you have been told is correct. I have business on the Barbary Coast and Jeremiah Adams was indeed contracted to take us there."

Again, this sounded like the truth and, taken temporarily aback, King looked to the girl who had remained seated. She appeared barely out of her teens and carried a natural beauty modestly, with a plain skirt that was not quite black and matching cloak and bonnet. On sensing his attention, she looked up and he noticed the deep brown of her eyes, so similar to her father's, while her gaze was just as direct and on the verge of hostile.

He returned to the man. "You have still to say exactly where you were bound. And why."

Palmer met his gaze and spoke evenly. "It is enough that my daughter and I were travelling to the North African coast; you need know no more."

King turned back to Adams. "You were proposing to carry these people to the Barbary States?"

"That was the arrangement," Adams agreed. "I have passed that way on several occasions and carried out trade. Having little in the way of timber supplies, they are sore in need of our wooden goods and there is much we can use from them."

"Then you have been lucky indeed."

"It was a luck won by the threat of my cannon and how I manage my ship, Captain. I only enter undefended harbours and keep away from any potential warships."

"But the waters are infested with pirates."

"Who are fast, though not as fast as my *Glad.*," Adams countered.

"It is a risk nonetheless."

"Maybe." Adams' tone was gaining strength. "But for as long as powerful nations choose to ignore the pirate menace, and even pay them to do their own dirty work, it is one I must take."

Once more, King felt he was getting the worst of the conversation and wished he had invited Cooper to join them. For Adams was correct; the British Government not only paid an annual tribute to the Barbary States, it was not averse to commissioning them to attack enemy shipping, which naturally included that from America. He sensed further argument with Adams would be futile – it may be better to speak with the passengers.

"I have no idea of your business, Mr Palmer, yet assure you the Western Mediterranean is not the place for casual travellers," he said. "Whatever Captain Adams may claim, few ships are safe, even those whose countries pay tribute. A captured vessel will be stripped of its cargo and its crew carried into slavery while any women found aboard must expect far harsher treatment." His eyes fell briefly on the girl whose face registered no reaction. "Some that are taken – the lucky ones – may be ransomed in time though such arrangements do not always run true, and many have been held ten years or more. In truth, they are the very devils to deal with."

Palmer lowered his head in acknowledgement. "What you say comes as no surprise yet deal with them we must."

"That is your choice, however, I shall not be assisting you." He glanced at Adams. "We are bound for England; once there, Captain Adams must be treated as a prisoner of war, although I expect you both to be set free to continue your travels. Nevertheless, I would most seriously warn about venturing into the pirates' clutches; they are brigands of the worst order."

"You caution is noted." This time it was the daughter who spoke; her accent was similar to the old man's and once more King was struck by the darkness of her eyes. "As my father has said, we are aware of the dangers yet have no option."

* * *

The moon was rising now, its rays picking out the clipper that had settled considerably and now lay wallowing in the swell. And, as the cutter drew nearer, none of its occupants held out much hope.

Since that last, fateful, broadside a good deal had happened. First a boarding party consisting of marines and seamen formally took possession of the prize. Then she was thoroughly searched, and her crew secured before being transferred to *Tenacious*, while her master and two civilian passengers were already speaking with the frigate's captain. And now it was the turn of the standing officers who were to make a thorough examination to see if she could be saved.

However, Morales, the carpenter, had already made up his

mind. Even in the current conditions and before he had set foot on deck, he could see the hull was well below her usual riding height; unless a simple repair were possible, she was doomed.

"Good evening to you, gentlemen." The voice was familiar and, as the cutter bumped alongside, Morales looked up to see Cook, the marine sergeant, smiling grimly down on them.

"Looks like we made quite a mess." Amon, the boatswain, was the first to clamber aboard.

"Aye, you could say that," the marine agreed. "Spars what was damaged have been chucked over the side, though some could 'a' been saved I have no doubt."

Amon shook his head; there would be no point. He agreed with the carpenter: the prize was beyond repair.

Morales followed the boatswain onto the sodden deck; he was familiar with Baltimore Clippers and this one seemed little different. Apart from a tiny poop over the officers' quarters, the vessel was flush decked and truly a schooner with few fixtures and a frame barely strong enough to face the Atlantic. Some measure of reinforcement had been added but hardly enough to support the broadside guns that were optimistic for her size. In two places the hull had been severely damaged; her top rails ran, bent and twisted, above deep gashes in the bulwarks and one of the cannon lay trucks up on its barrel. A locker had also been hit allowing round shot to roll freely about the deck. Even the vessel's bitts, usually the soundest of fittings, had crumbled under the force of eighteen pounds of iron and there was a deep groove in the strakes where another had scraped a trail.

"Worse below," Cook snorted. "Fillin' up fast an' no pump what'll cope, while for'ard it looks more like a charnel house."

"Only a couple of wounded were brought across," Amon said.

"That's as maybe, though there were several more not worth the takin'; they'll be feeding the fishes b'now."

Morales turned away and began to examine the damage more carefully. "All up top could be sorted," he said, "but I fancy it'll be different below."

"Without a sound hull, there's little I can do," Amon shrugged.

"And nothing to be gained from them weapons." Regan stood up from examining one of the cannon. "While any powder will be ruined, so it will."

Morales made no reply; they would have to check below although, after Cook's words, he was reluctant to do so. The strength of a Baltimore's hull relied on integrity; were any more than a couple of frames damaged they may as well leave her to sink.

"Never seen the like," Cook muttered, "But then I never seen a tiddler hit by a frigate's eighteen-pounders."

"Most of the shots went high," the boatswain pointed out. "Only a few flew wild."

"Why were that then?" the marine asked, and Regan shrugged.

"It happens," he said. "And it would be them what did the real damage."

"Aye," Cook agreed. "They was enough."

* * *

Since the action there had been much to keep Lieutenant Woodward occupied. His guns needed to be secured and their crews stood down, then there were the innumerable duties that appeared when taking any prize. As second officer he could have been called to board the capture but was elsewhere when *Tenacious'* cutters put out, and since then had been supervising the ship's return from active warship to her marginally more comfortable cruising stations. And throughout there was no chance to speak in-depth to another lieutenant; Summers having been sent to take possession of the prize while Cooper remained on the quarterdeck dealing with the captain's demands.

Although Woodward knew he had done nothing wrong; round shot might have been fired when bar was more suitable, but the guns were loaded a good while before. And he had ordered the clipper's tophamper targeted; quite why those shots strayed so might never be known though any broadside can contain a few wild ones. He certainly had nothing to blame himself for and didn't think anyone else would hold him responsible. Daniels might make a fuss, but he was still a mere midshipman, yet Woodward remained deeply troubled.

For the clipper had been at their mercy; he'd waited for some sign of surrender but, when none was forthcoming, fired anyway. Because of that, men were now dead. And however much he tried, Woodward could not convince himself that perhaps he had not waited long enough.

* * *

"It is truly kind of you, though I shall be fine with my father."

Suzie Summers shook her head as she opened the small door to her cabin and squeezed inside. "I would not hear of such a thing; he has been provided with quarters below, has he not?"

"I believe so," the girl confirmed, ducking her head further and obediently following the woman who seemed set on mothering her. "A storeroom downstairs has been made available for our use."

"Well, a storeroom is no place for a female, and neither is the orlop," Suzie sniffed, "that is assuming such a thing exists aboard this ship."

Once inside the room, Hannah blinked as she looked around. What light there was filtered in from the larger space they had just left, although she could see enough to realise the place had been made homely. There was a miniature desk, a single chair, two narrow beds set one above the other against the ship's side, and what looked like a canvas washstand. Everything appeared clean and tidy yet there was hardly room for one, let alone two.

"You share this space?" she checked.

"With my husband – he can bunk with Jim Woodward; the pair are friends, it will be no inconvenience."

"I-I am not sure..."

"Hannah – I may call you so, I hope?"

The girl nodded.

"Hannah, you must understand, the only other women aboard are seamen's wives or so-called partners and, without casting aspersions, they come from different backgrounds. It may be several weeks before we arrive in England and frankly the idea of spending my time with a crowd of boring men simply appals."

"If you're certain..."

"I am. Here, sit awhile." Suzie indicated the chair and

28

perched herself on the side of the lower bunk. "There will be luggage to bring across from your previous ship, we can arrange for that to be stored."

"No, all I have is in this bag."

It was a small cylindrical affair that she had been carrying throughout; Suzie regarded it in horror.

"But my dear, it cannot be. How do you...?"

"Oh, I have everything I need, though would appreciate the chance for regular laundry."

Suzie pulled a face. "That's another tale. I'm glad I brought my own soap, there's barely a bar aboard apart from what the purser sells, and that at a frightening price. Then there's fresh water, the stuff's hoarded like liquid gold; we aren't allowed any for cleaning clothes and what's used for personal washing is heavily scrutinised."

"I'm sure I shall do well enough and have sufficient soap."

The older woman considered her. "You seem very independent."

"Do I?" she smiled briefly. "It is how I was raised. My family are Quakers: we prefer to look after ourselves."

"Quite right; best not to trust anyone, I say."

"Oh, we trust others," Hannah assured, "though do not wish to be a burden to them."

Suzie leaned back on the bunk and jumped slightly as the back of her head hit the one above. "So, what brings a Quaker girl to cross the Atlantic?" she asked, rubbing at the spot and leaning forward once more.

Hannah shrugged. "It will all be told in time, I am certain. We are hoping to rescue my brother."

"Your brother?"

"Father has an interest in a fleet of whaling ships; it was his intention for Peter to join him in the business, but he had his own mind."

"I see..."

"Peter said the life was not exciting enough and longed for greater adventure."

"And hunting whales did not satisfy?"

Hannah shrugged. "He preferred to travel."

"But forgive me, your family's trade sounds somewhat violent; I had it that Quakers were peaceable folk."

29

"Oh, we are, and father is no longer physically involved," Hannah smiled, "though those of our faith do take part. We regard such work as permissible; some of the disciples were fishermen after all."

"I see... And your brother found the idea of hunting whales too mundane?"

Again the smile, but this time more genuine; the girl was finally starting to relax. "He had planned to travel the world and chose to ship with a merchant, one similar to that just destroyed." Her words were level and carried no blame. "Though sadly it ran across corsairs off the Barbary Coast."

"I have heard tell of them," Suzie confirmed. "Devilish people."

"Maybe so; yet we believe there to be good in all, even if some keep their light concealed. One of the crew was allowed to go free and carried back a demand for tribute; unless a thousand guineas is raised, Peter will remain a prisoner."

Suzie shook her head. "A considerable sum for one man."

"It is for the crew of Peter's boat," Hannah said. "Father would never countenance freeing him alone."

"So, what do you intend?"

"Of that I am unsure. Peter and father have not always seen eye-to-eye, though he will always be part of our family..."

"And is your father carrying money with him?" Suzie checked.

"No, he has other plans and claims them to be as valuable. He is confident they will see Peter and his friends safe."

"And you are in agreement?"

The girl paused. "He is my father and will always have my support," she said at last.

"And you do not feel he is taking a risk himself?"

"A risk?"

"Yes, if he intends to treat with the pirates, they may choose to hold him hostage also, especially if he comes empty-handed."

Hannah blinked. "I am sure the thought did not occur," she said. "And why should it, when what they demand is more than we have?"

Suzie considered this, then continued. "And what is your part in the arrangement?"

"Mine?" Now the girl looked surprised. "Why, as I have said; to support my father, and care for him also. Is that not any daughter's duty?"

The older woman smiled. "Some might not see it as such. I assume you did not intend going ashore?"

"Oh no, Captain Adams had agreed to send in a small boat, though forbade my accompanying father."

"Then he showed a deal of sense although Captain Adams is hardly in a position to fulfil his duties now."

"Then we shall have to seek a replacement. Once in England we hope to meet with others of our faith. It will be strange if another ship cannot be found. With the Lord's help, we are certain to succeed."

"And I hope you do though much may still go wrong. Most of all I fear you may be underestimating the barbarians."

"Think you so?" Hannah asked. "We believe otherwise and do not doubt Peter will be released; it really should be very simple."

* * *

Woodward had noticed the midshipman approach but wasn't quick enough to avoid him.

"Caused quite a mess didn't you, sir?" Daniels gave the last word special emphasis.

"A mess?"

"Of the American." They were on the half-deck just forward of the officers' quarters and Woodward had the uncomfortable feeling their conversation might be overheard. "Never thought you would target her hull like that, sir. Was it on the captain's instructions?"

"No, and neither did I target the hull, I ordered the..."

"Only I were for'ard," the midshipman interrupted. "On the prow, where you stationed me. Couldn't see much from there."

Woodward had stopped speaking.

"Right in the heat of things, I was," Daniels continued. "Facin' the Yank's broadside. But then you would have known that, wouldn't you, sir?"

"You appear to have survived."

31

"Oh, I survived," the midshipman agreed. "Only a couple of hands were hurt, though you had nothing to do with that either, did you, sir?"

"Of course not."

"No, of course not, sir. You were too busy knocking seven bells out of that little cruiser. And now she's sinkin', or so I hears. Shame, a craft like that would have made a tidy price at auction. As it is we'll be lucky to see a quarter of her true value, and doubtless will have to fight for that. I remember one case where they..."

"I am not answerable to you, Mr Daniels," Woodward erupted. "And you would do better not to question my actions or those of any superior officer."

"Oh, don't think that, sir." The midshipman seemed genuinely concerned. "Don't think I'm criticising you in any way; that's not my place. And there wouldn't be no point, not with you being such an experienced and respected officer..."

Woodward eyed him warily.

"Man like you'll go far – if you don't mind me sayin' so, sir. I shall make a special point to keep an eye on your career. And I'm sure there'll be others equally interested in how you turns out."

Chapter Three

King emerged onto the quarterdeck and looked about. All was as it should be, which is what he expected as Cooper had the watch and was standing by the binnacle. Next to him, the duty midshipman was marking up the traverse board although there would seem to be little of note as *Tenacious* remained hove to. It was a crisp, dry morning and both officers wore watch coats while the quartermaster and messenger were clad in heavy woollens with sennit hats pulled tight against their rosy faces. Dawn had broken and a succession of grey-black clouds passed quickly overhead while a gentle swell regularly lifted the frigate's hull as her backed main kept her trapped against the wind. King sniffed at the breeze, unconsciously detecting the faintest hint of rain though nothing that should detain them unduly; as soon as the capture had been dealt with, they might continue their journey home.

Having sensed his presence, Cooper turned and gave a silent salute which King acknowledged with a tap to the brim of his own hat before making for the weather bulwark. The commission had lasted long enough for all aboard to know his peculiarities and a principle one was an intense dislike of early morning conversation. Even after as many as four hours' sound sleep, King appreciated time with his thoughts; a chance to reflect and refresh, before responding to the demands of the day.

The first of these lay before him, and less than a cable off, so he was forced to consider it a little early. The captured Baltimore Clipper had settled further during the night and was now barely afloat. He watched as a party of hands made their way along the waterlogged deck carrying stores in various forms. One held a cask, others sacks that might contain anything, while another struggled to keep a live hen under each arm. The clipper was down considerably at the stern and, as they made their way aft, each began to paddle through the steadily rising sea, with one kicking up spray in an attempt to soak the others. Then, on reaching *Tenacious'* cutter moored by the taffrail, they handed their goods across, before returning for another load.

In daylight it was possible to see more of the damage and King was surprised the craft had stayed afloat for so long. Regan, the gunner, had long since condemned her cannon as too old for modern usage and ditched them over the side, while several tons of dry goods, stores and supplies were already sitting safely in his frigate's hold. It was a shame little could be made of her cargo; he understood why Adams was taking fence posts and hickory hoops to the North African Coast – a place where such things were scarce – though there was limited need in England.

England! In the excitement of last night and the sleep it evoked – the best since receiving Aimée's letter – his family were not forgotten, although recent events had temporarily forced them to the back of his mind. But now free to roam again, his worries returned, and stronger, as if to punish him for the distraction. The time saved by his former diligence had been more than countered by dealing with the American, and reminding himself he was a King's officer first and a father second had little effect. And neither did it help to remember his children would live, or not, whether he was there or several thousands of miles away.

"Come to admire your handiwork, Captain?"

King tensed: Adams was speaking to him directly and it was strange that a mere prisoner was free to break his most cherished rule.

"There is little to admire in a wreck," he replied without turning. "I am only sorry you chose for it to come to this."

"You mean you're sorry I chose to fight?" Adams asked coming alongside.

King glanced at him. "I am. Yours was the faster vessel and may have made a successful escape, though once I had wounded your masts everything altered. At that point, mine was immeasurably superior and it was your duty to surrender."

"As simple as that?" Adams seemed surprised.

"I have surrendered in the past." King's tone was flat. "There is no shame in defeat – not when the odds weigh so heavily against you."

"I would agree, Captain, though sometimes there may be shame in victory, perhaps?"

King's attention switched back to the capture. "What exactly do you mean?"

Adams pointed at his former command. "A broadside aimed at my hull; three men dead and several wounded, not to mention the destruction of one of the finest sailers I've had the fortune to command. I'd call that shameless."

"You failed to strike and had fired upon us," King told him curtly.

"Maybe, but why did you target my hull?"

"Your hull was not targeted; in case it missed your attention, the broadside was general and accounted for the remains of your tophamper. Now if you have further complaints about the manner in which your ship was taken you might wish to address them elsewhere; I am no longer interested."

Adams took a step back and King felt a pang of remorse. He too had been beaten in the past and knew the pain well. And it was one inclined to endure when victory was won through power instead of skill.

"If it is any consolation, I do regret the loss of your ship," King added, speaking slowly and with more care. "As I would the destruction of any craft that could sail so. And equally, I regret the loss of your men, and that two of my own now lie wounded below. However, everything is directly attributable to your attitude, which frankly does little credit to any ship's master." Once more he was looking directly at Adams. "You put out in the midst of a war and were prepared to expose civilians to the brutalities of brigands, then attempt to cast shame on me, an enemy, for having the temerity to fight you."

"I agreed to deliver the man only," the American insisted. "And at his specific request. It was a commission: the girl was to remain aboard my vessel."

"And this was out of the goodness of your heart?" King checked. "Or was it a financial transaction?"

Now it was Adams' turn to be silent.

"I may have destroyed your vessel, but we are at war and that was my duty. And rather than profiting from the act, my purse is now the lighter for it. Yet you intended to take money from a civilian; payment for a service that would likely have ended in his death. And you dare call me shameless?"

* * *

Downes was the only member of the clipper's crew to volunteer for the King. When asked, it had seemed like a good idea; he was British after all. Only a succession of accidents and misunderstandings had led him to America and shipping aboard the *Gladiator*. Once separated from his former shipmates, however, the doubts began and his new home started to feel decidedly hostile.

When the action ended there was little confusion aboard the clipper. From the moment their tophamper took damage, all were expecting their master to surrender and there was even a hint of jollity in the air. And why not; the British frigate was a hundred times more powerful than their humble *Gladiator*, yet she had sold herself well. But the suddenness of that final broadside shattered far more than their barky; in the space of a few seconds three shipmates also died, so when the British came for them, they went quietly and without protest.

The warrant officer that rounded them up seemed affable enough and on boarding the warship her crew appeared almost genial. There'd been a measure of catcalls and taunts of course, but that was to be expected and, when they were taken down to the orlop and placed in what had been a petty officer's mess, all were feeling more settled. A little way forward the wounded were being cared for – they had passed the line of waiting injured – and there was talk about rustling up some scran.

Consequently, when the same warrant officer asked if any of them would care to sign for the British Navy, Downes genuinely thought he would not be alone. The majority of *Gladiator*'s crew had been born in England, after all, and serving in a ship – any ship – was preferable to being held prisoner. His was the only hand raised though, and on sensing the sudden wave of hatred from his former shipmates, Downes knew he had made a mistake.

And on being taken up and questioned by an officer, then almost frog-marched to what was to become his new quarters, his feelings were confirmed. The sea of faces confronting him was anything but friendly and when a bundled hammock hit him firmly in the belly, followed by a muttered instruction as to where he could sling it, Downes found himself missing the crowded comfort of his former shipmates.

* * *

"To be honest, I have no idea what you are worrying about."

On discovering his wife had effectively evicted him and he would have to share Jim Woodward's accommodation, Summers was mildly put out. The cabin space for a fifth rate's second officer could never be considered generous and the addition of another cot – there had not been time to commission Morales to construct bunks – made it positively cramped. It could have been worse, though; Woodward had gone out of his way to be accommodating and, despite the slight difference in seniority, they were good friends. And when their off-duty times next coincided and they were able to sort the cabin out to their mutual satisfaction, it seemed a friend was what Woodward needed most of all.

"Well, should I have released that last broadside?" he asked.

"Were you told not to?" Summers had been in charge of the forward battery so was on the forecastle with the chase pieces and too far from the quarterdeck to hear all that went on. Yet neither was he bothered; they were still arranging the furniture and, after some thought, he moved the washstand nearer the door to give slightly more room. It meant they would have to avoid it on entering but added valuable inches to their space. He turned back to his friend. "I don't recall a general cease-fire and had been popping away for'ard like a good 'un."

"There was no command," Woodward admitted with an element of sadness. "Though neither is there always, or so it appears. Most times our dear captain prefers us to rely on intuition and our reading his mind."

"That might be how it comes across," Summers agreed. Woodward had the only chair and his feet were blocking the sea chest, which might have made a suitable seat. The cove was too wrapped up in his problems to notice, though, so he settled himself on the deck. "You must remember this ship was first commissioned some time back and has been through much since. We have become familiar with the routine and there is often no need for direct orders. But be assured, when Captain King wants something done, you shall know of it. And he definitely did not order a cease-fire?"

"Definitely."

"Then, as I say, there should be nothing to concern you." The deck was actually quite comfortable; he could stretch his legs out and still not quite touch the opposite bulkhead. "And what about the aiming mark?" he added.

"I was targeting the masts," Woodward replied. "And some shots went wild."

"Some occasionally will. And, though you are new aboard *Tenacious*, she's been on station too long. The men are eager to be home so a couple may have rushed."

"It has been mentioned that I should have changed from round."

"You mean load bar shot?" Summers frowned. "Who said that?"

"Daniels."

The younger man shook his head. "Take no notice of him; he might be matey with the First Lord though that don't count for much when we's at sea. And neither should he offer advice to a superior officer."

"But is he right?"

"I have no idea. Has anyone else said anything?"

"Not so far."

There was only a light partition between their space and his former quarters where his wife would be, and Summers rested his head against it. "Then I think you can safely assume that he is not. We were in action, Jim," he added. "The Yank had fired on us several times and caused injury; I'd have said you'd be deeper in the suds if you hadn't chosen to finish her."

"You don't think Daniels will make trouble, with his father, I am meaning. Word is he has a deal of influence."

It was a shame that Suzie moved him out so, especially when they had only been married a matter of months...

"Are you listening?"

Summers returned to the current problem. "Daniels has nothing to do with this," he said. "He's a midshipman; you have to keep him in his place. And don't concern yourself so; worrying never helped anyone; you must be more positive."

"I know," Woodward admitted, resting back in the chair. "Though it doesn't always come easy."

* * *

38

"Yank, is you?" one of the hands asked bluntly and Downes shook his head.

"Originally from Sussex," he said. "Mayfield."

"But we took you from the clipper." This was another seaman, one with a twisted ear.

"I knows Mayfield," the first confirmed, "an' it's a long way from Boston. Ain't that where your barky hailed from?"

"That's right," Downs agreed. "It's a long story."

"Don't bother then." Twisted ear treated him to a toothless smile and the tension began to drop. "Truth is, none of us'll care much where you comes from."

"'Sright," an older seaman, who appeared to be in charge, confirmed. "It's what you does from now on that counts. How you behaves: how you treats your shipmates."

"An' messmates," another added. "You'll find that matters a lot."

* * *

With the addition of Woods, the bird of passage chaplain, and Summers' wife, *Tenacious'* gunroom had already been full, so accommodating Captain Adams was not easy. Accommodate him they must, however, as the man was in the possession of a letter of marque. This gave him several advantages, although the downside was there would be no easy release in the event of capture; Adams must be regarded as a prisoner of war and treated accordingly.

In which case King could confine the American below and even place him in irons, should the prospect appeal. Times were changing, though; the nineteenth century was already well advanced, and it was now customary to accommodate enemy officers with their peers. Consequently, Woods, the parson, had been moved from his cabin and forced to share with the purser although that did not solve the problem of feeding. At meal times there was yet another mouth to fill, and when all the frigate's off-duty officers also gathered about the gunroom table it became quite a squash. Normally such crowding would have been taken in good heart and only add to the occasion's conviviality but the additional presence of the elderly Quaker, who had been invited to join them for meals by a charitable Cooper, was something of a dampener. It wouldn't have been so bad were their female guests present; since leaving Halifax, Summers' wife had been entertaining them splendidly and the prospect of a closer acquaintance with Hannah, Palmer's daughter, was a major reason for some to be at the table. However, it seemed both she and Suzie were put off by the crowd, and the men must accept purely masculine company.

But at least the food was good. Being only a few days out, the gunroom cook still had a reasonable supply of fresh vegetables, although they wouldn't last forever. Accordingly, their lobscouse – a concoction of salt beef, ships' biscuit and onions, and a meal more regular than popular – was supplemented by generous amounts of winter cabbage and carrots. Some had started to show signs of age yet were jumped upon by those more used to preserved, and the majority treated themselves generously.

"Of course, I would always be willing to say a grace," Woods announced in a suitably severe voice when the rush was at its height.

"I am sure that would be appreciated." Cooper spoke from the head of the table and there was a guilty pause while the chaplain muttered a few words. Then, after some added an 'Amen', the race to feed resumed. Heather, the purser, whose plate bore a veritable pile of cabbage, tried to engage Adams in conversation.

"I understand you were bound for the Barbary Coast, Captain?"

"That was the intention." Adams spoke grudgingly as he toyed with the mess on his plate; he was not accustomed to eating in such crowded conditions and the loss of his ship had hardly increased his appetite. The last thing he wanted was to be reminded of it.

"Dangerous waters," the first lieutenant commented.

The American looked up briefly. "Think you so? I have sailed them often enough and been safe."

"And never a brush with corsairs?" Cooper persisted.

"Oh, they were sighted, and gave chase on occasions," Adams admitted. "But the *Glad.* were a fine sailer an' always left them in her wake."

There was a moment of silence; most present could appreciate his loss.

"I gather you intended to trade with them also." Heather,

the purser, was always alert to fresh business opportunities.

"Mr Palmer was happy for me to do so."

"Caleb Palmer," the American corrected gently from further down.

"He financed our trip and wished to explore such possibilities," Adams continued.

Now all eyes turned to the darkly clad man.

"A bold move for sure," Heather commented with possible respect.

Palmer lay down his fork to address his audience. "I could not believe all those living on the North African Coast are pirates," he began, "so made a study of the area. And they are in sore need of goods and resources we have a ready supply of in America, while equally possessing much we lack."

"Such is the basis for good commerce," Heather nodded approvingly. "A tidy sum is to be earned I am certain."

"Perhaps," Palmer hung on the word for more than a second, "though that was not my intention. Were other countries more willing to trade they might feel less inclined to seek a revenue elsewhere. If I can change their ways for the better, it will be profit enough."

Having delivered his thoughts, the elderly man began to eat once more.

"One does not trade with pirates," Pocock, the senior marine lieutenant, announced. "They are little more than savages; the only thing they understand is force."

"Then it is a pity your Navy does not address them." Captain Adams again and the marine turned on him.

"You think we will do better where your ships failed?"

"I think you might try!" Adams snapped.

"At least our cousins addressed the problem, and generally to good effect," Cooper spoke from the table's head.

"And with barely a handful of frigates," Manton, the sailing master, added.

"I think we are wandering from the subject," the parson, interrupted. "I'd gauge our friend here has plans to solve the pirate menace without resort to arms, is that not the case?"

"That is so," Palmer agreed. "They hold my son hostage, and he is not alone; there are several thousand men and women from many nations being treated as slaves."

"A crime to be sure," Pocock grunted.

"And one repeated on a greater level by our own countries," Palmer countered. "At least those confined by what you call savages have hope of release, even if it is dependent on paying a ransom. Our own countrymen's slaves are given no such choice."

There was an angry silence that Woods, the parson, took advantage of.

"So, what do you propose?" he asked.

"Paying ransoms will not solve the problem, and neither shall guns and violence as has already been proved. An alternative source of revenue may do better, which is why I financed this mission."

"Though you must be intending to pay for your son's release?" Cooper checked.

"In truth, there is little left to give," Palmer replied. "Yet I may have something equally valuable."

"Which is...?" Heather prompted.

"Advice," Palmer replied. "Advice and assistance. If I can set up trading agreements with other countries – my own and those closer by – there may not be the need for continual bloodshed and robbery."

"A bold move, sir," Heather commented.

"And a waste of time," Pocock added.

"Maybe so." Palmer's dark eyes flashed to the man. "You talk of solving the pirate problem with violence, though that has been tried and seen to fail."

The marine glared back but made no reply.

"I believe trade and cooperation will do better and it is a solution that speaks to my condition."

All took a moment to consider this as the eating continued more slowly. Then momentum gathered as the dish of lobscouse was replaced by a handsome plum pudding – one with the distinction of actually containing plums. And as those about the dining table readied themselves for a further onslaught, the dark figure departed in silence.

"I see our gloomy friend has left." Pocock was manoeuvring a slab onto his plate. "No stomach for this fine fare it would seem – the sugar if you please, Holmes."

"I consider his ideas entirely worthy," Woods added.

"Worthy be damned, the man's as mad as they make

them."

"I'm not so sure," Heather said. "The Barbary States do not lack resources; nuts and dried fruit to name but a few, while there are also made goods; fine silks and metalwork. Were the market open to us it would prove lucrative for sure."

"The matter is not worth consideration," Pocock again. "They are savages through and through. Worse; they are savages with power. Years of collecting tributes have made them rich, and not all is paid in gold. Most have accumulated sizeable arsenals and their navies continue to grow. Quite what they make in ransoms can only be guessed at, though it will be considerable, and not likely bettered with a schooner's worth of hoops and fence posts."

"I still think he may have an idea," Woods mused, and the marine sniffed.

"And I still think him mad," he said.

* * *

Once more Woodward was controlling the frigate's larboard battery, and once more his target was the American schooner. However, rather than the dark of night, a faint sun picked out the empty hulk of what had so recently been a fine craft.

The lightened hull now wallowed in a gentle swell while the stunted masts, once so full and elegant, described irregular circles under an ice blue sky. Woodward had been given the task of finishing the vessel; a solid broadside to send her to the bottom and one that carried no danger to any man, yet still he viewed the prospect with more than a hint of uncertainty.

For this would be a far more public demonstration of his skills; the range was less than a cable while he would also benefit from the quarterdeck's thirty-two-pound carronades. And no more than a couple of lucky shots would be enough to send her to the bottom although it was not the prospect of missing that bothered him. The barrage would be watched – and watched carefully – by the entire crew, many of whom were skilled in laying a gun and could spot a tight spread of shot with ease.

"As you will, Mr Woodward."

It was the captain's voice; he was on the quarterdeck along

with most of the officers. And there were others; the American captain had come up to witness the destruction of his former command and more from the clipper were also present – damn it, even the women turned out to look.

Woodward raised his sword. "Be ready!"

"Have to make a good grouping, sir." It was Daniels. Woodward had not spoken to the midshipman since their confrontation on the half-deck, and none of his predictions had come about, yet simply having the cull nearby was enough to put him off.

"Ready," he repeated, and several of the gun captains glanced back in mild irritation. "Fire!"

The broadside was despatched with a credible crack. Even the quarterdeck cannon, often a second or two behind, were almost simultaneous. And from the start the spread looked good. Woodward hardly breathed as the iron shot flew across the water. Then the lurching hulk was momentarily hidden behind a wall of spouting white that encompassed it totally. He watched, not daring to believe, as the waters subsided; perhaps one shot strayed beyond, though it might have skimmed, or ricocheted off the vessel itself. Most had hit more or less centrally, forcing the hull to fold up, the stumps that had been masts seemingly to clash, before all was swiftly swallowed by the grey waters. A faint hum of appreciation, or sorrow, greeted the departure and then there was a general buzz of conversation as all returned to normal duties.

Woodward felt the joy of easy breath – it really could not have gone better. Then Daniels' impish face came back to taunt him.

"Sound broadside, sir," he said in all respects the loyal, supportive junior. "I'd say you got the measure of her handsomely!"

Woodward eyed the midshipman with caution, but he had more to say.

"Though I'd chance you benefited somewhat from the practice."

Chapter Four

King had not entered Spithead for many years yet he knew the anchorage could become crowded, and that morning it looked particularly so. However, *Tenacious*, making slow progress under an easy wind, appeared equally full. It was as if every hand had crowded into her waist or onto her forecastle while others jostled for position on the tops or hung like apes from shrouds. And the quarterdeck was almost as bad; in addition to those of the watch, all entitled to walk the sacred space were pointing and jostling as they lined the bulwarks. King considered them for a moment; such behaviour on what he considered his private area was annoying, although it would be a harsh captain who put a stop to it. Most were getting the first proper sight of their native country for an age while for others – those still to set foot on what they oddly referred to as home – it must be the revelation of a myth. England, the land of Shakespeare and Newton, Cromwell and Cook, finally lay before them as a crowded muddle of ships and lines of drab and distant houses, all of which looked little different from those on many other shores. The disappointment should have been great but King detected none on any of the faces.

Rumours that *Tenacious* was to be paid off had been circulating throughout the lower deck for the past week and their eagerness to be away was palpable. Many were full of brave predictions doomed to fade at the first touch of English soil. Men used to the confines of a ship and the familiarity of their shipmates could be daunted by strange crowds and open spaces, while the inevitable change in prices, customs and fashions would disorient even the hardest tar, making his patiently acquired wages easy for the taking.

"Place is a mite thick," Manton commented as they drew closer. "For the life of me, I wonder if there'll be room."

On other occasions King might have reprimanded the sailing master for speaking out of turn, but this was a special day. This was homecoming, the end of a commission and, though he hoped to sail with his officers again, chances were high he never would. Besides, Manton was right; the Portsmouth anchorage was large indeed and could easily accommodate several fleets, yet it did seem unusually full. Then, when he looked closer, King noticed there was little activity; none of the usual to-ing and fro-ing of lighters and tenders bent on the never-ending task of maintaining their larger cousins. Even the ubiquitous bumboats seemed in short supply. And of the warships themselves, none appeared to be making ready and many had topmasts set down while there was a shared atmosphere of lethargy and fatigue. It was clear most had not seen open water for some time and may never do so again.

"My father was sailing master in the old *Gorgon*," Manton continued relentlessly. "When she came back in ninety-four, he managed to snag *Invincible*'s anchor cable and shaved the *Royal William*'s quarter gallery."

"Should you be telling me this?" King asked and the sailing master looked abashed.

"It were a long time ago, sir," he said. "Matters have improved a deal since."

"If there is a problem, we may be directed to Mother Bank."

"The merchant anchorage?" Manton asked in surprise.

"It would appear less crowded."

And that was the other side of the coin; many of Britain's fighting ships might be in port, although the same could not be said for her trading vessels. With conventional war coming to an end, this should be the dawn of a new prosperity. Throughout the dark years of conflict, Britain's merchant shipping had steadily fostered suppliers in the east, generating and maintaining an income that made the fight against Napoleon possible. And now, when peace finally seemed attainable, the future looked bright indeed. Or it would be, King told himself, providing the word from home was good.

Being reminded of his family broke the mood and suddenly he had no interest in the ship, her officers or where they might find a berth. It would probably take weeks – months – for *Tenacious* to be assessed by the dockyard and then, if work were agreed, years before it began. By then he may not even remain her captain; he could have retired from the sea and be living happily with Aimée and his children. Once more, it all depended on the news awaiting him.

Palmer and his daughter were standing nearby and with

them Captain Adams, the latter looking strangely formal in his blue coat and britches.

"Our journey would appear to have ended," Palmer announced with a hint of awkwardness when King approached. "I thank you for your courtesy; my daughter and I have been well provided for."

"I was pleased to be of service," King said a little stiffly. He usually found those with a strong faith to be overly sanctimonious and Palmer initially appeared little different, although he had warmed to the fellow during their voyage. "And wish you luck with your endeavours."

"That is kind, though we do not hold with luck, not when there is something far more powerful to depend upon."

"Of course. And I trust you will have no trouble finding accommodation ashore?"

"There are those of our faith in England," the American assured. "They will provide for us."

King turned to Adams. "And I fear you shall be taken into custody shortly, sir."

"It is of no great worry," the man shrugged. "Our war will be over soon."

That was probably the case, although Adams would be bound for the new prison at Dartmoor which was hardly a pleasant prospect.

"Boat putting out from the shore," Midshipman Daniels announced. "It looks to be making for us."

That would be for their medical reports; Manning was already on deck and prepared. All King must do was wait for a berth to be assigned and see *Tenacious* secured before another round of goodbyes began. And then, only then, he might finally make his way home and learn more of his family.

* * *

Downes lost no time in getting to know his new messmates; the first few days packed cheek by jowl had created familiarity. He'd quickly recognised the shellback, Stokes, to be their mess captain and Bovey as something of a sea lawyer. Twisted ear turned out to be a Midlander named Early, although the former moniker still came to mind, and Longdon was an affable topman and his older tie mate, Lovemore, a curly-headed forcastleman. The rest remained a blur of faces for slightly longer before their personalities became fully defined. And despite the initial approach, they seemed an amicable bunch, and he was slowly feeling accepted.

Which was probably premature; it could take years for a man to be fully accepted in a mess, for membership was a powerful thing. When properly organised, the tight body of men that ate, slept and often worked together came to be a force in itself. Should a specific task be called for, they could be summoned in the certainty that all would work together, while a good messmate would defend another to the last and expect the same in return.

But as they finished their plum duff, Downes was feeling, if not accepted, then at least tolerated. With *Tenacious* having to wait for an anchorage, those below were allowed slightly longer to finish the meal. And Downes was not sorry; his portion of pudding had been generous and took a deal of digesting. Besides, he found it easier to socialise in the daytime; the berth deck could never be considered well lit, although at midday enough daylight filtered through the gratings for him to see all at the crowded table, and the air was cleaner without the scent of evening lamps.

"So, we're here in time for the spring," Stokes said. "Question is, do we stay an' see something of life on land, or sling our hooks and try for fresh seagoing berths?"

"I'm for another barky," Groom declared. "Most of what I want in England will be gone as soon as me clink's spent."

"I'm with him," Lovemore, the curly-headed seaman agreed. "Though would prefer another man-of-war."

"I'd be happy with a merchant," said Longdon.

"I'd be happy with anything," Bovey, the sea lawyer, added. "'Cept a fisher or a Guineaman o' course."

There were murmurs of consent from the others.

"Well, I'm for a King's ship an' all," Stokes declared.

"And me," Early agreed. "That or nothing."

"Then a King's ship it is," Groom confirmed.

Not being sure if he were truly part of the conversation, Downes remained silent, although the fact that the men were proposing to move as a body was impressive and he could not help feeling mildly jealous.

"We've come in at Pompey," Bovey continued. "Which is as

good a place to start lookin' as any. That is so long as some don't spend all their time in tap houses and pushing schools."

"Hold hard, Bove," Longdon cried. "When we got liberty in Halifax, Barrack Street were your favourite haunt."

"That were when we had a regular berth." The man's eyes flashed darkly. "If the barky's being paid off you can bet she won't be alone. There'll be man-of-war hands forming lines for the best an' I'm not spending my time in a guard ship, just 'cause you lot chose to dance the kipples."

"He's got a point." Downes noticed whenever Stokes spoke all turned to him with obvious respect. "There'll be Jacks aplenty lookin' for tickets, and not every Navy ship will care to take on an entire mess."

"Time was when we'd a' been sought after," Groom sighed.

"That were when we was at war." Stokes again.

"Terrible thing, war," Early added. "Least, terrible when it ends."

"If you'd wanted to stay in demand, you could have opted out at Halifax," Lovemore told them. "McKenzie did, and they was 'appy to let 'im go."

"He 'ad reasons to stay with the station – connections ashore," Bovey added mysteriously.

"Anyone could 'ave stayed," Lovemore maintained. "They made that plain."

"Thought about it, but I wanted to see a bit of England." Longdon again.

"No reason why we can't an' all," Bovey added, "long as it is just a bit; there'll be places for us whenever; regular tars is always in demand."

"Maybe not in peace time," Early said. "Not unless you want to ship in a merchant."

"I told you, no merchants for me." Stokes shook his head firmly. "Had my fill of poorly manned tubs on deep-sea commissions. It's a King's ship or nothing – even if we don't stay as a mess."

"A John Company vessel might be alright," Lovemore supposed.

"Well, what about a bargain?" Bovey suggested. "If we can't bag a man-of-war, take up with the colliers. We could damn near man one on our own and needn't stay for more'n a passage. Like as not this peace won't hold no longer than the last. Soon as they starts fightin' again, we jumps ship and land us a proper barky."

"How's that feel, Stokie?" Early enquired. "Chance a collier for a while, would you?"

"Better than two years in China," another pointed out.

"Very well," Stokes nodded. "We'll have a cruise round Pompey, then head up north and see what can be snagged."

"Might pick up in London," Bovey suggested. "Find an empty that'll give us free passage if we signs on at Newky."

"Then we can stay together," Lovemore added and again Downes felt vaguely envious.

There was a general nodding of heads, then Stokes apparently noticed him for the first time.

"And what about you, Yank?" he asked. Despite Downes' place of birth, the name seemed destined to stick. "Care to join us, do ya'?"

* * *

"I must say, I'm going to miss the old barge," Vernon announced as he folded his second-best shirt.

"We've been with her a long time," Brotherton, another midshipman, agreed. He too was preparing to leave although his chest was already packed. "And won't find a tighter crew, nor a better captain."

"Probably won't find a captain at all," his friend added, "not with the war finishing. Best we can hope for is a shore posting, and they'll be as rare as hen's teeth."

"You're forgetting the board," Brotherton added. "There's one at the end of the month and we're all due to be seen – Coops promised."

"The board's a possibility, though I'll wager there'll be strong competition."

"Daniels for one."

"Daniels is a certainty," Vernon agreed. "But I can't see the rest of us making lieutenant, not when there's no posts to fill."

"Aye, no one'll be giving out commissions, it'll cost 'em half-pay; middies are cheaper; middies come for free."

* * *

It wasn't until the following morning that King finally caught the Portsmouth Mail and, though one of only three passengers and with a clear road, he was restless for every hour of the journey. Like most sailors, he found reunions and the first taste of land uncomfortable; it usually took him several days before he could settle into the ease of family life, while there were always changes in society and conventions to be learned. In this, as in many matters ashore, he would be relying heavily on Aimée, and at times felt it strange to be so dependent on one who was not his legal wife.

Again, like most sailors, King found the act of falling in love dangerously easy, a trait shared with Juliana, the Dutch woman he married many years before. Little had been heard of her for some while although the chance that she may reappear at any time was enough to stop him from taking Aimée to the altar. But in an enlightened age their living arrangements were not so unusual, and any prejudice shown was usually confined to the occasional snide remark from those in higher society, the average working man being far more forgiving. Aimée did have another aspect that marked her out, however: she was also French.

They first met when King was held prisoner in the parole town of Verdun. Naturally, he became instantly smitten and, though less impetuous, she proved trusting enough to escape with him and set up home in what was ostensibly an enemy country. No one who truly knew her could think of Aimée as anything other than a loyal and loving partner, yet King supposed her life could not always have been easy, especially when he was away. And this time there had been another burden, again one known and understood by many sailor's wives: coping with sick children alone.

But he would make it up to her – he always did. While at sea, and even when *Tenacious* lay at anchor, King could think of little other than his family's well being although, now they lay so close, found it easier to believe all would be well. When he left the ship, Robert Manning was especially reassuring on the subject, so really he should concentrate on resuming his place as head of the household and prizing his way back into his children's affections. And Aimée's, of course.

His final stop at Eastbourne was almost deserted, but King was well known in the area and it only needed one enquiry before a hackney was found to take him and his dunnage the rest of the way. It was late evening when his carriage finally swept through the imposing stone entrance and he could view the house for the first time in years. He felt a sudden nervousness; soon they should be celebrating together as a family although a nagging doubt remained that they might equally be mourning a loss.

The carriage pulled up and he paused for a moment before clambering out. A strange youth approached and viewed him quizzically before removing his cap.

"Captain King," King grunted in explanation.

"Of course, sir," the lad replied, noticing King's missing arm. "It's Giles, stable hand."

"Stevens has left?"

"A while ago now, sir. I been here two year or more."

King nodded; Aimée probably said as much in her letters; he had no memory for domestic matters. Turning from the lad, he made for his front door which really should have been open by now if Robinson knew his business. But rather than the elderly butler, when the carved oak door was finally pulled back a woman stood behind it. And though the light came from behind, it definitely was not Aimée.

He stepped closer while preparing to ask the question that had been on his lips for more than a month. The greying hair was tied back severely, and her expression seemed as hard and censorious as always, yet now there was no mistaking Kate Manning.

"Kate, it is so good to see you," he began. "Robert sends his love. He will be joining us shortly; there were matters concerning the ship that..." And then he faltered.

"Aimée is inside," her tone was restrained, but there was nothing extraordinary in that; Kate had never been the warmest of folk. "She asked me to meet you."

Of course, Aimée would be caring for the children. King felt a wave of relief wash over him; they were probably having a rare old time.

"Tell me, what news?" he urged.

Now it was the woman's turn to pause and, for a moment, King thought she was not going to speak at all. And then, in a voice unusually hesitant, she did.

"Oh Tom, I am so very sorry..."

Robert Manning arrived the day after and for a week it was just the four of them in an otherwise empty house. Empty, that is, apart from small telltail signs of the children; the scrapes and marks that no one felt inclined to see repaired or wiped away. Both were buried nearby in the parish plot King and Aimée had inherited with the estate and never intended to use. King visited them twice, once with the other three and once on his own, before deciding never to do so again. And then Robert and Kate left to pick up their old life, leaving them to do the same.

And, for a time, it was easy. *Tenacious* was resting in the safety of her Mother Bank anchorage under the watchful eye of her standing officers: Morales, Amon and Regan. Each would guard the ship as if she were their own and, until the survey, there was little more for anyone to do. Accordingly, King set his mind on country life, throwing himself into various activities with a fever that owed little to genuine interest.

A few weeks remained of the fox hunting season and, though his missing arm gave an adequate excuse not to physically partake, there was nothing to stop him joining in the revelry afterwards. Aimée attended once before deciding such events were not for her, but King embraced them to the full and if, on occasion, he returned late after taking more port wine than was wise, no one was harmed.

Then there were the tenant farmers; the estate included three large holdings along with two part-time affairs, and King inspected them all. He found something innately constructive in a process that allowed food to be created from apparently nothing and, with the aid of a hastily assembled library, soon became a self-appointed expert on all things agricultural. And after a day spent imparting advice to patient tenants, he would return to sleep moderately well, although there the emotional ache – so oddly similar to that when he lost his arm – was more noticeable. Quite how Aimée dealt with the loss was a mystery he did not try to solve. At first, when the Mannings had left and there was more room for honesty, they had addressed the subject, though to little effect; both were far too tender to fully express their feelings and King's foolish suggestion to try for another family was greeted with horror and a silence that lasted several days. And then, when the April sun finally began to shine with true force and King was resigning himself to another day's solitary study, all began to change, for him at least.

He had been standing at the gallery windows idly watching the blanketed hunters as they were exercised on the heath when he saw the Admiralty messenger arrive. Rushing down the stairs, he almost elbowed old Robinson aside before grabbing at the parchment package. There were several vital seconds' delay when the butler's signature would not suffice – King himself must sign. A pen had to be found and then, resting on the patient man's back, he clumsily scratched his signature and could finally tear the document apart.

Aimée must have heard something of the commotion and made a more dignified descent of the stairs while King read. "Is it the Admiralty?" she asked when his lips had ceased to move.

"It is," he confirmed, looking up. "They want to see me at the earliest opportunity."

"Then you must go." Her tone was completely neutral. "The parson and his wife are joining us for our midday meal, I shall just have to tell them…"

"The parson?"

"We were to discuss the May Day celebrations," Aimée reminded with little hope. "But you should travel to London now," she added after a moment's thought. "Then it will not be quite so on your mind."

King nodded. "I think you may be right."

Chapter Five

Vice Admiral Fraser was an old-school officer, one of several who noticed the trend for a more enlightened Navy and beat a hasty retreat to the Admiralty. King shook his bony hand and watched as the elderly man lowered himself onto a chair as if frightened it might give way. Fraser was also one of the last to wear a horsehair wig; his sat oddly on a bald pate yet the eyes remained sharp and, when King appeared without an appointment, he had immediately made room for him.

It was a small, panelled office that carried a strong scent of polish and its fireplace, though laid with logs and kindling, was stone cold. And there were no preliminaries, "We will begin with the important matters," Fraser announced once King was seated opposite. "*Tenacious* is for the breakers."

"Indeed, sir?" There was a moment of grief for his old command but no more. She had been a fine ship and served him well although, of late, King felt he had mourned enough. *Tenacious* being broken up did not lack significance, however; without a command, he would be touting for work and suddenly the prospect of spending the rest of his life in the country seemed too awful to contemplate.

"Nothing else for it, I fear; she's rot in the frame and worm in her strakes. Were the war to continue much longer there might be a patch-up job, but with Blücher on the assent and the allies nearing Paris it is just a matter of time before Boney's ousted."

This came as a surprise. The last news sheet mentioned an action fought at Laon and, despite it being heralded as a great victory, King felt more might have been made of the opportunity. Though things had obviously moved on since and Fraser's information was yet to reach the press.

"Course it is his own damned fault," the admiral continued. "Fellow was given every chance at the end of last year. If he'd played his cards right the cove would have kept his throne, and the same boundaries enjoyed in ninety-two. As it is, our allies have already signed a treaty amongst themselves; no one will be making a separate peace with the blighter; this time he's for the chop and we sort out who keeps what later."

They were bold words and not unwelcome, while King was also mildly flattered that he, barely halfway up the captain's list, was privy to them. But all the knowledge and regard in the world would be of little use without a command.

"There are those who would have it he might make an escape across the Atlantic." Now those pale eyes were set on a point slightly above King's right shoulder and the old man could as easily have been speaking to himself. "Mind, we're aware of the danger and have made provisions. Napoleon will be ours within a month; then the only problem will be what to do with him."

King waited, there would be more he was certain.

"But that's as maybe," Fraser said, returning to reality. "First we have to set you up with a new vessel."

The words were spoken lightly; the admiral might have been deciding where they would dine, although King's heart began to pound.

"It will be another frigate though smaller than *Tenacious*," Fraser continued. "A capture and French, formally a commerce raider on the India run till she ran afoul of one of our escorts. Came in at the end of last year and was bought into the Service. They've pronounced her sound and rated her a thirty-two; fitted twelve-pounders so I believe, though you might wish to change them for something heavier."

King thought not, he had no wish to weigh down what would probably be a slick and nimble sailer: long twelves would suit him perfectly.

Fraser was leaning back in his chair. "Pretty little thing by all accounts; time was when they'd have been fighting to copy her lines, though there's no longer the need. By autumn we'll have more frigates in Ordinary than anyone knows what to do with," his eyes met King's, "and more captains come to that."

"I'm grateful to you, sir." To be employed at such a time was incredibly good fortune and it didn't hurt to show gratitude.

"Of course, you weren't the first choice," Fraser continued. "Henry Writer was appointed but had a change of heart. I'm not sure of the details though believe it to be a financial matter. You know the sort of thing: Treasury doesn't pay the wages he requires and with the war closing, there'll be precious little prospect of prize money. You've done alright on that score I collect?"

"I have, sir."

"Glad to hear it. Part of a captain's duty is to feather his own nest, that way his career can progress without regard to what might be gained; makes for a better officer if I'm any judge."

King said nothing; for much of his life he had been in want of funds, it was only recently that luck, and an exorbitant amount of prize money, came his way. And it was indeed luck; many senior to him had proved less fortunate and now would probably remain so. Yet, whenever King faced action, prize money was never a consideration – or so he told himself.

"Whatever, Writer felt he might make more in the City and his first officer has ambitions for Parliament. Saw her most of the way through the refit, then left us high and dry; though I collect this is not a new experience for you."

"I took over *Hare* from a prospective politician, and *Tenacious* belonged to George Wheatstone before…"

"I remember, I remember." Fraser nodded his head emphatically. "Rum business, yet he always was the indulgent sort. The word is you made a sound fist of both, which is why your name came up for *Viper*."

King vaguely recalled reading of her capture, although he had been on the North American Station at the time and fighting a very different war.

"She has her standing officers in place for now, though some are making noises about casting off – evidently a hint of peace brings about almost as many changes as war. Whatever, the man who takes her on will have to see to the final fitting out and manning. Then, after sea trials, she is needed in the Med."

"I see, sir." This was getting better and better, and only for a moment did the image of his home in Eastbourne come to mind, along with Aimée, alone in the empty house.

"Yes, Pellew has the station and is short of French speakers – you have the lingo I understand?"

"I do, sir."

"Excellent, such a skill is likely to come in handy. *Viper's* lying at Buckler's Hard. As I say, only a thirty-two, but of regular timbers – none of your pine and spruce nonsense – and armed with the latest Armstrongs. If peace does come, I think you'll find a frigate more in demand than any seventy-four."

That might be the case; the Med had always been a frigate's sea.

"You'll have to move quick, mind; can't afford any further delays even in these times." Fraser leaned back and considered him. "So, what do you say, King, are you game?"

* * *

Woodward had been sitting in the anti-room for two hours and, so far, no one had been called. There were thirteen other officers present, all lieutenants and all immaculately dressed. Some were reading news sheets and others might be asleep, although the sense of tension and expectation was strong, and he guessed the only difference lay in how well each hid it.

This was his third visit to the Admiralty in successive weeks. On previous occasions the wait was less – under an hour for the first with the second only slightly longer. And each time he had spoken to different officers who both read his journals with apparent interest and appeared genuinely sympathetic. The result had been the same, however; there was little available; even positions in the regulating service were non-existent. Each advised calling again in a week; ships were still being commissioned but it would be down to luck if a vacancy occurred while he was in the office.

Which would have been fine; Woodward had nothing else to occupy his time. Yet, accommodation in London was not cheap; on the previous evening a very plain mutton pie had cost over a shilling. Then there was the obligatory bribe to the clerk if he even wanted to be seen as well as other necessary expenses. Half-pay for a lieutenant worked out at four guineas a month; if he lived frugally in the country for the rest of the time, he might indeed present himself for work on a regular basis. But those of better means had an advantage; with the rest of the week to kill there was nothing to stop them showing their faces at several significant naval bases and still make the regular London interview. With the cost of basic transport now rising to over tuppence a mile, he could not compete with such industry so any chance of a posting would be slim.

His thoughts drifted; shortly after quitting *Tenacious,* he had run in with Daniels, the upstart midshipman. The cove was in a chop house holding forth to a table of cronies while Woodward ate a more moderate meal unnoticed and alone. It seemed he would be facing a promotion board the following day and the result was pretty much guaranteed, in which case Daniels must be a lieutenant by now and, with his connections, probably employed. The concept did not bother Woodward greatly, there would always be those who passed him in promotion due to *who* they knew rather than *what*, and at least he was no longer forced to share a ship with the fellow.

The door opened a crack and a clerk's head peeped through. "Lieutenant Collins?" One of the apparent sleepers roused himself instantly and was suspiciously alert as he brushed his tunic down before leaving those behind with feelings of hope and disappointment. And then the door opened once more, and two further fresh and eager officers were admitted.

* * *

Lieutenant Cooper leant forward on the crate that was his seat and unrolled the superintendent's drawings. He and King had already spent all that morning and much of the afternoon inspecting the ship and there was still a good deal more to learn. He smoothed the paper out with his hands and both men peered at the fine lines for some while.

"I'm not sure the cockpits are big enough," he finally commented. "Having two, a larboard and starboard, wastes space; if we wanted to combine them, now would be the time."

"It would make passing further aft more difficult," King pointed out.

"And the stewards will be accessing the bread room at least twice a day," Cooper agreed.

"No," King said finally. "We should rate no more than six midshipmen and volunteers with a similar number of master's mates and other eligible warrant officers. The two make poor bedfellows, I'd think it better to leave matters as they are."

Cooper nodded and they sat back on their makeshift seats. The interview with Fraser had taken place forty-eight hours before; since then King had contacted Cooper, then made his way to Beaulieu and taken a room. The journey from London passed nowhere near Eastbourne, though, had it been otherwise, he would not have stopped. And there was something else that made him feel mildly guilty: he had misled Aimée.

While sending for Cooper he also wrote the briefest of notes that simply told her not to expect his immediate return. No details of Fraser's interview, and nothing that might lead her to suspect a command was in the offing. Not that he was intending to deceive; King had her best interests in mind. Should Aimée guess his time at home was limited, that he would not be spending the rest of his life with her in their echoing mansion, she would be distraught. And there had been enough upset of late.

Cooper broke into his thoughts with a welcome distraction.

"The riggers expect to start work in three days, and the first fifty hands have been detailed along with our initial warrant officers. We can have them aboard when we like though, before then, I'd say we'd better look to appointing more senior officers." He paused. "That is, of course, if you intend taking the commission..."

"Regulating office said men would not be a problem," King temporised. "With ships being laid off as they are, we have our pick and no need of the press."

"Neither do we require a wartime complement," Cooper added, "yet we shall have to decide soon."

Or rather, *he* would have to decide, King knew that.

Cooper was eager to take on the new ship and, if King wanted others to join them –Summers, Manton, maybe even the new man, Woodward – he must start contacting them. There were also the standing officers. Fraser had been right in his assessment; a peacetime deployment was a different proposition, and both *Viper*'s carpenter and boatswain were keen to retire once replacements had been found while King sensed her gunner was likely to follow. Were he to take responsibility for the ship there would be much else to do, and most of it must be completed quickly. Yet this was a decision he could not make on his own and, once more, regretted the brevity of his message to Aimée.

He glanced at Cooper; the man was watching, waiting, ready to be started on a project likely to dominate both their lives for several years and possibly ever. But if King allowed himself to become ensnared, he would also be committing Aimée, so she should probably have some say in the matter.

"There are more kidneys on the sideboard," she told him. "Jenny knows them to be a favourite."

"That was most thoughtful," King replied, although he did not rise for more. This was just another of the small indulgences allowed since his return home and they were starting to disconcert.

Three days before, he had left *Viper* in the capable hands of Cooper; by now Summers should have joined him as well as Morales, who would be taking over from her current carpenter. And their old boatswain was also willing, although unlikely to be with them for another week. By then the riggers would have started, so Amon must pick up the traces extremely quickly. There was no reply from Regan, although King was not unduly worried; good gunners were easier to find and would be in less demand with peace imminent. And neither had he heard from all the midshipmen, or Manton their sailing master, but again, it was early days. Even if no more rallied to the call he had the core of a good crew while the ship herself appeared extremely sound. His only concern on that last score was...

"And can I pour you more *chocolat*?"

King looked up and blinked.

"Thomas, you were lost in thought," Aimée told him. "Are you sure everything is quite alright?

"Forgive me, my dear, it is fine."

Her eyes stayed upon him. "You were away for such a long time yet so far have told me nothing of your travels."

"There was little of consequence," he blustered. "The Admiralty was extremely busy and, of course, they had not expected me to arrive so soon..."

"Of course," Aimée agreed. "Though your note did say that an admiral made himself available. Was there much to discuss?"

"Oh, a great deal."

"And it took all of five days?"

"Was that how long..." King began, and she was smiling now.

"No interview takes such time," Aimée told him firmly. "You travelled on, and I think I can guess where. Or at least, for what purpose."

He felt like a child caught scrumping.

"The only subject that can *captiver* you so is a ship. I believe they have offered one, and you went to inspect."

"Aimée, I was going to tell..."

"Oh, I am certain I should have learned everything in time," she said. "But not perhaps until all was settled in your mind. And though you may have come to a decision, there is still much that concerns you – is that not correct? So, tell me, Thomas, what is it?"

He pushed his plate to one side. "There is nothing specific, although you are quite right; they are the usual problems when accepting a new commission."

"And that is what you have done?" she checked. "You are to take another ship to sea and sail away. Will it be for years as in the past, or is that one of the matters still to be decided?"

"Aimée, I really do not know," he confessed. "She's a frigate, slightly smaller than *Tenacious*, and bound for the Med – so not as far as North America."

"And she will be away – how long?"

He shook his head; there truly was no way of telling. He might make a guess, but it would be that, and suddenly King felt she had been deceived enough.

"It is of no matter." Aimée sat down and took his hand. "We have had some time together and it has been good, though perhaps not as good as it might have been. I think a change would benefit us both."

"I certainly need to be at sea again."

"I know. I have always known: the sea is your life. And this house has too many memories. Perhaps when we return, we shall find another?"

"We?" King asked cautiously.

"I shall be going with you," she said.

"Aimée, I don't think that will be sensible."

"And why not? I am guessing your ship is not ready for sea; by the time she sails there will be no war and no reason not to have a woman on board." She picked up a fork and examined it carefully. "And *en outre*, I have sailed with you before, and survived."

"War is not the only danger aboard ship," he said.

"Oh, I know that also, there are the storms, and perhaps

illness – maybe even accidents – the things that never happen on land."

"Not quite to the same extent, perhaps..."

"And do you think I worry about them? Do you think I would rather stay here, safe, in a house that is already full of so many sad memories?"

"No. No, I suppose not."

"And who is your admiral?" she continued. "Does he not sail with his wife?"

"As a matter of fact he does not, though I hear he cares for her dearly."

"Well then he is the *imbécile*." The fork was dropped with an impressive clatter. "But does he inflict such lunacy on others? Or are his captains allowed to behave like normal men?"

King was old enough to remember officers like Jervis, who placed an absolute ban on carrying females of any description; Pellew was of a later era, and more lenient.

"I think it would be permitted," he said at last. "And I for one should be pleased to have your company. But only if you are certain; you did not stay for long in Halifax."

"In Halifax we had a house like any other; I was not with you and neither did we see each other so very often. It is the terrible thing to say yet, without the children, I am more free."

"I understand." King closed his eyes, and they were quiet for a moment.

"So, I will be coming with you," Aimée said at last. "When do we depart?"

* * *

"Told you they'd give him another." Stokes placed his tankard down. "Man like that, and all he's achieved – it were a certainty."

"And a frigate you say?" Early checked.

"She's lying at Bucklers. Coops is aboard and masts are in place but there's still a measure of fitting to be done. Might not be takin' on all her people for some while though I reckons we'd better make our way down to be certain."

63

"There'll be competition, mind," Groom warned. "It were hard enough finding a collier's berth an' old Tommo's a popular captain."

"Aye but some of us knows him of old," Stokes reminded. "An' he ain't the one to forget a shipmate."

"Certainly be a better bet than them colliers," Bovey snorted as he reached for his own pint. "Worst scran ever an' I breathed enough coal dust to last a lifetime."

"Well let's hope you won't have to breathe no more," Stokes told him.

"'Sright," Groom agreed. "Powder smoke's better for the lungs, an' Service grub's a sight more 'ealthy."

Chapter Six

They'd done a lot in two months. Principally, *Viper* was accepted from the dockyard and officially became part of the British Navy. Now fully rigged, armed and warped to a holding anchorage, what were previously empty, lifeless spaces were now noisily alive with men, while the entire vessel seemed less of a project and was fast becoming a viable ship of war. But even as she was being made ready, King wondered if another frigate were truly needed.

Since taking command there had been as many changes to the world as to his ship. At the end of March allied troops finally entered Paris making Napoleon's abdication a mere formality. Then, with a speed that suggested forward planning, the man himself was transferred to an island off the coast of Tuscany; a pleasant enough place, yet unlikely to satisfy one so recently set on global domination. Napoleon would still be close to world events, however, and more importantly, physically near those who would see him returned to power. Elba had been chosen by some Russian politician; were King consulted, he could have thought of far more remote locations that promised greater safety for all.

He had his own problems, however, and, though the war with France was finally over, the pressure on him remained the same.

It might have been due to Napoleon's incarceration, or simply a whim of his new Commander-in-Chief, but *Viper*'s presence was required on station with some urgency. What was little more than a terse note from Pellew had ordered them to sea with all despatch; even the customary sea trials would have to be limited to the most cursory of checks with any major defects corrected at their first port of call.

Which was Gibraltar, a place he knew well and one whose dockyard was more than capable of attending to the teething troubles of a refitted vessel. But King's concern was not wholly with his ship; there were already a good number of frigates on the Mediterranean Station. *Viper* must be required for a specific purpose, and he was keen to know what.

And the sudden need to commission did have advantages; as soon as there was a place for her, Aimée had quit their Eastbourne house. Though smaller than his previous ship, the captain's quarters aboard *Viper* remained generous and, while King attended to his duties, Aimée and Millie, her servant, set to work on their accommodation. There were obvious compromises of course; Aimée could share King's facilities easily enough although Millie – a girl from the estate – must be quartered elsewhere. And, whereas King's stewards berthed together on the lower deck, she required private space safely away from the regular hands. With the ship still in a state of flux, this was more easily addressed, and a storage area outside the gunroom converted for her use. So, while King was consulting with Robert Manning over vital changes to the sick bay, Aimée and Millie could address more domestic matters. Consequently, the great cabin soon boasted soft furnishings and, in the sleeping area, even a carpet while at night the deadlights could be covered by curtains and there were considerably more lamps than was usual. It was all very different from the austere arrangements King was accustomed to, although the place already felt like home.

And great strides had been made with recruiting. In the past, filling the lower deck was a perpetual problem. However great a captain's prestige, and no matter what prize money could be anticipated, few raised enough trained men to properly man their command. But with war in Europe a memory and the American conflict certain to follow, there were seamen for the taking and Cooper found he could recruit who he wanted exactly when they were required. As the ship neared completion, she steadily took on more prime hands to the extent that, apart from the ubiquitous ships' boys – the third-class volunteers that must be trained up for tomorrow's Navy – few were landsmen. It was a feat rarely achieved in the past although King guessed it would soon become the norm and, of all the changes in his long career, this was one of the greatest. And there were familiar faces amongst the new men, those that had served with him in the past and were prepared to do so again, which was a sincere compliment indeed.

And he was equally pleased by the appointment of his standing officers. These, the boatswain, gunner and carpenter, were essential to the maintenance of any vessel and it was usual for all to remain with a ship throughout her service. Such commitment meant each came to know her more intimately than any land-based family and probably love her more. Cooper asked *Tenacious'* former standing officers to join them, and all agreed. As a result, there were now known and trusted men to fill these important roles and they were not the only warrant officers to have rallied to the call.

The trait had been copied by higher ranks; a captain would be truly inept for his senior men not to follow, yet still, King was gratified to note all *Tenacious'* former lieutenants were now installed in *Viper's* gunroom. As was Manton, which was a distinct bonus as a skilled sailing master could make far more serving aboard an Indiaman.

Many of the essential stores were already stowed with the final victuals due to start arriving the next day. Then, as soon as a sailing date was agreed, powder, shot and finally water could be taken on board and *Viper* would in all respects be ready for sea. Cooper reckoned that should be in under a week and, with an experienced crew and a ship so freshly set up, King could see no reason why they might not make Gibraltar by the middle of June.

The Med in summer; the prospect would have made him laugh out loud, were captains permitted to for no apparent reason. An end to frail British sunshine and clean, clear air without the taint of heavy industry, along with a tideless sea that he knew well and liked. At that moment he could not remember feeling quite so fortunate and to make his happiness complete, Aimée would be by his side. And then he remembered the reason for her presence, and his pleasure dissolved into nothing.

* * *

Even without having passed his board, Daniels would still have been the senior midshipman. After all, he was the oldest and had served under Captain King before. He was also experienced; three of *Viper's* other young gentlemen were first voyagers and rated only as volunteers while Edwards was barely seventeen. Only Williams, recently turned eighteen, was a competitor, the rest still had much to learn. Though whether they would from Daniels was another matter.

For he made it clear the midshipman's berth was just his

67

temporary home. The actual date of Daniels' board had been delayed twice so, by the time he was examined, most of the prime posts for young lieutenants were filled. Of course, his family put in a deal of pressure, and a place would have come up eventually, although he was loath to wait. Most home appointments were for shore positions, either at the Admiralty or one of its bases and Daniels preferred to be on what he claimed to be his natural element. So, when hearing his former commander was actively recruiting, he immediately applied. Captain King might not be as manipulable as some, but he had an enviable reputation as a successful officer, and Daniels was quick to acknowledge there were other ways of furthering a career than by influence.

And the final clincher had been *Viper*'s next deployment; informed sources told him she was due to join the Med Fleet. Other than another stint on America's Eastern Seaboard – something that definitely did not appeal – it was a station that almost promised action. Distant postings were also more likely to bring promotion; once his sponsors did their stuff, he would be next in line for a lieutenant's berth in any of Pellew's vessels, although Daniels had another course in mind.

With a little manoeuvring, it should be possible to serve as a lieutenant in his current ship and remain under Captain King's command. Obviously, for that to happen one of the existing officers would have to leave, something that might stretch even Daniels' powers of manipulation. Yet, it would be the ideal outcome so was definitely worth pursuing.

While at school he conducted a whispering campaign against a master and the fellow left in disgrace before the end of term. Something similar against a senior man should be equally successful. He would wait until they were at sea and away from any competition, then a few sparks of slander scattered amongst the tinder of the midshipmen's berth and warrant officers' mess would soon take light. After that, he might engineer opportunities to run the fellow down more publicly. Within a month, maybe two, all would either dislike or distrust the man sufficiently to make his downfall self-generating and, by Christmas at the latest, he would be on the beach with Daniels comfortably installed in his place.

The only question was who to choose as his target, although even that was easily answered. Summers, as the junior lieutenant, would have been the obvious choice, but he was well established and popular with all senior men as well as the captain. But Woodward was a different matter; the cove had only been with their last ship a few months when Daniels found him particularly susceptible to his own subtle brand of insubordination. With a bit of careful manoeuvring, he should soon be in the captain's bad books; then it would just be a question of whether he left willingly or found himself pushed.

* * *

Captain King did indeed know Michael Summers well. On first joining one of his commands the lad had barely been in his teens and, though now a lieutenant and rapidly gaining skills as well as seniority, King still found it difficult to regard him as anything other than a dew-eyed child. However, the formal manner in which the youngster had asked to speak with him was concerning and, as Summers took a seat in front of his desk, King regarded him cautiously.

And he was right to have been suspicious; Summers appeared ill at ease and for a moment King wondered if his pleasure in discovering so many of *Tenacious'* officers wanted to follow him was premature.

"Mr Cooper tells me the last of the beef is due tomorrow," he began, after searching for a neutral subject.

"So I believe, sir." Summers was obviously eager to play the part. "And then we can start with shot and powder."

"Which is faster than anticipated, while you seem to be settling quickly. So, tell me, Michael, how are you finding the ship?"

"Oh, I like her fine, sir. A change after *Tenacious* – no smell of rot!"

"Indeed," King smiled politely. "And why did you ask to speak with me?"

Now all traces of humour left; Summers appeared almost desolate and King's worst fears looked like being realised.

"It's my wife, sir," he began, and it was not a good start. This was a personal problem; King would have preferred something on Service matters – issues concerning women, and anything connected with marriage were not his forte.

69

"I trust she is well?"

"Oh yes, sir. The difficulty is, she wishes to ship aboard."

That could have been worse, King supposed; at least it meant Summers was not thinking of doing anything foolish like applying for an exchange, although it did bring up further complications.

"I see."

"I fear she has not taken to England," the lad continued. "Too different from Canada, or so she claims, though I can see many similarities myself."

King nodded, Aimée had found it equally hard to settle in Halifax.

"And you want for her to share your accommodation and be victualled?" he asked.

"I hoped she could," Summers said. "You were kind enough to allow it on the journey home."

"I did," King agreed. "But this time the decision doesn't lie entirely with me. Even if I were happy for such an arrangement, we have no idea what Admiral Pellew might make of it."

At that point there came the sound of female laughter from the other side of the light deal bulkhead; Aimée and her maid were unpacking his cabin stores in the coach and something must have amused them. Since abandoning their Eastbourne house, and the memories it contained, Aimée had been determinedly cheerful – something King was keen to encourage   although it was a shame they should erupt so at that point.

He cleared his throat and continued. "Obviously we have women aboard already, however I have no wish to start a fashion."

"Of course not, sir. Though none of the gunroom officers wish to bring wives."

"You are sure of that?"

"I have checked, sir."

"We have yet to receive our marines and there will be two lieutenants to take charge, how do you know they are not married?" King almost said 'encumbered' but thought better of it.

"They'll be marine officers, sir," Summers beamed. "They don't get married on the whole – least, not the kind what goes to sea."

King had no idea what Summers meant but decided to leave well alone. With Aimée and her maid already aboard there was little he could say, although his earlier stance remained correct. It was one thing for a captain to bring his lady; allowing Mrs Summers to join them was a step further and would be opening the door for others to follow. And then what – their new purser produces a mate? The gunner? Where would it stop? Before anyone realised, *Viper* would be a ship full of women. He paused and considered further; Summers was watching him intently and King could remember being in such a position himself; that awful period of waiting while a crusty old officer comes to a decision. He sighed; he had no wish to lose the services of a fine lieutenant.

"Very well," he said at last. "She may join and share your accommodation and be victualled accordingly; I shall give orders to that effect. You will have to come to an arrangement with whoever purchases gunroom stores."

Summers brightened considerably and his cheeks were positively glowing with pleasure as King continued.

"However, should Mrs Summers imperil discipline in any way, or if Admiral Pellew takes exception to our having ladies aboard, she will have to be put ashore."

There was a crash from the coach, followed by another outburst of laughter.

"They all will," he added.

* * *

Stokes and his mates had made their way to *Viper* and been taken on readily enough; soon it was as if they had never left *Tenacious*, and Downes was now totally relaxed in their company. This was by no means his first mess, and most he berthed with in the past became friends eventually. But Downes now felt totally at one with his messmates.

He supposed much had to do with them all being volunteers as well as trained men; he'd never known a crew so blessed with seasoned, willing hands although there was something more about the chemistry that bonded their small group. And this was emphasised when a fresh hand was appointed.

"So, where you from?" Stokes, the mess captain, enquired.

"Darlington," Healy, the new man replied. He was thickset

71

with deep dark eyebrows and a solid jaw. Downes understood he had been taken aboard in place of a forecastle man who suffered a rupture.

"Served in a man-of-war before?" Bovey this time.

"*Only* in men-of-war," Healy sniffed. "Mainly liners, though there was one other frigate: *Indefatigable*."

A murmur of respect flowed around the table.

"Pellew's old command," Stokes nodded. "Fine ship."

"An' a fine captain. It's why I'm here," the newcomer told them. "Tried for a berth aboard *Caledonia* but all were taken. From what I hear, *Viper*'s to join her and being in the same fleet is the next best thing."

For a seaman to show such loyalty was a recommendation in itself, and Downes sensed his messmates warming to the man.

"An' you're rated able?" Stokes again.

"Been able in the last three ships, and ordinary three years afore," Healy said. "They was considering me for quartermaster's mate in the last barky, then she were paid off."

Better and better; a regular Jack, although there was still something about the man that worried Downes.

"So, you got any niggles?" Groom asked.

"Niggles?"

"Aye, any bad habits we should be aware of?"

"We don't want no petty thieving," Longdon agreed. "And you'll be expected to keep yourself clean."

It was a relatively harsh welcome for a newcomer and Downes was reminded of his own admission into the mess. Nevertheless, Healy took the question in good heart.

"No fear on any of those," he said. "Only contest you might find is I tends to speak me mind. Some might say too much."

"I don't see that as a niggle," Stokes announced and there were grins and nods from most present.

"Well, that's fortunate," Healy shrugged, "'cause I wouldn't give a monkey's cuss if you did."

Chapter Seven

Manning considered the candidate; he was the son of an apothecary and knowledgeable enough medically.

"So, you've been working as a farrier." The surgeon was looking at his notes. "And appear to have been an unofficial veterinarian. You did not consider training with Odiham?"

"Sadly, I could not meet their fees," Bewley explained. "Money has never been a strong point with me; frankly, sir, I am in the mire financially."

"Which is why you have applied to be a loblolly boy?" Manning asked.

"Yes, sir." He had a pleasant smile.

The surgeon nodded. It was not such an unusual story; a commissioned warship could be a debtor's haven. Once listed on a muster, there could be no physical or legal pursuance for debts of under twenty pounds and, in Bewley's case, this was clearly a major attraction.

But he seemed bright with an air of confidence; useful attributes for anyone in the medical profession. He also intended to better himself – Manning could already see him as an assistant surgeon. However, it was the present that concerned him more and Bewley should make an excellent sick berth attendant.

"And how could you cope with surgical procedures?"

Even some trained to the nines proved useless when faced with physical operations and it was not unusual to see the brightest run from the horrors of combat surgery.

"They do not bother me unduly, if that's what you're meaning, sir," he said. "I have lanced boils or applied sutures when necessary and set the legs of cows, sheep and horses while assisting with the birth of many such animals."

Manning nodded and made a mental note to suppress some of Bewley's past, the hands might not take kindly to being treated by a horse doctor.

"You do realise this is a ship of war and might go into

action?" he continued.

"Shall I be required to fight?"

Manning smiled. "Lordie no. But during combat the patients can come quickly and in large numbers. And I fear there may be a deal of blood – which can come as a surprise, even to those supposedly used to the stuff."

"Blood I would expect," he nodded, "though would prefer not to shed any myself."

"There should be no need for that. And are you happy with the sick berth arrangements?"

The question had little to do with Bewley's suitability; Manning might even have been fishing for compliments. *Viper*'s medical department had only recently been completed and, though smaller than the provisions aboard *Tenacious*, was a great improvement. Rather than being consigned below, it was housed forward and benefitted from excellent light and ventilation. Manning had also been able to add a good-sized dispensary, which would double as a consulting room, while easy access to the roundhouses meant an unpleasant aspect of sick berth nursing would be eased.

"I like them fine, sir," Bewley agreed with a confident smile.

"Excellent, then there is little more to be said; you may consider yourself appointed."

* * *

Longdon edged along the main yard and glanced with mild contempt at the deck below. That morning the larboard watch had set the mats – the hefty pieces of canvas thrummed with rope that kept spars and lines from chafing, and it was customary for essential work aloft to be checked by the opposing watch. As a skilled topman, the task had fallen to Longdon and entailed him covering every yard on the main. It was work he especially liked and, though not exactly skylarking, there was nothing to say he couldn't enjoy himself. With luck he might even stretch it to last until the end of his watch and then there would be Up Spirits and the main meal of the day. The prospect of both appealed; they were still on petty warrant victuals, and Longdon was partial to a bite of fresh beef.

But for now he was content in his lofty perch. The view of the anchorage was impressive and would only improve as he made his way up the mast. However, like most of his type, Longdon took an unashamed delight in showing off his skills, and those of a seasoned topman could be impressive.

Currently the captain's wife and her maid were on the quarterdeck and he had a mind to attract their attention. Nothing so indiscreet as a shout, although he did let out a subtle cough before casually slipping off the horse – the line on which his bare feet rested – and hoisting himself onto the spar itself. Longdon felt supremely comfortable on a main yard and could stroll up and down all day long if he chose.

Such feats never failed to impress landlubbers and the fact that these were females was an added incentive. Yet however much he rasped and croaked, the pair remained fixed on the collection of small crates currently being transferred from a lighter to the ship. Stokes and Groom were manning the whip – its line actually ran from the very spar that held him, and it was clear both were taking full use of an opportunity to talk with the maid. Well good luck to them; the girl berthed with the officers, an area that would soon be protected by a permanent marine guard, and they would be lucky to get so close again.

There were no paunch mats on the lower yard, so little need for him to even be on the spar, although that hadn't deterred him any. One of the main delights in being aloft was the relative privacy; in a world where all worked, rested and slept within touching distance of another, any chance to be alone, and in the fresh air, was precious. A boatswain's party was in the foretop, with the man himself several feet above them on the crosstrees, but Longdon had exclusive use of the mainmast.

He raised himself with both arms extended scarecrow fashion. At sea it would be different, and he could never have been quite so casual; at sea walking along the yard, as he now was, would also have been noticed by the quarterdeck and might lead to some mild punishment. They were at anchor watch, though, so Longdon felt relatively immune. And besides, he was aiming for an entirely different audience.

The women below had now opened one of the cases and

were poring over the contents; he tried another cough yet still they ignored him. Disappointed, Longdon reached the mast and turned his attention to the breech and hanging mats placed below the top; both were freshly made and had been expertly tied: this truly was a waste of time.

Transferring to the maintop was child's play and, though he tried to make it look anything but, there was still no attention from below. Then he began to scamper up the starboard topmast shrouds, feet digging deep into the ratlines as he went. He arrived at the crosstrees in a matter of seconds, before reaching up for the futtock shrouds and hanging for a moment, body almost horizontal, with only the strength of fingers and toes to keep him from falling to the deck below.

When learning his craft, the thought of a bone-cracking meeting with death constantly filled his mind, although he was wise enough now to know how to keep such fears at bay; far better to accept the risk and concentrate wholly on staying secure. So, when Longdon pulled himself over the crosstrees and felt for the shrouds leading up the topgallant mast, he could do so without worrying overly for his own safety. From there he could climb onto the topsail yard and continue his inspection.

Of course, now he must be less casual; the spar itself was lighter and narrower by several inches; walking along the thing, though possible, was verging on reckless. And anyway, the women below had become barely distinguishable from any of the tiny figures; he might as well set his mind on the work ahead.

Which he did; on reaching for the topsail yard, Longdon was thinking of little else, and it was simply bad luck that caused the scream to come from below just as he was transferring his weight.

And it was loud – loud and penetrating; even Longdon, dangling a hundred feet or more above, jumped slightly as his right hand groped for the spar. His foot reached out to the horse for support but instead thrashed uselessly in free air just as his hand missed the yard and, for the first time in years, Longdon knew fear.

Laughter followed the scream – something unexpected must have been discovered within the linen – although that meant nothing to the topman who suddenly found himself fighting, lonely and unnoticed, for his life.

His body was falling away, there was now only one chance – one way to stop himself plummeting to the deck below – and he took it. With a push from his left leg, he dived for the spar, which had become his only hope of safety. The pine was burnished from years of wear and what fingernails Longdon possessed failed to gain a purchase. He raised his other hand and tried again to take hold, then that too began to slip before finally, mercifully, one foot found the horse.

The thin line was enough to steady him; soon he had a firmer grip on the spar and then was heaving himself over, the warm pine pressing reassuringly hard against his pelvis. Positioned so he had a perfect view of the deck and could see Stokes and Groom stamping their feet like a couple of madmen while the women held handkerchiefs to their mouths in shock. Longdon finally drew breath; he could not tell what was going on below, but when it came to capturing the women's attention, his messmates had beaten him hollow.

* * *

"We now have our final loblolly boy," Manning announced when he and those senior officers not on duty were taking a mid-morning beaver in the gunroom. "Name of Bewley – seems a likely fellow."

"I remember a Bewley aboard *Tenacious*," Cooper mused from the head of the table. "Would this be the same?"

Manning shook his head. "Never laid eyes on him before, though glad to have done so now. I'm still awaiting an assistant surgeon; until one's appointed, he'll be a real benefit."

"So, tell us more of him," Browning, their new junior lieutenant of marines, urged.

"Never had you down for a medical man," Davis, his senior grunted. Both officers had come aboard the day before with *Viper*'s full contingent of marines expected to follow shortly. But simply having redcoats at the gunroom table marked the final stage in turning her into a warship.

"Son of an apothecary," Manning said, "so is well used to making up medication. And though not quite twenty and five, he's

77

assisted with minor surgery and performed several procedures himself."

"Minor surgery is not what we expect aboard a warship," the senior marine declared. "Can he hold his own in the gore of battle? I don't want my leg removed by some pale-faced child who faints at the sight of claret."

Manning considered the officer; this was only the third time they had met and on each occasion the surgeon liked him less. Davis was old for a seagoing marine, yet behaved like a swaggering youth, and never missed the chance to delight in the brutalities of battle.

"He claims to be accustomed to blood," the surgeon replied, "though has no wish to shed any himself."

"Is that so?" Davis demanded in wonder. "Then what in heaven's name *does* he like?"

* * *

"'Undreds of the buggers, there were," Stokes told them later over their midday meal. "Must have been a proper nest. But these weren't babies, all was fully grown."

"Mice, were they?" Longdon asked absent-mindedly; until then he hadn't been listening to his mess captain's story – petty warrant victuals were being served and his portion contained a positive chunk of prime stewed beef.

"Na, spiders," Groom told them. "Chest must have stayed sealed long enough for them to grow big an' juicy."

"Rattled the captain's lady, that were certain," Stokes continued happily.

"And her bint," Groom smiled at the memory. "'Ung on to me like I was her long-lost love, so she did."

"That would have been it," Longdon exclaimed. "I was aloft at the time an' heard a kerfuffle." For a second those terrible moments came back, but Longdon's meal was truly good, and they were soon dismissed.

"Reckon most of the anchorage did," Stokes agreed. "An' the dockyard."

"I 'eard her and all, clear as a bell," Bovey added. "And I

was on the orlop."

"Give you the shakes, did it Longers?" Groom enquired.

"Aye." Bovey again. "Consider the quick way down, did ya?"

But the topman shook his head. "It'd take more than a couple of screeching biddies to see me miss a footin'," he said.

* * *

When *Viper* first left the anchorage, she made a glorious sight. Her pristine paint sparkled in the early morning sun and with crisp, matching canvas, gleaming metalwork and freshly blackened spars she was a vision to stir the heart of any patriot. Yet on her return, a bare fifteen days later, the frigate had taken on a more functional appearance and could have been mistaken for any other commissioned warship. For in that short period of thrashing about the Channel, there had been a series of exercises that pushed her to the very limit.

And not just the ship, all aboard, from the greenest third-class volunteer to King – who barely left the quarterdeck – had been through countless drills that left them weary, raw and breathless. All hands were turned out at a moment's notice with the waisters, afterguard and forecastle men set to exercises as diverse as clearing for action, fighting imaginary fires or manning all boats with armed boarding parties. And the topmen were equally tested; while their terrestrial colleagues laboured below, they took in, let out or replaced canvas, struck or set up topmasts and yards, and every other apparently pointless procedure that their evil officers could devise. During those hectic two weeks the ship had also been commanded by midshipmen and master's mates, her bilges flooded, then pumped dry, and the trim constantly adjusted while everyone lived with the echo of live gun drill ringing in their ears. And, even if the lower deck might not agree, they were blessed with the weather. On the third day a storm blew up which, though nothing like that expected during a Mediterranean winter, was enough to stretch the warship's seams – and her men – just that little bit further.

However, as they resumed their previous station in the anchorage, King knew the time was not wasted. Two weeks might be short for sea trials yet, with a crew already well-seasoned, it would suffice. There were some minor defects to attend to – the mizzen mast needed re-chocking and some caulking was proving insubstantial, but these could be addressed. What mattered more was that the men were basically sound, and it was far easier to repair a ship than her people.

So, when topmasts were set down once more, and *Viper* cautiously relaxed, King was in a better mood and finally able to appreciate his new quarters, the comforts of which extended far beyond soft furnishings. Yet when he and Aimée took their first civilised meal together, conditions were hardly ideal.

The rain, which had begun when they took up their berth, now beat a regular tattoo on the strakes above and, as some of *Viper*'s defective caulking was on the quarterdeck, several pails were needed to catch the drips. And despite the meal itself being good, they were still to be visited by the victualling lighter so there were none of the fresh vegetables all had been anticipating. For some reason, Aimée had also chosen to serve everything on standard shipboard crockery when King was certain something more elegant had been ordered.

"I did say you could have transferred ashore," he reminded when they were finished. "A ship undergoing sea trials is not the most agreeable of places."

"Oh, I found it otherwise," she told him. "It was a test for me as much as any of your sailors and I think I survived."

"Your servant is better now?"

"Millie is asleep," Aimée replied. "I think the *mal de mer* has gone for good."

King nodded; in his experience the condition might return when they put to sea once more though should not be so severe. "And were there many breakages?" Something at the back of his mind forced the question, which he instantly regretted.

"Apart from much of the dinner service, which you are aware of," Aimée added pointedly, "I think we were extremely lucky."

Once it was mentioned he did remember, but at the time *Viper* had been on a lee shore. And even now, in the peace of a sheltered anchorage, he could feel little regret about a few pieces of broken crockery.

"It was partly my fault," she continued. "I should have

realised Millie was sick and checked all was stored correctly."

"I am sure the damaged pieces can be made good," King said. "If not, we shall be in Gibraltar shortly and the rock has ample supplies of such things."

"So, we will be leaving so soon? Can I not go ashore in England to buy more?"

The look of disappointment brought feelings of guilt that King was quick to dispel. He had explained from the outset that this would be no pleasure trip; there was a perfectly sound house in Eastbourne, one that didn't leak and remained static at all times. If a few pieces of broken china were going to upset her so, she might have been better off staying there.

"I fear not," he said. "Once we have topped with water, powder and shot I expect us to be under way. The next time either of us steps on dry land we will be in the Mediterranean, and hopefully enjoying better weather."

"Of course," she said, once more the dutiful companion and King felt an unexpected wave of tenderness. Though not his legal wife, Aimée was in every other sense his partner, and he loved her dearly. Yet still there were times when she really could be quite thoughtless.

Chapter Eight

They were lucky with the weather; their passage south was pleasant indeed with even Biscay proving amiable and, when Gibraltar finally drew into sight, *Viper* took on an almost festive atmosphere. And King had more reason than most to be cheerful; they were due to call at the base to deliver mail and despatches, then collect the same for Pellew's fleet. But there were an inordinate number of warships at anchor and one looked like *Caledonia*, his new Commander-in-Chief's flagship.

"I believe we have struck lucky," he said, turning to his first lieutenant.

"It appears so, sir," Cooper agreed. "I shall advise the gunner of the flag's presence."

Pellew had recently been appointed Admiral of the Blue, although that made no difference to the number of guns *Viper* must fire in salute. What mattered more to King was he had also been made a Baron, so was entitled to be addressed as 'my lord'. He must be sure to remember that.

"Interrogative from the flag, sir," Williams reported.

"Make our number and the private signal if you please. And Mr Regan may begin." Having Pellew's flag to acknowledge along with government house would keep the gunner busy for some while.

"Good to come across them so," Manton murmured. "Saves a deal of chasing about – the Med's an easy place to lose shipping."

"Flag's signalling us to anchor," the midshipman announced over the first of the frigate's saluting guns. "And several shore boats are heading our way."

Only one would be official; Manning must produce their medical certificates and there would be the usual rigmarole of customs declarations and the like. The rest were probably just bumboats; local hawkers keen to relieve their crew of anything they would trade in exchange for fruit, trinkets and clothes, although it was the less innocent luxuries that were King's main concern.

"Lieutenant Davis, I'd be obliged if your men would assume their shore positions."

A word from the marine officer was translated into something far harsher by their sergeant, and two crisp files of red-coated sea soldiers took up position alongside both bulwarks before snapping to attention. King looked on with approval; there was no end to the lengths the average seaman would go to in pursuit of alcohol and it would be surprising if a little 'sailor's joy' were not smuggled aboard at some time during their stay. But, with armed marines in attendance, the chances were reduced.

"Beggin' your pardon, sir?"

King turned. It was Dob, their new purser. The fellow was appointed as soon as they started taking on supplies and, from what he could tell, performed his duties adequately. Still, King was always suspicious of any officer who made most of his income at the expense of his shipmates, and Dob appeared little different from others of his type.

"I was 'opin' to step ashore, soon as it is convenient, like. We was short delivered on tallow, whale oil an' rosin, an' the gunroom's in sore need of cabin stores."

"Very well, as soon as we are permitted to anchor you can have a cutter."

"Thank you, sir. An' may I be so bold as to take a midshipman with me?" Dob added. "Mr Daniels 'as expressed an interest in seeing how provisions is requisitioned."

That was a different matter; Daniels was the only midshipman to have followed them from *Tenacious*, something King privately regretted as he was also the only one he actively disliked. The lad always managed to combine the air of an admiral with the arrogance of an earl. King had even thought twice about taking him although, however secure he felt himself, it was better not to offend someone who boasted the first minister as a godfather. Still, Daniels had recently passed his board so would doubtless find a lieutenant's berth before long. Then they would be rid of him for good.

"I will be issuing orders regarding shore leave in due course," he replied. "Though you may take Mr Daniels now if you wish."

The purser saluted smartly enough but, as he turned away,

King caught sight of Daniels watching with unconcealed approval from the break of the quarterdeck. A spark of anger briefly rose into a flame, and he was about to countermand the order when Williams, the signal midshipman, spoke once more.

"From the flag, sir. Our number with the union at the mizzen topmast head: 'Captain to repair on board'."

There was a buzz of comment from the quarterdeck in general and Manton exchanged a glance with Cooper; this was what they were waiting for. Speculation had been rife in the gunroom for some time, but the next hour should tell them exactly why *Viper* had been summoned.

"Very well," King grunted as he cleared more mundane matters from his mind. "Call away my gig."

* * *

"You'll be going ashore I assume," Woodward told Summers.

"Soon as we're able," the junior lieutenant confirmed. "Suzie's never been to Gib: I promised to show her the town."

Woodward nodded; he was intending a shore trip himself and had hoped to pair up with his friend although didn't welcome the prospect of making a third with a married couple. The ship was still settling to her anchor and the captain had been called to the flagship so it was likely they would remain for a while, but something major might equally be planned. In which case, *Viper* may be ordered back to sea almost immediately, and Woodward was keen to stretch his legs.

Knowing Daniels was already ashore only increased his desire. On learning the cove had followed him to the new ship, Woodward seriously considered turning down Captain King's offer; the midshipman had been annoying enough before and, with a passed certificate for lieutenant in his pocket, was bound to be more so. Yet there was a lesson in discovering even one so connected could not find an immediate appointment, which finally persuaded Woodward to accept the commission.

His predictions were proving correct, however; the entire business of setting up *Viper*'s armament had been subject to criticism and comment. Woodward persevered and was now reasonably pleased with the result; each gun drill having proved

84

smoother than the last, although having a smug wiseacre hovering at his elbow hardly made the task easier.

But if Daniels were ashore, he may be applying for another position; his family's influence would certainly reach as far as Gibraltar, and it would be strange if some form of lieutenant's post were not found. In which case he would be quitting the ship and, as far as Woodward was concerned, the sooner the better.

* * *

HMS *Caledonia* was an impressive sight; over two hundred feet at her gundeck and nearly three thousand tons burthen, when launched she was the largest line-of-battleship in the British Navy. And it wasn't just her size that made her remarkable; the three full gundecks delivered a broadside weight of over fifteen hundred pounds and, though large enough to dwarf such monsters as *Victory* and *Royal Sovereign*, she was also rumoured to be an excellent sailer. And her size had another advantage; King's gig was approaching from the bows so her pronounced tumblehome was obvious. The ship rode easily in the flat calm of harbour and the sight of a bo's'n's chair already hanging at the main yard gave King a sudden urge for recklessness. To be plucked from his gig then dangled from a line and ultimately deposited on deck was not the most dignified form of arrival, especially when he had used an entry port several times since the loss of his arm. Admittedly, previous occasions had been more casual, and not with his new Commander-in-Chief and the entire Mediterranean Fleet on hand to witness. But the sky was clear, the sun blindingly bright and, as so much had already gone his way, King felt entitled to take a few risks.

"Bring us alongside," he muttered to the midshipman at the helm. "Starboard entry port."

"Alongside, sir," Williams repeated with what might have been the faintest hint of enquiry. Nevertheless, the lad laid a course to close with the mighty hull readily enough, while King suppressed his first qualms of doubt.

And, as the boat took up position and the massive ship towered above, those fears increased. Bright, white, canvas-covered man ropes were rigged to either side of the entrance steps, although he could only use one and must change his grip at least twice before gaining the safety of the entry port. Should he slip and fall back, it would not be the forgiving sea that caught him, but his own gig. He might break a limb – his back even – to say nothing of the loss of dignity.

"Shall I pull away when you've clapped on, sir?" Williams asked, obviously following his captain's line of thought. But King shook his head; he had no intention of clinging to a man rope while the midshipman manoeuvred his gig; better to take a risk and go for broke.

The boat rubbed gently against the battleship's side and King raised himself gingerly while checking those with boat hooks were keeping them secure. He reached out for a man rope and noticed the slight rise and fall of the gig that made the flagship feel unusually solid and secure. It was hard to believe so much bulk was actually afloat. Yet he must not delay; Pellew and his entourage would be waiting on the upper deck; it would be good to catch them out by boarding as an able-bodied person.

He stepped up to the first ledge and paused for no more than a second before shifting his entire weight onto the big ship. Behind him, Williams muttered an order, but, with more urgent matters to attend to, King had no mind for anything else

Now that both feet were on the lowest step he would have to move his grip. For most this would be a simple operation with one hand holding the left man rope while the other sought a fresh purchase on the right. There was no such luxury for King; he would have to release his hold then, before tottering backwards, snatch another as high as could be managed.

He gritted his teeth and reached up; the entry steps were generous though still did not take much of his foot beyond the toe and he only managed to advance his hand by a few inches. This was enough to bring him onto the next ledge, however, and he could raise himself a little higher.

Looking up it became obvious that, rather than two or three changes of handhold, there would be far more and, yet again, King questioned his own wisdom. Had he been sensible and accepted the bo's'n's chair, he might be safely aboard by now. But there was no sense in thinking so, he could hardly change his mind and, once more, imagined Pellew and the other senior officers awaiting his arrival. They would be expecting a cripple – the word had been overheard often enough for him to know how some considered him. This was an excellent opportunity to prove himself otherwise.

Once safely on the next ledge he sought a fresh hand hold, and this time managed one slightly higher. It was not enough to allow him more than a step, though and, looking up, there was still a long way to go. But as he continued it became easier; soon he was on the tumblehome's shoulder and, rather than falling backwards, he could keep his balance and even feel himself being drawn towards the liner's hull. And then his hand reached for the brass plate that was effectively the flagship's doorstep; one final pull and his eyes drew level with her deck.

A wicked smile came to his lips. Pellew would be caught out: they all would. He had proved he could be as agile as any able-bodied captain, and probably more than some. Indeed, there were those on *Steel's List* who would have taken the whip through indolence rather than physical disability. However, once King was able to stand in the doorway itself, all was not as he expected.

Rather than an empty space, there was a positive welcoming committee on hand. As he stepped into the darkness of the flagship's 'tween decks, a line of sideboys began to pipe him aboard in the customary manner, and there was Pellew himself with what must be his flag captain – King had temporarily forgotten the man's name. All were expecting him, indeed the admiral seemed especially welcoming; as he stepped forward and offered his hand there was a smile on his face as if he had been sharing a joke.

"Welcome aboard, King," he told him. "Glad to see you. Allow me to present Captain Sibly."

King shook hands with his fellow senior captain, who seemed just as amused. But Pellew disliked small talk and was already turning his back on his visitor.

"There is much to discuss. Join me in my quarters, won't you?"

Sibly shrugged. "We'd better follow. The admiral likes to see things done, and neither does he suffer fools."

"I have heard as much," King said as they made their way aft.

"Oh, do not concern yourself." Sibly paused for a moment. "You've already made a good impression. He was sure one of your reputation would reject the whip and board in the conventional manner, though I must confess to thinking otherwise."

"Then I am sorry to have disappointed."

"It is not being proved wrong that hurts," Sibly confessed as they set off once more. "I have only served with his lordship a matter of weeks yet am already accustomed to that. But your high jinks at the entry port cost me a guinea wager."

* * *

"There will be no smoking of cigars in the cockpit," Daniels announced. "And neither pipes –Lord help us! And I do not approve of the taking of snuff."

His brief trip ashore had confirmed all expectations; they received him well and his name was definitely known but, despite the clerk trying to move heaven and earth for him, there were simply no vacancies for a junior lieutenant.

"The introduction of pets is also forbidden, and I will have no truck with any form of gambling."

That being the case he would remain aboard *Viper*; Pellew was a fine admiral and well known to his family – a message from his father should see him filling the first available post, although Daniels still had his other plan that should see him suited without having to move ship.

"Formal arrangements are also needed to see to our laundry; marine servants may be all very well, though cost money and do a lackadaisical job. Far better to undertake such tasks ourselves."

It was one of the rare occasions when all *Viper*'s young gentlemen were present in the midshipman's berth, so the ideal time for him, as senior, to set matters straight.

"To that end, I have made out appropriate notes which I would like you all to read." The berth's table was square, so it was difficult to be at the head, as such, but Daniels had an entire side to himself, whereas the other five were squashed about the remaining three. He shoved a paper across for them all to consider.

"I think you'll find there isn't a smoker amongst us," Edwards said, angling for a view of the sheet. "And standing orders already rule against naked flame below decks."

"I, for one, have never taken snuff," Williams, added a little sanctimoniously. He was closest in age to Daniels and, though he recognised his seniority, didn't care much for the bounder's manner.

"Which is how it will stay," Daniels grunted. "Foreign postings can lead to a change of habit, and I won't have such filth in my quarters."

Edwards looked up when the cockpit was referred to as such, although there was already enough room for contention in Daniels' paper. The three youngsters were still studying each word as if it were the very Gospel itself, but he had read enough.

"Sweeping the deck twice daily," he said. "Is that truly necessary?"

Daniels relaxed in his chair, glad to have been challenged on an incontrovertible point. "I know the first luff of old," he said. "Coops is a stickler for cleanliness and shall back me to the full."

"Maybe so," Williams conceded, "and I take your point about the washing of crockery. Yet do not see your name against any of the duties."

"And neither will you, Mr Williams. Do I have to remind you again; I am a passed midshipman: a lieutenant in all but name?"

"A lieutenant when you have a posting," Edwards pointed out. "And that might not come for some while."

"And until it does, I remain the senior midshipman," Daniels agreed. "*Your* senior midshipman and expect my orders to be obeyed."

* * *

"Mrs Summers will be joining us shortly," Aimée announced.

"Mrs Summers?" Millie, who was in the process of combing out her mistress' hair stopped suddenly.

"Yes. Is that a problem?"

The girl shrugged. "No mum, though she has a funny way about her."

"A funny way?"

Millie considered for a moment before deciding to confide. "It was when we first met, what she said to me..."

"And what did she say?"

89

The girl braced herself. "It were, 'Have you got a name, dear?'"

Aimée smiled. "And was that so *terrible*?"

"Well, it weren't very nice." She began to address the hair again. "Everyone's got a name; wouldn't be natural otherwise. Does she think I were born without one?"

"It's Millie." Aimée's expression was now mildly wicked.

"I know it's Millie," the girl said, tugging slightly with the comb. "Just a funny way of askin' for it, that's all."

"Well, she may be accompanying me ashore," Aimée said.

"Not going with the captain, mum?"

"Oh, I expect I shall eventually. Captain King knows Gibraltar well, but both he and Lieutenant Summers have their duty to attend to."

The girl gave a wry grin. "From what I hears, not all in Gibraltar is fit to be seen," she said.

"Is that so?" Aimée was smiling also. "And what do you know of the place? This is surely your first time away from the estate?"

"First time," the girl agreed, taking a ribbon and threading it through the thick curls, "Though not the last; I hear-ed a lot about it and many others. I tell you, mum, there's so much more to this travel lark than I ever thought – when I thinks of all them years a-wasted!"

"How old are you, Millie?"

"Seventeen, mum – or as near as makes no difference."

"Then there is much more to come. And you would do well not to listen to stories the *matelots* tell you."

"Oh, I don't pay them no notice." The girl seemed insulted. "Them's only after one thing, and I ain't giving it. It were the boys what told me."

"The boys?"

"Them what lives downstairs. Officers they are, and oh, so smart!"

"They may be smart, but most are hardly older than you, and some a good deal younger. Take what they say with the piece of salt."

"Oh, you don't want to worry about me, mum; I grew up in the country and can look after miself."

Aimée considered her servant in the mirror. Her face was

undoubtedly attractive, yet it was a puppyish beauty and destined to fade, while her figure, though by no means plump, was dominated by shoulders made strong by the annual harvest. A shout from the marine sentry stationed outside made them both jump.

"I wish they wouldn't do that, mum," the girl sighed.

"I have mentioned it, Millie, but Captain King said it has always been so and cannot be changed."

The door to the coach opened and Suzie Summers entered.

"Good morning to you, my dear," she said, then, looking pointedly at the servant, "And to you, Millie. Am I early?"

"No, it is I that is late." Aimée sighed. "Time is so different on a ship. For days there is nothing to do, then suddenly everything must be done at once."

"And we will hardly be welcomed on deck," Suzie agreed.

"Yet we can stay here and maybe have some tea?"

"Very well, mum," Millie said, taking the hint and handing the ribbon back to her mistress.

Once the two were alone, Suzie brought her chair closer. "Is it truly alright to talk?" she asked.

Aimée smiled. "But that is why you have come!"

"No, I mean *talk*," Suzie said. "You see I have news – important news. At least I think I have…"

* * *

For much of the time *Viper* had lain at anchor, Stoke's mess was on watch and manning the whips – the light tackle used for seeing small loads on or off the ship. So far they had distributed mail to boats from every warship currently in harbour and those stationed at the fore were now swaying up casks of rosin that Dob, the purser, had ordered. A lighter was approaching that Stokes' team, at the main, would doubtless deal with but until it came alongside, they were free to catch their breath and watch their messmates further forward.

"Grumpy old bugger," Stokes muttered, his eyes falling on Healy. The new man was leading those at the foretackle and doing it well, yet there was little of the relaxed humour expected when seamen undertake monotonous and undemanding work.

"Ain't he just?" Groom agreed. On first learning their new

messmate was a fellow northerner he had been pleased, although the newbie was still to endear himself to anyone aboard, and certainly his messmates.

"Handles himself well," Downes added. Both working parties were stripped to the waist but of all on deck, Healy had the best show of muscles.

"Fellow has the body of a prize-fighter," Longdon said in grudging respect.

"Got the brain of one an' all," Stokes sniffed.

"Oh aye, he's strong enough," Groom allowed. "And keepin' the lads in order, though there's nothing to say he couldn't do it with a smile on 'is face."

"I've known a few Yorkshiremen," Downes said. "All've been as nice as pie."

"I'm from Bradford myself!" Groom beamed and his messmate shrugged.

"There can always be exceptions."

"Well, I messed with a Yorkie, an' he were a right old grump," Bovey volunteered. "Fellow never had a decent word to say for anyone."

"What town was he from?" Groom asked.

"Never found out," Bovey replied. "No one asked, no one cared, just wished he'd sling his 'ook."

"And did he?"

Bovey shook his head. "Didn't have to, surgeon fixed him."

"The surgeon?"

"Aye, seemed he had a number of bad teeth; sawbones noticed and pulled 'em. In a week he were a changed man."

"You reckon Healy's got sore teeth then?" Groom pondered.

"I hope so…" said Stokes.

* * *

Pellew had aged since King last met him; it was hard to believe the heavy, full-jowled admiral seated behind the desk in *Caledonia*'s coach was once a lithe officer famed for an ability to perform headstands on a yard. But though the hair was thinning, and several front teeth had fallen by the wayside, there was no mistaking the fire still burning within, and King tensed slightly as

92

the great man treated him to a brief, yet frank, inspection.

"You made good time, Captain," he said at last.

"I understand *Viper* is needed on station with some urgency, my lord."

"That is so," Pellew confirmed. "All my ships are necessary, but frigates especially." He relaxed slightly. "You must not think that just because Boney is safely tucked away on Elba there is nothing to do."

King remained silent; frigates were the ideal ship for the Mediterranean and the lack of them had been an issue since before Nelson's time. Yet this was starting to sound like a regular deployment and not the specific mission he had been expecting.

Caledonia's coach adjoined the great cabin, although the space was as large as many City offices. The comparison was especially apt, in fact, as much of the business of managing both the ship and Pellew's entire command was conducted there, and considerable time spent fitting it out.

Ornamental panelling covered the spirketting with every section highly polished, as was to be expected. For this was a true flagship, intended not only as a base for a Commander-in-Chief but, on occasions, a floating embassy. Beyond the gleaming bulkhead would be a dining cabin suitable to host the grandest of state functions; in times past, world affairs had been decided in similar areas and vessels such as this used to convey both royalty and tyrants.

"We have two ships keeping an eye on the blighter at present," Pellew continued. "Would it were more but it don't do to make too much of our force. Campbell is monitoring Boney's individual movements, of course, and we are intercepting his mail, though he is bound to have discovered other ways of communicating with his sympathisers."

King knew of several prominent men who proudly proclaimed themselves pro-Bonaparte, although why anyone would want to follow a broken autocrat was beyond him, especially one whose plans had ultimately brought little other than death and misery.

"Yet, for the time being, he seems to be confining his activities to playing at soldiers." This was Sibly, Pellew's flag captain. The man was seated next to King and also faced the admiral.

93

"Indeed, he appears to be sprucing up the island's defences," Pellew confirmed. "Utter waste of time, of course; can't see anyone trying to attack, but that's not to say he wouldn't welcome certain visitors." The elderly man leaned back in his chair.

"I don't mind telling you, King, the situation is not one I welcome. France may be back under Bourbon rule, though that could fold at any moment, while Boney's brother-in-law is King of Naples, easily within reach and just waiting to be manipulated. And we know Boney of old; he could land pretty much anywhere and talk up an army, then the whole darned circus would start over."

"But he has no ships, my lord," King chanced, and there was a dubious look from his right.

"Not at his command, perhaps," Sibly said, "though France hardly lacks a navy; even as we speak two national frigates are patrolling to the north of Elba."

"Which obviously cannot be trusted," Pellew cut in. "And he also lacks colonies. Remember, gentlemen, all the ingenuity and bluster in the world will not create a fleet nor restore San Domenico. Yet still I think him a threat and still I wish him gone."

Sibly stirred uneasily.

"Oh, I know," Pellew allowed. "It is a long-ridden hobbyhorse though one that continues to attract and, you will forgive me, Edward, but Captain King must know my mind."

"Of course, my lord."

"I shall be sending *Viper* on independent patrol," the admiral continued, and King's senses sharpened. "She will be stationed to watch over the Sicilian Channel, on the lookout for any vessel or vessels likely to be heading for the Tyrrhenian. Stop and search whoever you like; I shall be pleased to deal with diplomatic issues that might arise. If you sense even a hint of sympathisers, have them sent into Malta for further investigation."

King nodded. It was hardly the independent command he envisaged yet should prove lively enough, and there were worse waters to sail than the Med in summer.

"You shall not be alone, of course," Pellew added. "Other ships will be carrying out similar duties both in that area and elsewhere, however I trust you to avoid acting in concert unless

94

absolutely necessary."

It was a strange statement but there would be more, King was certain, and Pellew did not disappoint.

"The action of any individual ship might avoid notice, though should battle squadrons be formed, it will be a different matter." Pellew let out a sigh. "If it becomes obvious we consider Boney vulnerable it will upset our allies, to say nothing of the encouragement given to his sympathisers."

King supposed that was true yet, again, wondered why somewhere more secure could not have been found to house the fallen emperor. Even when beaten, the man was proving troublesome.

"Considering the area Captain King will be patrolling, he might also be interested in the corsair problem?" Sibly hinted.

"Of course," Pellew agreed, although his eyes remained on King. "You will be aware of the difficulties our Barbary friends have been causing over the years?"

"I am, my lord."

"It is an irritation that should have been addressed some while ago. The Americans tried though little good did it do them: I think we might fare better. However, for as long as there is war in the west I am unable to give it my full attention, so it is possible you will run in with them and should know our policy."

King was now listening intently.

"It's no secret that we have used the Barbary Pirates to our advantage in the past," Pellew continued. "In truth, they have proved almost as helpful as they have nuisance. Our regular tribute not only guarantees the safety of any British ship, it also keeps smaller trading nations in their place."

That was an angle King had not anticipated.

"Their constant drain on other nations' commerce is considerable; were their presence removed, or the Barbary States effectively neutralised, commerce, in general, would flourish and specifically the market for cheaper American goods. For as long as we are at war with Washington that cannot be allowed, and the Med must remain a closed sea to the Yanks."

"Which is not to suggest they are never found hereabouts," Sibly pointed out.

"Of course not, but any Johnathan entering these waters has to pass by the Barbary Coast and effectively run the gauntlet,"

Pellew continued. "America will not, or cannot, pay sufficient tribute, so a fair number regularly fall victim to the corsairs, which is to our favour. Later, when there is universal peace, I intend to address the problem myself, and for all time, although that will not go down well with the City."

"The City, my lord?"

"As I have said, the Barbary Pirates present more of a problem to smaller nations, due to their trade being suppressed. Consequently, any action I take to neutralise them would benefit others more than ourselves and such acts of benevolence are not approved of by our friends in Capel Court."

King supposed it was a measure of Pellew's responsibilities as Commander-in-Chief that he must concern himself with commercial matters as much as military and, not for the first time, was glad to be free of such worries.

"So, I am to avoid contact?" he checked.

"Do not seek it, for sure; whether the men of business approve or not, the problem will eventually be addressed but it would be better not to give any indication of our intentions. *Viper* is larger than your average corsair and, even if some take to operating in squadrons, they know which side their bread is buttered so will flee at first sight."

King nodded; that was gratifying to hear. In fact, his entire future looked incredibly rosy. With France effectively neutralised and every American warship safely blockaded many thousands of miles away, he would have nothing to fear from any other vessel and could roam the seas in freedom. Even the danger of an illegal seizure had been taken from him, while there remained the chance of a stray Yankee trader to sweeten his finances further. For one who had spent so much sea time at war and on the defence, this would be a novel experience, although one he felt he could get used to, given the chance.

Chapter Nine

Viper had been on patrol for less than two weeks and travelled fewer than a thousand miles but already the calm and peace of Gibraltar seemed far distant. A storm had risen that morning and came down upon them within the space of a watch. Now, more than eight hours later, the wind still blew strong and hard, while carrying with it raw red sand from the African desert for an extra touch of misery.

"I would say it were the Sirocco, sir," Manton informed his captain, one hand covering his mouth in a futile attempt to keep out the driving grit. The pair were on the quarterdeck as King had been throughout. "Though that is more to be expected in spring or autumn."

King nodded but made no response; whatever it was called, the storm would have to be ridden out the same way. And so far they had done well; Woodward was officer of the watch when the first signs were noted and summoned him in good time, allowing the ship to be safely hove to long before the abrasive wind began. And although this was their first proper blow, nothing significant had carried away. There might be work to do on her paintwork later, but *Viper* was proving an excellent sea boat with a crew equally up to the mark. In truth, now they were in the ninth hour, King was growing slightly restless; his presence had not been required for some time and Manton had only just returned from a spell below.

He glanced about as the wicked idea formed. The first dogwatch had been set half an hour before and Summers was now at the conn; it would be three hours at least before dusk began to settle and King had already resigned himself to the storm lasting well into the night; there really seemed little need for him to remain on deck.

He manoeuvred himself so his back was facing the wind as he spoke to Summers; *Viper* was riding easily yet he still must cling to the binnacle.

"Are you happy to remain, Michael?"

The young man nodded emphatically though did not smile; such a wind hardly encouraged open mouths.

"Very well, I shall go below."

On entering his quarters, he submitted to the rigmarole of Aimée brushing him down and complaining about so much dust, although the contrast between the two lives was curiously welcome. And when he settled into one of the upholstered chairs they had installed in the coach, the strain of the past few hours began to ease.

"You have not been too inconvenienced I trust?" he asked while accepting the cup of warm chocolate. "The storm has caused no damage?"

"I have never been better," Aimée replied a little sharply, "and all your crockery is safe." Then she paused as if considering, before turning away.

"Was there something more?"

She looked back.

"It is a small concern, Thomas, and probably best if we do not speak about it now, but yes, there is illness in the ship."

King sipped at his drink; thanks to the flying grit it was the first fluid tasted since breakfast. "Millie, I suppose?" he said.

Aimée shook her head. "No, it is not Millie... Perhaps when this bad weather is over, we may all talk?"

"*All* talk?" That was vaguely worrying.

She shrugged. "Everyone will know soon enough and there is little that can be done. If you insist on speaking further now, perhaps we should send for Robert?"

If some form of illness were rife that was definitely the case. In any vessel packed so, disease could spread and, war or no war, *Viper* might lose a large proportion of her crew.

"I shall send for Manning forthwith," he said, setting his cup down, "though perhaps you might give me an insight?"

"It is Mrs Summers," Aimée admitted finally. "She is with child." Then, before King could react, added: "As am I."

* * *

98

"Sail to windward!"

The call came less than two hours later when there was still plenty of light and Summers was preparing to hand the watch over to Woodward.

Both officers looked up to the masthead fully aware that, whatever misery they endured on deck would be a hundred times worse aloft.

"What do you see there?"

"Two-masted," the reply came several seconds later. Overton must be staring directly into the grit-filled gale. "Hove to but driftin' down on us. Wait, I think she's comin' back to the wind."

A lighter vessel was bound to be pressed more easily than *Viper*, although the fact that she was making off when a British frigate came into sight might be significant.

"Go below," Summers snapped at the duty messenger. "Tell the captain we have a suspicious sighting."

"I'd say she were a schooner," Overton continued as the lad shot off. "Main tops'l's back in the wind, she's on the move!"

Summers and Woodward exchanged glances. To that point their patrol had been uneventful, every merchant stopped having proved innocent. It was just their luck the first true suspect should turn up in the teeth of a sandstorm.

"A sighting, Mr Summers?"

Summers touched his sou'wester as both the captain and sailing master approached. "To windward, sir; masthead believes her a schooner."

King instinctively glanced south as he fumbled with his oilskins, but nothing could be seen from the deck.

"I think we'd better take a closer look," he shouted. "Can you take us in, Mr Manton?"

The sailing master drew nearer. "I doubt that, sir," he replied, "not in this wind. Just to try would be taking a risk."

That was so; *Viper* might be safe enough hove to although, once underway, the chances of damage to her tophamper would increase significantly. And it was likely to be a waste of time; a schooner would lie closer to the wind and probably turn out a good deal faster.

"Very well," King bellowed and, even in the atrocious conditions, they could see his disappointment.

"Wait, she's in trouble!" Overton's call came just as King was preparing to quit the deck once more and all waited.

"Topmast's all ahoo, she must have rushed it."

"Midshipman of the watch!" A heavily shrouded figure that might be Williams sprang to attention. "Get aloft and tell me what you see!"

The lad responded instantly and, grabbing the deck glass, made for the windward shrouds and was soon flying up them. Watching nearby Woodward was sorry Daniels had not been the duty mid. – a bit of exercise would have done him good.

"Topmast looks to have sprung," Williams reported a few minutes later. "They're takin' in the tops'l but the fore's set and she's still underway."

That might be the case, though her efficiency was bound to be impaired.

"Then we may have a chance, Master!" King roared. "Bring her back to the wind, and we'll see if our spars prove the stronger!"

* * *

They did. Even before dusk was fully upon them, *Viper* had closed to the extent that the wounded schooner was in plain sight from the deck. In a couple of hours – maybe less – they would have her in range, although night would close on them long before.

"I think we might show our colours," King announced. *Viper* was already flying her commissioning pennant, so those aboard the schooner would know they were dealing with a British warship, but hoisting an ensign was almost an indication of intent.

"Nothing in reply," Cooper, who had joined them, reported. And then: "No wait..."

All on the quarterdeck were silent as the schooner continued to labour against the wind. Williams was correct, her main topmast had been reset lower in the housing, but the foreshortened spar would only take staysails, and the vessel's performance was suffering as a consequence. Yet an ensign was running up the jackstay, and there was a murmur of anticipation as it broke out. Though nearly flying against them, it was undoubtedly the stars and stripes.

The news brought mixed emotions to those on the quarterdeck; all now knew the chase was an enemy and one whose hull alone would return a pretty penny, but still they had to catch her. And with the wind, rain and sand continuing to beat against them, and a shaded sun already dipping in the west, that would be no easy matter. The schooner lay a good three miles off their starboard bow, they would have to narrow that considerably to make any impression. King glanced up, they were under fully reefed topsails, and he could almost see the canvas straining, but the question was unavoidable.

"Can we not close faster?"

Manton shook his head. "We're stretching matters as it is, sir," he said, "and so far have been lucky. It wouldn't take much to shake a spar or split a sail, and then we'll lose them for certain."

Which was correct, of course, yet there were several hours of darkness to come when something so small might make good her escape.

"Double the lookouts and change them with every bell," King told Woodward. "Likewise for the midshipmen: I want one at the masthead at all times."

"Very good, sir."

"And as soon as the sun fully sets, pass the word to darken ship."

The light was unmistakably fading now, if there were no change in the weather the schooner would shortly be invisible. It was always easier to hide from a known enemy however, so *Viper* must also disappear. After that, it would be down to luck, with perhaps a little intuition and a whole lot of guesswork. But nothing would happen for the next few hours, so he might as well get what rest he could. Besides, there was the small matter of Aimée's news that had not been properly discussed.

"I'm going below," he announced, "and recommend those not on duty to do likewise; this might prove a long night."

* * *

For Daniels, Captain King's instructions for midshipmen to be stationed at the masthead was particularly hard to take. Doubling the lookout was reasonable enough although why junior officers had to be inconvenienced was beyond him. The wind had lessened slightly but still came with a full load of sand so, by the time he reached the maintop and was starting on the topmast shrouds, the grit had already found its way inside his clothing. And he was a passed man, so a midshipman only by post; truly he should be excused the menial duties of a common reefer. The arithmetic was against him, however; with only six young gentlemen aboard, and the need for them to change every half-hour, he could not avoid at least one trick in most watches. Yet as he continued to climb, Daniels felt the resentment steadily build.

And having to relieve Williams didn't make matters easier. Of all in the cockpit, he was the closest to Daniels in both age and experience. Damn it, the cove was eligible to stand before a board himself: they might soon be competing for the same posts.

Williams was waiting as he clambered onto the crosstrees. "When last seen she were a point to starboard," he announced while Daniels secured himself to the topgallant mast. "Mind, I've not seen hide nor hair of her throughout my trick, and neither has anyone else."

Daniels cast a disdainful glance at the other occupants of the top. They were trained men admittedly and likely skilled at lookout duty, though having to share the cramped space with those of the lower deck was a further annoyance.

"Probably be Armfield relieving you," Williams said as he prepared to quit the crosstrees, adding, "that's if he isn't needed on deck."

"Needed on deck?"

Williams nodded. "The kid's barely thirteen and Woodward's officer of the watch: he'll probably take pity on him." Then his expression brightened. "Better prepare yourself for a double trick," he said, added a wink, and was gone.

* * *

"And there is no doubt?" King questioned.

"Oh, there is plenty of doubt," Manning assured. "I head the medical department of a warship; fellows such as me are not known for their ability to diagnose pregnancy."

They were in the surgeon's dispensary, which was the closest to a private space available; King had no intention of carrying out such a conversation in the echoing enormity of the great cabin.

"I'm reasonably certain in the case of Mrs Summers,"

Manning continued. "And she gives me the greatest concern. Were this the sixth or seventh, her age, and size, might not be a barrier, but I understand it to be her first."

"Indeed," King grunted without enthusiasm; the woman had been a nuisance since coming aboard. "Though you are more confident of Aimée?"

"Of a good outcome? Most certainly. She is younger, healthier and..." he paused, "...and has given birth before."

"Of course." King swallowed.

"However, I should add that diagnosing pregnancy in her case is especially tricky."

"How do you mean? Are not such things obvious?"

"Oh, there are several factors that indicate the possibility; in time these will increase, and my judgment can be confirmed." Again, the pause. "Or not..."

This was excruciating, King began to squirm in his seat.

"What I'm trying to say, Tom, is it's too early to be certain she is even with child. If so – as I am inclined to think – it can only be a matter of weeks and you might expect an offspring well into the New Year, whereas Mrs Summers is likely to produce before Christmas."

King nodded, that was news of a sort, though it hardly made what he must do any easier.

"I cannot have a pregnant woman aboard my ship," he said.

"Of course not," Manning agreed. "Leaving aside any chance of us seeing action I say again, the necessary facilities do not exist aboard a warship. I trust the days of giving birth between the cannon are long gone, though anything I might arrange would hardly be better."

King closed his eyes; the idea of Aimée being inconvenienced so was utterly repugnant.

"Then I shall have to put them both ashore," he said.

"In Mrs Summers' case without a doubt, but you may wish to wait a while before deciding about your good lady."

No, that wouldn't work; if Summers' wife were forced to quit the ship, he could hardly keep his partner. Yet Manning was correct, they had no facilities and no one skilled in such matters; even basic privacy might present a problem.

"Malta?" he suggested.

"Or Gibraltar," Manning said. "Though truly, Tom, they are both outposts, certainly as far as medical resources are concerned. Were it my child I should opt for England, and the care of a competent practitioner."

"Your wife?"

"I'm sure Kate would be happy to oblige in both instances. And if you did not delay there should be time for Mrs Summers to be cared for as well as Aimée."

"Then it is agreed, our current cruise will end in a little over six weeks, we can land them at Malta; there'll be a packet heading home from there before long."

"That's hardly guaranteed, Tom."

"Maybe not, but something will be making for Gibraltar; they can pick up an Indiaman from there."

"You're asking a lot from two women," Manning said. "Especially those in a delicate condition."

"They will have a servant," King countered.

"You could not consider an additional escort?"

"Out of the question, I need all my officers and sending a hand would be inappropriate."

"I suppose so..."

"Well, there is nothing else to do, they have instigated this mess and must get themselves out of it."

The surgeon raised his eyes. "Think you so, Tom? I would suggest you and young Summers might have a hand in the situation."

A knocking came as King was about to reply and the messenger entered before he was even summoned.

"Mr Cooper sent me," the youngster announced breathlessly. "Masthead reports the chase in sight again. An' she's closer than anyone expected."

"Where away exactly?"

"Still to windward, sir," Armfield replied before his confidence faded, "An'... An' I don't know..."

King bit back the reprimand; the lad was their most junior young gentleman and he had to make allowances – even a captain should show a degree of sensitivity on occasions. "Very well, I shall come. But we must speak of this again, Robert," he added, before following the youngster out of the room.

"A mile an' a half off," Cooper announced when King reached the quarterdeck. "And the wind's dropping; you can catch her quite plainly from the deck."

King took the proffered glass and struggled for a moment before handing it back. He had his own, foreshortened, telescope below although, if the American were that close, he doubted either instrument would be needed. Instead, he stared into the dust-filled wind, hand raised in a futile attempt to shield his eyes.

"Yes, I see her!" he said at last.

The schooner was on the same course and still to windward but only just; the damage to her rig meant she had been unable to claw as tightly as *Viper* and now lay off their larboard bow. The moon was not quite due, yet some stars were already beginning to appear, and the storm itself was definitely easing.

King conjured a mental image of the North African coastline; unless he was very much mistaken, they were heading directly for the Gulf of Tunis. The area was wide and deep, but any hunted vessel would be foolish to trap themselves in any way, which meant the chase must shortly change course.

"Can you bring us any closer to the wind?" he snapped. Whatever the schooner's captain intended, it would do no harm to seize as much of the weather gauge as possible. But Manton shook his head.

"Near as we can hold it now, sir." And there was a grunt of agreement from Duckworth, the quartermaster, at the wheel. "Though we're gaining on 'em," the sailing master continued. "Long as they stay disabled, we'll have them under our guns by morning."

By morning. That was still a long way off and the American must surely have spotted them; it could only be a matter of time until...

"I believe she's preparing to change course."

King suppressed a smile. It was Cooper, the first lieutenant was better equipped to handle the deck glass and must be able to see more in the poor light. And he was proved correct as, with a flutter of canvas, the schooner began a slow turn; soon she was taking the wind more on her beam with a perceivable increase in speed.

"Follow her round," King ordered, and *Viper* was taken onto roughly the same heading. And now it was a toss-up; close-hauled his frigate had the legs on the injured schooner, whether that remained the case with the wind further aft would soon be seen.

"We're closing," Manton's words came after what seemed like an eternity and all on the quarterdeck relaxed. The wind was dropping further and now carried less grit – the next question was, would it remain strong enough to see this brought to an end?

"Strange they did not come fully 'round." This was the first lieutenant again. Their captain's dislike of direct comments or advice was well known, yet only an absolute tyrant would ban all speculation from the quarterdeck and Cooper's words were meant for the sailing master. Besides, he had a point, and King found himself straining to catch the response.

"You mean, why has she not opted to take the wind more on her quarter?" Manton clarified.

"Exactly. There's room enough to do so and be free of our guns." Cooper shook his head. "On such a course I'd say she'd be faster than us – wounded or not."

"What lies to the south?" King demanded, interrupting his officers' conversation. Manton turned to him.

"The Gulf of Tunis, sir. Though that is many miles off: there is no danger."

No danger from the weather perhaps and, with the wind set so, there never would be. So why had the chase turned now? Or rather, why in such a direction? Cooper was right: if the American wanted to shake off his pursuer, he had only to head further north.

He took a turn along the quarterdeck as his mind struggled with the problem. If the schooner's captain was reluctant to steer to leeward, despite the advantage it would give, greater safety must lie to the east.

"Take her two points closer to the wind."

Both Cooper and Manton reacted to this. King's order would effectively slow *Viper* while possibly allowing the American's eventual escape. The only advantage it gave was to secure the windward gauge, and that would be of little use if the chase remained out of range.

Cooper caught his eye and seemed to draw breath. "You think them unwilling to head north, sir?" he chanced.

106

King gave a grim smile. "I do, Jack," he said. "And believe it more likely they are making for a safe harbour. Mr Manton, I recall the island of Zembra being close by?"

"On the eastern leg of the Gulf, sir," the sailing master confirmed. "We are heading in that direction; at our current speed I would expect to raise it by morning."

"But that is Tunis territory," Cooper protested. "And probably pirate held."

"Maybe so, yet I think our friends plan to seek sanctuary there. And I intend to stop them."

* * *

Midshipman Daniels was feeling quietly smug. He had spotted *Viper*'s chase within fifteen minutes and that was after Williams wasted half an hour searching. Admittedly Carling, the Welshman, first made out the schooner and then it was mainly down to luck, as everyone else had been concentrating on an area further forward. But Daniels intended taking full credit. Such attention to duty would not go amiss when applying for other posts, although remaining aboard *Viper* was still a favoured option.

Of course, he could do little now to add to his kudos; the weather was definitely easing, and the American could be spotted from the deck. But the ship wouldn't be going into action for several hours – time enough to quit this current perch and take up a more befitting station with the guns. And if Jimmy Woodward's performance proved as inept as before, he may even shine there – that or change places with the fellow.

* * *

Whether King had been correct in his guess or not, when the moon finally rose it revealed the schooner to be holding both her course and lead. The latter was due almost entirely to *Viper* clawing deeper into the wind; had King matched the American's heading they would soon have been able to reach her with their bow chasers. But he remained comfortable in his choice; the wind, though holding in strength, now blew free of sand and the sky had cleared to the extent that Manton was able to get a reasonable fix on their position. Zembra should be less than forty miles off and slightly to the north. With the schooner now on their larboard beam, it was time to make his move.

"Very well, Mr Manton. Take us three points to larboard and add what sail you think proper." Most on the quarterdeck had already realised his intention and were expecting the order; *Viper* fell smoothly onto her new heading and, to men attuned to such things, the increase in speed was immediately obvious. Those in the schooner had tried to effect repairs although, apart from an extra staysail, she carried no more canvas. And with *Viper* now firmly in possession of the windward gauge, it should only be a question of time before she swept down upon her. Then, rather than a couple of light round shot, the British frigate could deliver a full broadside.

* * *

They had beaten to quarters but not cleared for action; engaging a small schooner that may turn out unarmed hardly called for such measures. Instead, Woodward was told to make his guns ready, although privately he would have been happier had Captain King ordered full preparations for battle.

Not that he was concerned about taking damage; even at cruising stations *Viper* was well protected with hammock-stuffed netting topping many of her bulwarks while the surgeon's team would be able to cope with a small number of injuries in the regular sick berth. However, Woodward felt being fully prepared for combat instilled a greater spirit in the men; knowing every measure had been taken was a definite encouragement.

And that was not his only concern; Midshipman Daniels was blessing them with his attendance and now stood casually assessing the situation. Woodward had hoped to be spared the young man's assistance but, once the chase was in clear sight, the midshipmen were relieved of their masthead duties. So Daniels would be with him for the duration, and even now looked keen to impart some of his wisdom.

"Do you anticipate a change of shot, sir?"

Woodward sighed. "We have received no orders," he told him curtly. "Five rounds of both bar and canister are on hand, though the guns were already loaded with round. And that's how they'll stay unless the captain requires otherwise. The extra range may yet be important."

As soon as he added the final sentence, Woodward regretted it, but Daniels jumped on the opportunity.

"Ah yes, the range..." he agreed. "It were why you kept to round shot aboard *Tenacious*, as I recall."

"I kept to round shot because the captain did not order otherwise," Woodward snapped. "And you will call me sir!"

Daniels treated him to a look cast from pure malevolence and Woodward turned away. He had never been skilled at arguing: the best lines always occurred long after a confrontation. And, with action imminent, neither did he wish to be distracted; the schooner lay off their larboard bow and *Viper* was closing noticeably. Soon, certainly within the hour, she would be in range of their chase guns and not long after they might reach her with the broadside cannon. If nothing changed, the distance would be less than half a mile so Captain King may then call for bar shot, yet the American was just as likely to turn with the wind and make a northerly chase of it.

"So, will you have me stationed at the chase guns?" the midshipman persisted. "I recall that being your plan in the past."

Woodward spun back. "I would have you obey orders when they are given," he said.

Daniels gave a shrug. "An offensive manner will get you nowhere, Mr Woodward. I am assuming you wish to progress..."

Woodward drew breath; *Viper*'s commission would not last forever and, backed as he was, Daniels probably could influence his future. Perhaps if he confided more they may come to an arrangement; he was clearly on his way up and bound to make commander before long. Yet did he really want to spend the rest of his career playing boot-catcher to a prig?

A sudden anger rose up, one Woodward had rarely known and, before he fully realised what he was doing, he began to speak.

"What I want or intend is of no concern to you, Mr Daniels. When I or any officer issues an order, it is to be obeyed, not commented upon or discussed." His words came out slowly and he looked the midshipman in the eye as he spoke. "Anything else will see you in the deepest trouble, and your influential friends may not be as keen to back a man who has been seized to the rigging or made to kiss the gunner's daughter."

"You would not dare!"

"I would not have to. Should your current behaviour continue, I shall have no hesitation in reporting you to the first lieutenant who will take the appropriate action. Until then, consider your words more carefully and, if you do feel the need for speech, address me as sir; is that understood?"

Daniels paused and might have looked abashed – in the current light it was hard to tell. But Woodward did notice him making to speak again, before thinking better of it. And then, as an afterthought, he muttered a barely audible, "Yes, sir."

* * *

Matters were certainly moving on apace; in the east, the sky was starting to lighten; already a dark mound that must be Zembra could be made out on *Viper*'s starboard bow. But the schooner was nearer, and they were continuing to close on her. King could sense his officers' impatience; Summers was waiting by the forward-facing cannon; it would only take a word from the quarterdeck and two six-pound round shot would be sent spinning towards the American.

But King was in no rush. It now seemed certain their chase was making for the island and to reach it would mean crossing *Viper*'s path. It was something the schooner's captain was putting off, presumably in the hope of a miracle. When the time came, King wanted to be as close as possible so emphasising the steadily reducing distance by firing off light cannon would not be wise.

He took a turn across the deck and breathed in deeply. Yes, dawn was imminent; in twenty minutes it would be daylight when they might really expect action. However, it turned out the American had other ideas...

"Chase is altering course!"

The cry came from the forecastle lookout yet all on *Viper*'s deck could see as much. And yes, the schooner had thrown her helm across and was clawing manfully on a more southerly course that would take her to the island.

"Hold your fire, Mr Summers!"

The lieutenant was no fool, and King didn't truly think he would be panicked into action; the ideal time for a barrage was still several minutes away.

110

Silence now hung heavy over all on deck; the American was proving game enough although there was a morbid fascination in watching any doomed vessel attempt escape. Even if she made it safely across the frigate's bows, *Viper* could catch her close-hauled. She would be in their hands in no time, and the more optimistic were already spending their prize money.

King glanced up at the sails, then across at the schooner once more; if it was to be done, it may as well be now.

"Very well, open fire, Mr Summers. Mr Manton, lay us further south; I want her taken before breakfast."

It was a bold statement and one he might live to regret, yet it drew grunts of approval from those serving the nearby carronade and even Cooper seemed amused by it.

The light cannon snapped out loudly in the silence of morning and were followed by shouts and whistles as the ship was turned closer to the wind. King had never expected much from their chasers so was not disappointed when the shots went unsighted. *Viper* would soon be matching the schooner's course; the next time she spoke it would be with her great guns and to far more effect. But before that could happen, the American had one more surprise in store.

"She's opened fire!" This time Williams, the duty midshipman, was the first to notice although most caught the final flash of what had been an unexpectedly large broadside.

"Carrying heavy metal for a schooner," Cooper muttered. "Though I'm surprised she's armed at all."

"It's the Med," Manton grunted. "Dangerous place for a Yank; they got a whole lot more to worry over than us."

King supposed the sailing master was right; the only enemy a British ship should expect to meet was an American and, with no sizeable warships nearby, the schooner before him presented little danger. Consequently, he had become complacent: soft. And he was just beginning to wonder at the wisdom in not fully clearing for action when the first shots began to land.

Chapter Ten

"Bo's'un believes them to be firin' nine-pounders, your honour," the seaman reported. "Hit us squarely on the 'sprit just aft of the dolphin so they did. Made a proper mess of the forestay, an' topmast stay 'ousin's all ahoo. Mr Morales is attendin' an' all."

"Did Mr Amon give any indication how long repairs will take?"

"They reckons it'll be three hours till all's put to rights," the hand replied before becoming more confidential. "Mind, that's a touch cheerful, if I'm any judge."

King bit back an oath. He had been overconfident, arrogant, a bull. Just because the schooner was smaller and already wounded, why should he think she could do them no harm? Like the cat bitten by a mouse, he had been taught a lesson.

"Can we not take her into the wind?" This was to Manton, and the sailing master gave no comfort.

"We might try, sir, though without proper support there's no tellin' what might 'appen to the fore."

That was it exactly; robbed of bracing from the bowsprit, the mast would be severely weakened. He glanced up at the schooner once more; she had settled on her new course and was battling on towards the island and sanctuary. There was nothing for it; a mistake had been made and he must take his medicine like a man.

"Very well, my compliments to Mr Amon and Mr Morales, I am sure they will do what is necessary."

The seaman knuckled his forehead and left; King turned to Cooper.

"I suppose we should have seen that coming, Jack," he said.

"It was a lucky shot, sir."

"It was several, by the sound of it," King grunted; the fact that the American's gunnery was of such a high standard had not gone unnoticed. "Though if we'd been cleared for action..."

"It would have made no difference." The first lieutenant

was refreshingly confident. "Harker said the bowsprit's been hit; any damage there would have taken out the preventer stays as well. Like I say, a lucky shot."

Cooper was right, although knowing that did little to stem the contempt King felt for himself. Perhaps there was nothing they could have done materially, but his mind had been distracted and equally ill-prepared. And the worst part was knowing he had made the same mistake before.

* * *

From a distance the island appeared much like St Helena: a mound of apparently solid rock that rose many hundreds of feet and was edged by ferocious cliffs. But whereas St Helena boasted a fertile heartland, one that contained some of the most memorable countryside, Zembra appeared universally brutal, with no visible vegetation larger than scrub. Even the harbour seemed less welcoming than most. King doubted that they would have discovered it, were they not led there. The boatswain and carpenter proved as good as their word; within three hours of taking damage, *Viper* could be sailed on a bowline. However, sufficient time had passed to allow the schooner to make good her escape.

And there she was now, safely moored within the protection of the natural harbour; her main topmast had been set down and repairs were underway. Were they to prove satisfactory she would be difficult to catch, and a prudent man would turn away and continue his patrol. But King had never regarded himself as such and, though it might prove futile, was not prepared to give up quite so easily.

"Does anyone know these waters?" he asked, and Cooper cleared his throat.

"I understand the island was previously known as Aegimouros," he said, "and is mentioned by both Greeks and Romans: Pliny the Elder referred to it as Aegimuri."

King lowered his glass and straightened up. "Indeed?" He was aware of his first officer's interest in literature, though had not considered him a student of the classics. "And you have visited before, perhaps?"

113

"I regret not, sir."

"Can't say I'm much of a reader myself, though I've passed by often enough." This was Manton, the sailing master, and King turned to him.

"And landed?"

"No, sir."

"Our charts, how do they have it?"

The older man shrugged. "No soundings for the harbour or its approach, though you don't need to be a James Cook to know what the bottom will be like."

King waited.

"Look at them cliffs, sir," the sailing master directed. "There'll be deep water thereabouts for certain, an' probably a good few sharp rocks an' all. I wouldn't care to bring anything as large as *Viper* within a cable of 'em, not without decent charts an' regular soundings."

That made sense and almost came as a relief; King had no desire to simply crush the schooner with gunfire. It would be far more fitting to capture her whole, to say nothing of the additional benefit his people would receive for her hull and any cargo she carried. All of which rather pointed to a cutting-out expedition...

King raised his glass once more and returned to his examination of the harbour entrance. The one good point was there appeared to be no shore batteries, at least none directed seaward, although what might lie within was another matter. And neither could he tell if the place was even populated; there were buildings ashore for certain – small, ramshackle affairs though they might equally be for storage as habitation.

Which brought up another point: Zembra was officially Tunis territory. Pellew had been quite clear; the Barbary States were a problem to be addressed at a later date – King was to seek no contact with them. How did that sit with attempting to steal a ship potentially under their protection?

And that may be the case. The island lay only a few nautical miles off the Tunis mainland, and less than fifty from a principal port. The manner in which the schooner sailed almost directly for the harbour suggested some familiarity yet, even if it proved to be deserted, would the Americans really seek sanctuary where they were unwelcome?

Of course not; of all the Barbary States, America enjoyed

the best relationship with Tunisia; a friendship treaty was signed last century and, if he were not mistaken, they had official representation in Tunis itself. If he attempted to cut the schooner out, there may be more than her crew to fight; he should expect assistance from the shore, and quite possibly artillery. A badly staged attack could cost the lives of many men and put him in bad favour with his Commander-in-Chief. Was the possible capture of a single armed merchant worth such a sacrifice? Again, a prudent man would think otherwise, but at that moment King was not so certain.

* * *

"Mark my words, there'll be a cutting-out expedition tonight," Midshipman Williams announced as he unbuttoned his shirt.

"Think you so?" Edwards was already comfortable in his hammock; Williams might have six hours of rest ahead, but he only had the two and wished to make good use of them.

"Without a doubt; Old Tommo's got the needle with this one, he won't let it go without another crack."

"You seem to know a good deal about him," Malcolm, one of the older volunteers, chipped in.

"When you've served as long as I have," Williams sighed, "and known as many captains, you get an instinct for such things."

"I'll take your word for it," Edwards grunted, snuggling deeper. It was rare for them to have the berth to themselves, Daniels being on duty, yet he still didn't wish to waste a moment of potential sleep.

"So, what happens on a cutting-off?" Armfield, the youngest, enquired,

"A cutting-out," Edwards corrected, and Williams shrugged.

"We goes in, board the vessel in question, and... cut her out."

"You mean tow?" Malcolm asked.

"If need be. We get to choose the time, so there's usually an agreeable breeze."

"But not tonight." Edwards spoke from the depths. "Wind's holding an' blowing hard onshore; if you're right, it'll be the very devil and need more than a couple of cutters to shift her."

"That's as maybe," the older lad allowed. "Though I've heard of worse exploits and been involved in a few myself."

"You've been on such a venture?" Armfield asked aghast.

"They happen all the time." Williams was careful not to meet anyone's eye. "And our captain ain't the kind to let a contrary wind let him miss a step."

"So, some of us might be in action tonight?" Malcolm asked in wonder.

Williams nodded. "I should say so."

There was a groan from Edwards' hammock. "All the more reason to get some caulk," he added.

* * *

"You sent for me, sir?"

King looked up from his place at the head of *Viper*'s dining table. Despite a disrupted night, Summers looked unusually smart and was standing before him at something close to attention.

"Yes, do sit down, Michael." King indicated the chair to his immediate left – that on his right hand being reserved for the ship's first lieutenant. "Mr Cooper will be joining us shortly, as will our marine officers: I wanted to speak with you first."

The lad took a seat but, while King rested back against his, Summers sat bolt upright.

King considered him; appearances might be deceptive, and Summers could simply be suffering from too many hours on duty, still he had always regarded the young officer as particularly robust.

"Is anything the matter, Michael?"

"No, sir. Not exactly." The lad looked at him sidelong. "Though I think I know why I've been summoned..."

"Do you?" That came as a surprise; King had only decided upon the cutting-out expedition himself an hour before and, even now, nothing was set in stone. The next few minutes would either convince him to go ahead or forget the notion completely.

"Is it about Suzie?" Summers demanded.

"Your wife?" King blinked. "No. No, she has nothing to do with matters. I was contemplating cutting-out the American

116

schooner."

Summers exhaled loudly as his captain continued.

"As I recall, you've been involved in such missions before though have yet to lead one; am I correct?"

"Never in overall charge, sir." Summers' face was now a mild crimson.

"And what are your feelings? I ask because Mr Woodward is still relatively unknown, and the marine officers even more so."

Summers nodded; he was aware of the regard his captain held for the corps in general.

"As you know, such operations are always manned by volunteers; I didn't wish to make an offer if it were to be turned down."

There was a clatter outside the door and a bellow from the duty sentry announced the arrival of Cooper.

"Wait one!" King shouted in return before turning back to the lad.

"I-I would be pleased to lead," Summers said.

"Glad to hear it," King smiled. "As I have explained, we are still to decide if it is even viable. But, should we go ahead, I think you will do an excellent job. Now, you mentioned your wife. What did you wish to say about her?"

* * *

The moon was not due to rise for some time although most traces of the recent storm had vanished, and it was an annoyingly clear night. Consequently, *Viper* was forced to release the boats several miles off before stationing herself to the east. And by the time the island was in clear view, those at the oars were already tired. To maximise the element of surprise, Summers' flotilla was approaching from the west; the only time the harbour would be properly visible was when they rounded the headland and made their final approach. But that didn't stop the young man from gazing at the impending landmass with a fascination close to that of a rabbit confronted by a snake. He cleared his throat.

"Second watch to the sweeps." Midshipman Williams could have given the order; the lad was next to him in the cutter's sternsheets yet Summers saw no reason to delegate such a simple matter. And the truth of it was, he had been a midshipman himself for longer than he held his commission, so such tasks came to him naturally.

His voice echoed strangely in the night air. The wind had dropped though still came up from the North African coast and, as the harbour was set to the south of the island, would be dead against them when they came to leave. They couldn't even benefit from it on the run in, as masts and canvas would make the small force more obvious.

Summers looked back at it now. Behind him was another cutter commanded by Midshipman Edwards and, beyond that, Midshipman Daniels had the launch. In each, the hands were changing stations and even Daniels' command, a truly substantial craft and the largest boat Viper carried, was rocking like a child's toy.

Summers was in overall charge, so might have expected to be detailed to the larger vessel but accepted that King had appointed Daniels with good reason. As leader, Summers was expected to go in first, and a cutter would be handier when coming alongside an enemy. Once the smaller boats had established a foothold, Daniels could follow with the relatively mundane task of delivering their main force of boarders. Then, when all were safely deposited, the launch would provide much of the power needed to tow the schooner out of harbour.

Apart from its seamen, the launch carried twelve marines under a sergeant and every regular hand was an experienced Jack. Most, if not all, were well versed in such operations so, when the occupants of the cutters were included, he should have manpower enough to carry a moderately sized schooner. But then no one could be sure of the opposition they would face – the American had fired off a sizeable broadside so was more than a simple trader. There may be anything from thirty to sixty armed men waiting to meet them, yet his force was equal to the worst estimation and, for the twentieth time, he assured himself there was nothing to worry over.

Summers glanced at the men as they settled. All appeared to be looking forward to the night's adventure; with peace in Europe now established, many may have even welcomed the chance for one last stab at an enemy. Whether he shared their view was another matter, however, and one strongly influenced by Suzie's recent news. The prospect of becoming a father had hit

Summers hard and altered his views on many things: his future in the Navy for one. But if this was to be his last boat action, at least he would be leading it.

"Do you think there'll be any ashore?" Williams asked as the last fresh hand took up his sweep and the boat settled.

"There may be," Summers replied. "Though the island is more likely to be uninhabited."

It was a vain hope, yet one he had been cherishing since agreeing to head the operation. Despite his force, carrying a schooner that was obviously able to fight would be perilous enough, but taking on an unknown number, possibly professional soldiers and maybe artillery ashore, was another matter. The lightest of cannon could destroy any of his boats with ease; if a battery caught them on the way in, capture was the best they could hope for. And if they were struck leaving, with the wind against them and the schooner's rig already damaged, there would be little chance of sailing the prize away.

Then there was another thought, one unspoken – indeed one too terrible to discuss. Summers guessed most of his party assumed capture meant falling into the hands of Americans. It would be an ignominious fate, though no more. And any who thought further probably expected the gallant Captain King to either negotiate for their release, or take them back by force. However, Summers knew differently. Any stationed on the island were likely to be pirates and, even if those from Tunis were not the fiercest of their type, it would hardly be a happy outcome. There were countless tales of prisoners stripped of all they possessed before being sold as slaves in the open market. The last news sheet had gloried in the fact that several thousand Europeans were currently enduring such a fate while the few that had found freedom only did so after the payment of large ransoms. Summers didn't think the Admiralty would pay a great deal for him and as a husband, soon also to be a father, had no wish to spend the rest of his life in bondage.

For a moment the prospect felt too terrible and he seriously considered abandoning the mission. A reason could surely be found – or contrived. Or he might simply say he'd lost his nerve and let them make what they would of it. Captain King was a reasonable man and Summers felt he had already taken sufficient risks for his country. With luck, he would simply be dismissed the Service and left to pursue a different course with his new family. Not the finest ending to a naval career perhaps, though preferable to the alternative.

"We're about ready," Williams told him, and Summers' mind began to clear. On agreeing to lead the mission there had been no thought of crying off, and neither should there be now. However the odds turned out, he would face them, along with the consequences should he fail. Yet even as he braced himself for the final effort, Summers was aware of a strange reluctance. It was a job that needed to be done, and he was going to do it. But not for much longer; this time may well be the last.

"Sir," Williams hinted. "Fresh hands are in place; the men are waiting."

"Very well, we can get underway." Summers paused, then added, "You may give the order."

* * *

Stokes along with several from his mess had volunteered and, being as they were a known entity, been placed together in *Viper*'s second boat. The cutter was under Midshipman Edwards' charge, with Malcolm, a mere volunteer, as his second. Neither officer was born when Stokes and some of his men first went to sea, although they were accustomed to being under the command of teenagers. As speed was not of the essence, the craft carried a minimal crew at the sweeps, and those not actually at an oar were either squeezed alongside or sat huddled in the cutter's bows.

"Rum lookin' place," Downes said as they picked up speed once more. Until then he was one of the rowers, so could now inspect their destination for the first time.

"Aye," Stokes agreed. "No sign of the schooner yet, I'm thinkin'."

"No sign of the harbour, neither," Bovey added. "If we hadn't seen it earlier, I'd never have guessed anything were there."

"Least there won't be no confusion when we gets in," Lovemore said. "Jonathan were the only hull present."

"Rest of the island seemed a mite deserted," Longdon mused.

"Good job too," Stokes again. "On a night like this, we won't go unnoticed..."

120

That was truly the case. There was still no trace of moon, though the sky was awash with stars and every stroke woke ripples of phosphorescence in the dark waters. They were less than a mile off now and Longdon was sure he could see part of the scrub move as if disturbed by something other than the wind. It was likely to be nothing more than wild animals, but there were definitely living things close by.

"Anyone see signs of batteries?" Groom, now at the oars, asked.

"Give over," Stokes said. "We've not been goin' more'n a minute."

"Won't know for sure till we round the headland," Bovey added.

"*Viper* should be making her move afore long." This was the mess's newest member. All were surprised when Healey was amongst the volunteers; until then the Yorkshireman had done little to endear himself to any aboard the frigate.

"Not for a while," Stokes replied. "Idea was, she turns up just as we makes our approach."

"Distraction?" Lovemore asked.

"Somethin' like that."

"Be a while yet, then." Bovey was gauging the distance carefully. "I'd say fifteen minutes at the least."

"I see her now!" Downes exclaimed, pointing excitedly over his messmates' heads.

All who could, looked, and there was a hush as the warship came into view. She was as close to the island as they were and approaching from the east on a broad reach under reefed topsails alone. Even without the moon her canvas glowed; surely no one ashore could miss such a spectacle.

"Quite a sight," Longdon murmured and there was a muttering of agreement; they may not have been aboard the frigate long, yet already she was winning a place in their hearts.

"Maybe," Stokes said, "though the old girl's early. That or we're late..."

* * *

"Double bank the oars!" Summers knew there were mutterings of resentment at his order but to get any benefit from *Viper*'s appearance they must get a move on. He reached inside his coat and brought out his watch, then looked across at Williams.

"What time have you?" he demanded.

"Not quite a quarter to," the lad replied after fumbling for his own piece.

So, Captain King was slightly ahead of time, although that was not to be surprised at; all knew how hard it was to be entirely accurate when conning a ship. More importantly, *Viper* had yet to open fire, and Summers must be in position when she did.

Under the increased power, the boat soon picked up speed and he glanced back to check those following were keeping pace. He could see Edwards' cutter plainly while the launch commanded by Daniels was also close behind. And this, the largest of the three, was the most important.

Not only did the bigger boat carry their marines, it also held more seamen than both cutters combined. And, while it would be possible to tow the schooner out with the cutters alone, the larger craft's capacity for rowers would do so with ease. He had no desire to be sunk, and neither did he wish such a fate on Edwards, but if they were to lose one of their number, it must not be the launch.

Double banking the oars was certainly making a difference though; all three boats were fairly skimming across the water and Summers told himself King's early arrival might not matter after all.

"Bring us nearer," he muttered to Williams. The closer they rounded the headland the better, both for surprise, and to make the final approach shorter. He looked across at *Viper*. The frigate was still to fire yet must be obvious to those on land, and any shore batteries would surely find her.

"Captain's taking it close."

Summers considered this. It was not close exactly; *Viper* remained a good half-mile from the nearest land although Williams' comment had struck a chord. He remembered the sailing master's warning – could it only have been a few hours before? Rocks, exposed or otherwise, were expected near the cliffs so the frigate was on the very limit of caution and possibly slightly beyond. But that remained Captain King's problem, his was to round the headland at the same time as *Viper* took station across the harbour mouth.

The nearest cliffs were alongside now and he could study them properly. They towered above by perhaps eighty feet and were topped by a thick layer of vegetation that in places overspilled their jagged edges. That scrub might be concealing anything and his boats were well within range. As was *Viper*, fast approaching the harbour entrance from the opposite direction. Summers noticed Williams had tucked the tiller under one arm and was peering at his watch, held in the other.

"*Viper* should be opening fire at any moment."

Summers remembered how quickly the minutes passed when going into action and revised his earlier estimation; perhaps Captain King's timing was spot on after all? *Viper* was steadily creeping into position, and he was about to round the headland; they should indeed arrive at the harbour mouth simultaneously.

And then his boat was finally making the turn and passing under the most likely site for shore-based artillery. Ahead, the harbour opened up and there was the schooner, anchored in plain sight and less than a cable off. Edwards and Daniels were keeping perfect station behind, and he wondered for a moment if it would be easy after all.

They would be alongside in a matter of minutes and shouldn't take a great deal longer to carry her. He must allow a little time to set the towlines but, if their luck held, the enemy should be a prize, at sea and safe within the hour. As Summers breathed out, he felt the tension flow from him; there had been no activity from either headland and what he could see of the nearby quay was deserted. Then, just as he was berating himself for having been concerned, the heavens were torn asunder by a blinding light as a terrible barrage of fire and smoke thundered overhead.

* * *

"Strewth, they didn't tell us that were coming!"

Williams was wrong, all were advised that *Viper* would be giving covering fire, yet expecting a warship's broadside was very different from being directly beneath it. But beneath it they were, even if many later would swear they felt the wind of passing shot. The American, now less than a cable off, was momentarily hidden

123

by a wall of water that rose up close enough to soak them in its spray.

"Ready boarders!"

As Summers shouted the warning, he knew it was unnecessary; those detailed were already prepared. Each was armed with a cutlass either looped through a belt or allowed to swing alarmingly from their wrists, and some carried uncocked pistols. As the schooner loomed nearer, a few began to tentatively stand in anticipation and, despite the shock of *Viper*'s broadside, Summers' confidence was quickly returning. There were no shore batteries, the frigate's covering broadside had proved an excellent diversion and the schooner seemed reluctant to return fire. On reaching her decks there would doubtless be one hell of a brawl but, if his force could only approach unharmed, they had every chance of carrying her. And, if the American gunners did decide on a target, what could be better than the massive frigate lying off the harbour mouth? With that sort of a distraction, their little flotilla may still not have been noticed.

"You'll stay with this boat," he reminded Williams, "and make sure Malcolm pays attention in the other." There would only be fifteen men boarding from this cutter although, combined with the same from Edwards' craft, they should be sufficient to secure part of the deck. And when Daniels, with the launch, joined them carrying still more Jacks along with a detachment of marines, taking the ship should be a mere formality.

And then, just as they were creeping under her shadow, the schooner did speak. Her broadside was a fraction the size of *Viper*'s yet the proximity, and that it was fired by an enemy, added extra menace. Summers instinctively ducked, then looked back and at the frigate. But the shots landed far sooner than he expected and had been aimed at the launch. And while most only bracketed the heavy craft, one struck her neatly on the bows.

Chapter Eleven

"Carry on!"

Summers gave the order without conscious thought. The launch had received a direct hit to her stempost and immediately began to take in water, yet there could be no going back, not without exposing his own boat, or Edwards', to the same fate. But would he be able to capture an armed schooner with a handful of men?

To their credit, those rowing his cutter held their stroke and the boat continued towards the enemy. A glance aft told him Edwards was following while Daniels' launch had already started to settle. That was to be expected, but hopefully some buoyancy would remain and it might stay afloat a while longer. Williams was looking to him as if for instructions although nothing had changed. Except now they would be relying on the cutters more than ever.

"Daniels will have to look after himself," he snapped. "Once we've boarded, make for the enemy's bows as before, and be ready with the hawser."

Summers could not check whether the lad fully understood – there were other matters to consider. The schooner boasted a reasonable freeboard, so it would be a small climb before they reached the top rail when his boarders would be most vulnerable.

"Together lads!" he bellowed; a swarm of men arriving simultaneously would be far harder to fend off than if they appeared in ones and twos. Then he raised himself and checked the hilt of his hanger as the cutter scraped alongside.

He was opposite the schooner's starboard mainchains and took hold of a toe link before hauling himself onto the channel itself. A look left told him others were following while Edwards' cutter had ground to a halt nearer the bows and its men were already tumbling over the bulwarks. Soon he had his first view of the enemy's deck, and the line of dark figures awaiting them. But all were holding back and appeared oddly fascinated by their arrival.

Then he realised why; at a shouted command, pistols, muskets and what could have been a blunderbuss were raised and the sudden discharges blinded some with their flash, while others fell back under the wave of shot. The schooner's crew must have been expecting company and there might be more surprises, although Summers could not begin to imagine what. Yet there was little point in wondering; his hanger was at his side, he reached for it, chose a clear area of deck, and leapt.

The soles of his feet stung briefly and he staggered forward on landing, but quickly righted himself. A body was directly before him, though the lad was young – little more than a boy – and carrying a short-bladed sword that he handled awkwardly. Summers raised his own weapon and was about to strike when the child screamed, dropped the sword, and ran.

The next was less obliging; a bearded heavyweight charged toward him brandishing a cutlass. Summers parried the blow, then followed with a deadly hack that sent the seaman stumbling into the scuppers. Another – this time with a musket. The piece had been fired though still carried a lethal foot-long blade which was plunged in his direction. Summers dodged before slicing horizontally and cutting deep into the assailant's arm.

Another confronted him, this time with the hint of a uniform so probably an officer. In the half-light Summers also caught the glimmer of a smile on the clean-shaven face as an elegant, yet businesslike, sword was raised. The hilt glinted ominously, and Summers brought up his own hanger in response.

With a sideways swipe, his opponent advanced. A step to the right was enough to dodge the blow and Summers countered with his own. The blades clashed with an industrial clang, then the pressure suddenly relaxed, and Summers' hanger dropped. A glint of metal was enough to warn him of the next attack and he brought up his weapon fast enough to halt it in mid-air. Again, they tangled but this time Summers was prepared and pressed forward more firmly. The man resisted for a moment then, with a cry of surprise rather than pain, tripped before falling back, forcing Summers to take a further step to avoid tumbling also. He paused; the officer lay face up on the deck with one hand raised in supplication.

"Quarter!"

Summers' hanger was poised, ready to strike; nothing

would be easier than ending it there and then, and he struggled to control his fighting madness. But the contest was over: he had won. He nodded and the man rose slowly to his feet, before reaching down for his fallen weapon. Summers accepted the hilt gingerly, then glanced around.

All from his cutter had boarded and Edwards' party was in control further forward. The fight had been easier than he anticipated; they had captured the schooner's deck with ease and with the cutters' boarders alone.

His attention returned to the officer. "You are the captain?"

"I am."

"And are surrendering the ship?"

"The ship for sure." Again that smile. "Though I have men ashore and cannot speak for them."

That explained much, but there was no time to investigate further.

"Benton, Larkin, here a moment!"

The two seamen loomed closer and Summers passed the surrendered sword to one.

"This here's the captain; guard him closely."

"I shall give you no trouble," the man declared.

"Your word?" Summers checked.

"My word."

Men ashore meant a counterattack was likely at any moment and they did not have the numbers to mount any form of credible defence. Yet it would only need one to guard the captain.

"Larkin, get yourself aloft and keep watch; first sign of a boat approaching I want to know about it."

The seaman knuckled his forehead and made for the shrouds while Summers assessed the situation. They had been fortunate in catching the schooner without a full crew, although that luck might change at any moment. He must act while some remained.

* * *

Viper lay hove to across the harbour entrance. By approaching so, King was exceeding both Manton's recommendations and common sense, although he had yet to be punished. Still, with the wind on her beam, the ship was steadily drifting closer; soon they must seek more sea room, although for now he was content to let matters rest while he surveyed the action ashore.

He had witnessed the launch being hit – or rather, he had been partially blinded by the schooner's broadside and now could make out the result. Though waterlogged, the boat still floated and there looked to be men in the water – men who may distract Summers from his true objective.

Once more King wondered if he had been right in appointing the young man, and, once more, reminded himself of the options. Woodward seemed the only other likely candidate and, with him in command, Summers could have gone as his junior. Their second lieutenant remained an unknown quantity, however, and Michael Summers was a very different proposition.

King knew the boy well and that he could be trusted: this was an ideal opportunity to test his mettle further. The American was not a major threat and King's hunch about the absence of shore batteries had proved correct. All the lad need do was keep control and tow her out; providing the cutters remained undamaged, that should still be possible.

"Beggin' your pardon, sir, but I think we should put out to sea."

This was Manton – the man had been fussing in the background for some while. King lowered his foreshortened glass and listened as a leadsman called out the depth. More than three fathoms remained under the frigate's keel, although King was no fool; the sea bed would shelve suddenly and, even at the current pace and with the Med's lack of tides, *Viper* could still become snagged on an uncharted rock.

"Very well, Master," he said at last, and Manton could hardly contain his eagerness as he brought his precious charge back to the wind.

King raised his glass one last time as she clawed away. There were flecks of light from the schooner that might be small arms fire, but nothing was certain. Summers could be in possession or may have been driven off; a sudden burst of firing towards the stern suggested the latter though he trusted the lad would not risk his men unnecessarily. If the vessel proved too hard to take it were better left. Another occasion may present: the Americans would not get far with a damaged rig and *Viper* guarding their only exit.

He finally brought his glass down as the ship began to edge

away. In the past, when King had been fully able and could lead such missions, he gave little thought to those waiting in safety. And why should he? The concern he currently felt was nothing to the very real fear Summers and his men must be facing. However, King's previous experience did give him some insight; even without seeing everything, he could guess a good deal and readily empathised with those in danger. More importantly, he understood the value of an agile, yet focused, mind amid the madness of an attack.

Providing Summers kept his head they would either carry the schooner or retreat without losing too many souls. But once he abandoned control, or gave way to the lunacy that affected so many in the heat of battle, it could only end in brutal defeat. King felt he knew the lad well enough to gauge how he would react and only time would tell if he were right.

* * *

Summers was making for the bows; the anchor cable must be cut and towlines secured; only then could the schooner be moved. But as he pressed forward, so much more demanded his attention.

The prisoners were clustered in small groups with one or two seamen guarding each: they should be gathered together. And the wounded; there were several from both sides and some were being cared for yet, without coordination, the more serious might die while minor scratches were attended to elsewhere. Then there would be those below; at least one American had taken refuge down a companionway so before they called the schooner theirs the lower deck must be secured. And all the while the spectre of counterattack still haunted him; to be sure of beating one off he must reinforce his men with survivors from the launch. So, before anything else, they must get underway.

He caught up with Edwards who was already making progress; Groves, a holder with shoulders like a bullock's forequarters, was taking considered blows at the hemp hawser with a fourteen-pound axe while Williams passed up the towline from below.

On noticing his arrival, Edwards turned to him. "Shame the wind's not with us," he said. "Though there would never have been much of a breeze in such a place."

Avoiding the swing of Grove's axe, Summers glanced back. Edwards was right, the small harbour was dwarfed by surrounding hills. There was a quay with several storage sheds behind but little space for more as the rock rose steeply, as stark as it was inhospitable. And then he heard something that turned his blood to ice.

"Deck there – boat putting out from the shore!"

Summers looked again yet could see nothing in that direction. Then a hint of movement turned into something more solid, and the outline of a launch under oars formed.

"She's riding low," Edwards said, and Summers nodded in silence. It was a sizeable affair, generously filled with men, and it was also making directly for them. He tore his eyes from the sight as the tasks mounted up; that too would have to be dealt with. He turned his attention seaward where Daniel's stricken launch was immediately obvious. It seemed not to have sunk further but lay half-submerged and surrounded by a veritable crowd clinging to the rubbing strakes.

"First tow's clapped on," Edwards announced.

"Very good, when the other's made fast, get underway. And steer to pass the launch."

The midshipman touched his hat, although Summers was already heading aft.

His way was blocked by both prisoners and wounded – a voice called out to him, but he had other priorities and pushed past. None of his boarding parties carried a firearm larger than an ordinary seaman's pistol – this was when the marines would have come in handy. A bunch of fools were gathered on the schooner's tiny quarterdeck but doing little other than staring down at the approaching boat, now midway between them and the hard.

"You there, look alive! Load up your weapons!"

His sudden appearance stirred the seamen into action; all reached for their pistols and began to reload; soon there was the spasmodic popping of small arms fire.

"Second tow's secure, we're moving," Edwards announced, joining him. Then, on noticing the approaching boat, added. "The larboard guns are charged, sir – we might veer and reach them with a broadside."

"No!" That also needed no thought. Even if there were enough spare hands, firing strange cannon at night and expecting to hit a moving boat was absurd. "Round up those with pistols who can be spared," he said.

The deck gave a slight lurch: they were definitely underway. Summers turned back to see a quartermaster's mate at the wheel.

"Steer to pass the launch," he ordered, before making his way forward once more.

It was like a scene in some absurd play; wherever he looked men and matters were demanding his attention. The impending attack from the boat was important, but Edwards would have to hold them off; Summers' next priority must be collecting those from the damaged launch.

He reached the forecastle and almost tripped over the schooner's captain, now sitting disconsolately by the bitts. The American caught his eye and went to say something, but Summers had no time for conversation, he must see to Williams and Malcolm in the boats below.

"Make for the launch!" Even as he shouted, Summers realised the order was redundant. Both cutters were already pulling for the damaged boat, which now lay just off their starboard bow. He turned back to Benton, still guarding the captain.

"Help get them aboard," he ordered. "And direct anyone fit enough aft to Mr Edwards."

The sound of sporadic shots aft continued; those by the taffrail were doing a better job but all that could be hoped for was to keep the Americans at bay.

"There'll be twenty armed men in that boat," the schooner's captain called out. "Force like that'll take us back easy."

Summers had the image of an enemy boarding party swarming aboard like monkeys released from a barrel; in no time he and the rest of his party could become prisoners themselves.

"I'd give it up now were I you," the American continued. "There'll be no hard feelin's – I'll even guarantee you safe passage back to your ship."

But this time Summers had not heard; the first survivors from Daniels' launch were beginning to appear at the schooner's top rail. Tired, wet, yet evidently relieved, they staggered onto the firm deck with inane grins and muttered thanks. Summers addressed them as a group.

"All of you aft; the enemy is trying to board at the stern. Private, do you have a musket?" The bemused man shook his head and Summers snatched a pistol from a nearby seaman. "Never mind, take this; if the prisoner shows any sign of moving you may shoot him."

The marine wore no boots and his dark red tunic was completely soaked yet he took the weapon eagerly. And there was Daniels, equally bedraggled although the sight of another officer was more than welcome.

"Glad you survived," he said making for him. "Get the rest of your men aboard sharpish, we need to be underway!"

"In good time, sir, in good time." Daniels was drenched and looked shaken, yet this was not an acceptable reply when a lieutenant addressed a midshipman.

"Now, Mr Daniels! I realise you have been in the water, but the prize is in a..."

"I have indeed, *Mr* Summers!" Daniels was on the verge of screaming and had approached sufficiently for his nose to almost touch Summers' face. "And was forced to watch as my shipmates deserted me!"

"What the...?"

"Did your boats not continue when mine was hit?"

There wasn't time for this. "If you have a complaint, it can be made later and to the captain. Until then, you will do as I say!"

Daniels' gaze dropped and he took a step back. "I spoke in haste."

"That you did."

"Though I believe I am allowed a moment to recover..."

"Moment be damned, we must quit this place now," Summers snapped. "See the rest of your men aboard – I will hold you personally responsible for any left behind. Now move!"

* * *

Those of Stokes' mess were thoroughly enjoying themselves, but then taking potshots at an enemy boat was splendid sport and made the more so as little fire was being received in return. The craft itself appeared dangerously overcrowded; simply rowing the thing must have been difficult and loading firearms in near darkness almost impossible. Their midshipman had gone in search of further men, and all accepted the boat must not come alongside. Yet, like most seamen, they were disinclined to think beyond the moment, and found their current task particularly satisfying.

"Stand aside, there!"

Healy must have helped himself to one of the American's muskets and was now using it to lever a place for himself amongst his messmates.

"Steady on, Yorkie!" Stokes said as he was pushed to one side and there were grumbles from others.

"Pulled the bayonet off, didn't I?" Healey asked as he took careful aim.

The piece was despatched with a grunt of satisfaction, then Bovey, with a freshly loaded pistol, casually snapped off a shot.

"Must be makin' some form of impression," he said.

"Whether we is, or whether we ain't, we got to keep it up," Stokes muttered firing his own piece. Of them all, he appeared to be alone in understanding the situation. "They're still picking up them from the launch for'ard. These devils must be kept back till we're underway."

"An' for a bit longer after that," Groom supposed, although his words lacked conviction.

"Aye," Lovemore agreed as he carefully replaced his ramrod and checked all was well before finally raising his weapon.

"We won't make much headway with only a pair of cutters on the tow," Stokes insisted. It was a shame their midshipman had wandered off; this was one of the rare occasions when a strong dose of authority would have been welcome. "Yanks'll close on us easy, then we'll need all aboard an' more to keep 'em back."

But his words made little impression, and the firing continued with the same lack of urgency. Stokes glanced back at the schooner's upper deck; it was crowded with men, though all appeared to have equally important tasks. He muttered a silent oath; with their current attitude he would have preferred his mess not to be solely responsible for dealing with the American boat.

"Well, they can keep this up as long as they likes," Bovey grinned as he pressed a ball down the muzzle of his pistol. "Best jolly since our last run ashore."

"Need a proper piece for real shootin'," Healy announced. "An' a proper man to handle it." His musket was ready once more and all watched with interest while he selected a target. The Yorkshireman was becoming accustomed to the weapon and its flash was more subdued this time, while the boat had neared the point where they could almost pick out individual figures. As soon as the shot rang out, one of the leading rowers fell forward on his oar causing consternation around him.

A cheer rose from the taffrail, and Healy stood back, musket held aloft in triumph.

"Did you see that?" he demanded. "Like potting chickens in a pen!"

Then a rare shot was returned, and the Yorkshireman fell back, blood already spurting from his face. And after that, it stopped being quite so enjoyable.

* * *

Twenty minutes later the moon was starting to rise and Summers could finally take stock. Generally, he was satisfied; the last man had been plucked from the remains of the launch some time before, both towlines remained secured and the cutters were pulling them clear of the harbour entrance. Their prisoners had proved docile, and the wounded were strapped up sufficiently to see them to *Viper*'s medical department. And Daniels was behaving like an officer again.

After seeing the last of his men aboard, Summers detailed him to lead a party of marines and some of their burlier hands to clear the lower decks. By their nature, those seeking sanctuary below would not be the fiercest fighters, yet there were still numerous opportunities for ambush and Summers privately admitted Daniels was appointed as much out of punishment as necessity. But the midshipman had made a reasonable fist of things, and the lower decks could now be considered safe. Summers still felt a measure of resentment at his earlier outburst yet was prepared to forgive a moment's indiscretion. Having charge of a crowded launch struck by cannon fire would probably have shaken the stoutest of hearts.

And that piece of bad luck was more than outweighed by good; the American's boat had finally pulled back. Summers could find no definite reason for this; powered only by the cutters the schooner could easily have been caught and boarded when matters would have turned out very differently. But the firing party aft had suddenly become far more deadly in their aim which must have swung the balance – something he would have to remember when he came to write his report.

Write his report – the concept seemed unreal, and it was only then that Summers realised the enormity of what had been achieved. Until that point, his role was always in support of others; this was his first independent command and it had gone surprisingly well.

In which case it was strange to feel no elation; he had been on the winning side more times than not and there were usually a few moments of pure exultation – or perhaps relief – at the end of a successful action. Yet the hands seemed chipper enough, there were jokes and mutterings of conversation all about; even some of the marines had been seen to smile. No one said very much to him of course, that was to be expected; he was in overall charge, and this must be what was meant by the loneliness of command.

But Summers knew there was more to rejoice in than a simple successful operation. The last few hours had proved he could keep his head and lead men in action – a major test for any young officer – and one he would seem to have passed; such a thing could not be shared with junior men. It might be different once they rejoined *Viper*, when he could talk with Woodward, Cooper, even the captain; those who had been through such an experience and may understand. And perhaps one of them could explain why the passing of such a crucial marker was so lacking in satisfaction.

Chapter Twelve

"It's not what I would expect from one of His Majesty's officers," King agreed. "After all, Daniels is a passed midshipman..."

"He may have been shaken by the loss of the launch," Summers added.

"Yes, yet to have behaved so – to almost refuse your order – truly Michael, it does not bode well for the future."

That was very much the point, for any man to show reluctance in action was deplorable and contravened the Articles of War; had Daniels held a commission, he would probably lose it.

"Maybe so, sir, but he made a first-rate job of securing the lower deck. And he is still effectively a midshipman."

That was also significant. As a junior warrant officer some latitude could be granted although, if noted, the incident would not look well on his record.

King sighed; Summers appeared especially keen to let the matter rest, which was understandable; as the senior man and only commissioned officer present, any action taken would be entirely on his report. And King knew the lad of old; he would have no wish to blight another's career simply because of one unfortunate incident.

"Very well, let me think on it," he said. "And I shall be interviewing the schooner's master later."

"I'd be interested in knowing why half their crew were ashore, sir."

King nodded although he had his own ideas about that. On dropping anchor in any strange harbour, most captains would wish to check for water and green stuff ashore, while the fellow may also have been planning to set up a temporary battery. "I'm more concerned about discovering if they are in league with the pirates at Tunis," he said.

"They appeared to be making for the island when first sighted," Summers agreed.

Of all the North African States, America was on the closest terms with those based in Tunis while the country may even have come to terms with the Barbary Pirates in general. In which case, when King's actions became known, there could be major political repercussions – that or a flotilla of brigands sent to seek him out. Either would hardly make him popular and it was all a long way from his original brief of watching out for vessels likely to offer aid to Bonaparte. He closed his eyes for a second aware that, yet again, he may have let his heart rule his head.

"Sir?" The polite enquiry brought King back from his thoughts; his personal problems did not concern Summers or his actions. The lad had done well and deserved to be praised.

"Doubtless we shall know all in time, but first you are to be congratulated; your performance was outstanding, considering the circumstances. And we lost six men in total, is that not correct?"

"Yes, sir," Summers agreed. "Three of the boarders and three from the launch – the latter apparently drowned."

That was another thing against Daniels; his boat had actually proved a hindrance, although the man could hardly be blamed for it being struck by enemy shot. And neither was he responsible for the fatalities; few seamen were able to swim after all. Yet the launch did not totally sink, and an active officer should have done more to save his people.

"And the wounded?"

"Nine, sir; Mr Manning expects all to make a full recovery."

Again, that was good news, as was the fact that the *Mary Anne,* a prime armed schooner, now lay off *Viper*'s beam. Cooper's initial appraisal suggested she still carried her American cargo, which would add to her value at any prize court.

King nodded. "All are regrettable, of course, though it could have been worse."

"Actually, sir, there were moments when I wondered if I could carry it off," the lad admitted. "There just seemed so much to do – so much to think of..."

"Which is not uncommon," King smiled. "I think most of us have known such times." That was true; however careful the planning, few actions go smoothly or totally to plan. To King's mind, an officer should be judged on how such difficulties are overcome and Summers had exceeded on that count.

Yet even as he spoke, King was no longer thinking of the past but the future. Were they at war, Summers would steadily rise in seniority as a lieutenant and probably be given a command of his own before long. During peacetime, such a chance was less likely though that also had advantages – at least from King's point of view. It meant he would retain the services of a fine officer for many years to come. And, more than that, the company of one who was fast becoming a friend.

* * *

"Well, he came, and he went," Stokes said and there was a moment's silence from all around the table as they considered this. Those making up the boarding parties had quitted the prize at first light and spent the following watch asleep. There was little chance to talk over their morning burgoo, or throughout the following trick of duty. It was only when the noon issue of spirit was still warm in their bellies and after eating a less satisfactory portion of cheese and pickled cabbage – it being a banyan day – that they were finally able to discuss the previous night as a mess.

"Can't say I ever liked the bugger," Bovey added. "Though that don't mean I wished him gone."

"None of us *liked* him," Stokes agreed, "an' none of us wished 'im gone."

"Fellow played a fair hand of cards," Downes suggested in an attempt at compassion, but the remark was greeted in silence.

"Gonna be a different place without him." Lovemore this time.

"Gonna be quieter," said Early.

"At least you always knew where you were with the old sod," Longdon supposed.

"Aye," Bovey agreed. "Yorkie was never known to hold back with an opinion."

"Hold fast there," Downes protested. "Fellow's dead, we should be more respectful."

"That so?" Stokes seemed unconvinced. "He never had a good word for any of us."

"That's right, always spoke his mind," Lovemore agreed.

138

"You could rely on him for that."

"So why should we be any different?" Groom added.

"Well, I hated the bastard," Early stated with apparent detachment.

"That's honest, I suppose," Bovey shrugged.

"Aye," Stokes agreed. "Healy would have liked that."

* * *

"My name is King, I command this ship. This is Lieutenant Cooper my first officer. I believe you have already met Lieutenant Summers."

The American captain nodded to each and added a smile for Summers.

"Indeed, Mr Summers bested me in a fight," he said. "I suppose a rematch would be out of the question?"

Summers met the grin and was about to reply when his own captain broke in.

"Absolutely. You are our prisoner and would do well to remember that."

There was an awkward silence that King privately welcomed. What with a sleepless night and the nagging concern over Aimée's condition, he knew he was not in the best of moods to interview the schooner's master. Such things could not be delayed, however, especially as he had just discovered they must spend several days away from their patrol while repairs to the prize were completed.

But his mind was already made up about Captain Goodman; as soon as the fellow entered the great cabin he had assessed him. Not more than thirty and likely a good deal younger, educated and well groomed with neatly cut hair in the modern manner. But he had a direct look that took in each of his captors before joining them at *Viper*'s dining table and there was an aura of confidence about the cove that came dangerously close to arrogance. It was an attitude King had come to associate with the next generation and not one he liked.

"So, what is it?" he demanded, "Or shall I guess? You are a simple trader whose sole intent is honest commerce?"

"The carrying trade is certainly part of my remit," Goodman admitted.

"And you hold a letter of marque, though only to allow access to weapons and ordnance?"

Goodman held his head erect. "The status of privateer is one acknowledged by both our countries as well as much of the civilised world."

There was something about the man's accent that King found familiar, although he lacked the inclination to think further.

"And you had no wish to raid British merchants or disrupt their legitimate trade in any way?"

"I have made no such claim, sir."

"I am glad to hear of it, for your vessel is equipped with cannon that would credit many a man-of-war along with gunners evidently well versed in their trade."

The American closed his eyes and nodded.

"And I am expected to believe such provisions were merely for your defence?"

"No, sir, the guns carried aboard the *Mary Anne* were so I might prey on my enemy's merchants, while I also intended giving any smaller warships a run for their money."

King nodded. "That is an honest answer at least."

"I have no need to lie to you, or anyone else," Goodman continued. "And neither do I appreciate this form of interrogation."

"I shall speak as I choose," King snapped.

"That is your prerogative, Captain, though I should prefer a more polite conversation." There was the hint of a smile, "Such as might be enjoyed by civilised beings."

King glanced to his officers; Summers may have been out of his depth and was maintaining a neutral expression although Cooper was watching the exchange with obvious fascination. And he knew his first officer well; there might also be a hint of amusement lurking somewhere.

"I am sorry you do not consider me civilised," he began.

"Captain, my opinion of you is irrelevant," Goodman interrupted. "Nevertheless, I do wish you would give me a chance; rather than making bold assumptions why not ask outright what my intentions were? You may be surprised by the result."

"Very well," King conceded. "What is your business in

these waters?"

"In the main to trade," Goodman replied, "though were a spot of privateering to have come my way, it would not have been discounted."

"In which case, your victims would have been British?"

The American raised an eyebrow. "Our countries are at war; I'd consider that inevitable."

"And how would you have enticed such prey?" King demanded, his tone strengthening once more. "False colours and concealed armament?"

"Now there you go again," Goodman sighed. "Always assumptions."

"So, you deny it?"

"As a matter of fact, I do. Since arriving in the Med I have sighted several potential prizes but with my holds already filled, none were pursued."

"Where are you from, Captain?" Cooper asked the question, while King drew breath.

"The *Mary Anne* was seven weeks out of Baltimore," Goodman replied. "And I hail from the East Coast myself."

"So, a New Englander?" Cooper again.

"Born and bred."

"I knew another from those parts." King had suddenly placed the accent. "He too was a naval man."

Goodman considered this. "Am I right in guessing the United States Navy?"

"You are; Robert Walton, commanded the *Delaware*."

"I know the name, and of the action though was never fortunate enough to meet the man himself. His ship was overwhelmed, as I recall?"

"That is so," King admitted, "though not before he had taken my own."

At this Goodman raised his eyes. "Your name was familiar, Captain, and now I can place you. That would have been *Tenacious* and, from what I recall, you fought a gallant action."

"Thank you," King said only mildly grudgingly.

"And your friend – I'm assuming he was your friend – is very much a hero where I come from."

"Oh, he was a friend," King confirmed quietly.

Goodman's eyes had softened slightly. "Then we have

found something in common, Captain King," he said. "What say we start again? And perhaps, if both of us try to be a little more constructive, we may get somewhere?"

* * *

"Well, it would appear you will have to manage without me, for a spell at least."

Daniels' announcement was not greeted in the way he expected; Williams, seated at the cockpit's table, took on an expression of frank delight while Edwards, currently at the washstand scratching at his down with a razor, seemed almost amused. But Daniels never cared much for the opinion of inferiors, his mind was set on the impending adventure.

"Captain announced it, has he?" Edwards enquired through the soap.

"Not in so many words," Daniels replied. "Though it would stand to reason. Such a command is hardly large enough to warrant a lieutenant, and I am by far the senior mid."

Both statements were undoubtedly true, even if the younger men would have been keen to dispute them.

"Of course, I shall be wanting another to accompany me. A junior, for the more menial tasks."

At this, William's took on a look of distant contemplation, while Edwards began to rinse his razor so feverishly it raised quite a foam in the bowl.

"Oh, do not concern yourselves, I shall be speaking with the others."

"But they're just volunteers!" Williams exclaimed. He had no wish to join Daniels in the prize yet was strangely offended that an untrained lad might be chosen in his place.

"Maybe so, maybe so," Daniels said. "Though there is something in willingness to learn; an attribute I fear you both lack."

Now that was adding fuel to the fire and, despite a line of light brown fluff remaining on his top lip, Edwards began to scrub at his face with a towel.

"Yes, I'm afraid attitude is all-important," Daniels continued. "It's what got me through my board and will guarantee a successful career." He treated his fellow midshipmen to a look rich in both pity and disdain. "Whereas you, my friends, are somewhat remiss in that department. You lack my approach and are doomed to a life of junior ranks and servitude."

And that was his second surprise; rather than encouraging more despondency, the pair seemed quite buoyed by his prediction. Edwards might even have been sniggering slightly.

* * *

"I'd been in command of the *Mary Anne* no longer than two months," the American continued.

"So, you are not the owner?" Cooper checked and Goodman shook his head.

"Not me, I was to be due a portion of what was earned though soon discovered it to be a raw deal. These waters are not as rewarding as some would have and what profit there might be hardly matches the risk."

"So, you have not been active as a privateer?"

"Or a trader," Goodman said. "After a bad crossing, I had been trying to make up time when we chanced upon your ship."

"And were you heading for Zembra?" King recognised an easing in the atmosphere; Goodman was finally proving cooperative, although he privately accepted his own attitude had hardly encouraged this.

"Only when we took damage aloft; I figured it would be the nearest place of refuge."

"Then it wasn't your original destination?"

"As I said, it was to get away from you fellas."

"And where were you bound?" Cooper asked.

Goodman gave a brief smile. "Now that I would rather not say; though assure you it was a legitimate port. And for trade; I was not intending to rely on privateering for profit. You have my word that our eventual customer has no relevance to you gentlemen or your country."

There was nothing unusual in this, instead Goodman's reticence only reinforced his status as a merchant; most were cagey about revealing their suppliers and buyers were kept equally confidential.

"So, you are not in league with anyone in Tunis?"

At this, the American laughed aloud. "No indeed, sir, no indeed. The pirates are our enemies and probably always will be. Whatever made you think so?"

King shook his head. "It is a strange world," he said. "And one in which enemies and allies are inclined to switch back and forth. It wouldn't have been so surprising to hear of an alliance with America."

Goodman inclined his head. "I guess you're right. Yesterday this gentleman and I were fighting to the death." He gave a wink in Summers' direction. "Yet today we can sit at the same table and enjoy a civilised conversation."

The two young men exchanged a grin.

"If there is an alliance, nobody bothered telling me," Goodman continued. "A couple of my men knew of Zembra from previous visits, yet I can tell you I felt mighty uncomfortable in that harbour. Which is why I despatched my first officer to investigate setting up a battery."

"That would be the shore party?"

"Indeed, Mr Summers. The one your men so efficiently saw off."

"Then you had decided to stay for a while?" Cooper chanced.

"The decision was forced upon me; our topmast is badly damaged, as you will have no doubt discovered. We reckoned on two days at the least to put matters right and in that time could have faced an attack by yourselves, or the barbarians. Though I'll admit, none of us expected you to act quite so quickly."

King acknowledged this with a slight nod. Since being alerted to the connection, there were other similarities to Bob Walton beyond the accent. Goodman was a completely different build, of course – and a good deal younger – yet still he found himself warming to the chap. "I suppose they're safe enough," he mused.

"Pardon me?"

"Your shore party," King expanded, "they must still be on the island."

"Oh sure, though I know Davy White of old. If there's wildlife around, he'll have found it. And they have a decent boat; soon as you fellows take off, they'll be heading for the nearest neutral harbour."

"We don't intend to move for some time," King said. "As you mentioned, your tophamper requires significant repair."

Goodman shrugged. "Then I guess they'll wait."

"But, if Tunis learns what's been going on..." Cooper began and now the American became more concerned.

"You mean if they hear about you taking my ship?" he stiffened further. "You think they'll come and take a look-see?"

"It is likely."

The American eyed King cautiously. "And you couldn't stop them?"

"It's not that I couldn't," King said. "There are few pirate vessels that can match *Viper* in size or fire power. But I have specific instructions not to interfere with any from the Barbary States."

"Can I ask why?"

"Let's just say my C-in-C has plans in that direction."

The American accepted this, although his expression remained thoughtful.

"So, I guess Davy and his men are in danger," he said.

"Indeed. If Tunis do send a ship, and if they choose to land on the island, it might not go well with them."

Goodman shook his head. "It's a big place with plenty of cover. Most of my men grew up in such an environment; they'll keep a bunch of 'Turks' at bay, just you see."

"I hope so," King said. "Because if any of them were to be caught..."

"What is the alternative, Captain?"

King shrugged. "We might send a boat," he replied. "Our countries are at war which officially makes you and I enemies, but I've heard stories of how so-called infidels are treated on this coast. If your men are willing to surrender, I'll bring them aboard and grant protection. As privateers, you must be considered prisoners of war, of course, although I don't expect us to remain opponents forever. As soon as this foolish war between us is over you will be free men."

"And we might be friends?" Goodman chanced.

"It is a possibility."

"And what of my ship?" The American questioned.

"She is my prize," King said. "I cannot alter that."

Goodman considered this for a moment, then seemed to come to a decision. "I think you are right, sir, they are likely to come lookin'," he said at last. "So yes, I agree to your terms. And thank you."

* * *

"Do you hear the buzz?" Groom asked as the mess were slinging their hammocks that evening.

"News, is there?" Stokes was mildly interested.

"I'd say, about our prize."

"*Our* prize?" Bovey gave a quizzical look.

"Well, we was the ones what saw that Yank boat off," Groom pointed out. "If they'd gotten aboard, we'd all be in the suds."

It seemed a moot point, but they let it pass.

"I hears she needs more work than they thought," Downes said. "Whole topmast housing wants replacing."

"It's not that, they're talking of takin' her to Gib," Groom announced.

"That bad is it?" Stokes asked.

"Won't be, not after Morales and his mates've finished. Though they'll be wantin' a prize crew."

"Likely one'll be appointed," Early said.

"Maybe, but that don't mean we can't put up for it."

"Can't say the thought appeals," Bovey sniffed. "I crewed aboard a capture afore, an' 'tain't no holiday."

"'Sright; too few doing the work of too many," Longdon agreed.

"P'raps, though Gib bound you say?" Stokes again. "They won't be takin' her to Malta?"

"Na, it's Gib for sure." Groom was certain. "Skinner, one of the master's mates, told us. That said, wherever she's heading, there'll be nothing doing for them aboard once she makes harbour. They'll be kickin' their heels an'll have the place to theirselves whereas *Viper*'s got more'n a month of cruisin' ahead. Given the choice, I know which I'd prefer."

* * *

It actually took three full days to make the schooner fit to sail and *Viper* stood by her. They remained close to the island throughout, and on one occasion Lieutenant Woodward took Captain Goodman back to its harbour in a cutter. There they were initially met with a hail of bullets, but the American stood up and bellowed to his former shipmates. The cutter was then allowed to approach and shortly afterwards the schooner's own boat followed them back and a further seventeen were added to *Viper*'s prisoners.

These proved to be the expected mixture of native-born Americans and British who had adopted the country, with a couple of Spanish and a Lascar thrown in for variety. King arranged for the general hands to be quartered in what was little more than a screened-off portion of the orlop, while the *Mary Anne*'s two former officers were given a cabin in the gunroom to share. Soon all were allowed limited freedom on deck, then on the second day, security was lifted further. Some, who had struck up friendships amongst *Viper*'s regular crew, were allowed to join the lower deck for meals and, when the monotony of waiting for the schooner was broken by a mess night, the Americans became welcome guests.

But it proved a lonely vigil. Apart from the occasional sighting of small craft – fishing vessels, local traders and the like – they were left very much to themselves. It was only as the repairs were coming to an end that a true ship was sighted.

The light, graceful hull and distinct yet equally elegant lateen rig immediately identified her as a xebec. Such craft were a common sight in the Mediterranean where they were used for a variety of purposes although their speed and agility made them particularly suited to pirating. This one was the size of a small frigate and an elegant sailer; she sliced through the blue-grey waters, drawing wary, yet admiring, glances from the seamen. King guessed she had put out from La Goulette, the nearby Tunis port, and was concerned. Pellew's advice had been clear; the Barbary States were to be given a wide berth, yet he had already crossed the line by effectively invading their territory and snatching an enemy from under their noses. He had no wish to add to his sins by engaging one of their warships in combat.

Besides, it might not be the easy conquest the xebec's light and fragile hull suggested. Those of her type regularly carried a sizeable armament that might be equal or even superior to *Viper*'s, and the pirates' habit of cramming their vessels with the toughest fighting men was well known. Accordingly, he cleared for action and had his guns run out while marines manned the bulwarks and the main body of prisoners obediently retired to the orlop. But, after passing just out of range, the vessel continued and they watched as she entered the island's harbour and dropped anchor. There was a delay of just over an hour in which any number of things might have happened before the xebec left once more.

"Guess that might have been uncomfortable for our boys," Goodman said when the xebec was underway again. He had been allowed on deck and was standing with Cooper and the sailing master as the vessel passed by.

"I dare say they would have remained hidden," Cooper supposed, although the American was unconvinced.

"Not Davy White," he said. "Fellow can't hold his fire for no one; there'd have been a fight for certain and, though a few 'Turks' might have been taken, it could only have ended one way."

"Do you take it they'll be back?" Manton asked.

"I was thinking the same myself," Cooper admitted. "Xebecs can prove a difficult enemy; I shouldn't like to face more'n one at a time."

"It's not the fighting that would worry me," Goodman mused, "it's the prospect of being caught. Those fellas treat their prisoners worse than dogs. They've a system similar to your Navy's prize money."

Cooper raised an eyebrow. "How so?"

"The dey – that's their ruler and similar to our president – he takes the lion's share of any cargo and keeps the vessel itself. The owners are entitled to half of what's left, and the crew share any that remains."

"Seems a reasonable arrangement," Manton commented.

"Ah, but personal possessions are the sole property of the pirates themselves. They takes what they want and anyone who complains is likely to be butchered, especially so if they've put up a fight. And most times it won't be a pleasant end."

"And the rest?" Cooper didn't care much for the conversation even if there was something compelling about it.

"The best any prisoner can expect is to be sold into slavery, in which case some could win their freedom back in a few years, providing those at home are willing to shell out a small fortune. But have no illusions, gentlemen, they enter servitude with nothing, not even the clothes on their back."

For a moment all digested this, then Manton cleared his throat.

"Accordin' to the carpenter she should be underway by mid-morning," he said. "And her next stop will be Gib. The housing's not totally sound though, as long as she keeps the wind on her counter, should serve."

"And you'll be going back with her," Cooper checked. "Along with your men, of course."

"So I understand," Goodman agreed. "And the time can't come quick enough for me. Speaking personally, I've had my fill of these waters."

Chapter Thirteen

Before they could move on, there was one more item for King to address. News of Aimée's pregnancy had overtaken that of Summers' wife; until that evening he had forgotten the woman was also with child. That presented yet another problem and one that would be awkward to handle. He might consult with Cooper, or Aimée, although both were liable to be biased and, when it came down to it, he was the captain and must make up his own mind. The coward inside wanted to sleep on the matter, but a decision was forced on him when the lad requested an interview that evening.

Of course, it might have nothing to do with his wife; Summers had just completed his first independent mission and was yet to submit a report; such things could be daunting to the uninitiated; it would be natural for him ask for advice. That was certainly the subject King would prefer, he knew most of his limitations and coping with officers' personal problems was definitely one.

But when Summers entered the great cabin and took a seat, King sensed from his flushed face and anxious expression that this was not a professional matter.

"You will know about Suzie, sir," he announced almost immediately.

"I realise she is expecting a child," King agreed. "And I am sure you understand the difficulties such a situation presents."

"It was not what we planned..." Summers began although King stopped him.

"There is little point in debating that, Michael, we have a situation that must be addressed. You realise she cannot stay aboard this ship?"

"I expected something on those lines, sir."

"In the normal course of events I should put her off at the next port, which would be Valletta and at the end of our patrol, though I think we might reconsider that."

The lad waited.

"You will keep this to yourself, Michael, but I am also to become a father – a father once more," he added a little self-consciously.

Summers' face lit up. "That is good news indeed, sir, and I wish you joy of it." The words were undoubtedly sincere, yet King sensed something more in the lad's manner. After the initial enthusiasm, he became awkward, embarrassed even; although it must be hard to congratulate a man who had already lost two children.

"Thank you, Michael," King began, before falling equally aback as he realised his failure to properly acknowledge Summers' approaching fatherhood. "Aimée will be returning to England," he continued quickly, where Mrs Manning will be taking her in hand. "It would seem sensible if both women travelled together, and I think you might have provided the ideal craft."

Summers blinked.

"The schooner," King said. "Your capture."

"Oh, the *Mary Anne*?"

"Indeed. Amon and Morales believe her rig will be workable by midday."

"And then, sir?"

"Then she will be liable to raise a fair sum at the prize courts."

A light smile played upon the lad's face as King continued.

"Obviously she cannot take them all the way to England, and usually I would simply despatch her to Malta. But there are better auction facilities in Gib, and I think that alone justifies our sending her there."

Now Summers had taken on a look of pleased expectation.

"And I was considering Daniels to command her."

"Daniels, sir?" His face fell.

"Yes, he is reasonably experienced and, even if we were still at war with France, such a prize would usually fall to a midshipman."

"Though you will remember how he behaved when she was taken, sir?"

"I do, which is why I am mentioning the matter."

If he were honest, King had given the choice of prize master very little consideration and long since decided on Daniels. Try as he might he simply could not warm to the fellow and he was not alone. Even from the exalted position of captain it was obvious his attitude, combined with supposedly good connections, had made him unpopular with those of every rank, and King would be mightily pleased to be rid of him. With luck, Daniels should find a better posting in Gibraltar, which would leave room for a more agreeable midshipman to be appointed.

"If I may suggest, sir..." King nodded, he was prepared to listen to Summers, yet doubted anything would change his mind. "I could command her."

At that King had to smile; Summers must have forgotten his own commission. Maybe the lad had spent too long in the cockpit?

"You are a lieutenant, Michael," he reminded, "and have an important post aboard this ship."

"I realise that sir, but... but when Suzie delivered her news – well we wondered about making a change..."

"A change?"

Summers nodded. "In my career."

"You are considering resigning your commission?"

"I am, sir. With the French war over so much has altered. Positions are already harder to find, and promotion has come to a halt."

"You have a responsible position here."

"Yes, sir, but only for a time. This commission may last a few years, or it might be over by Christmas. And then what will happen to me?" He paused. "What will happen to any of us?"

King knew the lad was right. He had been exceptionally lucky in landing the command of *Viper*; many senior to him were already on the beach and when the war in America came to an end, there would be more. Before the start of hostilities with France, Nelson himself had been unemployed for five years. King was quite likely never to get another ship while, even if Summers remained in the Service but unemployed, he would probably die a lieutenant.

Yet were he to go now things could be very different. For some time it had been possible for lieutenants to retire with the rank of Commander, and benefit from an increased pension. Why, he would even be better off financially; from what King could recall a retired commander's allowance was six shillings a day, sixpence more than the most an active lieutenant could earn aboard a first rate. Summers was a youngster, but the Admiralty were desperate to reduce their numbers; he may well be offered such an arrangement and, if he truly had doubts about continuing, would be a fool not to take it.

And he could go to sea again; positions were available with the East India Company or any of the new merchant ventures that were starting to appear. Opportunities even existed to serve aboard other nations' warships where Royal Navy trained officers carried a definite cachet. He sat back and considered the lad more carefully. It was a shame, a dreadful shame, yet totally understandable; in his shoes, King felt he would jump at the chance of leaving.

"So, what are you suggesting?"

"I resign my commission and see the *Mary Anne* to Gibraltar." Summers spoke with the air of someone who knew his own mind. "If it made matters easier, my resignation could become effective once I arrive."

It was not impossible: a good solution in fact. King would feel more comfortable with Aimée under Summers' care, and, in the circumstances, Pellew might allow the schooner to continue to England. In which case both women would be certain of their child being born at home. However, that did not alter the fact that he was losing a talented officer.

"Let me give it some thought," he said, although both already knew what the answer would be. "But I must say I'm sorry."

"Yes, sir," Summers agreed. "I'm sorry too."

* * *

"Can't say I'm surprised," Manning sighed.

"But he is an excellent officer," King insisted. "And capable. The cutting-out expedition proved that."

"It might have proved something," the surgeon supposed. "Though will his talents be needed? There have been so many changes since you and I first joined, Tom, and peace with France will bring more. Rather than fighting officers, they'll be wanting diplomats and politicians; the old regime won't stand a chance."

King shook his head. "Young men with spirit will always be in demand," he said.

"Michael Summers has spirit, yet he is seeking to leave. I'd say let him go and, more to the point, let him care for his wife – and Aimée, of course."

"He'd do a better job than Daniels," King admitted.

"There you are. And Daniels is a passed Mid., or so I believe?"

"He is."

"Then you have his replacement all lined up."

King nodded; he supposed his friend was correct, although exchanging Summers for the stuck-up Daniels was no bargain.

"Sadly, there will be another departing at the same time," Manning added, and King frowned.

"I trust you are not thinking of deserting us?"

"Not me: Bewley, one of my loblolly boys."

"The former farrier?" King asked in surprise. "I had thought him settling well."

"And I; he took to the life perfectly and was a Godsend with the recent casualties."

"So why?"

Manning shrugged. "There is no specific reason, least not one he will own to. The lad just wants to move on."

"We are not exciting enough for him?"

"Hardly that, though I sensed he did not enjoy our recent spell of action."

"The same would apply to many," King grunted.

"Sure, yet combat surgery is a different discipline. I sense Bewley to be a peaceable chap and happier looking after animals. Still, it is a shame; I had him down as a potential surgeon's mate."

"You could not persuade him?"

"Lord, Tom, I would not try; this is medicine, you cannot press a man to heal others!"

"I assume not. You wish him to go with the prize?"

"It would seem sensible; he enjoyed Gibraltar and wishes to try his hand there."

"Then it is settled, and I dare say someone with medical knowledge would be an advantage, considering the state of the women."

Manning pulled a wry face. "That may well be the case. Tell me, when exactly is the prize leaving?"

"Tomorrow, probably around midday. *Viper* will

accompany her as far as our regular patrol area."

"And I assume you have advised Aimée?"

"She knows she has to go, though not exactly when..."

Manning sighed and slapped his forehead. "Lordie, Tom, sometimes you amaze me!"

"But she will not need time," King protested. "Her luggage is minimal, and the maid shall see to that."

"All the same, she might appreciate some warning. You must remember, Aimée's in a delicate state. And she'll be leaving her husband..."

"The house will be waiting for her in Eastbourne."

"Oh, for sure, and it's a fine place with good people; they will make her welcome. Yet there may be memories..."

King sighed, yes there probably would... "I was hoping Kate might see her through the later stages," he said.

"Maybe you should think about joining her yourself?"

"Me?"

"It's a thought, Tom. As we have said, the Navy we joined is fast disappearing; better to go willingly than find yourself pushed."

"Thanks, Bob, though I shall see out this commission."

Manning smiled. "I wouldn't expect anything else," he said. "But bear it in mind; for the future."

* * *

A final problem rigging the schooner's new futtock shrouds put off their departure until later in the afternoon watch, although the delay did at least allow King to take one last meal with Aimée. In honour of this he had chosen to eat in the great cabin, rather than the coach where they usually dined when alone. However, the grand surroundings hardly added to their intimacy and neither did eating at *Viper*'s massive table. So, it was almost a relief when the midshipman interrupted their pudding to announce the schooner ready to depart.

Summers had already officially transferred yet was waiting for them on the quarterdeck, having made the journey back to bid farewell, although King noted his wife did not accompany him. And when it came for his turn to say goodbye to Aimée he found himself regretting wasting their recent private time. But while his officers looked pointedly elsewhere, they managed a brief embrace. Then a handshake for Summers, who muttered something King did not catch and, all too soon, the pair of them were clambering into the schooner's cutter while King strode to the starboard bulwark. Glancing down he decided Aimée looked as composed as ever, although her servant clutched at the gunwales as if frightened of being tipped over the side. At a word from Summers, the boat put out and was soon on the short journey to the waiting schooner.

Captain Goodman was already on board, as were the majority of his crew – three having opted to serve King George. Half of *Viper*'s contingent of marines had also been transferred along with eighteen hands from her lower deck and a couple of midshipmen to keep them in order. Such a sizeable prize crew was justified by the number of prisoners, although King sensed there would be no trouble from Goodman and his men. With little chance of meeting with a larger American vessel, they should have a trouble-free run to Gibraltar. Even the Barbary Pirates presented no threat; whatever plans Pellew might have to address the menace were far in the future. Right now, Britain remained a cautious ally and one sight of the Union flag should be enough to dissuade the fiercest corsair. The winter storms were also a long way off; even the famed Sirocco wasn't due to rise for at least another month and, with Summers in command, they should make Gibraltar with the minimum of fuss. After picking up an Indiaman for a further short but luxurious cruise, the women would be in Eastbourne long before winter set in and then Kate Manning would care for them.

He stole away from the bulwark careful not to catch the eye of anyone around him. *Viper* would now continue her patrol, before eventually making for Valletta. After which there may be another detachment, or Pellew could have something else in mind, although King was equally aware that would also be the first chance of mail from home. But Manning's words continued to echo within him; he may indeed be coming to the end of his career, in which case was there truly any point in continuing? A jobbing captain could be found in Malta, and he may yet spend Christmas at home with Aimée.

And then sense was allowed to take over. He was being a sentimental fool; if this truly were his last commission, he should make the best of it. The previous week had proved there was still work to be done, enemies to fight and men to command. Aimée and the schooner would have a safe passage and Summers might even reconsider and return to *Viper*. The next time he visited Eastbourne there should be a fresh family awaiting in a house no longer cold and echoing with memories. He had still to speak with Daniels, it could be promotion would improve the fellow and, if not, he would find reason to ditch him and to hell with his connections. The future was incredibly bright, if only he allowed himself to see it that way.

* * *

There was no child, there never had been: Aimée had concocted the entire story although for the very best of reasons – to make things easier for them all.

And there was no one to blame other than herself; the time she and Thomas had spent together in Halifax was pleasant enough even if, on the rare occasions when he stayed in their rented house, his mind remained with the ship. And it had been much the same later in Eastbourne; as long as his uniform remained safely stowed, they were happy, but as soon as word arrived of a fresh command, she once more lost him for good.

Which is why Aimée had chosen to accompany him. At the time it seemed the ideal solution; they would still be together and, with his precious ship all around, every chance of a compromise being reached. It proved otherwise however, and now she understood it would always be so.

Her plan was simple: see Suzie safely to Gibraltar and installed aboard an Indiaman. She would be home in no time where Kate Manning was waiting. Meanwhile, Aimée would head back to her family home in Verdun. With all of Spain to cross it would be a long journey, but she was well provided for and, though alone – she intended sending Millie back to care for Suzie – it would be done in time. Then she might review things properly before contacting Thomas and attempting to explain. And after that everything would depend on him; he could choose between living with her on land – she didn't mind where – or at sea aboard a ship and fighting his endless battles. But if he chose the latter, he would spend the rest of his life without her.

Chapter Fourteen

Ten days later Summers had the feel of the schooner and was equally happy being her temporary captain. The wind stayed moderate and fair, so much so that they were now more than halfway to their destination with no sign of strain to the repaired topmast. This was his first truly independent command and he had been reluctant to stray too far from the coast. The Mediterranean sky could be a navigator's dream, yet he preferred to rely on known geographical features to fix his position. Which some might consider cheating, although that hardly bothered him. Summers' appointment was only temporary, but there was still no one to answer to officially and he soon began to enjoy the autonomy of command. However, neither was there any chance of him becoming aloof, not with Suzie on hand to keep him in check and two spirited midshipmen watching his every move.

Nevertheless, the atmosphere aboard the *Mary Anne* remained pleasant. Goodman, her former master, had been cordial throughout and, on the odd occasion when Summers needed to seek advice about the vessel herself, gave it readily. Equally, there were few problems with the prisoners. Before they set off, secure accommodation was constructed on the forward berth deck and the marine contingent messed between the Americans and the schooner's prize crew. But for much of the day, a third of the prisoners were allowed on deck and casual socialising between both nation's seamen became common. Yet Summers was not tempted to relax security entirely and instructed Marine Lieutenant Browning to divide his men into watches; at all times armed guards supervised both groups while any ready-use weapons were moved to the great cabin.

Which, despite the stash of cutlasses, pistols, tomahawks and boarding pikes it now held, had become a decidedly feminine area. As soon as he was offered command, Summers wondered what to do with three female passengers, and the fact that one was his wife, and another the captain's lady, gave the problem extra spice. Accommodating them in what would normally have been the master's quarters made the most sense and gave both privacy and space – valuable assets in any vessel and especially one as small as the *Mary Anne*. Summers was comfortable enough sharing the tiny gunroom and had become used to travelling separately from his wife.

And at least the women seemed to be thriving; they were even hosting a dinner that evening. As he paced gently across what was now his quarterdeck, Summers could hear the sound of preparations through an open skylight. Goodman would also be attending, along with Marine Lieutenant Browning, both midshipmen and Bewley.

The latter represented the vessel's entire medical department. Summers was not exactly sure why the loblolly boy was returning to Gibraltar although there were no complaints about the man's presence or abilities. Two days into the voyage he had set the arm of a topman who, in a moment's inattention, fell from a yard. All feared the seaman's work aloft would be over, but Bewley did a fine job, and the limb should be saved.

The brief experience of command had not altered Summers' plans, however; as soon as they made Gibraltar he remained set on resigning his commission. And then, perhaps, a few months on land; time to see Suzie through her confinement and get to know their child. Even without newspapers or fresh gossip for so long, it was reasonable to assume the world remained in a state of flux. He and Suzie had sufficient funds to support them for a year, and the return from this current prize would stretch that further, so he could afford to sit back and let everything around him settle. Then, once something approaching normality was established, he would seek out a seagoing post. Whether this would be in a trader, or a foreign navy's warship, was still to be decided; his first task must be to convince Suzie of the wisdom of the act. Yet inwardly he was sure this current passage would not be his last and there may even be other commands after the *Mary Anne*.

Williams had appeared on the main deck and was making his way aft; Summers paused in his pacing as the midshipman approached.

"All well below?" he asked.

"Absolutely, sir," the youngster beamed. "Not sure what the ladies are up to in the pantry, but the place smells like a regular chop house."

The first dogwatch would soon be called, and Williams was due to stand it. With the meal scheduled for two bells, he would miss only part, whereas Edwards could enjoy an hour before being called on deck for the second dog. It was an example of the relaxed atmosphere that prevailed; rather than delivering a capture, this might almost have been a yachting excursion. Summers was about to make an appropriate reply when a call from the masthead brought both officers back to their duty.

"Deck there, sail to the west. Off the starboard bow and making for us."

They had encountered a good deal of shipping on their brief journey, mostly local coastal trade and fishermen although, five days before, one of Pellew's frigates had been sighted carrying out a similar duty to *Viper*. It was a nervous time for Summers; the warship must have noted the schooner's rig and, despite their colours, believed them to be an American. It took that day's private signal followed by a bellowed conversation with her captain before their current status was accepted, and then a boat had come across with mail intended for Gibraltar. The whole incident delayed them more than half a day and Summers would prefer not to repeat the process.

It was usual to send a midshipman to the masthead in such situations and he glanced speculatively at Williams. But before an order could be issued, the lookout gave more information.

"Looks to be a frigate; a three-master for sure and probably a man-of-war, as she's showin' royals."

"What heading?"

"She's clawing toward us, sir." The lookout had recognised Summers' voice. "An' settin' a fair old rate."

That was an important point; there was a moderate wind on the *Mary Anne*'s larboard quarter and she was also making good speed; it would be a shame to alter course in the hope of shaking the sighting off. Besides, if this were yet another British warship, any evasive action might be taken the wrong way.

"I suppose it all depends on the length of her tack," Summers remarked, and Williams nodded sagely. To make any progress in their direction the mystery warship must be close-hauled. Depending on her captain, and his need for speed, each leg might cover fifty miles or five, but the *Mary Anne* still hugged

160

the coast, so the sighting was likely to turn and head deeper out to sea at any moment.

She remained on the larboard tack, however. Even as the new watch was set, the lookout replaced and Williams officially took charge of the deck, the sighting continued to make directly for them, and Summers resigned himself to yet another delay. And this time it would be more complicated: this time they would probably meet in the dead of night.

At two bells – the time Summers was due to go below for the meal – there was no change and occasional glimpses of the sighting's canvas could be made from the deck. Sunset was due in under two hours although it should be possible to communicate before. Then movement caught his eye; someone was coming up on deck and, with a mixture of pleasure and guilt, he realised it was his wife.

"Michael, have you no idea of the time?" she asked approaching, "There's a meal below getting cold."

Summers usually felt awkward when speaking with Suzie in front of other officers, and this time was no exception. "I am aware my dear," he said, "though my presence is required on deck."

"But you are the captain!" she announced, before glancing to Williams then the helmsmen as if for confirmation. "You can come and go as you please; Simon is perfectly capable of sailing the boat."

Williams remained impassive, although Summers had been a midshipman recently enough to know the youngster would be thoroughly enjoying his discomfort. He glanced across to where a flash of canvas signalled the sighting's position; it might be hours before they began to communicate and there truly was little advantage in being on deck, not when a messenger would summon him quickly enough.

"Very well," he said, as if it was his decision. "I shall leave you to it, Mr Williams; call me if the sighting changes course or shows colours or signals."

The midshipman touched his hat, the model of respect.

"I shall merely be on the deck below," Summers assured him.

"Of course, sir. Enjoy your meal..."

But despite only being separated from the quarterdeck by a single thickness of pine planking, Summers found he could not enjoy the gathering. Suzie had done wonders of course; the cabin was transformed from the masculine space the builders intended. Sailcloth, gaily decorated with painted flowers and a country scene, covered most of the spirketting and, as the light was already starting to fade, an inordinate number of candles gave the place a flickering cheerfulness. Goodman made no comment about his former home being altered so and entered fully into the spirit of the occasion with polite conversation. He even volunteered a case of his own wine – a sweet white – that was stored in the bread room and had avoided detection. A thick pea soup was served first and proved excellent while the smell of roasting hen from the pantry promised much. Yet a good proportion of Summers' mind remained on the sighting.

No word came from the deck, which was almost as frustrating as bad news, and he did his best to chat with Suzie and the captain's lady – since becoming his passenger, he could not bring himself to call her Aimée – while sipping sparingly at the wine. But eventually he could stand it no longer and, when Edwards left to relieve Williams, found himself standing as well.

"You will excuse me, my dear," he told his wife. And then to Aimée, "Madam, I must see all is well on deck."

"You will return directly?" Suzie checked, and Summers promised he would.

However, as he met the fresh air, all thoughts of the party and his commitment to it vanished. Sunset was due in under an hour and the sky was starting to darken, yet the warship was in clear sight and steadily edging closer. And now there could be no doubt she was indeed a frigate and equally little question of her intention; she clung stubbornly to the larboard tack and seemed intent on running them down.

He moved to the binnacle and helped himself to the deck glass while Edwards and Williams completed their handover. The telescope told him little more; the rig appeared regular enough and, apart from a disparity in colour of the canvas – something easily explained and almost expected – there was nothing untoward about the vessel. What appeared to be a commissioning pennant flew from her main top and the whales had been picked out in the manner now common in many nation's warships. Yet it was while he continued to study her that the first doubts began to materialise.

He caught Williams' eye as the lad was about to depart.

"Do you notice anything unusual about the sighting, Simon?"

The midshipman considered this. "I can't say I recognise her, sir," he said.

"The lines are French perhaps?"

Williams shrugged. "They may well be," he agreed, although this was hardly a revelation. The British fleet contained a great many French-designed ships; some were captures – such as *Viper* herself – while others had been blatantly copied from enemy drafts. And there were still a few British-built vessels designed by Frenchmen who had escaped to England the previous century. At his young age, Williams could not be expected to distinguish such subtleties, but Summers found more to concern him than just the origin of the vessel approaching.

"Would that be all, sir?" The lad was keen to join the merriments below.

"Yes, thank you." And then, as an afterthought, "Actually, could you ask Captain Goodman if he would come on deck?"

* * *

"French design for certain," Goodman confirmed as soon as he raised the glass. "Though not sparred as such so possibly a capture."

Summers let out a sigh; they were at peace with France and, if indeed a former prize, she must surely be British. But either way, he had been worrying unnecessarily.

"That said, she's carrying more canvas than your usual Brit," Goodman continued, "and I'd have expected that foretopsail to be set slightly lower..."

Summers was now only half listening; the American had already reassured him sufficiently and he was prepared to dismiss the subject. With luck, some hen would have been saved although

163

he may already have annoyed Suzie enough for one evening. Yet Goodman was still studying the oncoming vessel and had grown strangely silent.

"Have you considered hoisting your colours?" he asked, finally lowering the glass.

"We are at a fair distance," Summers replied. "Though I could show an ensign if you think it wise."

"It may be prudent." The man spoke slowly and seemed to be considering. "Mind, I'm not sure I'd trust any reply you might receive."

"Not trust?" Summers' misgivings began to return.

Goodman closed the glass with a snap. "I'll be honest with you, Michael, I don't like the look of this one little bit."

"But she is a warship," Summers protested, and then a dreadful thought occurred. "You don't think her one of yours?"

At this, the American's face broke into a grin. "If I did, you'd probably be the last I'd tell!" Although his expression soon fell. "No, I still say those lines are unmistakably French."

"Then there is no threat," Summers began before the doubts increased. *Viper*'s mission had been to watch for Bonaparte sympathisers; supposing he had chanced on one, possibly filled with soldiers and maybe just part of a far larger force? What chance would he have of stopping such a vessel in a captured schooner?

"I said she started that way," Goodman continued, "though would chance there have been changes since."

"Which would tie in with her having been taken," Summers insisted.

"I'd like to think so, Michael, but I'm a Yank," Goodman said. "We've no treaty with the Barbary States. In fact, they have still to forgive us for standing up to them a few years back. So on my passage here I had to be wary of anything even approximating a corsair. Of course, most I could have handled, yet some have appeared of late that your old *Viper* should be wary of."

"This isn't a jape?" Summers checked but Goodman was deadly serious.

"You can forget galliots and polaccas, the devils are movin' on. There are rumours of several sizeable frigates currently in refit at Algiers and they took a Portuguese forty-four not so long ago."

"A forty-four?"

164

"Sure, and it's only a question of time before we see her under their flag." Goodman nodded towards the approaching vessel. "This one may be totally innocent, though I don't believe her to be British. Were I you, I'd hightail it out of here while you still can."

* * *

They had the windward gauge and, despite Goodman's warning, a considerable distance remained between the two ships. Summers glanced to the west where the sun was close to setting; within minutes it would be gone completely with no moon due for several hours. But the previous night was filled with stars so there seemed little point in waiting. They were already under topsails and forecourse; unless the wind varied significantly that should suffice. The only real question was the heading.

Summers felt there were two options; he might turn the schooner about and steer to the east. With such a rig and a lighter hull, he was confident of leaving the frigate in his wake. Such a course would hardly shorten their time to Gibraltar though and sailing close-hauled must put extra strain on his repaired tophamper. Besides, even when the mystery frigate was well over the horizon, there would be the thought that she may be lurking nearby and blocking his path to safety. The alternative was to try and make it past. Again, he had the faster vessel and it should still be possible, even without the cloak of night.

Of course, with both options, he had to consider the possibility that Goodman was wrong – wrong or deliberately misleading him. Were the frigate a legitimate British vessel nothing would attract attention more than an attempt to evade. And the schooner was American designed and American built; all the colours and private signals in the world may not be enough to convince a stubborn captain she was in British hands. Yet if he were to allow the warship close enough to inspect, and it did turn out to be a corsair, the outcome could be fatal. Or, remembering there were women aboard, something far worse.

Chapter Fifteen

"I have no idea what's keeping the men," Suzie declared. "They have been upstairs for an absolute age; their dinner will be stone cold b'now."

Midshipman Williams was just as unsure and, off watch or not, felt he should also be on deck. Leaving the party would not be easy, however. Bewley had been called away to tend to the seaman with the broken arm so, apart from him, the only man present was Browning. And the marine lieutenant was presenting a problem in himself. After being the main consumer of Captain Goodman's wine and an equally generous portion of roasted hen, he now had one elbow on the table and was unashamedly resting on his hand with sleep apparently imminent.

"We might send something up," Aimée suggested. The difference in rank between a lieutenant's wife and a captain's lady was as distinct as that of their husbands', even if there was little likelihood of her dominating Mrs Summers in any way.

"I should say not!" Suzie declared. "We spent all afternoon cooking and preparing; if they can't come down and eat like Christians, they can go without!"

"Lions," Browning muttered, surfacing for a moment. Suzie turned to him.

"Whatever did you say, Lieutenant?"

"Lions," the man repeated. "Christians eat lions." He paused to consider this. "Or is it the other way about?"

"Well, I think we should save what we can," Aimée said. "They are sailors and will enjoy it whatever the temperature."

There was a loud knock at the door and a curly-haired seaman entered.

"Beggin' your pardon, Mr Williams." The man appeared mildly aback as the cabin also contained two women in their finery along with a semi-comatose marine lieutenant. "Mr Summers says 'ed like you on deck sharpish."

"Tell Mr Summers not to be so rude!" Suzie erupted.

"Tell him nothing of the sort, Mr Lovemore." Aimée did not

166

know the name of every hand, though Lovemore was almost a friend. She turned to Williams, now every inch the captain's lady. "Simon, you had better go; thank you so much for your company."

The midshipman's chair fell back in his haste to stand although he had the sense to nod respectfully to both women before leaving.

"But the meal!" Suzie wailed, as Browning's jaw slipped off its rest and he slumped face down onto his dinner plate.

* * *

"What's the private signal for today?" Summers demanded as soon as Williams appeared on deck.

"It had better be night," the midshipman replied after considering the light. "A single red at the maintop, sir, and two blues on the tops'l yardarms." The prompt answer was impressive.

"Very good, set that up if you please and place a reliable hand alongside each."

It had been a difficult decision as well as something of a compromise, and Summers was still not entirely happy with it. There was one advantage in signalling by lamps, however, messages could be read at a greater distance. On the other hand, signalling meant maintaining his current course for longer than he would have liked. Even being the faster vessel, and benefiting from the wind, it would be harder to make it past if the warship was determined to intercept. And the option of turning back would still be there, it was just a question of whether Summers were willing to trade that for a slow passage.

Goodman remained on the quarterdeck and, now a decision had been reached, it felt natural for Summers to turn to him, a prisoner, for reassurance rather than one of his midshipmen.

"I have to be certain it is not a British ship," he said.

"Of course," the American agreed.

Williams approached and touched his hat. "Lamps are lit and in position, sir," he said.

Summers looked up; he could see the faintest of glimmer from each shielded light. "Very well, make the signal."

At a whistle from the midshipman, the lamps were exposed

and cast an eery glow on the schooner's canvas and deck. Summers tore his eyes from the sight and waited for full night vision to be restored. The reply might not be immediate; his opposite number was likely to be unprepared – why should he be otherwise, when his vessel was superior by far?

"Answer should be a green light from the fore shaded three times, sir."

Summers nodded and all on the quarterdeck waited.

"I think we should have seen something by now," Goodman said at last, and Summers could only agree.

"Very well, mask those lamps," he said. "And take her three points to larboard."

"Sail ho. Sail on the eastern horizon!"

The call came at the right moment as far as Summers was concerned; until that point, he had been dangerously close to despair.

"What do you see there?"

"Nothing definite, sir." Downes was at the masthead – a bright young man with good eyesight although Summers sensed the warning was premature. Yet even if that were the case, he cared little; the merest hint of rescue was welcome. "She comes an' goes, though still looks to be headin' our way."

"Any idea of size?" It was a foolish question, but Summers was desperate.

"Nothing substantial," Downes replied. "No more'n two masts though carryin' a fair head of sail. An' I've lost her again for now..."

* * *

The new course would send them towards land, although any danger would not be immediate. Even with the sun fully set, the dark hills marking the shore were visible and still more than four miles off. After ten minutes he would turn again and, heading due west, hug the coast until they were clear of the larger vessel. Summers understood the risks he was running; long before the *Mary Anne* left *Viper*'s protection, he had made a thorough study of the entire route and knew there to be both outlying rocks and dangerous shoals on this particular stretch. But the schooner would draw less than any frigate and, being as the warship was superior in so many other ways, he must make full use of any advantage. With luck, and if the other captain was at all cautious, they should slip by beyond the range of the warship's cannon.

"Sighting's holding her course," Williams muttered, then, "No wait, looks like she's turning!"

All strained into the gloom; there was a definite fluttering of canvas before the frigate fell back, although not just the few points Summers was expecting. He watched in disbelief as she continued to manoeuvre until the wind came onto her beam and she was equally tearing straight for the shore. Summers swallowed: his ruse had failed. If he were to turn now, they would meet in less than half an hour. He looked about the quarterdeck, and no one seemed prepared to meet his eye.

"Very well, take her about!"

It was the only solution; turning eastwards would delay their journey by at least a day and probably several while, if the frigate remained on their tail, he would still have to pass her eventually. Yet to hold his current course could only mean disaster.

The schooner turned neatly enough and soon settled on the starboard tack. Now close-hauled, her speed dropped considerably but the same would apply to the frigate, should she decide to give chase. Which she did – how could he have thought otherwise? Slowly her head was brought round until the warship was taking station off their larboard quarter.

"We're the faster." Edwards' words came after they had watched in silence for some time and felt like the only encouragement to come Summers' way for hours. The warship must still be four miles off but that would have doubled by daylight. And then, if nothing altered and the wind held, they should have run her over the horizon by the following evening. It would be up to him how long he left the next change of course, although Summers already knew it could not be immediate; maybe after half a day's sailing to the north, he could finally turn once more for Gibraltar. At which point they would be considerably behind; Captain King would hear of their slow passage and wonder at the wisdom of putting him in charge.

"Wind's freshening, sir." Edwards again, though Summers chose to ignore the remark. A slight increase may be to their

169

advantage, while he certainly had no intention of shortening sail. And then as he turned to Goodman in search of reassurance, it happened.

It started with a crack from above, a terrible sound that seemed to run through the schooner's entire frame. Summers' first reaction was to look back at the prize fearing some terrible miscalculation had allowed the frigate to draw into range. But even as he dismissed this, a cry came from aloft and he was in time to see the main topmast separate just above the top.

More shouts and what sounded like a woman's scream followed as the mast began to tumble. Line and strips of canvas flew up as a mass of timber plunged towards the deck.

Some took shelter behind fittings, others threw themselves headlong beside cannon and all instinctively protected heads with hands while all manner of debris rained about them. The schooner immediately lost way as the wind turned her broadside on, then what was left of the topmast began to slide noisily over the larboard rail.

Most of its bulk cleared the deck yet remained stubbornly clinging to their hull, fastened by a tangle of shrouds and halyards, while the schooner itself, no longer a living thing, took up a sickening wallow.

"Axemen, axemen there!" Summers cry was immediately taken up although, with every boarding weapon safely secured, no one could act on it. "You there, Edwards get below. Roust out the small arms!"

The midshipman threw himself down the companionway and, in a remarkably short time, reappeared with an armful of hatchets. Soon the air was filled with the clatter and snap of parting line while sparks and splinters flew in abundance. The schooner continued to wallow, though progress was being made and the mainsail remained in place.

"Bring her to larboard," Summers bellowed when they were finally clear of the wreckage. It would be impossible to remain close-hauled but, with assistance from the large aft sail, they may at least make progress on a broad reach. And they had been on the starboard tack, so the hull was now pointing out to sea, rather than the nearby land – as fortune went it was hardly the greatest, yet it seemed not everything was set against them.

"Beggin' your pardon, sir, we lost Downes."

170

Summers turned. The name was familiar, it was a hand, one from Stokes' mess – for the moment he could not recall the seaman's face.

"He were on lookout duty."

Of course, Summers had been speaking with the man so recently. He caught his breath as realisation came; Downes was the first to have fallen while he captained a ship. And then there was the uncomfortable feeling that he would not be the last.

However, they were starting to pick up speed; this was not the time for despair and Goodman appeared to be of the same mind.

"We might still fight!" the American roared.

Summers considered the possibility; the frigate was in plain sight, now less than two miles off their larboard beam and closing rapidly. His mind continued to wrestle with what had happened; the previous repair to the topmast housing must have proved insubstantial. No one could blame the carpenter or his team, such work should never have been undertaken in the open sea; if anyone was at fault it was him for not considering the extra pressure when sailing close-hauled.

"I cannot beat to quarters," he said simply, "I do not have the men."

"We can crew your cannon," Goodman replied. "I've a fine team of gunners who know the weapons well. You fellows tend the sails and keep us straight, we'll deal with the pirate."

Summers paused for no more than a second; the American's words made sense; they might not see off the oncoming warship yet could at least give her a bloody nose. And it was the use of the word pirate that finally swung him. Until then he had retained doubts; the frigate might still be a friendly vessel with an inattentive officer of the watch. But recent events would seem to discount this; the likelihood of his command being taken had gone from possible to probable, and suddenly there was every reason to defend her to the last.

"You will not retake the ship?" he checked, and Goodman met his eyes.

"You have my word, Michael."

"Very well," he turned to Williams. "See the prisoners released and open the magazine." His eyes flashed to Goodman; the Americans might not take to being directed by his

171

midshipmen. "An officer will be needed to supervise them."

"I guess Davy White'll do that; I shall speak with him directly."

Summers watched as Goodman departed; he could be making a mistake although, whatever happened, things could hardly be worse.

But there was more to be done and he may as well see to everything now. "Mr Edwards, the rest of the small arms if you please. Then we might clear for action."

"Very good, sir, and the ladies?"

Summers drew breath as his mind began to spin.

"See they are stationed below," he said quickly. "The orlop at the very least or if you can find space in the hold so much the better. And be sure they understand the importance of remaining hidden," he added as the midshipman made to leave. "I cannot spare a man to be with them."

Edwards saluted smartly and then was gone, although Summers' thoughts went with him. Exactly how Suzie would respond to such instructions was uncertain yet, despite her bluster, she was not totally without understanding. Whatever, he must not be distracted, it was vital that he put everything into keeping the pirates at bay. Were they allowed to board, the men would be treated badly enough but there was no telling what must become of the women.

Chapter Sixteen

King settled back after his supper – another solitary meal, as they all were since Aimée left. Somehow, he could not find it in him to invite anyone else to share his table. The prize had departed almost two weeks before and must be well on her way to Gibraltar by now. He wondered vaguely how Summers was responding to his first taste of independent command yet was not unduly worried. The lad was experienced enough, King did not expect him to fail in any of the duties of captain and neither was he concerned about his coping with so many prisoners. Goodman had given his word they would not try to retake the schooner and, despite the short time they had been acquainted, King sensed no trouble from that quarter. It was still Summers' first experience of such a position, however, and may also turn out to be his last. Were that the case the Navy would have lost a valuable officer.

But of his replacement aboard *Viper* he was not so certain. Daniels had taken to the rank with all the assurance King expected and was performing his duties adequately enough. Yet he retained an arrogance that annoyed his fellow officers as much as those on the lower deck. Woodward was suffering the most from this; the pair were close in age and almost equal in experience, yet there was no trace of friendship between them. Instead, Daniels never missed an opportunity to snipe and criticize his senior, showing little care as to the circumstances or who was in earshot. On several occasions King himself had been present and was forced to bite his tongue; if Woodward were not strong enough to fight his own battles, little good would be served by interfering. There may come a time for official intervention – have the two before him in the great cabin and give Daniels a proper dressing down – although he hoped not. In his experience such action rarely brought positive results; far better to let the junior man go at the first opportunity and hope the senior learned from the experience.

Yet that might not be the best move diplomatically; Daniels was known to be well supported and King's future career might depend on a good word from the Admiralty. He could even find himself recalled and another officer sent to finish the current commission, yet, terrible though that might be, he felt comfortably immune from such a threat.

Almost as soon as he waved Aimée goodbye he began to miss her. Miss her and regret the wasted opportunities when they could have been together. Having her aboard was undoubtedly a diversion although feeling her absence was proving more so, and far less pleasant. And despite not having spoken with Robert Manning since, the surgeon's words remained with him. Perhaps he had come to the end of his time and maybe an honourable departure was called for?

There were plenty of precedents for such a change; should he choose to resign his commission no one would be so very surprised. Another captain could be found for *Viper* and much would continue as before. He might even pick up a fast packet at Valletta and, if the wind were with them, be in Eastbourne before the women.

King pushed his plate aside and called for his servant – another who must be missing Aimée as the cove was properly earning his money now. For a moment he wondered again how they were faring in the schooner yet remained unconcerned. King knew the difference a young captain could make to any ship's company; they were probably having a high old time of it.

* * *

The moon was finally starting to rise making the already star-filled night seem almost bright and highlighting the frigate, now less than a mile off their larboard bow. The warship had altered course to intercept; she was currently on the starboard tack and setting a pace that should see her approaching their beam when she came into the reach of the *Mary Anne*'s broadside.

"They're making it easy for us," Summers said as he and Goodman regarded the enemy.

"It would appear so, though I don't hold up much hope," the American replied. "These fellas are skilled seamen, and anyone given such a vessel will know how to fight."

174

That made sense but Summers did not feel the need to reply. Even after being in command for so short a time he had the measure of the *Mary Anne*, at least as far as sailing her was concerned. However, he had yet to bring the schooner to battle, or any warship for that matter, in which case he must allow the American some say in what was about to happen. To do anything else would be foolish. And besides, he had nothing left to lose; the Americans were already in position at the cannon; should they choose or if Goodman ordered it, the schooner could be retaken with ease.

"What do you see there?" Summers' call was to the foremasthead which had become their principal lookout station. With the moon creeping steadily upwards, more was being revealed and the Med could be a crowded sea. His hopes were still firmly on the earlier sighting. That, or meeting with another British vessel, or a warship from almost any other nation if it came to it; Barbary Pirates had few friends.

"Nothing new, sir." Even from such a distance, the lookout's voice sounded faintly apologetic. "Though there's movement from the sighting," he added.

All on the quarterdeck looked over to where the frigate was indeed manoeuvring. They watched in silence as the warship swept into a neat and orderly tack. In no time she had settled on her new heading and was taking the wind to larboard so, rather than aiming for the schooner's bows, she was now steering to pass their stern.

"I might turn to larboard," Summers pondered, although it was more a question.

"You might," Goodman agreed, "though are most likely to meet with another vessel if you continue heading north. And, even without her main topmast, the old girl's making a reasonable speed; t'would be a shame to risk that by manoeuvring until you must."

Again wise words, and Summers took note of them. He reckoned they had under an hour; in that time the frigate would pass their stern and be in a position to launch a broadside. It would be at long range, yet anything more than a minor hit could only disable them further. Though by then they may have spotted help, or some misfortune might occur to their pursuer to balance that of their own damaged rig. But if not, that would be the time to turn and see what impression the schooner's nine-pounders could make. Her American gunners fared pretty well before and disabled *Viper* for several hours although, in the end, the *Mary Anne* had been taken. And it seemed likely she would be again.

* * *

It was a black rat and quite handsome, Suzie decided. Even the naked tail seemed somehow fitting and a suitable contrast to the fur that glistened in the light from their single lantern.

"Get away you filthy beast." Millie, the servant, kicked her stockinged feet in the animal's direction. It scuttled out of sight, but they continued to hear it move behind the bales of cotton that lined their dismal hole.

Suzie glanced at Aimée, sitting closest to her against the wall of hessian. Both still wore full dresses, fine garments specially chosen in honour of that evening's entertainment; even Millie's cotton frock was her best. Only a couple of hours before, the girl was joshing with seamen as they served food or cleared the table in the captain's cabin. It seemed incredible that such a short space of time could separate a convivial gathering from their current wretchedness, while Suzie was uncomfortably aware the misery could soon become a great deal worse.

As yet, no one in their small group had mentioned the word pirate, though each accepted they faced a terrible enemy. And none of them was particularly stupid; all three knew about the waters the schooner was sailing in and what dangers they might hold.

There was another rustle: it would be that rat again. Or another – there could be a hundred hiding close by. Suzie shivered slightly and wrapped her arms about herself. In some ways it had been less frightening to have sight of the rat: a hidden enemy – one that could be magnified by just a little imagination – was so much worse.

* * *

Though expected for several minutes, the broadside still came as a shock and dazzled all who saw it.

"Take her to larboard!" Summers roared even while the memory continued to fog his eyes. Holding their previous course was sensible as long as the pirates remained out of range; but now the schooner had come under fire, they must manoeuvre.

A torrent of water erupted barely pistol distance from their taffrail and one ball – lucky or not – struck them low on the hull. But as the schooner began to turn, all aboard her remained composed. The wind was on hand to help them round and, as they finally headed westwards, hardly any speed was lost. The pirates were probably expecting the turn, though it would take the heavier ship longer to follow and Summers may yet be able to reply with their own broadside.

"She's on the edge of wearing," Goodman commented, "still I think it worth a chance.

"Sail ho!" It was the foremasthead. "Fine on the starboard bow."

That must be the vessel Downes had seen earlier. Summers' spirits rose, and it was with difficulty that he kept his voice from cracking. "What do you see there?"

"Only a tiddler," the lookout replied. "Post Office packet, more'n likely."

The disappointment was immense; all that could be expected from such a craft was for it to summon help, and that could no longer come quickly enough.

Summers exchanged glances with Goodman; both men knew the situation was becoming hopeless, yet they might still make a fight of it. The frigate was to larboard and within reach of their long nines' arc while the range was slightly less than when the pirate had fired. Summers shrugged, he supposed it was up to him to give the order – he was still the nominal captain after all.

"Fire!"

Even in the all-pervading tension, he wondered if American gunners had ever before responded to a British command. Those manning the *Mary Anne*'s cannon showed no reluctance, however, and the guns spoke almost as one. And they were well aimed, spouts erupted on either side of the frigate, although no one could be sure of any hits.

"Send the next higher, Mr White!"

177

Again, Goodman was right on the money and Summers could not object to his order. A nine-pound ball could always bring down a major spar, even if that only delayed the agony.

"They're not making any move to return fire," he said.

The American pursed his lips. "That does not surprise me."

Summers was about to question this when the reason became apparent; they would want the schooner whole and must intend to take her by boarding.

"Ready, sir!"

White's men had done well to reload so quickly while the frigate had closed to the extent that the gun captains could remove the quoins and target her masts.

"Fire!" This time Goodman gave the order, and it seemed appropriate that he should.

The change in angle meant no splashes were visible, but neither did the frigate's tophamper alter in any way. Summers was coming close to despair; however fast the Americans worked, there could not be many more broadsides before the pirate came alongside. He turned away from Goodman, too depressed to even meet his eye, and was looking elsewhere when the next barrage was despatched. But a gentle moan from all around told him it had been unsuccessful.

* * *

"Well, I can't say I blames them for tryin'," Stokes grunted as the latest attempt achieved little more than a hole in the frigate's foretopsail.

At first, he and his men were mildly disgruntled by being replaced at the schooner's cannon, but it took no time for them to realise her original crew knew the light pieces well, and quietly adopt the role of interested spectators.

"Think that'll rile the heathens?" Bovey spoke with apparent indifference. "I heard they're inclined to butcher any crew what stands up to them."

"Maybe it will, an' maybe it won't." Groom was gripping his

cutlass tightly. "Either way I 'tend to take a few with me."

They could see Groom's potential prey now. The frigate was less than a cable off and those gathering at her bulwarks were easy to pick out in the moonlight. All sported beards and many wore the most exotic headgear along with shirts cut more generously than those of British seamen. And they seemed just as ready for a fight.

About them, the American gun crews were throwing themselves into reloading as if it were their last act on earth, which seemed likely. Enemy musket shots regularly thudded against the *Mary Anne*'s bulwarks like the first solid drops of rain before a thunderstorm. Then, with a cry from White, the schooner's cannon gave forth a blistering reply.

The hull had been targeted and Stokes' mess watched in awe and delight as their opponents were cut down. But for every one that fell, two more were ready to take their place and, as the warship closed further before finally scraping against their hull, a torrent of robed assassins began to drop onto their decks.

Groom was as good as his word; when the first landed, he waded in with oaths and a swinging cutlass. Benton followed and was soon downed by a silk-clad monster wielding a curved sword that cut like a razor. Vincent Early, the Midlander with a twisted ear, was armed with a pike and for several seconds kept three at bay before one dodged past his reach and knocked him to the deck. Marine Lieutenant Browning, still groggy from Goodman's wine, advanced at the head of a line of marines. Yet even the ordered menace of his men was no match for the terrors they faced, and all were soon overrun. Of their mess, only Bovey, Longdon, Lovemore and Stokes himself survived long enough to be captured, and, as the pirates began to manhandle them, all four soon began to curse their luck.

And from the quarterdeck, Summers watched it all as if witnessing another man's nightmare. Like Bovey, he now wondered if firing on the pirates had been wise, yet equally did not regret the action. And as soon as the first enemy came aboard, neither did he doubt they would be taken. Goodman put up a fight but was soon knocked cold by a bearded devil wielding a club, and Edwards' young body proved too fragile for the lance that neatly impaled him. Williams was cut down in a similar manner and soon Summers stood alone. So, when two silken warriors approached with raised swords and clear intent, he did not hesitate.

And the universal signal of surrender was respected to some extent. As Summers held his hands aloft, then smelt the sweat of his captors when they knocked him to the deck, he supposed it was the right decision. Although his thoughts were mainly for the women below.

Part Two

Chapter Seventeen

Valletta was as beautiful as ever. King knew the place well and had once even called it home yet, as *Viper* felt her way through the crowded harbour and a bright sun picked out the light brown of her packed buildings, she seemed especially welcoming.

And there was *Caledonia* at anchor: he could make out Pellew's flagship along with others of the Med Fleet. As well as saluting the fort, they would have to give the admiral his fifteen guns. He turned to a messenger.

"Advise Mr Regan the flag is in port."

Pellew might have come in to re-victual, or diplomatic duties may have demanded his presence while, with peace in Europe, there should no longer be the need for a returning captain to waste time hunting for his own fleet. But having his Commander-in-Chief to hand, as it were, would make what King proposed to do a darn sight quicker.

"We're being directed to the victualling anchorage, sir," Malcolm, the signal midshipman, reported. That was not so good and meant, rather than a spell in harbour, *Viper* was needed back at sea almost immediately. She must physically reprovision first, of course, so there would still be time to appoint a fresh captain in his place.

"Are you ready, Tom?" The voice came from behind and made King start. It was rare for anyone to address him so aboard ship and especially on the quarterdeck where others were within earshot. However, the expression on Robert Manning's face explained much. It was the surgeon's duty to be there; he must present his papers proving *Viper* free of infection and likely to remain so before anyone went ashore. But Manning's thoughts were obviously with King, which explained his casual mode of address. "You will be meeting with the admiral, I'd chance?"

"His ship is in." King nodded to where the first rate currently lay off their starboard bow. "So all will be easier than expected."

"And your mind is made up?" Manning checked.

"It is, Robert," King confirmed. "My course is set, and the wheel secured; I can think of nothing now that could dissuade me."

* * *

Caledonia had been snugged down at her anchorage and, in a well-protected harbour with topmasts lowered, mounting her boarding battens was simplicity itself. But as King heaved himself through the starboard entry port and touched his hat in acknowledgement to the pipes welcoming him aboard, the admiral was not there to meet him. Instead, Sibly, Pellew's flag captain, stepped forward and extended a hand.

"Pleasure to see you again, King," he told him. "His Lordship's in the coach though keen to meet with you straight away."

King mumbled an appropriate reply; it had just occurred to him that, despite having become accustomed to being piped aboard countless commissioned warships, that was probably the last time he would enjoy the compliment. The marine sentry snapped to attention as they approached the hallowed inner sanctum of the flagship – a place only senior officers frequented – and, again, King wondered if this would be the final occasion.

"Ah, King – glad to see you." Pellew rose from behind his desk and after the briefest of handshakes, indicated the pair of chairs facing him. "Be seated, gentlemen, please. I own I am behind with matters." The admiral caught King's eye. "You will not be aware, but I am to haul down my flag in a matter of weeks."

That certainly came as a surprise. "I'm sorry to hear that, my lord." They were trite words and doubtless expected, although King meant them sincerely. He may not have spent long under Pellew's command but the man was a legend in naval circles, and it had been a privilege to serve under him.

"Can't be helped, though I'll admit there are several matters I'd wished to attend to. Maybe Charlie Penrose will see to them, who can tell? He will be my replacement and your new C-in-C."

King knew little about Penrose other than he was a capable officer, if one that lacked the kudos of a Pellew. The change of Commander-in-Chief hardly affected him, of course, yet still he felt more than an element of regret.

"I am relying on you to address one of the more important issues," Pellew continued. "In fact, for a number of reasons, you are the ideal man. But I'm jumping the gun. First, you must tell me of your patrol."

"There was little of note beyond my earlier report, my lord," King began. Shortly after the prize departed, *Viper* had spoken with a Navy victualler bound for Malta and entrusted King's journal to her master. But then it rarely hurt to raise an ensign and King could not resist reminding Pellew of their capture. "Though we did cut out that American privateer."

Put like that the minor conquest sounded more impressive and King expected some emotion from Pellew. However, the admiral remained neutral.

"I do recall your mentioning that and it is connected with what we must discuss."

King was mildly put out; presumably Pellew reasoned that, though heavily armed, the schooner's holds were full and she was being used in the carrying trade. But a prize was still a prize; she and her cargo would fetch a fair price and, as the station's Commander-in-Chief, an eighth would flow straight into Pellew's pocket.

"Your capture was sighted off the North African Coast some weeks back," the admiral continued, his tone distinctly businesslike. "And I regret to inform you, she has been taken."

"Taken?"

"I fear so; these things happen."

King's mind began to race; he must have misjudged Goodman, that or been wrong and Summers lacked the skill to captain a prize. But, whatever the cause, the original crew must have been allowed to reclaim their ship.

"A Post Office packet reported seeing a schooner showing that day's private signal. She stood off and witnessed the entire affair and sadly yours is not the first we have lost in such a way."

King shook his head; hearing his Commander-in-Chief was

to go, then learning their prize, along with Aimée, was back in American hands, had left him stunned. "I'm sorry, sir – my lord – I..."

"It seems she were snapped up by a corsair," Sibly added. "And a large one at that, though I've no doubt a suitable match for *Viper*."

Now King was positively reeling. His mouth was open, but the words would not come, although the others seemed unaware that one of their number had been struck dumb.

"More recently we received this from our embassy in Lisbon," Pellew continued, passing a sheet of paper across. King reached for it with a shaking hand.

It was a short note, and the poor hand suggested its contents were not considered suitable for fair copying by a clerk. And the message was brief yet apposite: a British prize had been taken along with its crew and three female passengers. All were being held by pirates active on the Barbary Coast. Letters from the captives had been provided to prove their identity and a tribute requested. The Ambassador was seeking advice from London.

"The report is dated ten days ago," Sibly added. "We assume it was forwarded to England at the same time so it may not have arrived yet."

"That is so," Pellew agreed. "Though, as I have already stated, my time here is limited, and I intend to act now."

King's mind continued to spin; Aimée in the hands of barbarians, it was just too horrible to contemplate.

"Don't take it to heart," Pellew huffed. "As I said, the fortunes of war. However, I did consider you the ideal chap to take her back."

"Take her back, my lord?" Mercifully his voice had returned. "But surely... surely we are at peace with the Barbary States?"

"Peace you might call it, though one that comes at a cost," Pellew sniffed. "As soon as we settle the mess in America it will be a price we need no longer pay."

"But Aimée," King began. "She was aboard the prize..."

"Aimée?" Sibly questioned. "Would that be your wife – was she a passenger perhaps?"

King nodded. Wife was not an accurate description, though one he hardly intended to explain.

Pellew let out a sigh and Sibly looked aghast.

"You did not mention that in your report," the admiral said.

"I-I must have omitted it, my lord."

"Yet, it makes little difference." Of them all, Pellew was the first to recover. "We have some indication as to where the schooner was taken; if it proves correct the prisoners are likely to be close by – your wife included," he added as an afterthought.

"You see, we believe the ship that captured your prize does not come from the Barbary States," Sibly explained. "At least not officially."

Now King was totally aback and must have appeared so.

Pellew cleared his throat. "Look here, King, I'll make no bones about it, the pirate problem has been a concern since I took up this station. I was hoping to take direct action against the whole darned lot of them, but my hands were tied. Still, for reasons that will be explained, we can act in this instance and, though it is regretted, your wife's presence only gives us more cause."

"I see," King lied, but Pellew had more to say.

"There's a gentleman I want you to meet," he continued. "He's a Jonathan, yet not of a military cut, and I think will prove of use. I sent for him as soon as *Viper* was sighted and he's awaiting us in the great cabin. What say we step through and hear his mind on the subject?"

* * *

At times it grew unbearably hot although, when all else was considered, Summers could almost ignore that. Their cell was the size of a midshipman's berth in a third rate yet, as it held twelve adults, felt impossibly small. And there was no furniture, not even hammocks to raise them from the earthen floor – ground built up by years of caked filth. Their food was delivered once a day and never deviated from the bucket of pulped beans that was universally despised and equally craved. This was supplemented by a more regular supply of brackish water. On one occasion an emptied bucket was used for a personal function and the offender beaten soundly for his gall. Illumination came from what might generously be called windows, though they were little more than

185

slits cut into the raw stone wall. These were set just below the high ceiling and let in an insignificant amount of air and light, although were a reliable method of estimating the time.

Each morning Summers explored the openings by clambering onto Goodman's shoulders and a reasonable view of the harbour was possible. He had seen the place in greater clarity when their party was delivered in triumph by the Dutchman who captained the pirate frigate. The man spoke perfect English, yet hardly addressed more than a couple of words to any of them. Still, it was clear he regarded their capture as something of a personal triumph and led the procession that brought them to the ruler's palace.

It was a long and humiliating walk and one made more so by the chanting, jeering mob that ran alongside. The crowd increased in size and anger as they went; before long they took to spitting and snatching at the captives' raw bodies and were barely kept in check by guards who had already taken their own pleasure sufficiently. Summers tried to memorise the place in the hope of later escape until the strain and distractions became too great, and after their brief interview with the bey – a small man with a sharp tongue who ruled the place – it was obvious that freedom, however earned, lay far from their grasp.

But Summers' group were faring better than the seamen. Both the British and American hands had been taken for use as slaves. The bey went to great pains to explain this, and the fact that only ambitious and unlikely commitments from their appropriate governments would secure their release. Until then, they would remain beasts of burden and regarded as expendable. There was no mention of any wounded seamen, and Summers held out little hope.

The rest – those like him and Suzie who had been singled out for this cell – also included Goodman, Aimée Silva, the captain's lady, and Millie, her servant. Then there was, Bewley, the loblolly boy, and an injured Midshipman Williams. As they would appear to have been selected by the superiority of their original clothing, Summers assumed some form of individual ransom was intended and this was confirmed when they joined those previously captured.

The stench hit them once the door was opened and some immediately gagged, although most soon ceased to notice. And

186

there was plenty else to learn from the cell's original occupants.

Summers quickly met up with Peter Palmer, son of the elderly Quaker captured when *Tenacious* had taken the Baltimore Clipper earlier in the year. Summers was able to pass on news of his father, and young Palmer told him more about their current circumstances.

He, along with three officers from his original ship, had heard nothing from the outside world since their capture. They were allowed to communicate, however; at least once a month writing materials were provided for letters home which Palmer felt certain were being passed on.

Summers had also been introduced to the French officers from Palmer's late ship, who were genial enough even though space was at a premium and the extra bodies not entirely welcomed. Of greater concern were the wounded.

Goodman had received a severe blow to the head; Bewley examined him and could find no trace of fracture, yet the pain and giddiness only began to subside after several days. And Williams was worse off with a left arm sliced between shoulder and elbow. They were only allowed the most fundamental clothing which left nothing spare for bandages; consequently the wound was not healing and must soon start to fester. At which point Williams would be removed – or so Peter Palmer, believed. It seemed severe illness was regarded with deep suspicion by their guards and, if spotted, they acted quickly and without concern for the patient.

So Summers was equally worried about Millie. The servant had been fortunate to some extent and, like Bewley, was well dressed when discovered. Exactly how quickly their lack of support from home would be recognised remained uncertain, especially as the girl was rarely in a state to write a sensible letter. Instead, much of her time was spent alternating between gentle, monotonous sobs and high-pitched screaming – something else that hardly endeared them to the other prisoners.

And then there was Suzie. She had never been exactly slim – Summers once decked a marine officer who described her as 'Dutch built' – but at least her state of pregnancy was barely noticeable when they were captured. Nevertheless time and limited rations was making it more obvious and no one knew, or could guess, how their captors would react when they finally noticed.

And that was just one of many imponderables; their letters must be going somewhere, and the outside world should eventually respond, although how was yet another concern. The British government was more likely to do so with force than hard currency and, positioned as their cell was, so close to the harbour, any attack from the sea could mean death for them all. And though Peter Palmer was sure his father would be more considered, the family had little money. Summers remembered both the man and his plan to bargain for his son's freedom; at the time such notions appeared as nothing more than mildly eccentric, but now he knew how dangerous they might prove.

For, even in a few short weeks, Summers had learned a good deal about his captors. Rather than the disparate band of brigands previously assumed, they were surprisingly sophisticated. And there was every reason for the primitive conditions he and the others were being subjected to; what better way of encouraging a sizeable tribute? Consequently, he was now convinced that, until money was paid – and *only* until money was paid, or nature took its course and they fell ill or worse – all were doomed to remain in their misery.

But however easy it might be, worrying would help them little; all they could truly do was block their minds to the heat, the stench and the sound of Millie's sobs, then count the days on a scratched calendar and look forward to the next bucket of beans.

Chapter Eighteen

Caleb Palmer was the last person King expected to meet although, after everything he had experienced that morning, it was as if nothing could shock him further. The old Quaker looked no different and rose from the table at his approach before greeting him with a firm look and what was a surprisingly warm handshake.

"I trust you have fared well, sir." King's use of the honorific was more than expected politeness; the man had a presence that demanded respect.

"Well indeed, thank you," Palmer told him, "We have both been cared for throughout."

For the first time King noticed his daughter sitting quietly at the table and muttered a greeting.

"It is my understanding that you know these people, King," Pellew interrupted.

"We are old friends," Palmer confirmed.

"And do you have news of your son?" King enquired.

"It is why I am in Malta." The old man had regained his seat. "And probably causing a nuisance to you gentlemen."

"It is no nuisance," Pellew assured. "We have always sympathised with your predicament though could do little to assist. However, now Captain King has made an appearance, your advice would be appreciated."

"So, you refused help us before, yet when my father's knowledge is needed, you feel free to ask for it?" It was the girl. King struggled to remember her name and was surprised that she should speak.

"The situation has changed, Miss Palmer, and may have turned to one where each may help the other." Pellew's eyes switched to her father. "You know much of how these heathens behave. And I recall your mentioning a substantial warship, which would appear to be what we are seeking."

"If it is the same that took my son, I know a good deal, and of the regime whose flag it sails under."

189

"And your knowledge includes where she might be based?"

"It does, and I would be happy to cooperate with you."

"Splendid, then we have a ship and men ready to act so let us get down to business." Pellew took his place at the head of the table and Sibly joined King facing Palmer and his daughter. The admiral's eyes flashed to King. "You will know, of course, that Mr Palmer is something of an expert when it comes to the barbarians?"

"Both he and his daughter were guests aboard my previous command," King confirmed.

"Of more importance, he has made a special study of the ones who would appear to be holding the schooner," Pellew continued. "And your wife, of course."

"Your wife?" Palmer questioned, looking directly at King.

"She is also held hostage." Those penetrating eyes were really quite disconcerting. "Though in truth she is not my wife, as you seem to remember," King added, mildly flustered.

"I recall your having come to an arrangement," Palmer agreed. "And the pair of you are partners for life, which is all any of us can ask."

"That's as maybe, yet she is doubtless a British subject," Pellew grunted. "And as such must also be rescued."

"The prize master was one of my lieutenants." Despite his confusion, King sensed it better not to explain Aimée's nationality. "His wife was also aboard, and there is a female servant..."

Sibly scratched at his chin, "Lord, King, your prize is sounding more like an Indiaman with every breath!"

"I am sorry to hear your news, Captain," the girl said, "but maybe now you can properly understand our situation?"

"That was always the case, Miss Palmer," King began.

"Though now His Majesty's officers are involved," Pellew interrupted, "– and their women, of course – we have more reason."

Palmer closed his eyes briefly. "Well, as it so clearly serves both our purposes, I am happy to assist," he said. "What do you wish from me?"

"You can start by telling us what you know," the admiral grunted.

"Very well, then perhaps I should begin with some background. You will be aware of the main Barbary States or

Regencies," the old man began. "They are Algiers, Tunis, Tripoli and then there is Morocco, which is more correctly a Sultanate. All remain nominally part of the Ottoman Empire though the ties are steadily failing. And none are intrinsically rich; their only truly fertile land is on the northern coast, that to the south being mainly barren. Which is why they choose to finance their economies by extracting tribute from other nations."

Pellew made a mildly discontented noise as Palmer continued.

"This tribute can come in the form of physically seizing shipping or charging for licences to allow safe passage. And then there are what is quaintly referred to as 'customary presents'. These personal bribes are paid to specific individuals in addition to any other demands." He paused and regarded Pellew specifically. "And finally I understand some nations also treat the Barbary navies as hired assassins," he said, "commissioning them to wage attacks on their enemies in return for payment."

Now Sibly scratched more awkwardly at his chin.

"Forgive me, Mr Palmer, we are aware of the history," Pellew said. "It is this specific case that interests us."

Again, Palmer closed his eyes and this time there was a slightly longer pause before he continued.

"Each state is governed by a dey or a pasha: rulers who live precarious lives and are frequently overthrown. This is usually by assassination, often at the hands of those closest to them although it is not unknown for the head of a smaller sector, known as a bey, to launch a *coup d'état*. Which is what we are dealing with in this instance."

"You mean the hostages are being held by rebels," King confirmed, and the old man nodded.

"I believe that to be the case."

"Which puts a different light on matters, as I'm sure you will agree." Pellew was now speaking directly to King. "For the present, we have to retain peace with the recognised rulers but there can be no objections to our attacking those likely to usurp them."

"It would be doing them a favour," Sibly confirmed but Palmer remained impassive.

"My son, and your ship – and your companion – are being held in a small port on the northern coast of Algiers," he

191

continued. "Land that is officially under the rulership of Hadj Ali Dey. I have communicated with the Danish consul who confirms a minor rebellion has taken place and the bey concerned is regarded as a thorn in Hadj Ali's side. Such incidents are common on the Barbary Coast, the most famous being the city state of Salé, which was a base for the notorious Salé Rovers."

"And this ruler," Sibly began. "Hadie..."

"Hadj Ali Dey," Palmer corrected. "Oh, it can only be a matter of time before the situation is addressed, although he is at a disadvantage. You see, the Barbary States tend to rely on maritime power for their primary defence."

"No armies?" Pellew questioned.

"Few of any great size," Palmer replied. "Such things are an ideal tool for insurrection; the ground forces that do exist are more an extension to the palace guard. And the bey in question has a powerful warship that was captured some time ago. As long as this remains within call the rebels can regard themselves as impregnable."

"Tell us more of this warship," the admiral urged.

"It is what you call a frigate," Palmer said. "And originally French, though she was taken from her owners after running aground close to her current base. She was refloated and repaired and now sails as a privateer under the rebels' flag."

"Do barbarians have such skills?" Pellew asked and Palmer turned to him.

"Oh yes, those living on the Maghreb Coast are well acquainted with shipping. They can build, repair and maintain craft of all sizes extremely efficiently, and it is only due to a shortage of suitable material that they lack a larger navy. This particular ship is now captained by a European named Visser; a Dutchman, formerly the master of a merchant ship though I understand he also had man-of-war experience with the Batavian Republic. From what I gather he sails his ship well and has made many captures in addition to the vessel that carried my son."

"Yet we might easily deal with such a craft," Pellew insisted, "and little damage can be done diplomatically with the official ruler if we do. Heavens, we shall be helping the fellow – he should be grateful!"

"And you know where this ship is based?" Sibly suggested.

"I do, and have done so for some while," Palmer replied. "I

believe my son to be held there, and possibly those equally dear to yourselves."

"Then be so kind as to tell us, sir!" Pellew roared. "A ship will be despatched without delay, and everything done to see your son safely returned."

"I don't think I have made myself plain." The Quaker's voice was the epitome of calmness. "I wish to pursue this matter without violence and prefer a more civilised form of negotiation."

"Then you will be wasting your time," the admiral growled. "There is nothing civilised about such people; the only thing they understand is force. To make them listen you must be stronger and prepared to prove it."

Once more Palmer held his peace, although his eyes were now fixed on Pellew. "Then I cannot continue to assist you," he said at last.

"Very well," Pellew rose, scraping his chair back noisily on the deck. "In which case we shall seek out this place, and this ship, by our own means, though I must say I am disappointed. There is more now at stake than just your son." He pointed at King. "This gentleman's wife – or woman – for one. Think on that and, should you have a change of heart, I may yet be prepared to hear you out." Then, with a nod to Palmer's daughter, he left.

* * *

They had been active since before first light and knew the work would continue long after sunset. And those final hours, when the narrow track became hard to make out and the first chill of night made itself known, would be the worst. Although Lovemore longed for cold now, the sun was at its highest and beat down with a ruthlessness that suggested permanency. Sweat flowed from his brow, running into his eyes and onto his chest as every joint in his wrecked body ached.

"Watch her head!" Stokes ordered and the four of them pressed the two-wheeled cart further up the incline. They had already made three journeys from the quarry and there was another mile to go with the fourth. Each trip moved several substantial rocks: chunks of granite that had been roughly hewn into cubes and would be finely smoothed to a workable size by more skilled hands. However, they would not belong to Lovemore, Longdon, Stokes, Bovey, or any of the prisoners guiding the constant line of carts to the master masons. Their role was that of dumb animals and, though many might be proficient seaman, only their muscle was required.

Working the carts was one of the better tasks and preferable to hacking out raw stone. All began at the quarry face; only in the past week had Stokes' men been moved. It seemed that, despite an obvious cruelty, their masters were no fools and their system for getting the best from a workforce was almost clinical in concept.

Every man would begin with the heavy iron picks that, with a skill soon acquired, cut deep into the stone. For as long as their belly muscles and rag-wrapped hands held out they would continue there and only when whips and clubs no longer had effect would they be moved to working on the constant line of carts. But there was little for them beyond this; as soon as their journey times slowed sufficiently, their exhausted bodies would be heaved over the cliff and finally given freedom in the waters below. Stokes and his men had witnessed this on two occasions and the knowledge of what finally awaited them was more effective than any beating. Privately, Lovemore felt they could expect another month; it was not a precise study, but few manning the carts lasted longer than six weeks, and they had already been working them for two.

"No sign of shipping," Stokes grumbled. It was the same statement each time they mounted the peak and just before the gradual descent to where the upper of two batteries was being constructed. This was the only part of their task that was at all easy, and the men welcomed it as much as they had Up Spirits or a run ashore in the past.

"Can't expect nothing for a while," Bovey grunted, and once more it was a well-rehearsed response. "Navy takes time to plan this sort of operation."

"And what sort of operation would that be?" Longdon sighed.

"Landin' party," Bovey replied as if it were the easiest thing in the world.

"I'm beginning to wonder if they'll bother," Stokes said. The downward incline made their work easier; the cart almost went with its own momentum and needed minimal guidance to keep it on the rough track. "What would be the point?"

"The point? A bunch of British Jack Tars is being 'eld as slaves which is something that can't be allowed," Bovey insisted.

"Can't it?" Stokes again. "War with France is over, we done our stuff an' ain't needed no more. Last I heard, the rondys were all empty and men was starving on the quays; why should anyone put theirselves out for a bunch like us?"

"Even the schooner's gone," Lovemore pointed out, and that was perfectly true. After attending to her damaged rig and making other changes, the *Mary Anne* had left her berth the morning before.

"Wonder where she's bound," Bovey pondered.

"A cruise," Stokes replied. "She'll be passing up an' down the Strait in sight of the rock an' probably dippin' 'er ensign to our Navy boys bold as brass. And all the while we's stuck in this hell hole shiftin' their boulders."

"I still says they'll come for us," Bovey insisted.

"Aye, an' you go on doin' so, if it makes you feel better," Stokes told him. "But I been a Jack longer and knows something of the ways of them what orders us about."

"They may not come for us, though they might for Lieutenant Summers," Lovemore suggested.

"Now that's a notion," Stokes said brightening. "An' there's his wife – an' the captain's lady."

"Navy won't stand for them being held by heathens," Bovey agreed. "Ask me them's our best chance."

"Our only chance." Stokes again. "And it ain't the strongest."

But as they continued along the path, their cart did run a little easier.

* * *

"The Admiral has his own way of doing things," Sibly said when Pellew had gone. "Yet I might talk him round – that is, if you truly have the information you profess."

"Oh, father knows all you need," the girl said. "He will not tell you this, but no one has learned more about these people. We have spent weeks – months – writing to various consulates and embassies and amassed what must be the most comprehensive study on the States, with special emphasis on Ali bey ben Hamoudad."

"Forgive me," Sibly said, "I do not know of him."

"There are few that do," Palmer spoke softly. "But he is holding my son, and it is with him I wish to speak."

"And say what exactly?" King asked.

"Explain our situation," Palmer replied. "I understand he is a father many times over so must possess a measure of humanity. And am equally sure he will look kindly on an officer wishing to be reunited with his partner."

"That I doubt," Sibly murmured.

"That I intend to prove," Palmer countered quickly. "At least I had hoped to. The man has not been in power long; indeed, his resources are believed to be small and centre mainly on a minor port. His principal assets are that one substantial warship, a consignment of American-made ordnance given as ransom and a harbour that, though natural and well protected, is currently undeveloped. I have the location and details of the latter."

"And his other means?" Sibly was showing more interest. "Military installations and the like?"

"I know something of those," Palmer confirmed. "There is currently no army to speak of, but sites are being erected from which to fire their cannon."

"Then you must see," Sibly insisted, "it is doubly important that we attack without delay."

"And your mighty engines of war may well overpower him," Palmer agreed. "Yet that will not stop another taking his place. And another after that."

"And the alternative?" King asked and Palmer lowered his head.

"Perhaps the words of an older person might change things for the better?" he said. "And for all times?"

Sibly sighed. "Surely you cannot believe a pirate will alter his ways simply with words?"

"I believe it should be tried," the old man insisted. "My own business was built on little more than communication: communication combined with cooperation and trust. I rely on others as much as they do me; the result is a trade that supports us all. We need only discover something similar – an alternative source of income for these people, one that does not involve piracy or ransom – and all would benefit."

Sibly sat back. "As I recall, you are a whaler," he said.

"I come from such stock," Palmer admitted, "though no longer hunt myself."

"And tell me, sir, when your men go after whales how do they arm themselves?"

Palmer was visibly confused. "Forgive me, I do not know what..."

"I mean, how do they win their prey?" Sibly interrupted. "Is it with words? Or do they rather use harpoons?"

Chapter Nineteen

It was three days later when *Viper* finally set sail, the time having been spent taking on the many supplies consumed during her last patrol. And while her senior officers supervised this, King, Pellew and Palmer met several more times when the logic and logistics of what they were to attempt were fully discussed.

For all had compromised and, in the admiral's case, time had been the deciding factor. There was nothing Palmer knew that could not be discovered in a matter of weeks, yet Charles Penrose was due at any moment and Pellew's tenure of office must then end: he simply could not afford to wait the old Quaker out. Besides, they were taking no great risk in indulging him; if Palmer chose to stake his neck on speaking to a madman, Pellew was prepared to allow it.

And with Palmer, the intervention of his daughter had done the trick. Sailing aboard the *Gladiator* – a trader armed for her own protection – had been one thing but *Viper* was a dedicated warship; a concept that offended him greatly. More than that, she would be setting out with little in mind other than death and destruction. To allow the latter, should his own powers of persuasion fail, felt beyond the old man's capabilities and it was only Hannah's steady persuasion, backed by an unspoken confidence, that finally convinced him otherwise. With a plan eventually devised, the frigate swept out of Valletta harbour and added her royals, carrying with her a sense of optimism.

With King, the latter was heavily bolstered by desperation; Aimée had been in danger before, but this instance topped them all. For years, reports of Europeans held hostage on the Barbary Coast had made popular reading in papers as varied as *The Sun* or *The Times* and, even allowing for hyperbole, such horror stories must have some basis in fact. Soon every half-remembered tale of the brutal practices returned to haunt him in vivid detail. Some were based on letters from those still held, in which case more could be allowed for exaggeration, although a good many came from the few already freed and their accounts were no less gruesome. Most, the majority, were told by men accustomed to the coarseness of life at sea, but women had also been taken and, though a different pen might have embellished these accounts, their experiences were undoubtedly the worst. Instances of humiliating public markets and subsequent consignments to harems were common with captives being sent as far as Constantinople or beyond. Soon images of Aimée's potential fate began to prowl about King's mind; he became abrupt and reclusive, struggling to eat while the little sleep he managed was won by ambush and came with accompanying nightmares.

Those who knew him well understood yet could do little to help. The best his officers managed was to care for the ship with as little reference to him as possible while Manning maintained a regular supply of sleeping draughts and all held him in their thoughts and, in some cases, prayers.

Probably the only one aboard not unduly anxious about the mission was Daniels. His plans to advance by denigrating Woodward might have failed as the man proved more resilient, and popular, than expected, while his unfortunate outburst on the deck of the prize hardly raised his own profile. Nevertheless, Captain King had grudgingly seen fit to promote him to lieutenant, albeit temporarily, which was a major milestone on his personal journey to success.

And their time in harbour had not been wasted; Daniels was able to call twice on the commissioner's office where wheels were beginning to turn. He was greeted genially and various appointments as lieutenant were offered elsewhere although Daniels eventually opted to stay with *Viper*. He might have failed to create the required impression, but the ship would be heading for almost guaranteed action – a rare thing in such peaceful times. And there was more: a letter from a friend of his father's pretty much promised promotion to commander. All he need do was complete a successful deployment, preferably one that included some form of combat, and he would be made.

So that was now Daniels' sole preoccupation. He cared little for Summers or any held captive and neither did it bother him that *Viper* was likely to do battle with some of the toughest fighters ever known. Further promotion should ultimately mean a vessel of his own, likely a sloop at first although any command would mark him out as an officer to watch. A year perhaps, maybe less, and he would be given something larger, perhaps a fifth rate like *Viper* which would mean being made post. And once he had that all-important rank of captain, he might even relax a little.

In fact, from that point his sponsors would become less effective as only the death or retirement of those senior to him would see his flag raised. Still, as long as he remained on the active list, the wait could be endured as easily ashore with his hounds, as performing the mundane duties of a warship captain during peacetime. Or, if he were determined to find further excitement at sea, those of his type were starting to enlist in foreign navies where honour and wealth were there for the taking. But, whatever the turnout, it looked to be a good one; his career was on track and, with a tasty little action in sight, rarely had Daniels felt more optimistic.

* * *

As soon as he accepted the post of loblolly boy, Bewley began to read extensively, so much so that Mr Manning often complimented his newfound knowledge. However, it was one thing to learn from a book and follow the example of an experienced practitioner, quite another to be the only one present with any medical understanding.

Williams, the young man he had just been attending, was a case in point. The wound was not healing, and neither would it in the current conditions. He knew the theory well enough; it must be attended to, bathed regularly and dressed with fresh bandages and liniment, while the patient should be fed a sparse, balanced diet to encourage a restoration of the humours. Yet when all of that was impossible, there must be something else and, without personal experience, or a mentor to guide him, Bewley was at a loss.

Then there was his next patient; what affected her was completely different, though equally beyond his expertise. Bewley had learned much since joining *Viper*, and not just that he was unsuited to the life of a naval surgeon: a calling that demanded far greater dispassion than he possessed. Primarily he now believed medical science should not simply be concerned with treating wounds and curing disease, and the more he read about physical ailments, the more it became apparent that conditions of the mind were woefully neglected.

When Mr Manning allowed his release and agreed for him to travel back to Gibraltar, an unspoken reason had been to care for the two pregnant women he would be accompanying. But both were proving amazingly robust; it was Millie, the young servant girl, who taxed his abilities.

"Come now, you can't take on so," he told her. She was lying near the wounded midshipman and her constant sobbing hardly aided the lad's recovery. And neither were the cell's other inhabitants finding her perpetual moaning agreeable; soon complaints would be made and the last thing their little hell hole needed was disagreement.

"Try to calm yourself, crying will only make you more tired and we have to conserve our energy."

The sobbing stopped momentary, although Bewley could tell the pause was fragile. "I'm frightened," she told him. "I want to go home."

He went to respond then decided against it; Bewley was still to come across any book that dealt with such a condition, yet common sense told him stating the obvious would do little good. Instead, he scoured his brain for something more positive.

"I think our captors want us to go home as well," he said, and the eyes opened wider.

"They do?"

"It's why we are here and not being worked hard," he swallowed. "Or worse."

"So, when will it happen? When will they set us free?"

"In time. Until then try to get some sleep."

"Will you stay with me?"

"There is nowhere else to go," he smiled and, rather than continuing what had come to be his evening rounds, Bewley eased his body next to the youngster. It wasn't a solution; that was far beyond his reach, yet he had learned enough to know even palliative care had value. And soon they were both fast asleep.

* * *

201

Their journey was just over eight hundred miles, though the wind was favourable and they made reasonable time. So much so that, less than two weeks later, *Viper* was standing off the coast near Mezmada, the port Palmer had stipulated, with the harbour in plain sight. Daniels had the watch although every officer and most of those officially below were on deck surveying the land.

Which was singularly unremarkable. The harbour itself bore a strange resemblance to that encountered on the island of Zembra. The cliffs that had been an occasional feature of the shoreline for much of their journey, dipped only slightly to give way to the narrowest of entrances and what lay beyond appeared equally forbidding. King had been surveying the area since first light yet, even when the sun rose further, there was little visual clue as to what may lie within. Or even if it were a harbour at all; from outward appearances, this could be nothing more than an outlet for one of the occasional rivers that ran for a few months of the year and might only have worn out the meanest of bays.

"I believe I can see buildings," Cooper announced. The first lieutenant was nearby and sharing the deck glass with Manton. "And there is activity atop the western cliff; a new construction within maybe?"

"Any habitation is likely to be to the south." The sailing master was consulting part of a rolled chart. "There is no town or structures of any type marked, though the land is low and level there before rising steeply. It is the most logical place to build."

"And I think I spy a tower," Cooper added.

King's own glass showed less detail, he lowered it and moved to join his officers. But Manton's chart proved a disappointment and gave only a vague representation. There was a rough outline of what might be a usable harbour along with a few grudging soundings about the approach. The hydrographers had not ventured further and neither did they consider the place worthy of additional comment.

King pursed his lips. The depths indicated were sufficient and, with the Med's lack of tides, there was little apparent danger of grounding. But his seaman's senses predicted a strong current and to that point the coast had been littered with shoals and sandbanks; he would be foolish to take *Viper* closer without proper investigation.

Which was not to say a boat could not be sent, and that was

the plan, after all. Before any show of force, he had agreed that Palmer would be delivered ashore to negotiate with the bey and King had no intention of going back on his word. If the old fool were determined to risk his neck in a place where even a white flag might not be respected, it was entirely his choice.

At that moment, the man himself appeared on the quarterdeck with his daughter following dutifully in his wake. The girl carried a plain canvas bag that held something large and shapeless, and both seemed unusually preoccupied. They were dressed as always although this time their drab clothing was topped by half jackets that appeared ridiculous in the glare of an early morning sun.

"I see you are ready to go ashore," King said as Palmer approached. "And must repeat my earlier caution; those you will meet are heathens and unlikely to negotiate with Christian folk."

"Christian or not, we believe there to be good in all people," the older man said. "And it is only by extending the hand of friendship that it can be taken."

"Very well, it is your decision, though you will not be accompanied by your daughter."

Palmer's eyes rose. "There has been no objection to Hannah's presence until now," he said.

"Because the subject was not raised." Knowing Aimée could be close by – almost within sight, in fact, and possibly suffering the most brutal of treatments – had made King's nerves especially raw. Something of this must have been communicated to Palmer as he lowered his head in acknowledgement.

The girl was less easily swayed, however. "I am prepared to go with my father." She spoke softly yet could be heard by all on the quarterdeck. "And shall make my own decisions."

"I have no doubt, ma'am," King snapped. "Though do not propose to discuss the matter further. No boat of mine will carry you and it is surely too far to swim."

The remark brought a ripple of laughter from the hands waiting to board their cutter although it was clear King was not speaking in jest and, colouring slightly, the girl looked away.

"Very well," Palmer said. "I cannot force Hannah's attendance though am disappointed that our obvious intent has been ignored."

"No one would assume a father should willingly take his

daughter into danger," King told him curtly. "If you insist on pursuing your own folly, a boat will be provided. Otherwise, I am quite prepared to skip that part of the arrangement and take more forceful action myself."

Again, his determination must have been obvious. The day was bright and clear; with careful use of the lead, it would be relatively easy to bring *Viper* up to the harbour entrance. Any seaward-facing batteries could be identified on their approach, and the embrasures swept. And then, once inside the pirate's lair, they could begin a very different form of negotiation.

From what Palmer had already told them, this was no established stronghold and, if the buildings had escaped notice from the hydrographer, they were probably new or still under construction. A fifth rate could play merry hell in such a situation, and do the same to any sheltering shipping. The barrage would be both devastating and decisive; within hours he should have forced this tinpot leader to parley, and Aimée, along with all those currently held, could be saved. But even if not, even if they were killed by his own fire or became victims of a cornered madman's spite, it would be over for them. As it would for King; he may continue to mourn and might do so for the rest of his life, but Aimée would no longer be in pain.

Once more Palmer seemed to understand and took a physical step back. A pipe from the boatswain alerted the larboard cutter's crew and all on the quarterdeck watched as the boat was made ready. Lieutenant Woodward was to command; seeing a passenger ashore would normally only require the attention of a midshipman, yet this was no simple ferrying operation and King would feel better with an experienced man in charge.

"You will be unarmed, Mr Woodward," King reminded him. "And as you know it is against international convention for measurements to be taken that may later assist us. Consequently, you will not use anything obvious such as a lead or sounding rod. However, that does not mean you go in blind; should there be shoals, you will make note with accurate bearings of their position. And if batteries are obvious, I wish them to be recorded also along with any principal buildings that may be pertinent to a later attack. And pay particular attention to those that might contain hostages."

Palmer remained close by but said nothing although King

sensed he was hanging on every word.

"At the first sign of danger you are also to retreat," he continued. "And will do so whatever the state or position of Mr Palmer, do you understand?"

"Yes, sir," Woodward replied, and King had the impression Palmer also gave a nod.

"Then I wish you luck," he added before turning to the older man, "And you also, sir."

"I am grateful to you, Captain," Palmer said. "Though, as to luck, reject the concept vehemently; I have something far more powerful to rely upon."

* * *

Woodward held the tiller himself while Malcolm, a midshipman only recently promoted from volunteer, attended their twin sails. Woodward had commanded cutters a thousand times when a middy himself and Malcolm steered the very same boat when cutting out the American schooner from the harbour at Zembra. It was a task that surely called for greater courage than ferrying a civilian passenger to an unknown shore, yet their present duty felt every bit as dangerous.

They would be more exposed for a start; a shore battery would have the cutter in their sights long before they could be spotted while the enemy would have both time and opportunity to launch their own boats – boats filled to overflowing with armed fighting savages. Woodward had read the accounts of seamen captured by North African pirates and did not wish to add any himself. And the final point was that his cutter's crew were unarmed. He knew himself to be relatively unskilled with either pistol or sword, although the handful of men currently seated at the oars were experienced fighters and would have made a decent show were they adequately equipped. But all they carried was the strength in their arms backed by the occasional pusser's dirk, and the thought was not reassuring.

There was one encouraging aspect to the duty, however. His nemesis, Daniels, might have made it to lieutenant and was doubtless due to progress, but for now remained the most junior commissioned officer in *Viper*'s gunroom. As such he would normally have been the captain's choice yet, instead, Woodward was selected. There might be a dozen reasons for this; Daniels had been the officer of the watch for one, although Woodward preferred to think otherwise. He preferred to think the captain trusted him in what could easily turn out to be a delicate, and dangerous, operation. And thinking so was a comfort; to be given such responsibility was actually a compliment, albeit a dubious one.

To the other side of him Palmer, the civilian, sat in restrained silence. Of them all, he would be in the greatest danger; the man was intending to step ashore and hoped to speak with whoever ruled this savage country in his lair. But then the entire enterprise was down to him, and he could have ended it at any moment, which was a luxury denied a mere lieutenant.

"Shoal water to larboard," Malcolm said.

"Very good, mark it down."

The green-blue sea was as clear as glass and quite still; even without the usual measuring devices they could judge the depth with ease and Woodward turned the cutter's head slightly to starboard and deeper water. They were closing on the harbour now and a positive channel was being revealed which would be useful were *Viper* ever called to attack. And, as he drew closer to the harbour entrance, there was more to see ashore. To the south they could make out a town; buildings of a regular height and size covered most of the distant hillside. And, just above the skyline, was a tower, probably some form of religious construction, with a copper-domed building set just below; if he kept the two in line, the boat continued in the midst of the safer water. It was a point that Captain King would find useful, and Woodward was encouraged.

Then movement ashore caught his attention; an elegant and substantial vessel was putting out. He watched in silent fascination as it was rowed to the mouth of the harbour before two graceful red sails were hoisted and the craft took to the wind. Such a craft would be both fast and relatively seaworthy while holding any number of men; certainly enough to swamp their tiny cutter.

"The heathens are coming to meet us, sir," Malcolm pointed out.

"See that pennant's kept free," Woodward snapped in reply. The wind was from the east, which at least allowed the white flag to fly clear of their own sails. But whether or not it could be seen was hardly the point, would barbarians honour such a convention?

The vessel was making good speed, far more so than Woodward's clumsy cutter, and soon they could pick out individual figures and faces. Most – all – were heavily bearded and there was a fluttering of light garments that suggested silk and robes rather than the more traditional seaman's garb.

"I should say they intend to collect you, sir," he told Palmer and the old man nodded.

"Doubtless they do not wish Navy men to survey their defences," he replied, and Woodward privately hoped that were the case.

Then the boat was within musket range and, though weapons were raised aboard her, none pointed in their direction. Soon high-pitched chatter could be heard and a growl from Woodward silenced any mutterings in his cutter. The time came to spill the wind; their sheets were released, and the two boats closed, powered only by momentum. Then a tall figure stood up at the pirate's prow.

"What business have you here?" it demanded, and Woodward was surprised to hear an apparently European voice that carried only the faintest of accents.

"We have a gentleman who wishes to treat with your ruler." As Woodward spoke, he felt a gentle pressure on his arm.

"I am Caleb Palmer," the Quaker declared in a surprisingly loud and clear voice. "I would wait upon Ali bey ben Hamoudad."

Even from a distance, Woodward could sense indecision.

"Very well, we will come alongside," the man replied at last. "But be warned, we are armed and can take a boat such as yours in an instant."

* * *

"And you know no more?" King checked.

"Nothing, sir," Woodward replied. "They took Mr Palmer aboard and headed straight back. I was uncertain whether to wait though thought you should be advised of the situation."

"Indeed, and your observations on the state of the sea bed may come in useful; a good job, Mr Woodward."

Woodward touched his hat and turned away. Inwardly he was glad the task was over and especially that he had been able to give good news regarding the harbour approach. And he supposed collecting the old man – were he called to do so – would be less of a concern. But he had now seen the pirates close up and the sight was not reassuring.

Rather than the ragged specimens that haunted other waters, all had been immaculately dressed in well-cut robes with some sporting magnificent, jewelled turbans. And the boat that pulled alongside was expertly handled and impeccably set up. Again, this was unlike any pirate or privateer Woodward had previously known. Their leader was clearly a man of some intelligence and seemed familiar with European dress as he regarded Palmer's drab garb with some surprise. And all had been heavily armed...

The ornate muskets presented little threat, even though their presence went against the ancient conventions of a white flag. But their edged weapons were far more intimidating. Most had a markedly curved blade and were highly decorated with precious stones embedded in the hilts and pommels. Yet these were no cheap ornamental pieces, but made by craftsmen, which belied the assumption they were dealing with savages. While Palmer was being helped into the larger boat, Woodward was able to examine one in some detail; the blade had been expertly forged with a myriad of small marks – presumably the result of hammer blows – along its length. And there was an edge that glistened silver in the sun; without touching he could tell the thing would cut like a razor and had the weight and balance to do so with awful precision.

The boat veered away before Palmer was fully settled, and Woodward's last sight of the old man was him hunting for his dropped bag before being pressed down onto a thwart as the pirate vessel took to the wind. But it wasn't the rough treatment or the fact that these were men who knew their business that left the deepest impression; it was the memory of that beautiful, terrible, sword.

Chapter Twenty

"It's definitely *Viper*." Summers' fingers dug deep into the rough flint walls, yet he felt no pain. "She's standing about three-mile offshore, but I'd know the rake of that bowsprit anywhere. An' her gaff."

The sight had awoken many emotions in the young man and it was some time before he could speak again.

"Anything else?" Peter Palmer demanded at last. Though unshod, Summers' feet were bearing into his shoulders and the lieutenant was no lightweight.

"There are two boats in the water." To make up for the pause he spoke quickly. "One looks like a naval cutter and is heading for *Viper*, the other's a galliot making for the harbour. Reckon they must have been parlaying and we missed it."

"Have you seen enough?" the American gasped, and Summers obediently slipped down.

"Talk is good," he said, his eyes once more becoming accustomed to the cell's gloom. "It means folk are aware of our existence." He glanced around at the crowd of watching faces; hope was on some although others had the empty look of long-term captives.

"They might be aware," Williams spoke from his bed place – a corner of the cell reserved for him since the wound began to fester. "But what can they do about it?"

"Doubtless we'll discover in time." Summers caught Palmer's eye; this was one of the minor inconveniences of their accommodation. All forms of dignity had been abandoned a long time since; their very clothes were little more than loincloths, and everyone was now accustomed to personal functions being performed in public. Yet what Summers still missed was the chance for private conversation, and none more so than at the present time. "Do you think, perhaps... Your father?" he asked softly.

The American shook his head. "Pa's had his chance," he said. "If he'd anything planned it would have been done months past. Besides, he would never willingly board one of your warships."

Summers nodded, that was very much as he expected and not encouraging. When aboard *Tenacious,* the Quaker impressed him with his strength of character; if anyone could negotiate with the bey, it would be him. However, he'd later learned the man had little in the way of hard currency, and they were dealing with a culture fixated on the stuff.

And *Viper*'s presence told another story. For her to have been despatched meant the British government knew of their predicament and was prepared to act. But they had sent a frigate: the largest warship capable of entering the harbour with any thought of safety. And despite having funds, he could not see the British government releasing any for officers and men when there was a surplus of both.

Though neither would the Navy take such an affront lying down. Which meant *Viper* was likely to attack and may be successful – at least what might be regarded by some as a success. For the cramped cell he and the others shared was close to the quay, and if *Viper* chose to bombard the port it was unlikely any of them would survive.

* * *

The bey's palace was not what Palmer expected, yet that was just one in a succession of surprises that began as soon as he clambered aboard the foreigners' boat.

For one, the men that manned the vessel were not savages. He was treated roughly for sure, although British seamen – or Americans if it came to it – would have been little different and the tension aboard the larger vessel was similar to that in the Royal Navy cutter he had just left. And there was a recognised order of command. The silk-clad man who spoke first was their leader with two juniors under him to enforce his wishes. Each did so with respect and the regular sailors – who were cleaner and better dressed than many Palmer had encountered in the past – carried out their duties efficiently. Consequently, his journey passed quickly; in no time they were through the harbour mouth and the town within was finally revealed.

Which again came as something of a shock. The buildings were exclusively of stone and matched each other in their red-brown hue. And, though each was smaller and the total area far more compact, the general impression was similar to Valletta, with tightly packed houses rising up from the various quays and wharves that ringed much of the harbour. There was also far less shipping in the basin itself; a mere handful of boats were huddled to the east and appeared identical to that which collected him, though all were under oiled sheets and apparently in storage. Then, when their own craft had been competently secured and he was able to clamber onto the hard, he noticed few people in the town itself. But as he was marched along the narrow lane that led up from the sea, more began to appear. The guards to either side were heavily armed though Palmer could not tell if this was for his protection or theirs, and soon several interested civilians began to follow.

The crowd kept pace and even grew as his small group climbed further, and several came close, attempting to touch his clothes. They remained until the palace came into sight – an austere structure that looked more like a government building – at which point all quickly dispersed allowing him and his escorts to pass through the outer gate unencumbered.

And as they approached the building itself there was still more to amaze him. A line of armed men stood guard over the double front door, only grudgingly allowing admission, and when they were in and could enjoy the relative cool of the stone building, the security remained as tight. Still without a word, the boat's captain led him along a succession of short corridors then up a staircase and, though only two of his guards remained, there were armed men at every doorway. All eyed him with deep suspicion and an apparent longing for the chance to use their long and wickedly curved swords.

Finally, he was led into a bare dark room that lacked windows or furniture; the place was little more than a cell and might have lain unused since the palace was built. Palmer was still taking this in when the white-clad figure left, taking the guards with him, and closing a heavy wooden door in his wake.

Sealing the room effectively cut out much of the light, only cracks in the frame and a slightly larger gap below and above the door itself gave any illumination, yet not enough for him to see the back of his hand. Carefully he reached out for the wall and, feeling its cold presence, rested against it. And then, as the minutes turned to hours and the hours passed so slowly, Caleb Palmer settled on the floor and resigned himself to a long wait.

* * *

Lieutenant Summers was not the only one to notice *Viper*'s arrival; as they topped the cliffs on their first trip from the quarry, Stokes and his men spotted the warship at once and were equally quick to identify their former home.

"Told you she'd come for us," Bovey said, "We'll be aboard by sunset an' spend tonight in our 'ammocks – see if we don't."

"Wouldn't count your chickens," Stokes warned. He was equally pleased to see the frigate, although age and experience had taught him much, principally the better the news the more closely he should question it.

"Too right," Longdon agreed. "They gotta land firs' and that won't be easy."

"And get past that little lot." Stokes was glancing down the steep slope. About thirty feet below, a terrace housed the lower battery, a structure completed before any of them arrived. It must have been a recent addition, however, and stood proud with naked stone still to be concealed by brush or undergrowth. And within its rocky embrace, six slick new cannon lay ready to sweep the harbour with devastating fire.

"Odd choice for a shore battery," Bovey commented. "Must be thirty-two-pounders, but look at the length of them barrels!"

"Aye," Longdon agreed. "More like carronades."

"Yank built," Lovemore added. "Probably supplied in place of clink."

"Fine thing, givin' your enemy weapons." Bovey again. "What were the Jonathans thinkin' of?"

"Well, they gave 'em the wrong sort," Stokes said. "However high them's mounted, pieces like that won't have no range."

"'Spose they've learned that," Longdon said. "Which is why they're stationing 'em so, to cover the harbour. Though it'll be plunging fire," he added glancing now at the water beneath. "With no room to speak of in the bay, any ship entering will be easy meat."

Stokes nodded wisely. "While their gunners'll find it hard to reach up to such an' height."

A shriek of unfathomable instructions assailed them and a sunburned hand slapped the back of Bovey's head as a guard passed by. All four turned their attention to the cart which was now running downhill yet had slowed slightly during their conversation. Stokes looked up when the required speed was achieved.

"They're lettin' us get away with more," he said.

"Aye," Bovey agreed. "Ain't watching like they used to."

"Maybe it's the progress?" Longdon suggested, glancing down at the completed battery. "Cannon below are ready to use, and they'll be setting more up here in no time; reckon the pressures off as far as they're concerned."

But the guard had reached the next cart and was berating its team far more sternly. Stokes shook his head. "This lot won't be happy till all's in place," he said.

The cart lurched to one side, and it took the combined strength of them all to persuade it back onto the rough pathway.

"So why they givin' us an easier go?" Longdon asked when it was running normally again.

"'Cause we're getting' past it," Stokes said. "Week ago, the truck would have held its course or, if it did fall off, one of us'd be sound enough to set it straight. Face it, we're gettin' slower. Only a matter of time afore they replaces us with fresh from the quarry."

"Replaces us," Longdon mused. "You mean..."

"I mean we'll be goin' on a one-way trip off the edge of that cliff," Stokes confirmed. "That is, unless the barky takes some action firs'."

* * *

They came for him that evening; Caleb Palmer had been able to judge the time as less light was filtering into his small domain and, when the door finally opened, the corridor outside was lit by candles. He stumbled more than once and nearly dropped his bag as the guards rushed him along, but when two large doors were swung back and he was propelled into a vast room, the glare from countless lamps was almost blinding.

It was several seconds before he could take everything in. The same white-clad man who had commanded the boat was there; he stood at the head of two rows of armed guards that lined a carpeted path leading to a raised platform. On this, a slight figure sat in an oversized chair that was itself sheltered by an embroidered canopy. The seated man was dressed in a plain white gown with numerous heavy gold chains draped about his neck. He wore a bejewelled turban and an ornate dagger glinted wickedly from a crimson waistband. The air was thick with a sweet aroma that was at once attractive yet equally repugnant, and the entire room felt unusually hot, even without any visible form of heating.

"Approach!"

Yes, that was unquestionably the boat's captain although there was no sign of recognition in the heavily tanned face. Palmer took a cautious step forward and soon reached the carpet. He felt the tightly packed fibres compress slightly under his weight and, when no more was said, continued along the strange pathway. He walked on, conscious of the steady eyes of those to either side, then paused at a previously unnoticed wooden bar that blocked his way.

"Approach!" The order was repeated with slightly more menace and Palmer examined the beam. It had been heavily polished and stood three feet from the ground while being as wide as the carpet; the only logical way to continue was to step to one side and into the line of waiting guards, something Palmer sensed would not be approved of. Other than that, he could clamber over or crawl underneath, and he chose the latter.

Holding the bag tight, he lowered himself to the carpet and, childlike, made his way under the obstruction and to the edge of the dais. He looked up; the seated figure must surely be the bey although this was not how Palmer imagined they would meet. The man was standing now and regarded him from above; Palmer was struck by the whites of his eyes that stood out like beams of light amidst a bronzed and mildly pockmarked face.

"What brings you here?" he demanded. It was a high-pitched voice yet in no way weak; the shrill tone cut like a scalpel.

"My name is Caleb Palmer; I came to speak with Ali bey ben Hamoudad."

"And what business do you have?" Though heavily accented, Palmer fancied he could detect a measure of

214

sophistication in the man's speech.

"He holds my son," Palmer declared. Speaking so made his neck hurt although this was not the time for such concerns. "Him and several of his shipmates. And there may be others."

The bey appeared to consider this, and, despite the indignity of his position, the old man could feel strength returning. "Men who wish him no harm yet are being held against their will," he added.

"You are aware of the price for such a concession?"

Palmer raised himself slightly until he could stare more boldly into those eyes. "I have no money, though might pay in other ways."

The figure remained silent, so Palmer continued.

"I am older than you and have learned much; I am willing to pass that knowledge on."

Again, no movement, no response.

"My community has survived with limited resources other than the skill of our hands and the strength of our faith. And though you and I may hold differing beliefs, we both trust in a higher being, which should be sufficient to form an understanding."

"I want nothing from you or any infidel," the bey told him. "Nothing, other than the tribute that is mine by right."

"But it is not your right." Palmer found the authority came easily and he began to stand. "You have stolen my son and others. That is theft and against your own teaching."

"They were taken by my privateers; a custom your countrymen practise and are pleased to benefit from."

"Some may," Palmer allowed, "though I do not, and neither do those of my community. We seek only peace, and the chance to help your country." He raised the bag. "Here, I have brought a gift, one that was made by our womenfolk."

Palmer was fiddling with the opening when the side of a decorated sword blade fell flat upon his hand. He looked back and into the set eyes of a guard.

"It is a quilt – a blanket, no more," he said. "My wife and the wives of others made it: a present."

The bey appeared mildly amused; he nodded and the sword was withdrawn. Palmer carefully removed the quilt and allowed it to roll out before him. The coloured threads caught the light, dancing in its glow while each separate piece of cloth took on a greater depth. The old man drew breath; never had the work looked so marvellous; whatever his personal tastes, the bey must surely be impressed.

"Show it to me," he commanded, and a tanned hand snatched the cloth which was held out for a full inspection.

Palmer's glance switched to the canopy above and inspiration stuck. "Your people are undoubtedly as skilled," he said. "Such things may be sold or exchanged, and perhaps there will be others."

"Others?"

"I see this gentleman's sword is well made and highly decorated: a work of art."

The bey eyed him wickedly. "You suggest that we should trade in weapons?" he asked.

"That would be my last wish, though the same skills could be used elsewhere; there are those who would pay high prices for fine jewellery or furnishings. And you have natural resources that are in great demand and could be exchanged for timber or other supplies you lack. With honest trade, there would be no need for piracy, and you may benefit further."

The bey said nothing.

"There could be an exchange in medical science," Palmer continued. "Our physicians are making discoveries all the time; their knowledge could be shared to improve the health of your people. And there have been breakthroughs in navigation that would benefit your seafarers. With good supplies of timber and ready markets to hand, you could be at the head of a vast fleet of merchant vessels, one that would make your country rich beyond all imaginings. Once wealth was attained there would be no need for slave labour, your people would prosper and reflect their gratitude in their respect and love. The name of Ali bey ben Hamoudad will be spoken of with awe and wonder, and I can help you make that happen."

"And in return?" the bey enquired.

"In return, I ask for my son."

The old man now took a step back. Speaking so had exhausted him and he would have welcomed the chance to sit. But the bey was considering his reply, and all thoughts of physical weakness were forgotten as the slight figure drew breath.

"I have heard enough." The tone, though still shrill, now carried an air of finality. "And been insulted in many ways. First, you call at my palace without invitation, then stand in my presence and ask for charity. And, finally, you bring no customary present," he glanced contemptuously at the cloth.

"But there is so much I can give!" The bey's eyes grew wide, yet Palmer could not remain silent. "There can be introductions to foreign markets and, if it is funds you lack, that might also be addressed, many will gladly help finance your kingdom."

"You are speaking usury?"

Palmer retreated further until he felt the wooden beam at his back. "That need not be so, we can find other ways. Truly, friend, there is so much I can give."

"There is nothing you have that I want; certainly not your friendship and certainly not this rag." The quilt was instantly dropped to the floor. "That is the worst insult of all, for it contains images that offend me as they would anyone with knowledge of the true light. You may be an infidel, so perhaps cannot be blamed for your ignorance, but I will not listen to you further. Take him away."

* * *

King had called a meeting in *Viper*'s great cabin. Cooper was there, seated to his immediate right, with Woodward and Daniels further down the dining table, while Marine Captain Duke – sent to command the double detachment of marines Pellew had authorised – sat opposite them with his two lieutenants. And, as action seemed imminent, there was an atmosphere of tense anticipation.

None present held any hopes for the old Quaker or his hair-brained schemes and, now night was upon them and it was likely they had indeed failed, decisive measures were called for. A landing party could be arranged within the hour, or they might take *Viper* in and see what mischief her cannon could make in the enemy's harbour. To King's mind, the only question was which course to follow.

"There has been no sign of Mr Palmer," he began when they were settled. "Indeed, little activity of any kind from the port."

He glanced over to Woodward.

"That is so, sir," the second lieutenant confirmed. After returning to the ship, he had spent much of the day in the red cutter waiting in hope; the man had been a nuisance from day one yet, now he was gone and apparently for good, Woodward felt surprisingly sorry.

"But you were able to reconnoitre the harbour approach?" King checked.

"Yes, sir. There is a channel that would likely accommodate *Viper*," he said.

"And shore defences?" Cooper asked. "What sign of them?"

"Work is being carried out deeper inside the harbour. It is on the western clifftop though I could see little detail.

"A building perhaps?" Cooper suggested. Woodward shook his head.

"More like a battery," he said. "One that would cover the inner harbour; stonework is certainly being erected."

"You could not be sure?" Marine Captain Duke demanded.

"To learn more would have meant entering the harbour," Woodward replied. "And with Mr Palmer in the hands of the pirates..."

"Of course," King allowed, although it was with effort. In truth, he could not have cared less about the old man; Palmer was a fool to go and not listen to reason. And, while he was being totally honest, no longer did the concept of Summers and the others being held captive trouble him greatly, his thoughts were now entirely focused on freeing Aimée.

But first, they needed a plan of action and, with negotiation and diplomacy having been seen to fail, the emphasis must indeed be on action. King was a fighting officer; it was time to put his particular skills to the test. In fact, quite how he had restrained himself for so long was beyond him.

"Even without established defences, we can expect opposition," Cooper chimed in with what, to King, sounded like pessimism. "We know the pirates are equipped with cannon and the harbour area itself to be limited; in the darkness, *Viper* will be in danger of being trapped."

"Cannon?" Duke, the senior marine, questioned. "How do savages obtain cannon?"

"And if they do," Marine Lieutenant Davis added with a

smirk, "are they able to use them?"

"Barbary Pirates are known to be well armed, Major." Cooper was replying to Duke, though aboard ship it was customary to address marine captains as Major to avoid confusion with the vessel's official captain. "Ordnance of every type is often extracted as tribute and we would be foolish to underestimate them in terms of ability, or the determination to fight."

"But *Viper* is a well-equipped warship," Davis reminded.

"Absolutely," Tyler, the second marine lieutenant and Browning's replacement agreed. "A ship like this could cause all manner of devilment."

King closed his eyes. At least this was a more optimistic attitude although, by wanting nothing other than an all-out fight, the marine officers were confirming his opinion of their corps. The idea of charging in with all guns blazing was not totally abhorant, but Aimée could be at the other end of that shot. And, where her life was concerned, he was not prepared to take chances.

Briefly his thoughts returned to Palmer. The man's naïve plans for negotiation would never have worked, yet, now free to use the force at his command, King was unsure how and regretted the lack of a more peaceful end to matters.

"Go in now and let 'em have it," the marine captain continued. "Show the blighters what we've got. Them heathens'll soon knuckle down."

King cleared his throat. "I would remind you, they are holding our people. We cannot tell where – indeed, we do not know how many are left. And Mr Cooper is correct, we are not dealing with fools; they understand the value of hostages and will use all such advantages to the fullest extent."

There was silence as most considered this although King's mind was elsewhere; none could know the pain he had caused himself when speaking of the captives so lightly.

"So, do we try a harsher negotiation?" Cooper suggested. "Place *Viper* in a position where the destruction of property and shipping is inevitable and see what can be arranged?"

"It is a possibility," King allowed, even if the prospect of manoeuvring his ship in a strange harbour at night was not attractive.

"Though surely much will depend on what we find on entering harbour." Cooper again. "As we have discussed, there is likely to be ordnance mounted within and in the dark..."

"The enemy would have us at their mercy," Duke announced with sudden understanding. "It would be like entering a tenaille."

Cooper looked up. "Forgive me, major..."

"It is a military term," Tyler, the new marine officer, explained. "An attacking force is allowed limited access to a fortification; only on entering do they realise hidden defenders can fire upon them from three sides and the place becomes a killing field."

"From the French," Duke added slowly. "For pincers..."

The sea officers digested this for several seconds before Cooper spoke again.

"Then what is the alternative?"

"Why, we must send in troops," Tyler declared.

"Absolutely," Duke agreed. "We have sixty of the finest fighters that can be ready in an instant; any one of them is worth a dozen savages."

"I say again, we are not dealing with savages." Now they were finally discussing the possibilities, King was finding this torture. "And your men will know nothing of the town, nor where the prisoners may be found. A detachment of bootnecks blundering about a maze of narrow streets at night would be of little benefit."

Again, there was silence and King felt mildly guilty. Though only mildly; in such situations he usually welcomed comment, but the marine officers were set on a single course of action. And even if the concept of meeting force with force held some attraction, he could see the foolishness in it. He glanced about the table; Daniels had added nothing, although King felt in no need of suggestions from that quarter. However well-connected the cove might be, he was not developing into an officer to be depended upon. Their second lieutenant was a different matter, though and might have more to contribute; King caught his eye.

"What about you, Mr Woodward?"

The lieutenant jumped slightly on being singled out, yet his response was almost immediate. "I'd say we should wait, sir."

"Wait?" Cooper clearly expressed the thoughts of many. Even in the candlelight, Woodward coloured noticeably.

"Yes, sir," he persisted. "Mr Palmer has only been ashore a

matter of hours; what he was planning would never be agreed in a single afternoon."

The atmosphere eased slightly at the apparent truth, although remained mildly hostile.

"And there is no telling what stage his negotiations have reached," Woodward continued, "and having *Viper* attack can surely not aid them."

"So, what do you suggest?"

"We leave it for tonight, sir. But close up to the shore and send a boat in at first light."

"A boat?" King repeated.

"Yes, sir. And this time it must enter the harbour. If Mr Palmer is ready to return it can collect him, and if not – if the pirates are hostile – I can think of no better way of identifying any inner harbour defences."

"You mean draw fire from the shore?" Daniels asked, appalled. "Sound out their batteries?"

"But it may be sunk," Cooper protested. "In truth, the likelihood is great."

"Then that will be obvious from *Viper*." Woodward's tone was surprisingly cool. "And she can enter knowing what must be faced."

This time the silence felt more contemplative, and it was a while before Duke broke the spell.

"I still say we move in now," he declared. "Batteries are more easily sighted in the dark and we won't be such a clear target."

"We shall be just as clear when we return fire," Cooper countered. "And if it comes to street fighting, I would rather that by day than by night."

"Then it is agreed." King's words may have been spoken on impulse and certainly went against his need for immediate action. Yet even in his heightened state, he could see the sense in Woodward's suggestion. The only downside was Aimée having to endure another night when she had already withstood so much.

Chapter Twenty-One

The days were hot but at night it grew cooler and by the time dawn broke, the cell could be incredibly cold. And on that particular morning, Summers had become stiff; he awoke resting against the hard stone wall after being in roughly the same position for much of the night. Sleep had mostly been light and fitful; only towards the end did he lose consciousness completely and as a result now felt strained and slightly groggy. Beside him, Suzie had been luckier. Though equally squashed she seemed far more composed and, on one occasion, even began to snore slightly. Now she rested comfortably at his side; her body keeping his tolerably warm as the light gradually increased and the crowded room began to stir.

Still, despite the pins and needles, Summers felt no regret at what some might consider a wasted night. There had been the chance to think – a rare luxury in the noise and confusion of daytime – and, though no conclusion was reached, his mind now felt more settled.

And there had been no interruptions. This was hardly surprising; the last bucket of water was issued at dusk, and another would arrive shortly, followed by their solitary meal of the day, but Summers was expecting quite another form of disturbance. Once he saw *Viper,* he knew she would come for them, the only question was when, and he was glad it had not been in darkness.

Due to the warship's proximity, he spent the previous day keeping an almost constant watch on her, Palmer and Goodman having taken turns in supporting him. However, apart from a solitary cutter drifting aimlessly about the harbour entrance, there was little to note. That could not continue; negotiations may be underway ashore, but Captain King was not the kind to waste time. If the bey were willing to release them, they would be gone by now, and if *Viper* had not come last night, she would do so this morning.

There was a whimper from Millie. The girl was on the opposite side of the room and seemed to be waking. At which point her monotonous moaning would resume and Summers was eager to get his thoughts properly in order before that happened. Yet Millie remained quiet; maybe she sensed a change in the air or perhaps Bewley, fast asleep close by, had more to do with it, but Summers was able to think on.

Any ideas of escape from their cell had been rejected long since; the guards often came in pairs and the sound of an outer door being unlocked always preceded that of their own, so the place was evidently secure. And besides, even if one or two made it to the outside world, where would they go? Now though, with help literally within sight, all that had changed and plans for breaking out of their prison were once more foremost in his mind. Despite *Viper* being close by, there was probably little chance of joining her, although he could think of a far better reason for wanting to get away.

The battery covering the inner harbour was now partially active – he witnessed the first test shots from the lower level only a few days before, and it appeared much of the area could be swept. Such intense fire would come as a shock if Captain King chose to bring the frigate in, and Summers would need his freedom to give proper warning. And not just of the battery; their cell lay close to the waterfront. Should *Viper* enter sufficiently to bombard the town, their cell would be in the forefront of her fire.

Or perhaps he could signal their presence from inside? The only logical way was through the tiny slits of windows which, with no means of ignition or even a reasonable amount of cloth to hand, offered little prospect. As the light slowly increased, he continued to think and, though no ultimate decision was reached, the time of quiet also enabled him to consider what personal prospects remained.

Certainly, if he were ever free of this place it would be the end of his career in the Navy; he had better things to do than be boiled, or frozen, in a cell. And Suzie – would she wish to stay with him? Her life might have been dull in Nova Scotia, but the excitement he had introduced could hardly be regarded as an improvement. No, meeting him had only brought her misery and adding pregnancy to their current inconveniences must be making them so much worse. Of course, they could not discuss the situation; without privacy, nothing could be spoken of above the necessities of keeping alive. Yet were they ever to win their freedom, Summers knew their life together would never be the same.

It was a harsh thought to end on, although Summers had little choice as he could hear the sound of footsteps and a lock being turned. That would be the morning water and an official end to the relative peace. He raised himself in expectation; there was no telling what the day might bring but it was certain to be a lot more active than those that had gone before.

* * *

They launched *Viper*'s cutter at first light and by the time she was at the harbour entrance, the sun was fully clear of the horizon. Aboard her, and in his customary position in the sternsheets, Woodward was still unsure why he had spoken out the previous night; his suggestion had been spontaneous and prompted solely by logic. It was also made without regard for his personal safety, though there was nothing brave in that; Woodward hardly expected to be entering the harbour himself.

For the cutter had drawn her crew from the opposing watch with Malcolm having been replaced by Balaam, the midshipman who assisted him with the long guns. Of them all, only Woodward had spent the previous day outside the enemy harbour; even the boat was different, they being in the green cutter rather than the red, so surely it should have been someone else's turn to command?

But apparently not; whether Captain King was impressed by his previous performance, or simply enjoyed a twisted sense of humour, remained a mystery although, again, it occurred to Woodward that Daniels was not to be trusted with such a mission.

"Nothing in sight," Balaam reported. The midshipman had the tiller and was staring into the harbour itself; this was closer than he had come the previous day, and more was being revealed with every foot. Apart from three separate quays and several galliots laid up in ordinary, Woodward could make a closer study of the town's square, flat-roofed buildings that rose up from the harbour in apparent uniformity. One might house Summers and his fellows, or they may be held further inland. Or they could all be dead: from such a distance there was no way of telling.

And there was no sign of seaward-facing batteries,

although they may still exist. The cliffs continued right up to the bay's narrow entrance and any number of lighter pieces might be concealed on their summits. The cutter was being allowed to approach the harbour itself though, and, as she crept cautiously in, another earlier sighting was confirmed.

To the west, and just inside the bay, there was definitely a structure. From their current angle, it looked partially built, although one hefty stone wall, with gaps to mark placements for heavy cannon, was already finished. Positioned so, it would only sweep an area inside the harbour, but the fire would be intense. And worse, the height must make it difficult to reach with any ship's gun. Woodward could not tell what weight of ordnance lay concealed behind those boulders, but even light shot, when sent plunging so, would be devastating.

He collected the handheld compass and took a bearing. It would be valuable information for those aboard *Viper*, providing he was able to relay it.

He exchanged a nod with Balaam; for some while the only sound had been the ripple of water at their stem and an occasional cry from an early gull. All in the cutter knew the danger they were approaching.

And the silence continued as they slipped deeper into the sheltered bay. The sun was temporarily shielded by the eastward cliff, a faint chill ran about the boat and barely a breeze gave them steerage way while the white flag set on the cutter's foremast fluttered listlessly. Woodward considered setting the men to work at the sweeps before deciding against it; they were in no specific rush; it would be better to conserve their strength should a hasty retreat be necessary. Instead, he continued to examine his surroundings. To the west, an industrial quay with a variety of commercial buildings, hoists and a primitive dockyard was being revealed, while the town that lay to the south could now be seen in greater detail. If the prisoners were housed there, finding them would be almost impossible; even if they sent a force ashore, the narrow streets might have been designed with ambush in mind.

Other than the batteries high above, there was no sign of a military presence. On the industrial quay a group of dockyard workers were unloading a small cart while, deeper into the town, brightly dressed civilians could be made out, although no one paid the cutter any particular attention and they eased further into the bay unchallenged.

The sun was now rising above the eastern cliff; slowly the harbour and all about became flooded with light. Woodward's attention returned to the construction on the western cliffs. A string of carts could be seen on the summit. They were probably being drawn by slave or convict labour; a practice common in much of the civilised world. Truly there was little to distinguish the pirate's lair from a thousand other small harbours.

"Definitely up to something there," Balaam said, following his gaze.

The midshipman was right, Woodward could now see more of the batteries themselves; a further emplacement was under construction on the upper level but that directly below appeared finished. And now he could properly gauge the size of the bay, he realised neither could be reached by the guns of a normal warship. The lower battery was manned, he could see figures and the mouths of heavy cannon peeped through the embrasures. A warship subjected to fire from such a position would be in mortal danger, although at that moment Woodward had another question in mind. Would those cannon be used on smaller fry, such as a naval cutter?

* * *

King was watching from *Viper's* quarterdeck; Manton had brought the frigate in closer than before and discovered Woodward's channel; now she lay, hove to and broadside on to the harbour, as a hundred pairs of eyes followed their cutter's progress.

"She's well in," the first lieutenant reported, lowering the deck glass for a moment. "And so far, there appears to be no response from the shore."

King's personal glass was in his pocket, but the foreshortened instrument was less powerful. And if the pirates decided to fire on Woodward's boat, he had no wish to witness it.

"Wait, she's altering course!"

King could see as much with his bare eyes. The cutter was now under oars and steering to starboard, presumably in response to a signal from the shore. He watched as the boat turned broadside on before disappearing behind the western headland.

And then there was nothing. Robbed of their subject, the watchers turned to each other and began muttered conversations. Cooper lowered his telescope once more and glanced hopefully at his captain. But King looked away; the boat could be heading for anything; the elderly Quaker might have made progress, right now he and the prisoners may be waiting on some unseen quay to be collected: he could be reunited with Aimée within the hour. Or Woodward may be heading for an ambush; in the same time another eighteen might be added to those held prisoner, or they could all be dead. Whatever the outcome, they would have to wait to discover it, and King was not in the mood for pointless discussion.

* * *

No individual word could be made out, although they were definitely being hailed and the robed figure ashore was now beckoning, so Woodward did not hesitate in ordering the boat across. There were four men in the small group, and none appeared to be armed while a wrapped bundle lay before them on the wharf. With the nearest cover a good way off, the lieutenant did not think his men would be in any greater danger. There may be marksmen nearby, and this was a hostile harbour, yet if the enemy had wanted them sunk, they would have fired by now.

The cutter fairly danced across the still water, though by the time it drew near, the wharf was deserted, all that remained was the package. And it was a large one, wrapped in heavy cloth.

"Might be anything," Balaam said as they approached. "Bolt of silk, or maybe foodstuff?"

Woodward didn't know, although he was mildly encouraged. Chances were strong it would be nothing more than a gesture – an offering perhaps; the forerunner to negotiations. But the very fact that something had been presented meant the pirates were willing to communicate; a faintest glimmer of hope that this might not all end in bloodshed.

"Give me the helm," he told the midshipman as they drew closer. "Then take a couple of hands and investigate."

The lad nodded and singled out Lesley and Corke; the men were stationed at the bows and shipped their oars early while the hand pulling stroke slowed the pace. Then Woodward pressed the tiller across, and the boat drew up against the wharf. But instead of stepping ashore the midshipman froze, before turning back to Woodward with a look of raw horror.

"It's the old man," he said. "The Quaker who..."

Woodward had begun to suspect something on those lines so was more disgusted than shocked. "Is he dead?" he asked.

The lad shook his head. "No, alive. At least I think so, I can see movement." He looked back briefly for confirmation. "And they've wrapped him in some sort of skin."

Chapter Twenty-Two

"I must admit I was wrong and assumed too much," Caleb Palmer confessed when he had been seen by the surgeon and allowed to clean himself up. "Most of all I believed that, though we are of different faiths, a common thread would bind us."

King had ordered Palmer brought to the great cabin where he and Cooper awaited him but, despite their need for information, the man was deeply shocked and this was not the time to press questions. It was even doubtful if he would have answered; Hannah had been with her father since they recovered him from the cutter, and her presence was the only one he seemed to register.

"William Penn had it best," the old man continued. "You will remember his letter to Lord Arlington when imprisoned in the Tower? *'The humble, meek, merciful, just, pious and devout souls are everywhere of one religion...'*"

"*...and when death has taken off the mask, they will know one another,*" Hannah Palmer continued, "*though the diverse liveries they wear here makes them strangers...'*"

King and Cooper exchanged glances.

"Here, father." The girl held up a china cup. "Take a little more of this tea, it will restore you."

"I gather you were able to speak with the bey?" King enquired gently.

Palmer turned and apparently noticed both officers for the first time. "The bey?" he asked. "Yes, I saw and spoke with him."

"And was there progress?" Cooper this time.

"News of Peter perhaps?" Hannah added.

"No," Palmer waved the cup aside. "No news of Peter, no progress at all. I failed on every count. The man's trust lies in material things and, while he might play at being the devout disciple, I fear the god he worships is man made and of this earth. In short, I looked for a light, though it were too well hid."

"You must not take on so," his daughter soothed while King and Cooper shifted uneasily. "You have done your best and can do

229

no more."

"I believe that to be the case, my dear." The man's eyes returned to the officers. "And now these gentlemen must do their worst."

* * *

The words acted like a benediction; at last, King felt free to act as his instincts demanded and he fled from the great cabin with a bemused Cooper trailing in his wake. Then, once on the quarterdeck, there was suddenly no time to waste. Daniels was officer of the watch; King approached him as Cooper finally caught up.

"Clear for action and beat to quarters," he snapped. "I want both cutters and the launch in the water and have Mr Duke join me this instant!"

The air was filled with shrill pipes, guttural bellows and the rumble of feet as all began to turn *Viper* into a true ship of war. Marine Captain Duke appeared, mildly dishevelled and in an unbuttoned tunic although the salute he gave was smart and there was a keen glint in his eye.

"Summon your men," King ordered. "They will be going ashore, probably in the launch, though I cannot be certain. Be ready to disembark on my command; you and your lieutenants will be accompanying them." Another salute then King was seeking out Daniels once more. The lieutenant would have an important job to do, and King would rather have given it to someone else, but commissioned officers were few; Woodward was needed at the guns, and Cooper on the quarterdeck.

"Mr Daniels, we shall be towing *Viper* into attack, and you will be in overall charge of the boats. See them manned with rowing crews and a midshipman; all are to be armed." King could see the look of confusion give way to partial understanding but there was no time to explain further. Others must be briefed, and the second lieutenant was already leaving to take up his station in the waist.

"Mr Woodward; a word if you please."

Woodward turned on his heel and appeared far more ready for instruction. "You remain confident the central channel will accommodate our draught?"

"I am, sir," the young officer met his captain's eye with reassuring certainty.

"And of the westward battery?"

"I believe the lower level to be armed and manned, sir. There is another under construction above though that should be no danger to us. And, of course, there might be others I did not detect..."

"Then we shall have to find them out. The first: can it be reached with our cannon?"

"No, sir. Not if we are to remain in the channel I observed; the harbour entrance is narrow and the basin itself small and may shallow." Woodward clearly hated to disappoint his captain, yet recognised King was only interested in the truth. "There was no time to check the depth elsewhere; it is possible *Viper* will become confined."

For a second the marine captain's warning came back to King; this may well be a trap but that would also have to be discovered.

"Mr Palmer claims the harbour is used by the pirate frigate," he said. "If this Visser fellow can manoeuvre her there is every chance we will also."

"And we may be able to, sir, though, as I have said, the harbour is small, and repeat, we cannot stand off sufficiently for our guns to reach that battery."

It was not what King wanted to hear and the doubts remained although at least Woodward was not trying to sugar-coat the problem.

"Might a landing party reach the enemy's guns?"

"That is possible, sir, though it would be quite a climb..."

King looked across to the cliffs; how long would it take for marines to scale such a height? And how many shots would *Viper* have to withstand before they did?

"Very good," he said at last. "We shall have to see what can be done."

Woodward paused for a moment and may have been intending to speak. Then he changed his mind, saluted, and was gone. King turned to the sailing master.

"Mr Manton, as soon as we are cleared for action, I'd like tops'ls and stays'ls set." The wind was from the east and

231

reasonable though likely to fade as they entered the harbour mouth, which was his reason for preparing the boats. "And station two reliable hands in the forechannels with leads; we may need to feel our way."

Woodward's obvious concern remained with him but King had other matters to consider, and Cooper was waiting. "I'd rather this were done yesterday, Jack," he said.

"Of course, sir. Nevertheless, we needed to give the old boy a chance."

"And I wish he'd been successful. If the bey were willing to negotiate it would have saved much."

"And been a more certain outcome," Cooper agreed. "As it is we shall have to take what we want by force."

King looked across and into the harbour itself; at such a distance the individual buildings merged into one vast expanse of brown stone that spread over much of the hillside. Behind one of those dull walls would be Aimée, along with the others they had come for. To find them at all would be hard enough, and then he must see them out of the hands of their captors and safe aboard *Viper*.

Now he was confronted with the task it seemed impossible and, yet again, he wondered if the old Quaker had been right. No specific funds had been made available although every ship on independent deployment carried a reasonable sum in specie. It may be enough to tame a madman and buy the time necessary to raise more from his private fortune.

But no, they must act. Now Palmer's efforts had failed, King had to demonstrate their show of force was more than just a sham. To do otherwise would be an admission of defeat and only attract ridicule and contempt, both from his fellow officers and those who held Aimée. Battery or no battery, *Viper* must attack, and the town would have to be destroyed, even if it meant the death of those closest to him.

* * *

232

The mood in their cell had lifted considerably; all apparently sensed the day would bring changes and, though some might not be for the best, they would still be welcomed. For it was equally acknowledged that an end to their misery – any end – was needed.

And it was generally assumed *Viper* would be entering the bay, although Aimée had been expecting nothing less since the ship was first sighted. Thomas was close by; she could almost sense his presence. And he would be coming to get her – to save her. The concept stirred both longing and trepidation for whether he would like what he found would be another matter entirely.

For a great deal had happened since they parted and there was so much – almost too much – to explain. Some, like that she was no longer carrying his child – and never had been – would be relatively easy, and the only element that could be laid directly at her door. But even ignoring every other indignity and humiliation, the time she had spent in the current conditions would be enough to sully her in the eyes of many men.

Aimée looked about the crowded room, at the squalor, the depravity that had so quickly become normal and accepted by them all. That day's ration of beans had been distributed earlier although her's remained untouched and unwanted in her hand. She understood Thomas better than most, and knew him to be both stubborn and insensitive, yet still she wanted no other man. But if, by some miracle, they were reunited, and should he ever get to hear her story and see how she had lived, would he still want her?

* * *

The channel was proving sufficient; *Viper* had reached the edge of the harbour with several fathoms of water beneath her keel. And neither was there fire from the shore, which meant they could surely discount any seaward-facing batteries. King hoped the good fortune would continue as he could now see deeper into the bay, and it was both narrower and smaller than he imagined.

"Those in the boats can take up the slack," he said. "And you may strike our canvas."

Manton touched his hat before turning, out of politeness, to bellow and King caught Cooper's eye.

"Peaceful enough for now, Jack."

"Indeed, sir, though I fancy it will not stay that way. Mr Woodward's battery has yet to be fully sighted."

The fact had not been forgotten, yet King remained determined and strangely optimistic. He still found it hard to believe any nation would be foolish enough to equip an enemy with heavy weapons. For all any of them knew, the cannon Woodward reported were no more than sham pieces – wooden barrelled affairs made to intimidate an enemy – and there was irony in fact that the common name for these was Quakers. But even if the pirates were conventionally armed, they would surely have placed their weapons pointing seaward, to defend the port, in which case *Viper* would be under fire at that moment. Besides, Woodward mentioned the inner battery was only partly built, so it may prove inactive while, as to the size of the harbour, he felt he understood his command well enough to manoeuvre her in the tightest of spaces.

For King was dead set on attacking; he had waited a long time for this moment and was not going to be put off by groundless fears or phantom gun emplacements. *Viper* was drawing closer with every breath, soon she would be in the harbour proper and he could finally see for himself and take positive action.

"Cliffs appear a deal higher than I expected," Cooper remarked as they passed into the shade of the nearest. "Though that is a common illusion, I gather."

"Of course," King muttered, although he too was surprised; the rock off their larboard beam was almost level with their mainmast cap. Were there truly ordnance mounted inside the bay it would prove more than inconvenient. Yet so far, the enemy was staying quiet and with luck that might continue. *Viper* was now under tow and her boats were setting a fair pace, in no time they would discover if the inner battery were fact or fiction.

* * *

There was no rest for Stokes and his men. Despite having a British frigate close by, work on the upper battery continued and they were making that morning's second trip with the cart when *Viper* began to nose her way through the harbour mouth.

Longdon was the first to see her; "Now there's a sight," he

234

said, as the ship made a stately entrance.

"Never thought Old Tommo would chance it," Stokes confessed; the cart was stopped, as were all in the line, but their guards appeared equally fascinated by the warship's arrival. Those manning the lower battery had noticed her as well and, goaded by an officer, a stream of robed men were making for the cannon mounted there.

"Will you look at 'em?" Bovey scoffed. "Runnin' about like a flock of 'eadless chickens."

The group watched in silence as wild yells filled the air; some of the gunners had even drawn their swords, presumably to do battle with a ship more than a hundred feet below.

"'Eadless chickins don't make such a din," Longdon grunted.

"You'd think they'd never seen a proper enemy before," Lovemore agreed.

"Aye, though brave enough when it comes to 'andin' out a floggin'."

"They're clearin' away the cannon," Stokes pointed out. "Won't come as a pleasant surprise, not to them aboard the barky."

All considered this for a moment, and then the first gun spoke.

Its discharge echoed around the bay for a good five seconds, before another added to the din and another shortly after that.

Stokes looked to the nearest of their guards who, feeling his eyes upon him, turned. There was a babble of indecipherable orders, and the man gestured threateningly.

"Looks like he wants us to move," Stokes muttered as the guard's tanned hand now closed about his sword.

"What do you reckon, lads?" the seaman asked quietly. "Think we should try an' stop 'em?"

"We ain't armed," Bovey replied, equally soft. "And there's only the four of us."

"More along the line," Longdon pointed out and the rest grunted in agreement. Dressed so basically and after weeks of backbreaking work, only faded tattoos distinguished the other prisoners as seamen. But however harsh their treatment since, years of hard work had made their bodies strong and some residual strength would remain.

235

"Not many of 'em is British," Bovey said.

"Maybe, though they all hate the 'Turks'," Stokes countered. "And most will know that ship is their only means of escape; I reckons they'll come alongside us soon enough."

"It's worth a shot," Lovemore agreed. "What have we to lose?"

* * *

"Would this be your first action, Mr Balaam?" Lieutenant Woodward's question was almost formal. They had seen the great guns cleared away and the crews were standing ready but, until *Viper* fully entered the harbour, there was little for any of them to do. The midshipman shrugged and tried to look nonchalant.

"It is, sir, though there have been the drills, of course."

"Of course," Woodward agreed, "and you have performed well at each. Nevertheless, I chance you'll find this a little different; empty casks make excellent targets yet are not inclined to fire in return."

The lad felt himself blush. "Yes, sir."

"And the position will be fully reversed today," the lieutenant continued. "You remember the battery we sighted earlier in the cutter?"

Balaam gave a cautious nod.

"We'll get plenty of attention from that, I'm thinking, an' there'll be no means of reply."

The midshipman certainly did recall the battery; it was one of several memorable sights that had impressed him on his first visit inside an enemy harbour. But at the time there seemed little threat. Of more obvious danger were the bronzed faces and full beards of those ashore; the white-eyed demons that peered surreptitiously while he collected the disgusting mess they had made of an elderly gentleman.

Once the old boy was returned to the cutter, Balaam had been fully involved cutting him free of the rancid hide that was bound so tight. And when he looked again the cutter was nearing *Viper* and they were out of danger. As a result, what he remembered was not so very terrible: a line of rocks on a steep hill set high, high above. There may well have been cannon though none had fired and, considering the height, neither did they seem likely to.

"Mind you, that won't mean we shan't be busy," Lieutenant Woodward was still talking. "There'll be other targets ashore within our reach, I'd chance we shall be conducting a few modifications to their waterfront."

"Yes, sir. Do you think we'll be under fire from elsewhere?"

"Probably not. From what we saw there's no army as such, though there might be the odd potshot from an enthusiastic guard or civilian."

Balaam nodded wisely.

"Whatever, I don't think you'll be bored," Woodward added. "That one emplacement will provide enough to keep us all entertained."

* * *

The lower battery was now in plain sight from the quarterdeck. Its stonework stood exposed and even shone slightly from the fresh working while the sinister snouts of heavy artillery peeped out from its embrasures.

"Woodward was right," King muttered as he and Cooper regarded the menace.

"Aye, it appears to be manned, while there's another under construction above."

King nodded, he could see a partial wall of rocks with a succession of carts presumably adding to them. That was a long way from presenting a threat, however; it was the emplacement below that concerned him.

He lowered his gaze and looked about. The harbour itself was every bit as disheartening. It appeared as tight as Woodward described yet, were there the depth, he may still manoeuvre, though not station the ship sufficiently distant for his gunners to reach either battery. And then the enemy cannon opened fire.

The first shot was pitched short and fell harmlessly off their starboard beam, yet the tower of water it sent up was impressive in itself. The second actually hit them, although much of its energy was absorbed by the starboard bower which rang out once before being sent to the harbour bottom. But the third might have been guided by a particularly malevolent spirit; it landed plum on the frigate's forecastle, taking out one of *Viper*'s chase guns and three of its crew as well as partially penetrating the deck.

"Warm work, sir!" Cooper exclaimed though King's mind was elsewhere. They had not sounded out the harbour yet there looked to be room to turn. And turn they must; fire their guns by all means and probably cause some damage to the town, but already it was obvious they could not remain to do more.

"Message to Mr Daniels in the boats," he ordered, "he is to take us about to larboard. Mr Manton, supervise if you will."

The lad ran off and the sailing master touched his hat briefly before following at a more sedate pace, while King turned his attention back to the battery.

"I can see figures." Cooper's tone was conversational; it was strange to be able to speak so when in action, but *Viper*'s own cannon were still to fire.

"Indeed," King agreed. The men who had been hauling the carts had stopped their work and were now watching from the summit.

"They appear to be slaves." Cooper was now studying through the deck glass.

King's smaller instrument showed less, yet he could make out movement on the lower battery. Even as he watched, the guns he had hoped to be fake or poorly handled were being competently loaded, then hauled back to bear on *Viper* once again. King felt his earlier optimism fade; this was definitely not going as he had hoped.

* * *

Overpowering the guards was easy; Longdon received a minor cut to the upper arm yet, by the time that fully registered, his opponent was on the ground and had suffered far worse. Stokes calmly collected the fallen man's sword while Lovemore ripped part of his shirt into a strip which he wound about his mate's wound. There was a shout from further up; other groups of prisoners were following their example while below a pitched

238

battle was being fought in which bare hands and anger were proving superior to any single blade. All along the line, each guard was overcome, before being neatly despatched with his own weapon.

"What's next?" Lovemore asked.

"The rocks," Bovey decided. "We roll what we got down on them below; take 'em by surprise so it will – won't know what's hit 'em!"

"Chances are none of them will," Stokes countered, "but surprise is the key for certain. Come on lads!"

Chapter Twenty-Three

Viper was now under serious fire. It was as if each of the shore-based weapons was taking a turn; every twenty seconds or so another round shot plummeted from above, landing heavy on her hull and the damage was already extensive. The binnacle lay in a thousand pieces, their main topsail yard was neatly severed, the starboard forechains struck twice, and that was ignoring the numerous splits and gashes in her strakes where plunging shot caused mayhem on her crowded decks. Men had also fallen; those hit by shot usually being killed outright, though more were caught by splinters – wicked barbs of wood that could tear a limb to pieces in an instant or leave wounds that festered indefinitely. It was clear to all that such a solid, deliberate, bombardment would soon destroy the frigate, yet in such a cramped harbour there was no obvious avenue for retreat. Even turning the ship was an exercise best undertaken without distraction. Lesser commanders may already have been considering striking their flag, although the thought was far from King's mind – not when a chance remained of their hitting back.

For *Viper* soon began to give as good as she got. Though still unable to reach the shore-based cannon, her great guns could reap vengeance on the harbour installations below. So, while King and Cooper sought ways to free them of the fire from above, Lieutenant Woodward was pointing out fresh targets to his gunners and several dockside buildings already lay in ruins. These included much of the warehousing backing the wharf itself although, as Manton was preparing to see the frigate about, they would shortly be able to concentrate on the gaily blinded windows and laundry-strung streets of the residential area. And while *Viper*'s starboard guns played on the industrial buildings, her larboard cannon lobbed shots across to the eastern side of the harbour where a collection of galliots were moored. Two of the small craft were already sinking, while a third had lost a mast and another was on fire.

And throughout it all, King's self-reproach was steadily

growing. He had been a fool and should have listened more carefully; Woodward had warned about the batteries, as well as the harbour's size, the latter being barely sufficient to turn a sloop, let alone a thirty-two gun frigate. The one advantage lay in the depth; both leadsmen forward were reporting a good four fathoms and with *Viper* drawing a little over two, there was room to spare. Manton was bringing her as close to the western wharf as he dared, and they should make the turn in one. Whether that good fortune stayed with them on the other side of the bay was still to be seen, but if this truly were the base of another French-built frigate, it must be worth a try.

And then another thought occurred: Visser may turn up at any moment. For the past two days the prospect of the pirate appearing had not been far from King's mind. Supposing the Dutchman's ship was to come into sight now, while they were trapped in her own lair? *Viper* was already weakened, by the time she made good her escape what remained would quickly fall victim to such a vessel. But there was little point in thinking so, Manton was already bringing them about, and Woodward had just released yet another broadside, reducing a well-to-do warehouse with lifting tackle and a loading chute to rubble.

In desperation he glanced up at his tormentors; the battery was continuing to release regular, paced shots and doing so with remarkable accuracy. Then movement above caught his attention.

The men gathered on the summit were starting to descend. Like children on a day's outing, they tumbled down the steep slope, slipping occasionally though making good speed. And as he watched he saw the first arrive. Arrive and land, physically, on one team of gunners. King turned to comment to Cooper, but the first lieutenant was watching also and let out a gentle oath.

"Looks like there is help from above," he said.

"I was thinking the same myself." Another shore-based cannon was despatched, but it may have been fired in haste as the shot fell wide and short. Cooper was now looking directly at his captain.

"Prisoners, do you think, sir?" he asked.

"I do," King said. "And would chance those we have come for."

* * *

Stokes and his men were indeed descending the short steep hill. It was the first time any had run so in weeks, their energy having solely been expended in brute strength. And though it had been a period of almost constant exhaustion, the sudden exercise enlivened them, and they felt ready – eager – for action.

Which followed almost instantly; the gun crews were set on serving their weapons and had no eyes for an enemy attacking from behind. One cannon fired as Lovemore arrived and he threw himself onto those tending the warm beast. He landed on the back of one, tearing the light cloth of the gunner's loose shirt and adding a hefty punch into the man's kidneys, an act that brought an agreeable grunt of pain from his victim.

Though wounded, Longdon, proved as effective and, armed with their former guard's sword, accounted for two more. And Stokes was only slightly behind; targeting the same team, he drove his fist into the face of a startled gunner, forcing the man backwards and adding a kick for good measure as he fell.

Bovey was more thoughtful; he arrived slightly behind his colleagues and, on noticing the gunners' swords left piled to one side, grabbed one. With the weapon in hand, he took a hesitant swing; the perfectly balanced blade flew with a reassuring swish, and he immediately addressed the nearest enemy. This turned out to be a heavily built monster who was laying in to one of the foreign prisoners. Bovey was accustomed to the axe-like hacking of a boarding cutlass so when the sword sliced through the air, then the man, with unbelievable ease, he was oddly elated and turned in search of more game. A further cannon was fired, its roar bringing the shortest of pauses before the fight resumed with even greater energy.

And the other prisoners had followed. Encouraged by such an example, and bonded by a common hatred, seamen from many nations joined as one to fight back against their oppressors. The stash of weapons was quickly discovered and so denied their owners; soon any pirate left unharmed was stumbling down the incline in a desperate attempt at escape. In minutes they were in total command of the battery, while the place itself had taken on the appearance of an active shambles.

"So, what now, Stokie?" Longdon panted; despite his wound, the seaman had accounted for himself well and had a blood-smeared blade to prove it. Stokes shrugged.

"Don't feel like leaving these fellas." He patted the warm barrel next to him.

"There's no one about," Bovey said. "Anyone who could 'as made a run for it."

At that moment there was a rumble from the harbour below; *Viper* had released another broadside and a little more of the dockyard was demolished. A prisoner from another group approached and addressed them in French.

"He's askin' what we're planning," Lovemore, who had a reasonable tongue, explained. "Seems like you've been appointed leader," he grinned.

Stokes assessed the situation; there were twenty of them in all and about twice that number would be working the quarry. Below them, *Viper* released her larboard broadside and a third galliot began to settle. But the frigate was being turned, for all any of them knew this was just a spontaneous strike, something to soften up the pirates before negotiation. She might be gone in no time, and then they would be rounded up and put to work again. Or worse. Yet, if they were to try for freedom there was one thing they must do first.

"We have to wreck this battery," he said.

"Wreck it?" Bovey pulled at his chin; each heavy cannon must weigh upwards of two tons and were securely attached to the stone embrasures. "And how we gonna do that?"

"Hand me one of them dirks."

Some of the gunners had carried short, ornamental daggers in their waistbands. Longdon retrieved one from a nearby corpse and passed it to his friend and all watched as Stokes examined the piece. Then, grasping the hilt, the seaman inserted the point into a touchhole. The narrow blade went deep and, once stuck firm, Stokes bent the weapon to one side until there was an audible snap. A murmur passed about the group and Stokes looked up in triumph.

"Maybe not as good as a regular spike," he said, "but it'll keep 'em busy a while – time enough to see *Viper* clear of the harbour at least."

"Never mind them lot, what about us?" Bovey demanded. "'Turks'll know someone's silenced the batteries, they'll be comin' for us."

"We'll be leaving on the barky," Stokes stated as he

continued to look down at the ship.

"Down there?" Longdon regarded the steep decline doubtfully.

"Won't be so bad," Stokes said with more confidence than he felt.

"An' the heathens managed it," Lovemore agreed; already the pirates that had fled were halfway down the savage slope.

"An' the others?" Bovey again; Stokes turned to Lovemore.

"Tell the frogs to come with us. Say they'll be welcomed aboard and safe." Next, he nodded at the Americans. "Same applies to you Jonathans."

Longdon was still considering the drop with uncertainty. "You reckons we can make it?" he asked.

"There speaks an upper yardsman!" Lovemore mocked.

"This is different," his tie mate insisted. "No tackle, nothin' you can rely upon." He rubbed a bare foot on the crumbling soil. "An' I'm wounded," he added.

"We're leaving on the barky," Stokes repeated. "All of us, which will mean headin' down that slope. Ask me, the main problem will be stoppin' but the sooner we starts, the sooner we finish."

* * *

Viper was halfway through her turn and lay broadside on to the town proper.

"Deep water anchorage for sure," Cooper commented, and King could only agree. How such a fine natural harbour had been neglected so was a mystery. It was hardly generous, admittedly, but as a base for small raiders, ideal. If the pirates had been allowed to fortify it properly, the place would have been almost impregnable. "And a fair-sized town," the first officer continued.

King supposed Cooper was correct there as well. The streets were narrow and though most individual buildings modest, they covered much of the hillside. Towards the top, the tower that had been part of their transit bearing stood out against a cloudless sky, with the second reference, the copper-domed building, slightly below. Closer to, and within reach of their guns, lay a single-storey structure that looked more industrial. With tiny slit windows set high on the stone walls, it might be for storage, manufacture or stabling and was the only non-residential building in sight.

Now they were no longer being bothered by the battery, an air of tense calm had settled over the frigate. She had already suffered significant damage and lost several of her crew though this was clearly not an end to the action, merely an hiatus. For *Viper*'s guns were also silent; her larboard broadside now faced the harbour entrance and the open water beyond, although several prime galliots had felt its might and now lay level with the water or deep beneath it. And her starboard cannon were equally quiet – King called a halt when the last of the warehouses was flattened as, apart from that one building, what lay before them now was very obviously residential.

In his current mood, he cared little about subjecting a civilian target to the stiffest of bombardments: with Aimée in danger, there were no such things as non-combatants. Still, common sense, helped in no small way by Caleb Palmer, had convinced him doing so would waste a valuable bargaining point.

The old Quaker was with them now and had been since the guns ceased to fire. King turned to him.

"So, what think you?" he asked. "Do we wait and see what those ashore propose, or take the initiative and land?"

Palmer gave a rare smile. "I am surely the last to consult on military strategy," he said. "Though suspect your point has been made with the destruction of those dockside buildings. I'd chance there'll be a delegation afore long, if you are prepared to wait."

And that was the question; the battery that had plagued them was silent for now yet might spring back to life at any moment while the threat of Visser's frigate returning remained ever-present.

Woodward was looking up from the waist, clearly waiting for the order to continue and King was sorely tempted; perhaps a single broadside, to demonstrate the power the ship still contained? That warehouse lay in easy reach and would be satisfying to demolish. Then Cooper interrupted with a shout.

"There's movement ashore!" he said, pointing to a ramshackle group of barely dressed men. They came hobbling and stumbling across the hard from the direction of the ruined dock and for a moment King thought them survivors from his attack. But some of *Viper*'s hands quickly recognised their own and took to shouting and waving.

"That's Lovemore," Cooper confirmed, pointing at a curly-haired figure. "And, if I'm not mistaken, Stokes."

King singled out the marine captain. "Mr Duke, prepare to land your men. I want a bridgehead established on the hard. Once that is done you are to supervise the embarkation of those prisoners."

Duke saluted then set to with commendable efficiency; in no time the marines were ready to disembark. Even if the bey was planning to send a delegation, it would do no harm to create a military presence on land. King summoned a messenger.

"My compliments to Mr Manton. He is to verify the depth and, if feasible, bring us alongside."

The lad repeated King's message then made off. The crowd of half-dressed men had reached the ship now and some were preparing to receive a line.

"If that's all the seamen, part of our job here is done," Cooper said.

"Indeed," King agreed. "Now we need only find the rest..."

* * *

It was Summers' turn to support Peter Palmer on his shoulders, and they were not alone at the windows, a pair of French officers had claimed another, while Bewley was suffering the not inconsiderable weight of Captain Goodman. Behind them, all waited in tense anticipation.

"Looks like your ship," Palmer said. "At least it's the one we saw earlier outside the harbour."

"Aye, that's *Viper* for sure," Goodman grunted. "I'd know them lines anywhere. She's taking soundings and seems intent on picking up a berth alongside."

"Where exactly is she?" Summers asked. Peter Palmer was lighter than him, and it was only fair that they took turns, although he would have given much to see.

"Broadside on an' just abeam of us, though not yet

246

secured."

"So, she can move at any time?"

"That's about it," Goodman agreed. "An' if there's going to be a repeat of what was done to the dockside warehouses, I hope she goes quick. Entire area is flattened, and them what caused it lie less than a cable off; I'd hate for us to be next."

Summers pursed his lips; a lot would depend on Captain King and his state of mind. He well remembered the black moods that plagued him when they were returning to England aboard *Tenacious*. Worry for his family almost took the man over and, now his lady was being held hostage, it must be as bad if not worse. However, the captain wouldn't know where she was, or how vulnerable they all were from his ship's broadside.

"If only we had some way of signalling," he muttered.

"We might show some cloth," Goodman supposed, "though goodness knows, we have little enough for ourselves."

Summers shook his head. "I can't see what good that would do; even if noticed by *Viper*, they could make little of it."

"Can you see movement?" Bewley was continuing to support the American captain. "Aboard the ship, I'm meaning."

"Nothing from that quarter," Goodman replied. "Though there's a bunch of slaves making for her."

"Slaves?"

He shrugged. "Or prisoners I guess, though I can't say I recognise any. Wait, I believe the ship's now fully alongside."

This was frustrating in the extreme; it was all Summers could do to keep still long enough to let the American look.

"Any sign of guards?" he asked.

"Nope, reckon they're keepin' their heads down." Palmer this time. "I know I would in their place."

Summers sighed, that might be the case, although the pirates would have to negotiate eventually. Otherwise, Captain King was liable to start firing again.

"And what's happening now?"

"Your soldier boys are comin' ashore and right pretty they looks too," Palmer chuckled.

"And the prisoners?"

"The *prisonniers* are being 'elped aboard ze ship." It was one of the French officers. "Zey include zome of my men."

"I see a few familiar faces now as well," Goodman again.

"And most are in one hell of a state. Let's hope your captain don't think his job's done."

"*Oui*," the Frenchman agreed. "With the *prisonniers* on board, 'e might start shooting once more."

"I don't think so." Summers' words carried more confidence than he felt. "He knows about us and wouldn't be so foolish."

"Maybe," Palmer said. "But he has no idea where we are. And right now our little homestead lies right beneath his guns."

* * *

"They're prisoners sure enough," Cooper announced when he had made his way back from the waist, "and a mixed bag, with quite a few foreigners, though some of our men as well."

"From the prize?" King demanded.

"It would seem so, sir."

Cooper drew breath; their own people were in the minority; he had met with far more French and Americans. Still, the condition of all had affected him deeply; even the strangers were in a shocking state.

Wounds from both hard work and beatings were obvious, and everyone was woefully undernourished while the few that he knew – what should have been familiar faces – seemed little more than shadows of their usual selves. And the journey down from the cliff had proved the last straw for some; several were leaning on their comrades for support and in others the first signs of hysteria was apparent.

"Were there any women amongst them?" King's tone was oddly cold.

"No, sir."

"...or officers?"

"I'm afraid not." Cooper was finding returning to reality a considerable effort. "All appear to be general hands or marines; I cannot speak for the foreigners."

"Foreigners?"

The lieutenant paused, wondering how much of his previous statement his captain had taken in. "There are French and American amongst them," he repeated. "Those from the schooner's original crew and I gather some who served with Mr Palmer's son, though he is not present."

"You are sure?"

"His father was with me when they came aboard."

Cooper supposed King must have failed to notice the old Quaker leave the deck, while there was something in his captain's expression that worried him greatly.

"From what I understand the officers and women were separated," he continued, "though we may learn more shortly. Our men will report to you as soon as Mr Manning is finished."

"Never mind, I will go to them," King turned and was about to quit the quarterdeck when something made him pause. "Remain on deck, Jack, and send for me if anything happens. Though if the pirates appear in force, I trust you to take the appropriate action."

"Very good, sir,"

Cooper went to salute, but King had already gone. He looked to the hard; Duke and his marines were commandeering a collection of barrels and crates and taking station behind them while anxious faces peered out from windows in the nearby houses. Every street was empty, though, and there was no sign of pirates or any military units. And then it occurred to him that, if any should appear, either as a delegation or in force to attack the ship, he had no idea what the appropriate action would be.

Chapter Twenty-Four

On clearing for action, much of the orlop had been turned into a temporary sickbay and the low, dark space was almost filled with wounded. Yet King was quick to notice that, rather than the victims of action, most of those lying on the canvas-covered deck were uncommonly decent, with barely a trace of gore or any of the grisly wounds he usually found so disturbing. That did not mean they were fit, however; even as he searched amongst the barely clad bodies, King could not suppress a growing pity. All were emaciated, and some had the glint of madness in their eyes, although each one was undoubtedly relieved to have found this place of safety. Then something about one of the recumbent figures caught his attention and he looked closer. The face bore an uncanny resemblance to a skull, yet there was also a familiarity about it, and he lowered himself to speak to the man.

"It's good to see you, Stokes," he said.

"Glad to be back in the barky, sir," the seaman told him.

"How many of you are there?"

"From the original lot? Just a handful. Lovemore's hereabouts, probably still with the sawbones... beggin' your pardon, Mr Manning. Bovey an' Longdon made it back an all, though I've not seen them for a while – not since we started down the hill, an' Longers was wounded an' all."

King supposed Stokes and his men were responsible for silencing the battery and would have questioned further, if other matters had not been more pressing.

"And what of the rest?" he demanded.

"The seamen, sir?"

King shook his head. "The officers – and my lady in particular."

"Can't help you much there I'm afraid, your honour. Prize was taken by a corsair frigate an' a well-manned one at that. The buggers stole everything we had, then separated the officers and women."

"And where did they go?" Stokes was plainly close to

exhaustion, yet the man must know more; even a clue to Aimée's whereabouts would be welcomed.

"Last time I sees them they were being 'erded into the town; there's no telling where they ended up, though I wouldn't give much for their chances."

"I see." King swallowed. "And yourselves, how were you treated?"

"Terrible, your honour." This was Longdon, the man must have been dismissed by the surgeon and now wore a bandage over much of his left arm. "No clothing, nor food to speak of an' treated worse than slaves so we were."

"I'm sorry to hear of it," King said, although his mind was elsewhere. "And you have no idea where the others can be found?"

"Not seen them since the day we landed, sir," Longdon confirmed. "But like Stokie says, I wouldn't be holdin' out no hopes."

"Captain, sir!" It was Cooke, one of the new midshipmen. "Mr Cooper reports a large body of armed men approaching. Mr Duke has formed his men up and they're ready to open fire."

"Very well, I'll come." Then, to Stokes, "You've done well, both of you. I'm sure Mr Manning's team will see you fed and cared for."

"Thankee, sir," Stokes said, knuckling his forehead, although King was already making for the companionway.

* * *

And once on deck he had no chance to think further. After the darkness of the orlop, the early afternoon sun burnt his eyes, yet even that could be ignored in his rush to discover what was about.

"Appears to be a delegation," Cooper said, pointing over the side to the nearby land.

King looked; Duke's marines were lined up behind their barricades with bayonets fixed and muskets held at the ready, while before them a group of robed figures stood fingering their swords.

"The man in white is their leader." It was Palmer, King turned his way.

"You know of him?"

"Name of Mehmed. He captained the boat that collected me, then saw me imprisoned in the palace and finally had me trussed up in that cow skin; I'd say I know him quite well." The words were spoken without a hint of condemnation.

"Then perhaps you wish to meet again?"

Palmer looked doubtful.

"I intend to speak with his ruler," King explained. "And then, if necessary, take my companion – and your son – by force. Providing that does not offend your principles, that is..."

"I have already tried my way," Palmer sighed. "And though I still consider it the right one, am prepared to accept there may be another."

"Then I would appreciate your joining with me, and we shall see what can be achieved together."

* * *

"Now it looks like they're talking," Summers was taking a turn on Peter Palmer's shoulders and matters had moved on since he was last able to look.

"Just talking?" the young man enquired.

"That's all I can see." It was annoying that the American should ask questions; his job was to give support. "Looks like your father's there."

"My father?" Palmer repeated.

"Hey, steady!" Summers gripped the sharp ledge of the window until his prop grew still.

"Why don't we try shouting?" Bewley asked. Somehow the loblolly boy had been persuaded to continue supporting Goodman.

"It's a thought, though they're a fair way off."

"And the windows are too darn small," Summers agreed.

"It vood also raise ze guard," a French officer at the third window added.

"We have to do something." The voice came from the floor and must belong to Williams, the injured midshipman. Summers glanced down; since the wound became infected the lad had been almost silent when awake, although his night-time groans could be unbearable to hear. "Unless they know where we are they might

252

do anything."

That was undoubtedly the case; Summers remembered Captain King setting about that schooner on their return from the North American Station. If the heathens denied holding further prisoners or prevaricated in any way, there was no telling how he might react. And their cell remained directly under *Viper*'s guns.

"I'd think it worth the try," he said. "If we all shout together..."

"Vot do we shout?" The Frenchman asked.

"Name of a ship," Goodman replied. "It's what every sailor hollers in a pickle." He turned to look at Summers. "An' seein' as yours is close by, I guess it'd better be *Viper*."

Summers still felt it unlikely Captain King would hear, though they would all feel better doing something other than watching in impudent silence.

"*Viper, Viper, Viper!*"

His feeble efforts were soon bolstered by others until the entire cell was echoing with the word. Even Millie ceased her complaining to join in, and Summers felt more alive than at any time since his capture.

He continued to stare out of the window, but there was no change; their efforts were being lost or perhaps masked by other sounds closer by. They continued to chant, however, and, though the blood rushed about his head, and he began to feel physically weak, their efforts were growing louder. And then another noise interrupted; one they had heard a hundred times and even greeted in the past. Yet now when the door was opened there was a sudden hush.

A familiar guard strode into the crowded room and glowered at them with angry eyes. And rather than carrying a bucket of meal or water, he held a drawn sword. It was a particularly evil-looking blade that glinted in the poor light and, as he swung it easily in his hands, the man's skill – and intent – was obvious.

* * *

253

King had never cared much for marines; their stiff discipline and automaton-like drill were poles apart from the demeanour of the average lower-deck seaman, many of whom were also able to think for themselves. Still, he was glad of their presence and, as he stood on the hard within the solid ranks of redcoats, felt safer than when aboard his own ship. Something of this must have communicated to the robed figure opposite. The man was exquisitely dressed and well supported by the line of heavily armed fighters standing behind. But, though both groups were similar in size, there was something verging on the apologetic in his opponent's stance which King quickly picked up on.

"Why have you come here?" the figure asked. "Why have you destroyed our fine dockyard?"

"That is definitely Mehmed," Palmer whispered. "I believe him to be an advisor to the Bey."

"I represent His Majesty King George," King bellowed. "He has sent me to retrieve that which was stolen from him."

"Then your master must treat with Ali bey ben Hamoudad and pay the usual respects; it is the way of things."

"I'll have no truck with such nonsense." King's anger was rising steadily and went into his words. "You have offended my sovereign as well as the president of America so must face the consequences."

Mehmed stared back blankly, and King wondered if he had been fully understood. He looked to Palmer.

"When you spoke before, did he have good English?"

"The best," Palmer confirmed. "I would think him well schooled."

"I wish to speak with your master," King announced, turning back.

"Ali bey ben Hamoudad does not leave his palace."

"Then I will address him there."

Once more the look of apparent incomprehension, although this time King sensed otherwise.

"It is not possible," Mehmed began. "Ali bey ben Hamoudad does not speak with any infidel who appears on his...

"Mr Duke, if you please!"

At a word from their lieutenant, the rank of marines raised their muskets with a simultaneous click. Those facing them tensed visibly, and some stepped back while Mehmed's face turned a

254

shade closer to that of his robes.

"My men are ready to fire," King said. "And when they do, you will die. You will all die. And then I will march on your master's palace. But either way, I will speak with Ali bey ben Hamoudad within the hour. You may choose how this is achieved."

* * *

Summers slipped down from Palmer's shoulders but continued to watch the guard. The man was staring about the crowded room with eyes wide and white, while his sword made slow, gentle sweeps from side to side. At any moment he might attack – lay into one or more of them – and then there would be carnage indeed. Of course, they could react and overpower the fellow. Summers knew no plan would be needed for such an action; they had been imprisoned for long enough, although that would not save those who fell to that terrible blade. And with rescue and freedom so tantalisingly close, it would be the final insult.

"Steady, friend!" The voice came from behind; Summers guessed it belonged to Peter Palmer. "Just take it easy and no one'll be hurt."

Summers noticed the guard's attention switch.

"Just leave us be," Palmer continued. "We won't try to leave, just want our colleagues to find us."

"'E does not speak your language," a Frenchman said.

"Maybe not," Palmer's voice remained soft and level. "But he'll get the gist."

The guard continued to stare, although his sword was sweeping slower now, and the look had softened.

"Leave us be." Peter Palmer continued. "Go back to your guardhouse or, if you're sensible, get out of town. But go and go now."

* * *

255

Despite the profusion of arms and military swagger, Caleb Palmer found walking amid the detachment of marching marines oddly reassuring. He and Thomas King, the frigate's captain, were together at the centre of the column and, though faces stared from many windows, and groups of armed men gathered to watch, they made steady, unobstructed progress along the middle of the road. And Mehmed headed the procession; it was one of the captain's stipulations; he had no intention of letting the man give warning or arrange a special reception for them. Instead, Mehmed and Marine Captain Duke were leading this strange parade, with the latter obviously not prepared to take chances, as both the marine's pistol and sword were drawn. Palmer instinctively rebelled against such a show of force yet the might and precision were impressive indeed, and it was proving a far more peaceful journey to the palace than his last.

Which, he suddenly realised, only took place the previous day; a lot had happened in a remarkably short time. And having already rescued so many hostages surely augured well, although Palmer would never be satisfied until Peter was with them and sensed the captain felt similarly about his partner. Only when both were safe could their mission be called a success.

Then they were approaching the palace proper; the building lay before them, and Palmer could see the outer guards apparently panic at the approach of so many smartly dressed armed men. The gates were hurriedly closed but, at a word from Mehmed, one, then the other, was cautiously opened and the column passed through unopposed. Nevertheless, as they drew near to the main door, his concern grew. Marching down the streets had been one thing, soon they would be in the enemy's headquarters where it might not be so easy to remain secure. He turned to King.

"The palace has many corridors," he said. "I should think it ideally suited for an ambush."

"Indeed?" Captain King appeared unimpressed and may have been amused. "Mr Duke is an experienced officer," he added. "Sometimes it is better to leave matters to those who know their business."

Palmer supposed that was right. This was his first experience of military strategy after all, although he had already learned a lot. Perhaps calling a halt and discussing the matter would have been a sign of weakness.

As it was, Marine Captain Duke allowed his men to come right up to the door before stepping back and preparing to bellow. But Mehmed was ahead of him and called out in his native language. In the pause that followed King and Palmer exchanged looks, then the door was opened, and they were allowed inside.

"The bey may not be in his receiving room," Mehmed told them, looking back.

"Then we shall await him there," King snapped, and they continued into the building.

Now the danger was obvious; the passageways would not allow more than three abreast so, as the marines silently regrouped, neither Palmer, nor the captain, had escorts to either side. The column continued at the same relentless pace, however, though now with the sound of over sixty pairs of boots echoing off the stone. At times they passed the occasional armed guard, men who had been roused by the noise, then driven into doorways or adjoining passages. And again, Palmer accepted the show of force was avoiding combat, rather than encouraging it. Then they were outside another set of doors and had reached the bey's inner sanctum.

Another pause while Mehmed demanded entry, although this time only one of the doors was opened.

"The bey will only treat with officers," Mehmed's tone was firmer, as if being close to his ruler was giving him strength. "Your guards must remain outside."

Captain Duke was looking back for orders, but King did not hesitate.

"Carry on, Major."

Once more the marines moved off and the second door was roughly pushed back as they marched in. The same slight figure was seated on the dais with the same hated wooden beam also in place, along with the carpeted path that led to it. Yet rather than the line of guards to either side, the room was empty apart from the bey.

"I am Captain Thomas King of his Britannic Majesty's Ship *Viper*." The voice was loud, Palmer supposed King might have been hailing another vessel as addressing a dignitary.

"You are welcome, Captain," the bey told him, and Palmer noticed those eyes flash wickedly for a second. "I assume you have brought the customary present from your sovereign?"

"I have not." King's voice was harsher still. "All you will receive from me is the destruction of your palace and town."

Again, those eyes twinkled, the bey might have been deserted by his guards, but he was not without a measure of moral courage. "You are aware that my servant is at sea, and has a vessel that can sink yours with ease? He is expected to return at any time, then we will see who makes the demands."

"In which case you will not object to my men taking you hostage," King said, and this time the bey's countenance altered dramatically. The eyes fell and lost much of their glow while the man's body slumped and suddenly appeared ridiculously small amid the ornate chair.

"There will be no need," he sighed. "What is it you require?"

Chapter Twenty-Five

HMS *Viper* was at sea though making slow progress. The damage received from the battery was greater than most originally thought, and it was clear that, had Stokes and his men not intervened, the ship could have been destroyed. As it was, many of her crew were called in to help with repairs and, under the direction of the carpenter, boatswain and other artificers, she was gradually being brought back to life. Inevitably, a good deal would have to wait until a dockyard was reached but order was slowly being re-established, and each day saw another knot added to the frigate's average speed. Still, there was no intrinsic rush to raise Gibraltar. Those spared work – the near skeletons who were so recently held as slaves or hostages – had much to recover from while even King and his fellow officers welcomed the chance to take stock.

And it was good for him to be back with Aimée. At first, the sight of her emaciated face had been shocking, and it was all he could do to look her in the eye as she was taken to their quarters. With Millie in an even worse state, it naturally fell to him to look after her; something he was keen to do, despite Aimée pulling back and seeming reluctant to stay in his presence. Yet, with a patience and sensitivity that would have surprised many, King gradually won back her confidence and soon she was relying on his care. With the damaged ship now overburdened with sick and hurt, Robert Manning's team was fairly stretched, although the surgeon did find time to check on them both and judged Aimée to be recovering.

However, she was no longer with child; Aimée announced the fact herself and neither man enquired further. Throughout their separation, King had avoided thoughts of her pregnancy, yet still he found the news difficult to accept. A lifetime of discipline topped by several years as a ship's captain had taught him well and, with willpower and an iron expression he was able to disguise much of his disappointment. And then one evening his grief became too much, and the real King was revealed.

259

For a man so accustomed to control, he felt ashamed at crumbling in such a way, though quickly realised surrender did have a positive aspect. Aimée seemed touched and encouraged by his reaction; it was as if she had wanted him to reveal his true feelings. Until then she had barely pecked at her food, with even milk, generously donated by the gunroom from their shared goat, being declined. But from that point there was a change and King knew something of the woman he missed would soon return.

"Mainly it was the boredom," she told him during one of the long, disjointed conversations that became increasingly common. "The days were so long, so hot and so without change, while the nights could be bitterly cold. We would lie together like the *animaux*..." she added with the ghost of a smile. "And, until you came, nothing ever altered. I felt the boredom would be the death of me."

King shook his head in wonder; of all Aimée had gone through it seemed bizarre to pick on monotony as the dominant evil.

On the lower deck the care was more brutal, if just as well-intended. After being deprived of a good meal for so long, it was possible Stokes and his men wanted food more than drink, although they soon discovered their previous diet of salt meat and preserved vegetables too harsh for what were now tender stomachs. But not so the alcohol; Mr Manning had officially banned any form of ardent spirits, though it was not long before their mates provided enough to keep them mellow for some of the day. And, being that *Viper* so recently victualled at Malta, the drink concerned was blackstrap; a heady wine often issued in place of rum. With this, together with a return to their familiar diet, and the company of shipmates, they soon began to thrive and within days were putting on weight once more.

Summers and his wife took their convalescence more quietly and in private. With unspoken sensitivity, Cooper had given up his cabin to the couple – a larger affair that included its own head. They gratefully retreated inside and were rarely seen or heard.

Meanwhile, finally reunited with his son, Caleb Palmer had taken charge of the lad and, with occasional help from Hannah, tended to him night and day. At first it had been like before, when Peter was young and dependent yet, as strength returned, so did

260

his character. Occasional gripes between father and son began to surface and when, on the fourth day, one developed into a full-blown argument, all knew Peter would soon be fully well.

However, there was no such transformation with Millie. She rejected care from anyone other than Bewley, who, though equally weak, accepted the responsibility with patient understanding. The storeroom that had been her quarters was restored and the familiar surroundings gave some comfort, although she showed no improvement, and neither was any expected.

And then there was Williams. Bewley's grim predictions were confirmed by Robert Manning; his wound was unquestionably septic, and action had to be taken without delay. The operation took place on the evening of his release and was completed within minutes. But it would take hours to know if all were truly well, and days after that to be sure every sign of corruption had been removed. Whether he would then recover remained very much in doubt, the midshipman's body was weak from malnutrition and, however fast the surgeon worked, a good deal of blood was lost. Still Manning retained some hope; simply being aboard ship and surrounded by their peers had done much to bolster many of his patients, and he trusted the same would apply to Williams.

But, however good the outcome, the surgeon would always feel he had failed in some way. He tried his best with the knowledge and tools acquired over many years of practice, yet an inner feeling told him more could have been done. For the lad could never make a full recovery and must always mourn the loss of his arm.

* * *

Morales, the carpenter, had also done his best, although *Viper*'s fore and main starboard channels had suffered badly from the shore bombardment. Both were essential to the ship's safety, being the securing points for vital shrouds, tyes and stays; without a firm anchorage, the masts themselves would be vulnerable and could easily be lost. Addressing such damage would have been hard enough if the ship were in harbour and accessible, but even the gentle swell of a placid Mediterranean made matters more complicated, and he was further hampered by the lack of suitable material.

Throughout their time on the North American Station, Morales was spoilt by the plentiful supply of just about any timber he required. But their current posting was not so well served and, after already carrying out several important running repairs, the carpenter's storeroom lay almost empty. And to top it all there was the private guilt he felt over rehousing the topmast on that American schooner.

Nothing was said officially, the Navy might not always be fair but did possess some degree of understanding and all knew the work was done under extreme circumstances. Besides, no one would ever be sure if it failed due to poor craftsmanship or rough handling. The end result was undeniable, however; the topmast had fallen, causing the prize's subsequent capture.

And this time it was harder. To keep the ship in any sort of motion each channel had to be addressed individually, with more than two days needed to see the work on each one completed. They ran out of thick stuff for the fore although doubling up with lighter timber and copious amounts of marine glue would seem to have done the trick and, now it was over, Morales felt cautiously confident. Of course, they would only know for certain when the ship was placed under strain, something he had been careful to explain to the captain. But the weather was holding for now and he would be on hand this time, if only to face a reprimand.

Morales had long since learned it didn't do to dwell on past work; worrying over the channels holding would not add anything to their strength and could only distract him from other tasks. Which were plentiful; even ignoring the number of decking strakes needing replacement, there were fittings to repair or rebuild. A new binnacle was needed as well as a belfry plus countless other smaller fixtures that made *Viper* a viable concern. Morales had no compunction about putting his junior men or even general hands on such tasks; temporary jobs were quite acceptable as they should be safe in Gib within a week. Then the entire ship could be properly put to rights, with his work on the channels the first to be rebuilt. And, with luck, there would be no storms or heavy weather to test them before although, despite his resolution, and even if the wind and seas kept agreeably low, the strength of those channels would never be far from his mind.

* * *

"I could do with a change from blackstrap." Stokes took a sniff at his tankard, then a cautious swallow. It was the start of the afternoon watch, and they had just responded to that day's first pipe for Up Spirits. But this was not the grog they all worshipped, nor even double stingo, beer issued in home waters and claimed to be every bit as strong. They were in the Med; it was blackstrap or nothing and the men were not happy.

"Aye, there's something about wine 'board ship," Lovemore agreed. "Just don't taste natural."

"Officers' grog, that's what it is," Parker, a waister, sniffed. "An' them's welcome to it."

Stokes' mess had altered considerably; only four of the original members remained, so they had been amalgamated with another equally down on numbers. But Stokes was once more elected leader, and when he suggested they enjoy their drink below, rather than in the open-air favoured by others less sunburned, all readily agreed.

"Whatever, we's bein' cheated," Bovey announced as they sat around the mess table. Like them all, he still suffered from his time as a prisoner; apart from raw shoulders and aching limbs, he had yet to properly digest his food and remained on light duties. Some things were returning to normal, however, and one was the seaman's innate concern for his personal rights.

"How'd you work that out, Bove?" Longdon enquired.

"Stan's to reason, man gets threepence a day temperance, that's if he turns down the grog issue. Works out fair when they're servin' rum, but this muck is five shillin' a gallon. We gets a pint each – that's seven pence halfpenny a day, yet they hands out less than half if we turns it down."

"Then we may as well drink the stuff, I reckons," Stokes said, trying another mouthful.

"Well, we got grog if you wants it," Parker told them quietly.

"What, the real stuff?" Lovemore was amazed.

"Not proper," Stiles, a holder and another new member, admitted. "But the next best thing."

"Bulls?"

263

Parker grinned. "The very same. Up you gets, Joey!"

The boy of the mess, who had been watching his betters from the far end of the table, raised himself from his seat.

"Picked this up last time we was in Gib," Stiles announced reaching for the lad's chair. The cask was well made and would have held two gallons of liquid.

"Full, is it?" Stokes enquired.

"It were once," Parker confirmed. "An' of the best Jamaica rum, so not for the likes of us: officers' consumption."

"An' now?" Bovey was positively licking his lips.

"Been filled with spring water for more'n two month!" Stiles grinned.

"I heard of this," Longdon said. "Water takes the strength from the wood, makes it like grog."

"P'raps not true grog," Parker admitted. "But better than this muck." He glared at his tankard accusingly.

"Bulls ain't strictly legal," Bovey warned.

"Maybe not." Stiles looked around. "Though there ain't no one about to notice."

"Drink up, lads, let's try a draught." So saying, Parker laid the cask on the table, bung uppermost. Then, bending down, he bit into the stopper and drew it out with his teeth.

The scent of spirit floated above them in an invisible cloud.

"Who's for the first draw then?" Parker asked, and all took to draining their tankards.

* * *

Viper was his first posting, so Williams had little experience of other commanders, although he knew Captain King to be one of the best. More than that, he had come to respect the man himself. But with a damaged ship and so many other responsibilities, he had not expected his sudden appearance in the sick berth and, as a consequence, felt awkward and mildly guilty.

"It's kind of you to come, sir." The midshipman attempted to raise himself from the bunk though stopped when signalled to rest.

"I try to make a point of visiting the wounded." Captain King sounded slightly uncomfortable himself. "Especially my

264

fellow officers. How are you feeling, after the operation, I am meaning?"

Awkward or not, Williams recognised genuine compassion. "Fairly well, sir; Mr Manning said the wound would hurt for a day or two."

"Mr Manning is correct." The captain gave a wry smile. "Though in my experience the pain lasts a good deal longer."

"How long, sir?" It felt strange asking intimate questions of his superior officer, even if it was what he seemed to expect.

"I was unfortunate enough to suffer several amputations," King replied. "It was due to infection and, believe me, they did not become easier. After the last, the wound only remained sore for a month or so."

"A month?"

"The pain gradually faded," he added quickly, "yet I would advise against too much laudanum. It may give immediate relief, though a devil to be rid of and there are some who never succeed."

"Yes, sir." Williams had relied on the green liquid for the first few days; the heady sleep it brought being a better alternative to constant pain. But Robert Manning recently reduced the dose and he was the better for it. "And afterwards, how soon did you feel like returning to duty?"

"A month, no more," King replied. "I was a lieutenant at the time, so was at something of an advantage."

Williams nodded; that would certainly have been the case. Even the soundest of commissioned officers rarely went aloft, other than of their own volition, and neither did lieutenants carry out many of the more physical tasks expected of midshipmen.

"You are right-handed, I assume?"

"I am, sir."

"Then we are the same and, though you will miss the use of your left, it will not be so much of a problem. Nevertheless, balance may be. Do not expect to fight with a sword. Or dance," he smiled quickly.

"I understand."

"And there will be a measure of compensation from the Admiralty."

"I was not aware of that, sir."

"As a warrant officer, you shall receive a year's pay, which is in addition to any pension afterwards awarded."

265

"But I wish to continue to serve," Williams said, "if I can find a suitable berth."

"There will always be a position for you aboard *Viper*, I shall see to that personally." The captain was not smiling now. "However, we are no longer at war with France, and the chances of further employment will be less."

"Of course, sir."

"Do not consider that now," Captain King continued. "Rest and be well; we shall be in Gib before long, and there will be shore leave for certain."

The pain had been growing for some while and his next dose of laudanum was at least an hour away. A sudden surge made Williams wince. "Thank you for coming, sir." It was barely a whisper.

"I wanted to," the captain assured him, stepping back. "And wish to return if I may."

Chapter Twenty-Six

"We may dine in the gunroom at any time," Summers reminded Suzie when their steward left. "And then enjoy a change of diet." He lifted one of the pewter lids.

"Is it fish again?" she asked from the bunk.

"I fear so. Mr Manning seems to think it suitable."

Suzie turned awkwardly and sighed. "I would not mind, but the place stinks so afterwards."

Summers dropped the lid and returned to his seat at the desk. He was still noticeably thin and even his wife, now very obviously pregnant, looked oddly gaunt and lacked the glow common in others of her state. Yet she was right, a regular supply of stockfish backed by portable soup and a surplus of goat's milk was hardly attractive, even if there were few meals he could think of that would be preferable. The hunger that tormented him when initially held prisoner had been dormant for some while; what he longed for most was rest; a time without demands and, if he were honest, the chance to be alone.

In truth, the concept was almost overwhelming; he would consider it at night when the two of them squeezed together in a bed barely large enough for one. The images usually began with an empty space, nothing in sight for miles, and him – only him – at the centre. Or occasionally he would be the solitary occupant of an open boat, one set adrift on a placid sea that was clear as far as the non-existent horizon. It wasn't that Summers disliked company as such, and truly appreciated being able to spend time with his wife in a room not filled to the gunwales. Yet still he craved for solitude and did so with the desperation of a penitent seeking absolution.

"You may eat with the others if you wish. I am sure they would provide better conversation."

"I have no need to talk." Summers said with total honesty. "Besides, there will be many there dining, I should be lucky to find a place."

That was also the truth, with the sudden influx of officers and important guests, *Viper*'s gunroom was almost as crowded as the cell they had just left, and with many of the same inhabitants.

"I am very happy being with you," he assured her.

"And I you, Michael, though it was hardly the start to married life we intended."

This was the first time she had talked beyond a few, scant words and the change was welcome.

"We shall be in Gib before long," he said. "Time then to plan the rest of our lives."

"And will you be as keen to leave the Service?" She was peeping out from the covers to see his reaction.

"I believe so; little has changed, at least as far as I am concerned."

"Nor me," Suzie agreed. "And yes, when we reach Gibraltar things will be better. Shall you find us a cottage?"

"A cottage?"

She nodded. "Somewhere away from the main town, perhaps with some land – and a garden?"

"I fear there will be few available, it is a crowded rock."

"I see." Again that sigh, "Still, I would prefer not to travel straight away."

"You are meaning by ship?"

"Of course, though suppose with the war in Europe at an end…"

"We may purchase a carriage and take a leisurely trip on land," he suggested, and her face appeared again.

"Could we so?"

Summers pondered; it would not provide quite the solitude he craved but was an agreeable alternative to another small cabin in another crowded ship. "We can do whatever we wish," he told her. "However, the child may be born Spanish."

"Or French," she added, smiling at last.

"French?"

"You have the language, as do I," she pointed out. "Though that spoken in Memramcook is more an approximation."

"You would live in France?"

"I would live anywhere with you," she said. "And France might be suitable, as it is neither your home nor mine."

"Then it is something we must explore." He reached for her hand. "I only want for us to be together."

"And I," she assured him. "Yet perhaps not all the time…"

Summers tensed. "Why do you say that?"

Now she shook her head. "You must not take this personally... but being incarcerated so has left me slightly altered."

He waited.

"It was just so full of people; no chance to talk, to sleep and everything so horribly public."

He nodded encouragement, although she was not looking, instead her eyes had become fixed on the deckhead above.

"And it is not that I do not love you, Michael, or have no wish to be your wife for always... But sometimes I just want to be totally by myself. Can you imagine that?"

* * *

In another part of the ship, another couple were talking with almost the same intimacy.

"It all sounds a long way from our village in Nantucket," Hannah said when Bewley, the loblolly boy, finished speaking.

"Because it is?" he suggested, and she raised her eyes to heaven.

"Well, I was aware! Still, many of us came from England, yet the life you describe sounds very different to my own."

On returning to the ship, Bewley resumed his duties almost immediately, one of his first tasks being to assist with Williams' amputation. But Manning had long since identified a sensitivity in the man and soon gave him responsibility for what were his fellow prisoners. Consequently, much of his time was spent calling on those put to work by the pirates, ensuring all were eating correctly and checking no minor wounds gave concern. Like himself, most were recuperating well with some refusing to be confined by light duties. Only Millie caused any real worry, although the girl would often settle for hours after one of his visits. And really, there was no cause to bother the Palmer family; Caleb Palmer had barely been in the pirates' clutches a day and Peter, his son, was following the lead set by other seamen in making a quick and uneventful recovery. Yet Bewley still called daily at the small room which had become the Quaker's home, and it was no accident that these visits occurred when both men were likely to be elsewhere.

"There is little whaling where I come from," he agreed, his

269

tone remaining light. "Wartling is now some distance from the sea, though in the past was near enough a port."

"So, what changed?" Hannah asked. She had started her current piece of needlepoint when they first began to travel and it was now quite substantial, though little was added during Bewley's visits.

"They drained the marshes," he said.

"As in the low countries?"

"Not exactly, there are no dykes, just sound land management; it has proved sufficient."

"And the extra land, it is used for crops?"

He shook his head. "Mainly grazing; it's where I used to earn my living."

"Managing cattle?"

"And sheep, pigs, goats – anything that needed medical attention."

"And you were happier then, than when humans became your patients?"

He laughed. "In some ways I find people more challenging, and in others less so."

"I suppose a cow cannot announce when she is in pain?"

"No, though you can usually tell. And yes, I was happier. Medical science has advanced of late with many diseases that would normally prove fatal now able to be treated and often cured. Surgical operations are being attempted within the body itself, and even such terrors as smallpox can be countered by the miracle of vaccines. Yet certain conditions remain beyond a surgeon's scope, and I believe they always will."

"You are thinking of the girl, Millie?" she suggested.

"I am, and others like her."

"She trusts you and always quietens at your presence."

"Maybe, though I cannot provide a cure. In truth, I doubt a remedy will ever come."

"It is something you might address yourself," she said. "Those of my faith have done much to investigate diseases of the mind. We have set up a sanctuary specifically for such cases, the sufferers are treated with respect and encouraged to work. But most of all, they are loved."

"And that is in Nantucket?" Bewley asked but Hannah shook her head.

"In Northern England," she said. "Yet its principles could be copied."

"It is something to consider I suppose, if I do not return to animals, who are far less complex."

"Then it is back to Wartling with you?" she asked, and he shrugged.

"Or anywhere I may be of use. And what of you?" he added, briefly enjoying those eyes.

"Me?"

"When not travelling about the world rescuing your brother; do you spend all your time sewing?"

"I should think not!" She seemed mildly affronted though Bewley could see through the brittle exterior. "There is so much else to do. We have a few animals that feed us and turn a modest profit: they need tending."

"Is that common in Nantucket?"

"Reasonably so," she replied, and both considered this for a moment.

"You were telling me of your life," he prompted finally.

"There is little more to say, with domestic duties, the time is well used."

"So, life aboard ship is less taxing?"

She smiled. "Oh yes, I need only attend to my father's wishes, and laundry – if it were not for the circumstances, I should regard this as a holiday."

"A holiday? Do you people believe in such things?"

She raised those eyes. "You people?"

He blushed. "That was clumsy, I meant to say..."

"You meant; do we allow ourselves pleasure?" she suggested and now the smile returned. "Why should we not?"

"I suppose it is your clothes, and your manner." Bewley waved a hand aimlessly. "You appear so... severe."

"Then it is an illusion, and regrettable." She stopped work yet again. "Our life is love, and peace, and tenderness; and bearing one with another, and forgiving one another, and not laying accusations one against another, but praying one for another and helping one another up with a tender hand. Believe me, Andrew, it is not such a poor way of living."

He sighed. "Indeed, it sounds nothing less than the perfect existence. But can you keep to such an ethos away from your

271

community?"

"It has not always been easy, though our Friends in England gave us much encouragement. And travel has taught me a good deal; on our return, I will be the better for it."

"You are determined to return?" he asked, and she seemed surprised.

"Of course, it is my home, though I freely admit, its limitations have been revealed."

"The different places you have visited?" he chanced.

Hannah lowered her eyes slightly. "Different places... and people," she agreed. "Sure, there have been one or two surprises along the way."

"Places or people?"

"Both, though I was thinking of people mainly." Again, that look. "And some have proved very acceptable."

* * *

With the gunroom crowded and its pantry in such demand, King and Aimée had taken to inviting others to join them at their table for meals in the great cabin. The traditional time for a captain to dine was three, although King usually brought that forward by an hour to ensure all were gone by the start of the first dogwatch. This was entirely for Aimée's benefit; she was recovering well and now had an appetite close to normal, yet he noticed how she tired after just an hour of light conversation and, by the time the last guest left, was ready for rest.

And especially so when the French officers were invited. Having been deprived of conventional female company and the chance to share their native language for so long, they competed for her attention with questions, stories and often over-sentimental reminiscences; by the time the meal was finished – and they were the least prompt to leave – Aimée was completely exhausted. But King could now notice this, along with other more subtle signals. In fact, since her release, he had become a different man, and far more attentive to her wishes.

However, there was no need for effort on anyone's part when the Palmer family paid a visit. Rather than lessen after his failure to negotiate with the bey, the respect King held for Caleb

Palmer had increased and, instead of the solemn atmosphere expected when dining with those of strong faith, the party proved particularly enjoyable. Summers and his wife joined them on a rare outing from their self-imposed isolation and, though neither ate much, King was now sensitive enough to note their reserve begin to ease as the meal progressed. And it was later, when the youngsters had departed, Aimée was abed and King went up on deck to check the watch, that the two men were able to talk properly.

Palmer had also felt the need for early evening air, and they soon fell to conversation in the relative privacy of *Viper*'s taffrail.

"It was an unexpectedly easy departure," Palmer said after they discussed the release of the prisoners. And that had certainly been the case, once the horror of the shared cell was revealed, and those imprisoned were seen safely back to the ship – Captain Duke having commandeered several small wagons along with blankets to cover the women – it had been a relatively simple matter. They did still have to wait for the return of those prisoners still working in the quarry; an interminable period which might at any time have been interrupted by the return of Visser. But then, when *Viper*'s boats finally hauled her clear, and a few cautious shreds of canvas were raised to catch the evening breeze, the empty sea beyond was almost an anti-climax. Even an occasional shot from the battery – the pirates having managed to bring one gun back into action – could be ignored and no significant damage was received.

For several days it was impossible to think beyond the next immediate obstacle of refitting at sea but, now much was put to rights, they were finally able to reflect.

"I had known your attempts to negotiate would fail." There was a note of apology in King's voice.

"And I also," Palmer admitted. They were looking eastwards, so blind to the setting sun, although the changing beauty of the water's light was entrancing.

"Yet you were determined to persevere?"

The older man nodded. "It was important to me that I did."

"Even when you felt it would be pointless?"

Palmer turned and looked King full in the face. "There was nothing pointless about my approach; I will always believe it to have been the right one."

"But if you knew it would fail…"

"Sometimes right must be done," the Quaker interrupted. "Not because it will work, simply because it is right."

King was silent for a moment.

"And I must say your part was appreciated," Palmer continued, relaxing again. "For all my life I have decried the use of force, yet you and your marines showed me that, correctly managed, it could yet become an instrument of peace."

"None of my men were injured while we were on land," King pointed out.

"And many were saved; you are to be congratulated, Captain."

King smiled. "In the course of my duty that has rarely been the case," he said. "Too often the praise is greater when more have fallen."

"And will you continue?" Palmer asked after another pause. "With your duty, I am meaning. I have sensed reluctance in the past."

"I have always been a fighting officer and will remain one…"

"Until?"

King shrugged. "Until I stop."

"And will you stop?" the older man persisted. "Forgive me, I have encountered many who serve aboard ships of war yet detect a sensitivity in you that is rare. I would say you were not born to fight."

"Perhaps, though it was something soon learned," King grinned. "And you do not know me well. When we first met, I was under particular strain. There had been bad news of my family and I was eager to be home. I must confess, capturing your vessel was an annoying diversion."

"Though capture it you did," Palmer pointed out.

"Because it was my duty," King confirmed. "Then, aboard *Caledonia*, once more I was under pressure; you cannot expect normal behaviour in such circumstances."

"And the second time, when your wife was again in danger…"

"Aimée is not my wife."

Palmer smiled and shook his head. "It is the same to me. When your wife was in danger, and you could do something about

274

it, was that your duty also?"

"Perhaps not totally," King admitted, "Perhaps not at all."

"And if it had been solely your duty. If Aimée was not at risk. If those imprisoned were unknown to you, would your actions have been different?"

"Different?"

"Would you have fired on the harbour, and perhaps set your marines to attack the palace, rather than negotiate with the bey?"

"It was hardly a negotiation," King said. "Figuratively speaking the fellow was at the end of my gun."

"Still, you did not choose to shoot. Instead, you spoke, and he listened. You used force, but not violence and showed strength though not aggression. I tell you, Thomas, I was mightily impressed. And the more so when, on leaving harbour, your ship was fired upon and you did not reply."

"The battery was beyond my reach."

"Yet you could have vented your rage on the houses. Were I accustomed to such a concept, I should regard that as a major victory."

King paused again. "Perhaps I was taught something from your example?"

Palmer bowed his head. "I should like to think so, for I have learned much from you."

King was about to reply when a call from aloft brought both men back to reality.

"Sail ho! Sail off the starboard bow!"

"What do you see there?" Woodward had the watch and was asking the question as King approached.

"Hard to say," the masthead replied. "She's dead against the sun else I probably wouldn't 'ave made her in the firs' place."

"Do you see anything at the fore?" King bellowed.

"Nothing from here, sir!" another voice answered from further forward.

"Mr Malcolm," Woodward snapped. "Main masthead if you please!" The duty midshipman grabbed at a glass before making for the shrouds.

"Do you have a course?" King again.

"I thought at firs' it were the same heading, an' we was forereaching," the main lookout said at last, "but no, she's bearing down on us."

King squinted forward, the light was fading fast yet would last slightly longer for those at the masthead, while Malcolm had already reached the maintop and was making good progress.

"She's showin' tops'ls and forecourse," the lookout continued, "though I'm losin' her quick."

There was a pause as the midshipman arrived and King fancied he could hear snatches of their conversation. Then the lad's call broke through.

"I have her," he shouted, the adolescent voice breaking with excitement. "Headin' our way for sure an' making good speed."

King collected the traverse board; *Viper* was currently steering northwest by north on a close reach and had shown four knots at the last cast. The oncoming sighting would probably be in better shape and, sailing as she must on a broad reach, might double that. Which meant they were closing at anything up to fifteen miles in the hour and would pass before the quarter moon was due. Were the sighting another warship it was likely to be British, or at least neutral, although the bey's threat of Visser's return still haunted him. They may have been empty words yet, if correct and the pirate had been raiding shipping in the Atlantic, they were plumb on her course back to Mezmada.

"Can you gauge her size?" Woodward was asking an unnecessary question: if the lad had any idea he would have said so.

"No, sir," Malcolm replied. "Only that she's headin' our way."

That was understandable, though no less frustrating, and the two officers were exchanging looks again as Cooper and the sailing master appeared on deck.

"Gentlemen, we have an unknown sighting off our starboard bow," King told them. "She is hard on the horizon but heading in our direction and I propose to avoid."

The statement was greeted with grunts and nods of approval.

"Take us three points to larboard if you please, Mr Manton."

"Three points to larboard, aye sir." The sailing master touched his hat. "An' we can maintain that heading for several

276

hours if you wish."

"Very good." King was about to add more when the midshipman called again.

"Deck there, we're losing the light, yet she's comin' up fast and I think I can gauge her size."

In such conditions, any estimation was likely to be suspect, but still they tensed.

"I'd say she were another frigate."

Chapter Twenty-Seven

When night fell it did not grow fully dark; the sky remained clear, the water phosphorescent and a thousand stars began to compete for brightness.

"If it stays like this it may as well be day," Cooper complained to the quarterdeck in general.

"And we shall have something of a moon before long," Manton added.

"Summon Mr Morales." King spoke softly and to the duty messenger, yet the request was enough to put an end to any further conversation.

The carpenter appeared promptly, and King noted he was alert and fully dressed. As an idler, Morales stood no watch and officially only worked during daylight hours. Something of the current emergency must have filtered down to his mess, however, and he was obviously ready for action.

"The repairs to the starboard channels," King began, and the artisan's face fell. "How confident of them are you?"

It was an unfair question. When Morales announced his work complete, he had listed the many compromises made, despite King fully accepting dockyard-standard repairs could not be expected on the open sea. What he truly wanted to know was, how cautious the carpenter had been?

"There's no sign of strain or joints opening," Morales replied. "An' I been checkin' every watch, sir."

This reflected well on the man, although it might also suggest true cause to doubt. For the past three days, the wind had been light enough to trust top and staysails, but with a potential enemy in sight, more may be needed, and ultimately it would be up to King to decide how much.

Yet this all might be a waste of time; a frigate emerging from the Strait of Gibraltar was a dozen times more likely to be friendly. The whole affair could turn into a ludicrous anticlimax, one brought about by excessive imagination following a period of intense strain. Except King's inner senses told him otherwise, and they rarely failed him.

"Very well," he said, turning away from the unhappy Morales. "Mr Manton, I'd like more sail; do you think she will stand t'gallants?"

That was another unfair question, as King quickly realised.

"Belay that," he added. "Set them, I shall take responsibility. And when we have tried the extra canvas, I propose turning further to the south."

The sailing master paused and there was perhaps a momentary look of respect on his face before he went to bellow out the order.

"Turning so will delay our arrival at Gib," King told Cooper, "but also reveal more about our present company."

That was so, with war in Europe at an end and the American navy unlikely to send a frigate to the Med, few national vessels would bother to investigate a fellow countryman's sudden change of course. And even if this did turn out to be the dreaded Visser, the pirate would be returning after a cruise and, whether profitable or not, must surely wish to make harbour without delay. The fresh canvas was beginning to fill and those with sufficient sensitivity detected an increase in *Viper*'s speed. Morales excused himself to inspect the starboard channels and, when he did not immediately return or send a report, King began to breathe more easily.

"Very well, take her to the south-west," he said, and Manton repeated the order.

"If only this breeze would shift," King added to Cooper. The wind had been blowing strong and steady throughout yet remained stubbornly in the north. Were it to veer, he might take it to larboard and so reduce the strain on those channels. Of course, they could turn further, wear, then retrace their steps. Such a move would reduce any risk of shaking their tophamper, though must also mean them remaining in danger from the sighting for longer. No, a south-westerly heading would serve, for a spell at least. Despite Manton's earlier assurance, the North African coast was relatively close by; they must not become trapped on a lee shore with a doubtful tophamper. As soon as the danger was passed, they should turn back and, though it would be a long claw, set course for Gib once more.

And *Viper* was coping with the extra pressure admirably;

even after the turn, and increase in speed, her channels continued to hold and the sound of water rising from the stem only added to King's optimism. In his youth, he frequently pushed the bounds of safety too far, although the habit had grown less common of late. Yet, though it was well to be wary, too much caution could be every bit as dangerous as thoughtless abandon. As it was, the ship handled well and might actually be benefiting from being sailed slightly harder; had he done so from the start, they might be in sight of home by now.

"How goes it, Captain?" It was Palmer who had broken the cardinal rule; the man must have crept past Cooper and the sailing master to address him so, and usually King would have been furious. However, the elderly Quaker's look of concern was for him as much as their predicament, and he could not be cross.

"A diversion I fear, sir," he said. "Such a move will add to our journey, though I think it worthwhile."

"If doing so avoids conflict and the shedding of more blood, then I am with you," the older man agreed.

"I trust there will be no more of that on this passage," King told him honestly. And then a call from the masthead wrecked all their hopes.

"Deck there – the sighting's altering course; she's steering to intercept."

* * *

"It could have been worse," Summers supposed. "The captain was good to invite us."

"Oh, I think the meal a success," Suzie said. "And a change from that damned fish."

"I shall speak with Mr Manning, perhaps he will allow us some remission, though until we both add a bit of weight..."

"Sure, I have never found that a problem in the past," she sighed. "Do we truly have to consult the surgeon?"

"I believe it customary in such matters."

"Yet he does not insist we dine in our cabin. And there have been several invitations to join the officers next door."

"You would eat in the gunroom?" Summers was amazed.

"I think so," Suzie said. "At least I think I would now, after

280

dining upstairs."

"It will not be the same fare," he warned. "The captain's table is always best aboard ship, there will be no roasted meat or syllabub."

"Lord, Michael, you speak as if I have never been asea!" She pulled a face and there was definite colour in her cheeks. "Ask me, a bowl of frumenty at breakfast and a double throw of lobscouse for dinner would go down nicely. And I'd not be averse to the odd spotted dog now and then."

"Why that's marvellous!" he beamed. "Shall I request we join them tomorrow?"

"And miss tonight's supper? I should say not!"

* * *

Now there was no longer any need to risk a lee shore, the sighting had made it plain they intended to investigate and must be considered a potential enemy.

"Very well, Mr Manton," King said, his voice perfectly level. "We may return to our previous heading and strike the t'gallants."

There was silence as the sailing master brought them round; all knew action was growing more likely by the second and, if so, they would be facing another frigate. Such single ship duels were a common form of naval combat and often depended as much on manoeuvrability as firepower. And they were equally aware that, though *Viper* was sailing sweetly at present, either of those channels could break under pressure, leaving the mast they served without support, and the ship effectively helpless.

But King was determined not to let that happen. Their weakness lay to starboard so for as long as they remained on the present tack they were in danger. Yet he had no wish to alter course now, only to be forced back when action drew closer. There must come a time when the larboard tack could be adopted, and then he would show what a British frigate could do.

He raised his personal glass and examined the oncoming ship. In the clear night she was easy to spot; even without a moon, he could make out fine detail as she bore down on them with the wind comfortably on her larboard quarter. She was also being handled well; whoever this Visser was, he must be a seaman.

"We will hold this course for the next half-hour, then see

281

about tacking to the north." As he spoke, King knew the words were committing him. But in half an hour both ships would be coming in reach of the others' long guns and that would be the time to make a further change. Until then there was nothing for him to do, so no reason to remain in public view on the quarterdeck.

"Those not on duty would be wise to seek rest below," he added. "As I intend to – this may be a long night."

* * *

When Aimée awoke from her nap to find Thomas gone it was no surprise; he regularly went on deck at dusk and often remained deep into the night. So, she had not expected him to return to the cabin quite so soon. But the distant look in his eyes told her something was troubling him and, though it would have been nice to know what, sensed it to be the last thing he wished to discuss.

"Is it a pleasant night?" she chanced when he had ordered a pot of chocolate for them both. King looked up.

"Forgive me, my dear?"

"The night, is it pleasant?"

"Wind is in the north and holding steady," King replied quickly. "A small moon is due, though the sky is clear, and it is already bright enough."

"Then it should be a good day tomorrow."

His expression was close to surprise as he repeated her last word. And then he smiled.

"Indeed; we should have sun. A bonus when the nights are drawing in."

"And Gibraltar – when shall we arrive?"

"There might be a slight delay." She could see he was choosing his words carefully. "A ship has been sighted that may cause us to divert."

Again, she sensed dangerous territory and hurriedly changed the subject.

"And when we arrive, what do you propose?"

"It is not for me to decide; have you anything in mind?"

A steward arrived with the silver chocolate pot and poured two measures into the giant cups that had been made to King's special order. They remained silent while the man was in the room, then relaxed when once more alone.

"I was speaking to Suzie Summers," Aimée continued with elaborate indifference. "She and Michael are planning to complete their journey home by land."

"By land?" Again King spoke as if awakened from a dream. "But she is with child!"

"They might deal with such matters in Spain," Aimée replied. "Or France..."

"France?" Distracted or not, he noted something in her tone. "Do you wish to return to France?"

"I do," she admitted. "Not to live, merely a visit. To see my family and my home; you probably will not..."

"No, I do see, I see most certainly," he said, suddenly attentive. "And we must, Aimée of course we must. Though you are..." He paused and seemed to change his mind, then added, "You are still weak."

"If I were so *délicat*, I should hardly have survived as long in that cell," she retorted with something of her old spark.

"Yes, we will return to Verdun." He was smiling now. "There may be others we remember there; I hear many former prisoners have remained and made it their home."

"If you are sure," she checked, and again his look warmed Aimée inside. If nothing else, she had taken his mind from whatever was troubling him.

"I am certain," King assured her. "It is something to look forward to, something to treasure."

He reached for his drink and downed it in one, before staring aimlessly about the cabin and Aimée knew her time was over.

"Do you wish to go on deck?"

Now the smile was more mechanical. "I fear I must, there is a problem in the offing though all will be settled by morning."

"And in the morning, shall we continue for Gibraltar?"

They had risen together, and it seemed entirely natural that he should take her hand.

"Gibraltar, and then Verdun," he promised. "And afterwards, wherever you wish to go and wherever you wish to live."

The embrace was brief yet warm and, after he left, Aimée felt they had never been closer.

The call to clear for action came as Stokes and his mess were ready to bed down for the night and, though all remained on light duties, each responded instantly and helped prepare the ship for battle. Yet when the deep rumble of a drum sent them to quarters, they assembled at their assigned cannon to find another team already in place.

"Some mistake here, Smitty," Stokes told his opposite number. "Eleven an' twelve are my guns."

"Might 'ave been once," the seaman agreed. "But you was gone a while; we were 'ppointed weeks back."

"An' Elsje's a weighty girl." Another Dutchman patted the larboard gun with obvious affection. "Too heavy for those still sick from the working ashore."

"We're all more'n capable of handling a long twelve," Longdon snorted. "An' have fired both 'em off many a time."

"An' she's not Elsje, her name's Betty!" Bovey added.

"Is there trouble?" The tone was that of an officer and all turned to see Lieutenant Woodward standing nearby.

"It's the squareheads," Longdon said. "Got designs on our guns, so they has."

Woodward referred to a small sheet of paper. "Smitt was appointed to this piece and the larboard number," he said. "An' fired them both in action when we took Mezmada."

"Maybe so," Stokes replied. "But we weren't about then."

"No," Lovemore agreed. "We was ashore, seein' to that battery."

"An' if we hadn't," Bovey added, "there wouldn't be no gun to argue over, nor no *Viper* either if it comes to it."

Woodward looked from one to another then sighed. "Are you sure your lads can handle the work?"

There was a rumble of protest from Smitt's men which Stokes spoke over. "Sure as eggs is eggs, Mr Woodward."

"Very well, you take these pieces, Smitt's mess can supplement where needed."

* * *

"If you have a moment, sir?"

King turned on the half-deck; it was Goodman, the American. On taking them aboard it seemed petty in the extreme to confine him and his countrymen when they had been through so much together. And anyway, King now liked and trusted the man. Yet they would shortly be in action; there were important matters to consider and this was not the time for small talk.

"What is it?"

"I have spoken with my people," Goodman said. "They are willing to fight."

"To fight?"

"Against the pirates. You lost a fair few men in securing their release, and some still suffer from being held prisoner. Though none of mine are exactly strong, they might serve as powder monkeys, or maybe act as waisters – if you was willin', of course."

King blinked; it was an unexpected offer. The Royal Navy rarely turned away foreigners; two years' service in a King's ship entitled a man to claim British citizenship and the simple act of stepping aboard would instantly free a slave. Dubois, the French officer, had already offered his men, who were now accommodated amongst *Viper*'s lower deck, but Americans were a different matter; officially they remained the enemy.

"I-I am not sure..." he began, and Goodman grinned.

"You are thinking maybe we'll turn against you?" he suggested. "Side with the pirates and help them seize the ship?"

"No of course not."

"I tell you, Captain, we have just as much reason to hate them as you, and happily give my word every weapon will be handed back as soon as they're beaten."

"Of course, it's just that..."

"We are at war?" Goodman chuckled and King nodded – it seemed indelicate to mention the fact.

"Maybe so, yet there were Frenchman at Trafalgar," Goodman pointed out. "Four served aboard your famous Nelson's flagship and one fell alongside him."

King knew Goodman was correct, and also that twelve British deserters were crewing aboard the French ship that first engaged *Victory*. Warfare could truly be an international affair.

"Very well," he said. "Apply to Mr Cooper; he will see them

285

suitably posted."

"Grateful for the opportunity, Captain," Goodman assured. "I know they won't let you down. Most of them were born British anyways…"

* * *

Now was the time for action. Both ships had stuck to their individual courses and the pirate lay a little over a mile off *Viper*'s starboard bow. The quarter moon was shining as bright as many far larger while a myriad of cold, sharp stars studded the sky. And, on the quarterdeck, King felt the thrill of an approaching action.

It was a sensation first experienced as a lowly midshipman when he had charge of a single battery of cannon. On promotion, the responsibilities increased until an entire warship was his to control, but the feeling remained the same.

The size and power of subsequent vessels varied, but all shared one common element; they were weapons of war, forged with a single aim: to fight those of their kind or weaker. And now he would be directing yet another and, more importantly perhaps, the men who sailed her. Some – most – he knew; many had fought with him before and, if this particular engagement followed the usual pattern, a good number would be dead by morning. But though each action was in many ways unique, the present contest stood out as markedly different, even if there was nothing solid to support this.

Viper was injured, and he remained unsure of the full extent of her wounds, although he had been successful with vessels in a worse condition. And they were doubtful of their opponent– it was still possible the frigate bearing down on them might not be an enemy, but there had been times in the past when ill luck, confusion or poor visibility brought him close to firing on a friend. Equally, this was hardly the first time defeat, and subsequent capture would mean something other than becoming conventional prisoners of war. Quite how Ali bey ben Hamoudad would treat any remaining from *Viper*'s crew was a mystery, but it would not be pleasant. Yet there had been other battles when more was at stake than his own life.

Or perhaps it had something to do with being so close to

286

safety? Or that the war with his old enemy was over, and he had almost ruled out another significant engagement? Did the number of foreigners amongst his people have something to do with it? Or possibly his personal state of mind: that combat was being forced upon him after deciding this would be his last commission?

King did not know and, on some levels, neither did he care, for action appeared inevitable and all the theorising in the world would not alter that. However, of one thing he remained inwardly certain; he was about to face his final enemy.

"Very well, Mr Manton, prepare to tack."

The sailing master collected the speaking trumpet; at a time like this, there must be no confusion. Meanwhile, King directed his attention forward.

"Mr Woodward, we will be using the larboard battery initially, and round shot for all unless I order otherwise."

From the waist, the young lieutenant raised his hat in acknowledgement. Marine Captain Duke had mustered his men along both bulwarks; with a double detachment of marines, *Viper* was well provided for in that department, and her general hands stood equally ready at their posts. King looked across to Cooper, then to Manton, before focusing entirely on the enemy in the offing.

"Very well," he said at last. "Take us about and we'll see how well a pirate can fight."

Chapter Twenty-Eight

Viper swept into the manoeuvre sweetly enough and, once safely on the larboard tack, replaced her topgallants. King eyed the distant frigate speculatively; there were no flags, nothing even approaching a commissioning pennant flew from her masthead and neither was there an ensign. And even if there had been, and it could be identified, he still felt they were facing a pirate and would take any reply with a pinch of salt. Yet their recent tack had been aggressive in the extreme and it might be prudent to make certain before closing further.

"Mr Malcolm, are you aware of the current private signal?" he enquired.

"Day or night, sir?"

"Night." The signal midshipman was young and could be excused the occasional foolish question although King supposed it was an indication of the excellent visibility.

"Two lights on the foreyardarms, sir, with one above at the main."

"And the reply?"

The lad paused. "I shall have to check."

"Do that, and see those lamps rigged."

Even if this Visser turned out a fool and allowed *Viper* across his bows, it would be a good fifteen minutes before they came into range and, though King did not expect a response, neither did he want any absurd mistakes. And it would kill time; now they were taking the offensive he very much wanted action to begin.

Their recent manoeuvre was made in no great hopes, its principal purpose being to take the wind to larboard. Still, it remained possible that the enemy would allow them to close further: stranger things had happened. After all, the pirates would be used to fighting smaller prey and not accustomed to meeting a warship of equal size. This might actually turn out to be an easy engagement; they could yet raise Gibraltar on time and in company with a near-perfect prize.

Or perhaps not, for there was still the chance of the enemy turning away and tempting *Viper* into a stern chase to the west. Were that to happen King must choose between tacking once more and risking his fragile tophamper in pursuit, or making an ignominious retreat to the east, leaving Visser between him and his destination.

"Lamps are alight and shielded, sir!"

"Very good." The lad had done well to see to that quickly, or maybe time was passing faster than he thought. "Make the signal."

Even in such conditions, the additional glow cast strange shadows over *Viper*'s upper deck adding a sense of unreality to the mix. King glanced forward; their larboard cannon were fully manned and Woodward stood ready to command them while, at the bulwarks, neat ranks of marines waited stoically for whatever the night might bring. But soon this quiet world would be split by the raucous sound of battle, a din that would only cease when one ship was forced to submit. And it may indeed be over quickly – such actions had been settled in minutes – or the agony might drag on for much of the night. Still, of one thing King was certain; with no sign of bad weather, other shipping or significant navigational hazards, there would be nothing to interrupt the combat of two ostensibly equally matched opponents. And long before the sun rose on their madness, all would have been decided.

* * *

"Well, you've fought a land action, now you'll get the chance to see how *Viper* performs at sea."

Balaam nodded seriously. Lieutenant Woodward was an excellent officer; he had learned much from the man, in fact it was mainly his good-natured confidence that saw him through when the shore battery was firing on them. However, at that moment Balaam didn't feel like being cheerful. With a hostile ship to windward and the imminent prospect of a savage fight, it was all he could do to keep his hands from shaking. And to make matters worse, his own ship was damaged; the scuttlebutt had it that *Viper* might lose either her main or fore at any moment. At which point they would be taken by the pirate and end up like those poor coves rescued from Mezmada.

"We'll be using both broadsides eventually," Woodward continued, "and will have Mr Summers to assist us this time; he has charge of the quarterdeck carronades." Balaam obediently looked aft to where the strange, and slightly frail officer was standing.

"And Mr Daniels will also be with us."

He could also see the third officer by the forecastle; next to him was Armfield, another midshipman.

"Mr Daniels will be looking after the forward batteries," Woodward added, and there might have been the hint of caution, or concern, in his voice.

"Though you remain in overall command," Balaam checked.

"Of the guns?" Woodward smiled, "Oh yes, they are my responsibility."

Balaam was glad; there was nothing overtly wrong with Lieutenant Daniels, but he did tend to talk a lot and throw his weight about, while Summers was something of a mystery, having spent much of his brief time aboard in his quarters. Of all three, Woodward was by far the more solid officer.

"If Mr Daniels gives you an order you must, of course, obey it yet he is definitely under my charge," Woodward continued, before adding something in a softer tone that Balaam missed.

But the youngster didn't need to know more, he would stick by Woodward, who had seen him through much in the past and would do so again.

* * *

Stokes gave an involuntary shiver. He was at his station as gun captain of one of *Viper*'s long twelve-pounders. It was a position he felt comfortable in, and would not have changed for the world, while the night was clear, bright and surprisingly warm for the time of year. He and the other former prisoners were pleased to return to apparent normality, although all still had a deal of weight to replace. And it was that – nothing more – which caused him to shake so.

"Be good to give them 'eathens a seein' to," Bovey

muttered.

"Aye," Stokes agreed automatically. "Taste of their own medicine."

"If that's the Visser cull it won't be no pushover," Lovemore said. "Took us easy enough afore, or don't you remember?"

"That were different," Longdon sniffed. "We was in a tuppenny-halfpenny schooner. Chances are he's never met a proper warship."

"Aye," Bovey agreed, slapping the cannon's cascabel. "A dose from Betty here will soon put him to rights."

"Well, we's about to find out," Lovemore grunted. Then, on noticing his messmate, added, "What's the matter, Stokie? Cold, are you?"

* * *

On clearing for action, King had spoken briefly to Aimée and it was not an easy conversation. After that precious time of tenderness in their quarters, she took the news of impending action surprisingly badly; King even detected an element of betrayal in her eyes and for a moment was confused and mildly hurt. After all, he didn't make the rules, and neither had he asked this Visser fellow to show up and spoil matters so.

Then he noticed something else in her expression, something that may have been missed in the past yet now seemed blindingly obvious.

"It is not my choice," he had told her, closing his eyes now with the memory. And then there was an understanding once more; without speaking Aimée reached out and touched him gently on the chest before turning away.

She should be safe enough on the orlop and not alone, he told himself, eyes still tightly shut. There would be her servant, as well as Summers' wife, and Hannah Palmer along with her father would also be sheltering there; even Bob Manning was close by. So, really there was nothing for him to worry about.

"No reply from the private signal, sir."

Malcolm's comment brought him back to the present problem. That was his last hope, but at least Visser had not tried to confuse the issue with false colours or attempting to reply to their challenge.

A messenger approached. "Mr Daniels reports the bow chasers in range, your honour."

"Very good." King had no intention of firing off their forward guns, but his prey would soon be within reach of *Viper*'s broadside cannon, while equally he could expect return fire at any time.

"Tell Mr Daniels to wait upon my word, though you may also advise Mr Woodward to open fire with the broadside pieces as soon as he thinks fit."

The lad was gone in an instant, leaving King feeling strangely alone on the crowded quarterdeck. It would do no harm to give Woodward autonomy; he knew his guns better than any of them and had proved to be a reliable officer. He raised his glass and considered the enemy again; *Viper* was drawing closer, yet Visser stubbornly held his course; it was almost as if he wanted to be raked. From the corner of his eye, King could see nearby gun captains signalling their pieces in range, although his focus remained on his opponent. The optimum time – the moment when *Viper*'s broadside was level with the pirate's bows – was still several minutes away; it seemed impossible they would be allowed that one perfect opening shot.

And so it proved.

"She's turning!"

King noticed the move as Cooper spoke; the enemy frigate was steering closer to the wind and slowing. Soon she must present her starboard broadside and, though they might still make an impact on the pirate, *Viper* had been robbed of her prime chance.

"Fire!"

The order came from further forward and was given sooner than King would have liked. A couple of minutes more would have put them in a better position, and he briefly regretted allowing Woodward such independence. Summers had also been caught out and so was late in despatching his carronades, which was equally disappointing. Yet several hundredweight of iron was finally sent flying across the spangled waters and King remained determinedly optimistic.

His hopes were soon dashed, however. Despite a tight grouping, most shots fell short while the few that pitched further would do little damage at such an acute angle. He turned away from the sight; there was no arguing the fact that the broadside was ill-timed with insufficient allowance given for *Viper*'s roll; Woodward had let them down.

But as soon as he acknowledged the fact, King wiped it from his mind. There was no sense in worrying further; the pirate frigate was continuing to turn and must soon repay the compliment.

"Take us to starboard, Mr Manton!"

Normally he would have thrown the helm across to chase his opponent's tail, then release his starboard broadside on their stern although doing so would place their weakened channels under strain. Instead, they must turn to the east and retain the larboard tack.

Now the enemy was coming back and, rather than returning fire, following them to starboard with the wind; Visser must be saving his first broadside which was oddly comforting. King supposed his usual victims were lightly armed merchants; fighting a true warship would be very different.

Woodward's men were rushing to reload the larboard guns, but King's attention remained on the frigate, now settled on a near parallel course. Both ships were on a beam reach, with *Viper* slightly ahead and less than half a mile of starlit water to separate them. And then his eyes were dazzled by rippling light as eighteen heavy cannon were released in his direction.

The first shot struck them seconds later and it was immediately obvious all were well laid. The hammock-stuffed netting protecting *Viper*'s quarterdeck was hit, causing tight-bound parcels of canvas to fly up before falling harmlessly, yet alarmingly, amid those at the conn. Of far greater danger were the round-shot aimed lower that punched straight through the frigate's bulwarks. A marine was killed outright, with the ball accounting for him also sending razored splinters that sliced into his colleagues. Three men fell at a carronade and the leading davit holding their larboard quarter boat was neatly removed at its base, causing the cutter to tumble, then drag in the sea below, and the base of the mizzen was struck a glancing blow that made the entire mast reverberate like some primaeval tuning fork.

King noted the damage with an air of detachment; there would be more further forward but the feel of the ship remained the same and he sensed her sailing abilities were unaffected. Woodward had also survived, along with most of his gunners and, despite the sudden carnage, their larboard cannon continued to be served.

"Heavy stuff," Cooper commented. King followed his gaze and noticed the spent ball that had struck the trunk of their mizzen rolling harmlessly in the scuppers. The blackened sphere was larger than the twelve-pound shot *Viper*'s long guns were firing; this looked more like an eighteen. And there was another important point, the pirate's first broadside had struck, and struck hard, whereas theirs fell harmlessly into the sea. Much could be down to luck, of course, although luck could win battles as easily as skill.

* * *

Even in the relative darkness of *Viper*'s orlop a good deal could be supposed. Every turn and change of sail was revealed by creaks and groans from the frigate's frame and the sound of her opening broadside had echoed in deafening magnificence. Then, when the enemy hit back, it sounded a slightly softer note, if no less daunting. It was actually possible to gauge roughly where each shot landed, then judge the damage by the moan and crack of timbers.

On clearing for action most bulkheads were removed, turning the area into a hollow shell that would serve as the ship's dressing station and hospital. Further forward, several sea chests had been gathered together and Robert Manning and his assistants were now laying out their various instruments and equipment, apparently unaffected by the sounds about them. But as soon as the enemy struck there was a change; without a word, the surgeons took up positions at what would become their operating tables, while loblolly boys straightened out the canvas partially covering the deck and all awaited their first customers.

Which arrived almost immediately; Suzie Summers heard the lad brought struggling into their lair long before she saw his broken body and quickly turned away as more followed. She caught Aimée's eye. The woman seemed oddly untroubled, as was Hannah and, mildly ashamed, Suzie looked back. But the dark space had already become a scene from hell with sights, sounds and smells that would stay with her forever.

"This is awful." The words were not intended to be heard, although both women glanced in her direction.

"It will get worse, much worse," Aimée said. "I think we may be needed."

"Needed?" The very thought shocked Suzie to the core, yet Hannah nodded quietly and rose.

"But what can we do?" Suzie demanded when Aimée stood also.

"Whatever is required of us," Hannah told her softly and, in a daze, Suzie found herself following.

* * *

"Fire!"

Viper's larboard battery was despatched again and this time with more effect. The pirate was neatly bracketed, and King registered definite damage to the lower hull. However, the broadside did little to stop her; even as the enemy frigate recovered, her helm was put across and she wore to starboard.

The sudden change of heading brought the wind onto her quarter giving more speed. That, and the fact that *Viper* had been marginally ahead, meant his ship's stern was now in danger of being raked.

"Follow her round, Mr Manton," King ordered. Then, to the gunners in their waist, "Starboard battery, Mr Woodward!"

King felt a wave of relief as he realised their gunnery officer did know his business. With one blast of a whistle and a bellowed order, the lieutenant moved their transit gunners to starboard. It meant leaving the larboard guns unloaded, although Visser's ploy would be countered, and another quick broadside added into the bargain.

However, that was not to be, even as the British frigate moved onto her new heading and her gunners prepared to sight their pieces off the starboard quarter, a ripple of fire spread along the pirate's hull. It was not quite a rake, but *Viper*'s stern took a pounding. Her leeward quarter gallery was hit in several places and, along with much of her stern lights, dissolved in a shower of crown glass and shattered gingerbread. The taffrail also crumbled and men fell at the sternmost carronades. Midshipman Malcolm screamed in sudden agony as a splinter ripped into his belly, and the flag locker was tossed the length of the quarterdeck, leaving a trail of bundled bunting in its wake.

"Further!" King bellowed, although Manton took no notice. The ship had yet to fully respond to her rudder; what would truly make a difference was a solid broadside from her starboard battery: it would be up to Woodward to provide one.

And this time the lieutenant did not disappoint. The gap between both ships had narrowed and *Viper*'s guns caused obvious damage to the pirate's prow and forward spars. The jib boom separated close to its tip, her jib was whisked away and there was an obvious slacking of tension to the upper foremast. But what mattered more was the simultaneous loss of her lower foreyard. The forecourse went the same way as her jib and there would be no further support for her foretopsail. Then, with the sudden imbalance, the entire ship began to fall back with the wind.

King knew this was the time to finish things. A shout to Manton saw *Viper*'s main backed, and she began to steer to starboard across the enemy frigate's bow. It would be some while before that battery could speak again, though when it did, the result must be deadly. He turned to Cooper and noted the look of satisfaction on his first officer's face; both knew it was now just a question of time.

But their relief was premature; the pirate recovered faster than any of them expected. Her foretopsail was secured in no time, then she was underway once more and making for *Viper*'s larboard side. Robbed of support from their transit gunners, that battery was only partially served and would not be ready. They would have to meet the enemy's close-range broadside with nothing more than muskets.

There were more whistles and shouts; Woodward was returning some of the larboard gun crews, though it could not be in time. The pirate's wounded bowsprit was already creeping past *Viper*'s quarterdeck; soon the enemy ship would be alongside and less than a pistol shot off. Now King and Cooper exchanged worried glances, Manton muttered something that both of them missed and then the enemy drew fully level, and her broadside was released.

Chapter Twenty-Nine

The damage was significant though not critical; all *Viper*'s masts remained intact but three of her larboard cannon were wrecked and many good men fell. And there was confusion, but not panic. Most tending guns remained at their posts and continued to work, the job of securing the ship, the splicing, or replacing of line and removing casualties falling to waisters or members of the boatswain's team. And soon – miraculously soon – what remained of her larboard battery was ready to reply.

Which Woodward did immediately; the need was great, and the enemy's proximity made careful aim less important. The pieces were despatched with an erratic clatter and in the general direction of the pirate's hull that lay so horribly close.

"They must not board!" King's shout came from the heart; he knew the corsairs' liking for over-manning their ships; should a swarm of fighting men land on *Viper*'s decks at that moment they would take her.

"Port the helm!" Manton's order was instinctive and would seriously endanger *Viper*'s stern were the enemy's guns served in time. Yet it was correct, and King remained silent. Steadily the distance between both ships increased though the pirate also put her helm across and obviously intended to follow *Viper* round.

"Take her further to starboard," King ordered, and the sailing master turned.

"You wish us to wear, sir?" he asked.

"I do."

"That will place us on the starboard tack."

It was every sailing master's duty to alert his captain to hazards, be they meteorological, navigational or concerning the state of the ship, although there was far more to Manton's remark than a mild warning. Once the wind was taken to starboard, her weakened channels would be under pressure again. And there could be no more nursing; they were in action, speed would be required and a deal of fast manoeuvring. Even if the pirates failed to land another shot, *Viper* might be dismasted at any moment.

"I am aware," King said simply. "Make it so."

* * *

Suzie had already tended to several men, one being a relatively simple matter of stemming the flow of blood. There were copious rolls of ready-use bandages to hand and the end result, though hardly orthodox, would serve until more competent hands made a permanent repair. Another had what might have been a broken arm; the marine concerned was in obvious pain and she knew nothing of splints or the like but further lengths of canvas secured the limb to his chest and, though he still whimpered gently, the fellow seemed thankful. But the third was the hardest of all; a shellback – the man must be fifty if he were a day – and with a deadly wound to the head. He had been earmarked for immediate attention, although every surgeon was involved with other patients. And Suzie could do precious little; the head was already bandaged tightly and, despite the dressing being horribly discoloured, she left it alone. Her patient remained conscious, however: conscious and almost lucid, apart from the absurd notion that she was his mother.

In her delicate state, Suzie found kneeling on the deck difficult, yet kneel she must to keep the old man's bloodshot eyes on hers. And though his questions were varied and far-ranging, she did her best to answer, keeping her voice soft and reassuring, the way a mother's should be. But when they finally came to take him away, she did not rise immediately, and neither did she seek another patient. The pain below had been troubling her for some while although other matters kept it from her mind. With less distraction it asserted itself once more, and Suzie gave an involuntary moan. Aimée heard and was instantly by her side.

"Are you hurt?"

Was she hurt? They were surrounded by men wounded most horribly; how could she answer such a question?

"Is it the baby?"

That was simpler; she nodded emphatically. Now there was someone to care for her, Suzie found it easy to become the patient.

"We must get you somewhere private," Aimée said and

298

again the statement struck her as ridiculous. "Let me help you stand."

Then Hannah was close by, and the two women were guiding her over the mass of writhing bodies.

"The baby?" This was Bewley, currently dosing a topman with laudanum. "Take her aft, I shall ask one of the surgeons to attend."

"Please, do not bother." Embarrassment forced the smile, which was short-lived; the pain was returning. "I shall be fine," Suzie added when the agony began to fade. "I just need to lie down."

* * *

Viper wore easily and by the time she was clawing back with the pirate off her starboard beam, her guns were once more ready to speak. They did, and significant damage must have been caused; the pirate's hull was peppered with some shot landing close to her own channels. But it was just as the last gun was despatched that King noticed the enemy's driver was falling out of shape and wondered if a truly important hit had been made.

And so it proved, even as they watched, the huge sail billowed up and began fluttering uselessly in the wind.

"Struck the boom!" the first lieutenant bellowed with delight. "That'll slow 'em!"

Cooper was right, yet a well-trained crew could correct such an imbalance quickly. What worried King more was that *Viper* must shortly face another enemy broadside.

It came little more than a minute later, and after Visser had managed to turn his ship almost beam on. And, though the total impact might have been less than before, *Viper* was sorely wounded. Numerous blows landed deep in her lower regions, two further guns were dismounted, and a small fire broke out just aft of the foremast. But the worst damage was caused amidships, where their starboard main channel finally gave way.

They would never be certain whether this was due to enemy shot, or if Morales's repair finally failed, although the consequences were the same. Shrouds, tyes and stays slackened and, even over the noise of battle, a chilling groan was heard from the mast itself. All stared up, expecting to see the entire structure topple but, though the wind continued to fill her canvas, somehow it remained.

"Let loose the main tops'l an' t'gallants!"

Again, Manton had given the order without reference to his captain, and again it was correct. Without that canvas, *Viper* could still manoeuvre to some extent but, should their mainmast fall, she would be doomed.

King looked across to the pirate; already the gap between them had dwindled and, with the wind in her favour, the enemy frigate was being pressed closer.

"To larboard!" It would place their forechannel under further strain, yet they had to bear away and do so quickly. The manoeuvre failed, however; Morales' work held out forward and the ship continued to move, although not fast enough to avoid the oncoming pirate.

"Independent fire!" King's voice cracked as he bellowed the order, but it was soon picked up and, after one more ragged broadside, their remaining guns began to be released as soon as they were loaded.

King set his glass on the enemy's upper deck and his worst fears were confirmed. The pirates were preparing to board.

Slowly, far too slowly, *Viper* tried to creep away, but Visser's crew were up to the mark; their streaming canvas was already tamed and the ship herself appeared under control and steadily drawing nearer. Duke's marines continued to fire on her, and a scattering of robed figures fell to their shots, although now King could see a positive crowd gathering by the enemy's bulwarks. Even in the poor light, full beards and strange headgear were obvious while flashes from the marine's musket fire reflected off a mass of drawn weapons. There must be eighty – a hundred perhaps – ready to board: more than enough to swamp them completely. King drew breath; until a few hours before he had known little about this Visser fellow and was ready to take him for a fool. But the man was proving an excellent seaman, and one that equally knew how to fight.

* * *

"What are you playing at, Daniels?" Woodward bellowed.

The junior man was treating him to that well-known look – something between a sneer and a smirk – and Woodward had to stop himself from removing it with his fist. First the cull had ordered their guns despatched, an act that wasted *Viper*'s valuable opening broadside, now – and not for the first time – he was disputing the choice of shot.

"We shall be closing with the enemy." Daniels was forced to time his response between cannon. "Canister is the only option."

"Then the captain will make it!"

Another gun was fired, momentarily deafening those close by; this was truly not the time or place for conversation.

"He has ordered independent fire," Daniels said, "so passed control of the guns to us."

"To me!" Woodward corrected. "And you are my junior!"

"For now, perhaps." Once more, that look and, once more Woodward's heightened senses tempted him to violence.

But this would not do, Woodward had made his point and now was needed elsewhere. And without saying more, he turned on his heel and left.

* * *

Midshipman Balaam was in turmoil; his every sense lay under assault and he felt stunned, bemused and slightly sick. However, enough of the routine practised so often in drills had permeated the fourteen-year-old's brain and certain orders were automatic. When too many men fell at one gun, he would supplement from another less affected and every other small emergency or minor complication was dealt with as easily.

Likewise, the injuries. Though young, he was no mothers' loll and the presence of blood or wounds in general was hardly a novelty. And besides, Balaam found it possible to look but not see those carried away. In this he was helped to some extent; for a night action the light was incredibly good, although convenient shadows still hid much. And truly his job was easy; were he called to physically clear wreckage, extinguish a fire, or manage a screaming seaman, Balaam would fail, yet he could assess a situation, and instruct men old enough to be his father. But then, of course, he had Lieutenant Woodward's example to follow.

For a good while there had been little chance of conversation other than the odd, shouted, order but, even in such noise and confusion, the officer radiated confidence. Occasionally Balaam would glance forward and see how his friend Armfield was getting on working under Daniels and was in no way jealous.

Woodward was talking with the other lieutenant now, or perhaps arguing, Balaam could not be sure. Both men were particularly animated, though, so he assumed the latter. Certainly, when Woodward returned, he had a face like thunder.

"How are we loaded, Mr Balaam?" he demanded.

"Beg pardon, sir?"

"Our shot, it is still ball?"

Balaam checked the nearest cannon and noted the five ready-use rounds of both canister and bar remained in place.

"Of course, sir," he confirmed.

"Very good," Woodward said, softening slightly. "Be sure to keep it that way."

* * *

The din of combat continued to permeate the orlop yet was hardly noticed above the screams and moans of *Viper*'s wounded while, further aft, Suzie's personal battle was proving almost as loud. Space was made for her outside the lieutenants' storeroom; only those rushing back and forth from the aft magazine came near and they had other matters on their minds. But Suzie was totally focused on the demands of her body, as were the women close by.

"Grip as hard as you wish," Hannah instructed, clasping the woman's hand tightly as an example. She had assisted with the birth of several children, two being her own sisters, and learned much, although all were far simpler than this. Or was it that she was no longer a spectator and now must take an active part?

Suzie's eyes were fixed on the deckhead above, but she nodded slightly and squeezed in reply. Then the gentle gesture turned instantly to spasm and her entire body arched as the pain returned.

"We shall have to fetch a surgeon." Hannah spoke quietly,

even if their patient did not appear to hear or be taking notice.

Aimée glanced towards the flickering lamplight forward. "But they are so busy," she said. "Men are dying."

Hannah knew that was correct and preserving existing life probably should take precedence over starting fresh. Yet there was something about the woman's condition that did not seem right. She knew a little of the various complications though was not experienced enough to identify any; that needed a trained eye, and someone with a deal more understanding.

And then an idea occurred, one that might prove fruitless, but Suzie was tiring visibly. She gently laid the hand down and looked across at Aimée.

"I shall return directly," she said.

"You are going?"

"We have to summon assistance."

"*Assistance*? Everyone is so busy; no one will be able to help."

"There may be one who can," Hannah said and left.

* * *

Balaam was surprised to see Lieutenant Daniels; the man had appeared from nowhere and literally tugged at Lieutenant Woodward's sleeve to get his attention.

"We must load with canister!" he bellowed.

"I told you, no!"

Balaam could see the fury on Woodward's face.

"But they are so damned close!" Daniels' hand waved vaguely at the impending warship. A nearby cannon fired, and both were forced to wait until the echo fully died.

"Then the captain will order it," Woodward replied when the ringing finally stopped. "Return to your station!"

"I have instructed my men to change," Daniels said.

"Then you will answer for your actions," Woodward snapped. "Now go!"

He did and Balaam felt a measure of relief at his departure.

"Carry on, John," Woodward told him and, once more, gave that faint smile of reassurance. However, the look soon faded to be replaced by one of surprise that immediately turned to pain.

Balaam instinctively stepped forward and reached out, but

Woodward did not appear to notice, his mind was somewhere else entirely. With a slight stagger, he stepped to one side, then collapsed to his knees and finally fell face down onto the deck.

Even amid the chaos, Balaam could take in what had happened, yet refused to believe it, and only when he knelt and picked up one limp hand did he truly understand. About him all was madness, although one he was attuned to, and the midshipman bellowed an order without hesitation.

"Simons, Bradshaw, see Mr Woodward below!"

The seamen had just finished extinguishing a small fire and approached the body with minds already blank. Another cannon was despatched but neither heard, instead, they hoisted the lieutenant onto Bradshaw's shoulder before carrying him to the main hatch. There he would be passed to those on the berth deck below, then down to the orlop. Balaam looked away, he had no idea if his senior still lived or even of his exact injuries and there was no room, or time, for grief. The one fact that mattered was Lieutenant Woodward had gone and from now on he must cope by himself.

* * *

Stokes and his fellow transit gunners were serving the starboard gun. As veterans of countless drills, and not a few actions, the work was almost automatic – even covering for other members of their team came to them naturally.

And this was becoming increasingly necessary; two of the tackle men had been called away to tend other pieces, their designated fireman was currently dealing with a small blaze further aft, and Bovey, the sea lawyer who normally rammed home shot and charge, was dead.

As gun captain, Stokes' role was to prime, train and despatch the weapon yet now he must also haul the beast into position, while occasionally passing fresh shot or wads to the loader. They had been hard at it for a good while and normally would just be getting warmed up although Stokes knew things were different. He had recovered remarkably quickly from his time as a slave and, along with the rest of his crew, regarded himself as in prime condition. But for the last few minutes his strength had begun to ebb; he was growing clumsy handling the powder horn and needed to draw breath more than once before heaving back on the train tackle. An occasional glance told him Longdon and Lovemore were suffering in a similar way and were still to recover fully.

Yet, tired or not, the work must go on, despite it being harder to maintain a steady pace without the discipline of broadsides. And neither did it help having a bunch of officers close by with nothing better to do than argue amongst themselves.

It began with Daniels, the junior lieutenant that Stokes remembered as a particularly cocky midshipman. To hear him now he might have been made admiral; the cull was remonstrating with Balaam – a youngster Stokes held far more respect for. Though just a midshipman and perhaps a little green, the lad had been handling them well. Stokes could not tell what had queered the senior man's pitch but wished they would keep it to themselves; he had enough distractions with serving the cannon and dodging enemy shot.

On that tack, it was a pity Woodward had fallen, the cove was worth a dozen Daniels. Then it seemed Summers, their second officer, was joining in. He had come forward from his station with the carronades and the three of them were going at it hammer and tongs. With a genuine enemy so close it seemed a waste of energy to fight anyone else.

"Charge home!"

Stokes felt for the flannel cartridge with his priming wire while a fresh round shot was rammed down the barrel.

"Shot home!"

Easing back the hammer, he dosed the touchhole with priming powder. The barrel itself was hot – too hot. They were lucky not to have had a misfire with that last priming and should pause for a thorough quench before the next.

With the enemy so worryingly close, there was little need for training, yet Stokes was a seasoned gunner who took pride in his work. Considering his recent experiences ashore, the groups of jeering heathens were tempting targets, but he was savvy enough to know they could do little harm unless their ship were allowed to close. And the best way to avoid that was to damage their masts. A wave of his right hand saw the weapon hauled over until the enemy's foremast lay comfortably in his sights. Then, with a quick order to stand clear, he eased back on the firing line and the gun was despatched.

305

The pirate frigate was less than fifty feet off and would be alongside in no time. With *Viper*'s gunners firing individually, there were barely seconds of blessed peace between each discharge and every one weakened King's numbed ears further, although his mind felt remarkably clear. He winced as a forward gun peppered the ranks of robed figures waiting to board.

"Woodward's switched to canister," he said. Presumably that was to wear down the enemy before they arrived. And the idea carried some merit, King supposed, though it would take more than a few buckets of musket balls to dispel the crowd awaiting them. Besides, he would always prefer to kill the ship than her crew.

"Woodward has fallen," Cooper corrected. Even such a brief exchange must be timed between shots and, despite both men bellowing, they were barely heard. "Summers has gone forward to take control."

King nodded; Summers would do a better job than Daniels.

The pirate had not fired for some while; King guessed Visser was saving his shot to land one last devastating blow before despatching his boarders. Were he facing a conventional enemy, King might consider surrender; little could be gained from delaying and more good men would be lost. However, he now knew much about the Barbary Pirates and had no intention of anyone aboard *Viper* becoming their prisoner. This final battle would be fought to the end.

The expected broadside arrived shortly afterwards and was devastating. *Viper* received further deep blows to her belly and her bowsprit was shattered aft of the martingale boom. Further shots pounded into her damaged channels and several on the quarterdeck were hit, including the quartermaster and one of his helmsmen, although the wheel was miraculously left undamaged. Two more guns were struck, and the capstan dissolved into a myriad of chips and splinters. But throughout the carnage and confusion, what remained of their starboard battery continued to be served and, while waisters grabbed at ready-use weapons, or spare spars to fend the invader off, *Viper* continued to fire.

And then the miracle happened: an aft long gun, still firing round shot, found the pirate's foremast. It was struck just above deck level and immediately began to totter. For a moment the delicate structure remained, unsupported. And then, with the snapping of line and a chorus of cheers from *Viper*'s marines, the entire mast came crashing down, dragging the main topmast with it.

For a few sacred moments, all anyone could hear was the ringing in their ears. And then the guns began again.

Robbed of forward movement, the pirate began to turn in the wind until her bows almost faced *Viper* and, spurred on by such a prime target, the British gunners renewed their efforts. In no time the enemy's prow was shattered, with greater damage caused within. Soon fire broke out, and when the flames began to rise above the frigate's deck, King reached for his silver whistle and blew one long blast that carried with it a ring of finality.

A carronade fired immediately afterwards but its team had been working like automatons for so long it could be excused. Of more significance, nothing was heard from the pirates other than confused shouts and the hum of panic. King turned to Cooper.

"I think we might assume the enemy has struck," he said.

Chapter Thirty

"Is all well here?" Manning asked. He had been aware of Mrs Summers' condition for some time but was fully committed elsewhere. However, the guns were now silent while the steady stream of casualties had dwindled to little more than a trickle. And it came as no surprise to see one of his assistants was already present.

"We are close to the end, sir," the loblolly boy told him, "and all is now as it should be."

"Now?" Manning questioned, and Bewley appeared awkward.

"The child was not presenting correctly," he said. "I was forced to adjust."

The surgeon nodded and laid a fatherly hand on the younger man's shoulder. Manning's wife was an experienced mother midnight, so he rarely involved himself in such procedures. It was good to have someone proficient on hand, even if Bewley were more accustomed to assisting farm animals.

Suzie Summers was looking up at him with tired eyes. "I'm so sorry," she said.

"Sorry?"

"For all the trouble."

"I think she means for giving birth at such a time," Aimée said, and Suzie nodded.

"It is not so unusual," Manning assured. His apron was thick with the gore from far less natural procedures, and he felt reluctant to approach an essentially well person in the midst of an entirely normal process. Besides, with Bewley he sensed she was in safe hands; he really should return to his patients. "From what I gather such a thing is a regular occurrence," he said.

"Giving birth during a battle?" Hannah was amazed.

"Oh yes, Miss Palmer, there are numerous instances," the surgeon confirmed. "In two of Nelson's actions at least, as well as many others, or so I am told. It is believed to be associated with the noise of cannon," he added vaguely, glancing back at the sickbay proper.

"I would never have guessed." Hannah shook her head slowly and Aimée looked equally surprised.

"There is also talk of a woman giving birth at Trafalgar…" Manning added with a wicked glint. "And she wasn't even pregnant."

The blank looks that greeted the surgeon's jape were enough to hurry him away, leaving room for more competent hands to continue.

"It won't be long now," Bewley announced, and Hannah exchanged a knowing smile with Aimée. Though lacking formal qualifications, the man was a natural medic who inspired confidence, and they returned to Suzie's care with renewed energy.

* * *

It was not a general feeling, however. On the upper deck, Stokes and his men were slow in securing their guns. And, though much else needed doing, neither did they fall willingly back to other work.

"Light duties, Mr Armfield," Lovemore claimed when the midshipman challenged them, and despite being little more than a child, the lad could recognise exhaustion and left well alone.

Others were more active. *Viper* was in a sore state and taking in water. Morales and his men made the hull a priority and spent the rest of the night shoring up frames or stuffing oakum and pitch into shot holes before nailing all tight under sheets of lead. Marine Captain Duke also came into his own. He, and a detachment of his men, accompanied Cooper to claim the prize where, though outnumbered many times over, their discipline and solid intent quickly pacified the pirates.

Who needed to be secured aboard their own ship – none could be brought back to *Viper*; there being too many former prisoners that might take vengeance on helpless captives. And neither was King willing to accept the parole of any officer, especially Visser, the turncoat Dutchman.

His opposite number had actually proved something of a revelation. The man purported to be a latter-day Jan Janszoon, having joined the pirates when his own trader was captured several years before. On being brought ashore he avoided slavery by renouncing his faith, then volunteered to join a corsair's crew and, with a mixture of skill and luck, finally worked his way up to commanding the frigate. For a European to 'turn Turk' in such a way was not unusual yet, rather than the mixture of privateer and adventurer common in his type, Visser was a bitter man with a profound hatred of the British. He carried no papers or letter of marque and legally King could have hanged the scoundrel. But, even before Palmer intervened, he compromised by setting him in bilboes; the authorities in Gibraltar could make what they would of him.

Visser's former ship also needed to be made safe. Much of her damage was to the upperworks and spars, but her prow was also wrecked and there were several lower wounds that, even when patched, meant both pumps needed to be manned constantly.

Duke organised this as well and did so with the same gruff efficiency that coloured all his actions and King, who had never felt any special regard for marines in general, was surprised, impressed and deeply grateful.

And with dawn there was relief of another sort. Morning brought news of a warship approaching from the east and, by the time the sun had fully risen, a trim, slick and strangely pristine frigate was taking station on their prize.

"*Humber*, thirty-six, Captain Scott," Midshipman Balaam reported.

"I remember her from the American Station," Cooper said.

"I also," Manton grunted. "And her captain; a stuffed-up prig of a man. See how he stands off the buccaneer as if it were all his doing!"

"Well, it were not," Cooper grunted. "We took her, fair an' square."

* * *

King supposed he would accustom himself to calling on the sick in time although the task was becoming no easier and his first call on Williams, whose injury was so similar to his own, had been something of an ordeal. But subsequent visits revealed the lad to be making a far better recovery.

And Lieutenant Woodward was showing equally positive signs. The musket ball that struck him in the shoulder had been removed with a bullet extractor and, though it was early days, and still uncommonly warm for autumn, there was equally no sign of corruption. Certainly, he looked well enough when King entered the officer's cabin. With the regular sick berth re-established and full to brimming, Manning had allowed those with private accommodation to recuperate elsewhere and Woodward was resting comfortably on his bunk.

"You feel well enough to talk?" King asked after making the expected enquiries and taking a seat.

"Perfectly, sir. Young Balaam has just left." Woodward nodded to where three apples lay on the bedside table.

"He was your midshipman during the action, as I recall."

"Yes, sir, and covered for me until Mike Summers could take command."

"Though I gather not all went smoothly," King added. He had no wish to tire his second officer, but one matter did need to be settled before they made Gibraltar.

"That is not my understanding, sir."

"Mr Summers has spoken of a confrontation between him and Mr Daniels."

Woodward's frown was replaced with a look of mild despair. "Which doesn't surprise me," he said. "Arguing over the choice of shot, I suppose?"

"I believe so."

"That old chestnut." Woodward shook his head. "Daniels thought we should change to canister earlier and I disagreed."

"And it is fortunate for us all that you did. However, do I take it Mr Daniels is free with his opinions?"

"Remarkably so, sir. Especially with regard to the choice of shot, though in truth little that is done aboard *Viper* meets with his approval." He paused, as if aware of saying too much.

"Very well," King sighed. "Tell me, James, are you happy serving alongside him?"

"Daniels?" Woodward seemed surprised by the question though gave it full thought. "I would hardly say happy, sir; as I have said, the man is highly opinionated..."

King waited.

"Though he also enjoys good connections. His father is well in with the Admiralty, and I believe an element of interest has helped him in the past."

"I had heard as much. And you are concerned he may attempt to usurp your position?"

"Not exactly. Only a court-martial can alter my seniority as lieutenant, yet I would predict Mr Daniels' eyes are set far higher and he does not envisage a future aboard *Viper*."

King nodded. "I gathered that also. What say we give him his freedom?"

"Freedom?"

"Mr Daniels' time as a midshipman did not lack issue while his subsequent appointment as lieutenant was due to necessity and purely temporary. In short, he may be dismissed at any time, in which case you will be rid of him."

"I'd like that fine, sir," Woodward admitted.

"Then it will be done," King said. "Though I doubt he will approve of it, or my subsequent report."

"A poor reference may not be well received elsewhere." Woodward appeared genuinely concerned. "And, as I say, he is well connected. If you will forgive me, sir, you have your own career to consider."

"If the truth offends, it is hardly my concern." King's tone was harsh, yet soon softened. "And in your case, it can only praise; your conduct throughout this commission has been commendable."

"Thank you, sir."

"I trust you will resume your duties as *Viper*'s second officer as soon as is feasible," he added. With Summers still determined to depart, Cooper would need experienced men like Woodward to see the ship through her refit.

"Yes, sir. I'm looking forward to it."

King had been about to rise but something in Woodward's manner caused him to pause.

"Is there something else?" he asked.

"Not exactly, sir." The young man appeared cautious. "But you did speak of *my* being rid of Daniels," he added. "Not *we*..."

King sat down properly. "I see little gets passed you, James," he said. "I shall be leaving the ship at Gibraltar, though that is still to be generally known."

"There are few I can tell in here," Woodward replied, "yet am sorry to hear of it."

"I have family matters to concern me," King explained.

"And feel I have done enough fighting."

"Run out of war, sir?"

"Some might say so."

"But I shall see you again before we dock?"

"Oh indeed, and I do not intend to leave the Navy as such, just retire from active service."

"I understand, sir."

"And I have acquired a measure of seniority," King added more thoughtfully. "Nothing approaching those caring for our friend Daniels, of course, though if there is ever a need for someone to speak in your favour, I hope you will remember me."

"Thank you, sir; I will be sure to."

* * *

"There can only be one recipe for hard tack, yet it always tastes different," Longdon declared. "Queer, ain't it?"

Stokes paused with his own biscuit inches from his mouth. "Can't say I ever noticed."

"Nor me." Lovemore shrugged, but Longdon was emphatic.

"This Maltese stuff's miles off what they gives out in Albion, an' you can tell how long since it were baked."

"Al'ays assumin' it *were* baked," Stokes grumbled. "Most tastes like it's been chiselled from a quarry."

They had still to return to their regular messes; the ship being in too disordered a state for such formality yet, by unspoken agreement, the three seamen remained as a group. And, with the galley chimney one of the many casualties, there had been no hot food since the action. Instead, they were enjoying a scratch supper of hard tack and cheese in a forward corner of the berth deck.

"You take this," Longdon directed, tapping his biscuit on the cask head that served as their table. "Been about too long, and light as a feather. There'll be weevils in it sure as a gun."

He smashed down hard on a piece that obediently crumbled to dust, revealing the ominous red worms it had been hiding.

"Nothin' wrong with a bit o' weevil," Stokes claimed through a mouthful of his own biscuit.

313

"Maybe not, though they'll have eaten all the goodness."

"An' then we eats them." Lovemore picked one up in his fingers and popped it into his mouth. "Where's the difference?"

"Difference is maggots," Longdon declared. "Get a fresher biscuit and it'll have the little white fellows; they won't have eaten so much and taste better into the bargain."

"You sure it weren't just your arm what took a knock?" Stokes asked.

"Well, I'll always be sure to ask for my hard tack good an' maggoty in future," Lovemore confirmed. "Don't want any more of 'em weevils..."

"We'll be lucky to get any form of bread afore long," Stokes added more seriously. "*Viper*'s for refit an' a long one if I'm any judge."

"You don't reckon they'll turn us over to another ship?" Lovemore helped himself to another of Longdon's weevils.

"Doubt there'll be anythin' about to take us. Navy's cuttin' down."

"There'll be a berth of some sort, surely?"

"Maybe a merchant," Stokes supposed. "Though you know what that'll mean; small crews and short commons. But whatever we gets, I can't see us lot stayin' together."

"'Tis a pity," Lovemore grunted, "after so long."

"An' there were so many of us," Longdon agreed, "to begin with..."

"Early, Downes, Groom, Healy..."

"Don't remember a Healy," Stokes said.

"Yorkshireman," Lovemore reminded. "Always called a spade a spade."

"Oh yes." The older man pulled a face. "I do recall."

"Well, I wouldn't put it past remaining aboard *Viper*," Lovemore said. "They always need a few regular Jacks; them what knows the ship proper."

"You think that's likely?" Longdon asked.

"Stranger things 'ave happened. Remember the standin' officers?"

"S.O.s stays aboard whatever."

"That's right," Lovemore agreed. "Someone needs to keep an eye on how the dockyard maties behave."

"So, what you suggestin'?" Stokes was almost defensive.

"I've helped out the carpenter often enough in the past, and Longdon here knows his way aloft, while you're useful with the great guns an' all forms of ordnance. I'd say we'd make decent mates."

"A warrant," Longdon said in mild wonder. "That would be a thing..."

"Maybe not a warrant," Lovemore cautioned, "An' it might not be official. Though each of the S.O.s knows and trusts us. I'd say we stands a chance."

"And'll be on hand when the barky's brought back into commission!" Stokes was definitely warming to the prospect.

"With a regular billet in the meanwhile," Lovemore agreed. "Together with a run ashore in Gib whenever we wants one."

"Well, it won't come about less we put ourselves forward." Longdon had now lost all interest in his biscuit. "I say we speaks up at first light."

"First light?" Stokes asked, rising. "I'm gonna smoke Paddy Regan out now..."

* * *

Viper had been in harbour a full week and Gibraltar was proving as welcoming as ever, although all aboard began to relax as soon as the rock came into sight. And of everyone, King was probably the most relieved.

Captain Scott obliged them by providing additional men and materials to see both ships secure and then the motive power to bring their partially dismasted capture in. But *Viper* showed more independence. Yet again, Morales performed miracles with her starboard channels and, though no great speed was possible and all kept watch for the first of the winter gales, she was able to enter the bay and release her one remaining anchor unassisted.

Three dockyard wherries appeared shortly afterwards and the wounded were transferred ashore, followed by any able-bodied men not required to keep her afloat. And then arrangements began to see *Viper*, and her prize, properly secured.

Those transferred included most held prisoner by the pirates, only the standing officers, and a dozen or so of the older hands, were being allowed to stay with the ship and see her through refit. And Goodman, along with his fellow countrymen, had been transferred to a suitable gaol. There were still no official accounts of the American War, and every news sheet King could find was several weeks behind, yet he trusted the madness could not continue much longer.

And the Palmers had been one of the first to go and did so with their customary dignity and restraint. During the journey back King enjoyed several more conversations with the old man, with both learning much from the other. But two days after arriving at Gibraltar a Danish brig was discovered to be leaving for America and, by the following evening, they were gone. And they did not go alone; King was not sure of the exact details and neither did he greatly care but, Bewley, one of *Viper*'s loblolly boys, left with them. As did Millie, Aimée's former servant.

Summers and his family would also be going shortly. Their child, a girl, was proving healthy; even on the brief journey to the rock, she had endeared herself to both gunroom and lower deck alike, while her mere existence had subtly altered her father. Almost instantly he appeared older, mature and far more confident so that, in all things from supervising running repairs to managing the crew, King depended on him as much as Cooper. He remained resolute in his wish to retire, however, and a replacement was already appointed. In some ways King was sorry, and the Service would undoubtedly be the poorer without him, although Summers' mind was set elsewhere, and it would have been wrong to persuade the lad otherwise.

And King was equally keen to be off. As soon as *Viper* was taken in hand by the dockyard, he would tender his own resignation. Then, after acquiring servants and a suitable carriage, he and Aimée could start their journey home. But it would not be Eastbourne or even Britain; King felt he had already put Aimée through enough. Now it was his turn to consider her wishes and they were to settle in Verdun.

Epilogue

There would only be one more overnight stop; by the following afternoon, their goal should be in sight and the long journey over. After years of fighting the French, to settle amongst them still felt strange although King was coming to accept the concept. The well-remembered countryside was as beautiful as ever, while Aimée's growing excitement had long since convinced him it was the right move. The only thing for them in England were memories, and they would make new ones – better ones – in Verdun.

Their carriage survived the journey with only one broken axle and two shattered wheels to slow them. But then they had not rushed; getting away from *Viper*, Gibraltar, and active service in general, proved harder than King anticipated and, not free to start until after Christmas, they'd chosen to wait for the worst of winter to be over. It was nearly March now, and spring was properly setting in; neither of them could think of a better time to arrive.

And Summers, along with his young family, was already there. They had taken the lease on a small property not far from Aimée's parents. The lad was actually proving extremely useful having provided King with details of three chateaux on the outskirts of the town, any one of which would seem to be perfect. There was even the chance that Robert and Kate Manning might join them, at least for a spell when all was settled.

The winter had brought some truly worldwide changes, the most important, to King's mind at least, being the treaty signed at Ghent before Christmas. This was now ratified, and they might finally call the American War at an end. It had been a conflict that many now acknowledged should never have happened, and much was being done to restore conditions to their pre-war status. When every promise was kept, a good deal would be as it had been at the start – apart, that is, from an inordinate number of graves.

Then there were other, more subtle, political moves that should have concerned him more yet strangely did not. In November a congress opened in Vienna with the bold aims of deciding the fate of Europe whilst also ensuring such large-scale wars could never be repeated. The fight against Napoleon had been long and hard with six international coalitions needed to finally defeat the tyrant. But though he would have liked to think otherwise, King could not see any country adopting worthy ideals for world peace unless a healthy material gain was also included.

However, there was good news from the Med. Despite the doubts of Pellew and his like, Napoleon was seemingly firmly ensconced on Elba. And with the former tyrant no longer posing a threat, plans could finally be made without considering him, although King had barely followed their progress. It was as if retiring from active service had left him immune to politics: the only news that truly interested him concerned the pair of them.

"If we are still in Verdun, when your time comes..." he began. Aimée had made her revelation the day before and both had been deep in thought since.

"Which I trust we shall be!" she interrupted.

"And I," he hurriedly assured her. "Though it will mean our child will be born French!"

She began to laugh, and after a moment of further consideration, he joined her.

"All those years of war, yet I shall end up the father of a Frenchman!"

"Or woman," she reminded him.

"Which we might call Josephine!" he added, succumbing further.

"And if a boy, Napoleon!"

At this King took exception. "I don't think we need go that far," he said. "There will only ever be one Napoleon, and we have seen the last of him."

Author's Notes

Napoleon escaped from Elba on the 26th of February, just as this story ends. A combination of personal bravery, charisma and promises for constitutional reform saw his initial force of a thousand men increase to that of a mighty army. He entered Paris three days later and the War of the Seventh Coalition (also known as The Hundred Days) began.

Foreign subjects aboard British Ships. Official records show that 59 native-born Frenchmen served in the British fleet at Trafalgar. One, Louis Davit, an able seaman aged 24, died aboard *Bellerophon* while Pierre Pellerin, Francis Jeanson and John Duggers received significant wounds. Also present in British vessels were natives of America, the West Indies, Africa, Prussia, Sweden, Spain (another enemy at the time) and many other countries. The crew of HMS *Victory* alone included over twenty nationalities other than British.

The **Odiham Agricultural Society** was formed in 1783 and proved to be the basis for Britain's first veterinary college.

The island of **Zembra**, a holiday resort until 1976, is now an important bird sanctuary which has been classified as a protected area by UNESCO since 1977. The port of Mezmada is fictitious.

The Sun and *The Times* were both popular newspapers during the early nineteenth century. *The Sun*, which originally ran from 1792-1876 was founded by Pitt the Elder to counter the contemporary pro-revolutionary press. It began as *The Daily Universal Register* in 1785, changing its name three years later. In 1815 it had a circulation of 5,000.

Towards the end of the eighteenth century, **The Retreat at Lamel Hill, York** was established by William Tuke (1732-1822), a Quaker and philanthropist, to offer an alternative to the brutal treatment then common in British asylums. Tuke was in no way a professional yet acted as superintendent for the first year until George Jepson (1743-1836) – an equally untrained man but one who shared Tuke's vision – was appointed. Although considered radical at the time, The Retreat's more humane care of those suffering from melancholia and other associated conditions showed positive results. It went on to inspire similar establishments, notably in America, while doing much to encourage a greater understanding of mental illness in general.

Round shot on canister. Despite officially being frowned upon, the practice of double shotting cannon was common. It was only truly effective at very close range, however, and a reduction in powder was required to avoid the weapon exploding.

"Our life is love, and peace, and tenderness..." is a direct quote from Isaac Penington's message to Friends in Amersham (1667).

Jan Janszoon (c. 1570 – c. 1641) was also known as Reis Mourad the Younger. Born in Haarlem in the Low Countries, he was captured by Barbary Pirates and taken to Algiers as a prisoner. After serving as a pirate himself he became a notable member of the 'Salé Rovers' helping to establish the independent Republic of Salé where he was made President and Grand Admiral. He was later appointed Governor of Oualidia, a small town on Morocco's Atlantic coast.

Following Pellew's reappointment as C-in-C of the Mediterranean Station in 1815, the elderly admiral finally got his wish and was allowed to act against the Barbary Pirates. This culminated in August 1816 with the **Bombardment of Algiers**. A combined Anglo-Dutch fleet comprising 5 line-of-battleships, 10 frigates and some smaller vessels including bomb ketches, faced a smaller force of shipping and 224 land-based cannon. The action exhausted nearly all of Pellew's ammunition although, at its end, only four pieces of Algerian artillery were left standing. The Deylik of Algiers, Omar Agha, himself a former pirate, finally sued for peace and 3,000 European slaves were released. The trade in human flesh continued, however, only ending when the French invaded Algiers in 1830.

Alaric Bond
Herstmonceux 2022

Selected Characters

HMS *Tenacious*

Thomas King	Captain
Jack Cooper	First lieutenant
James Woodward	Second lieutenant
Michael Summers	Third lieutenant
Manton	Sailing master
Pocock	First marine lieutenant
Holmes	Second marine lieutenant
Robert Manning	Surgeon
Heather	Purser
Daniels	Midshipman
Joseph Morales	Carpenter
Patrick Regan	Gunner
Timothy Amon	Boatswain
Duckworth	Quartermaster
Sturridge	Gunroom cook
Downes	Able seaman
Stokes	Able seaman
Groom	Able seaman
Bovey	Able seaman
Healy	Able seaman
Early	Able seaman
Longdon	Able seaman
Lovemore	Able seaman

The *Gladiator*

Jeremiah Adams	Master
Caleb Palmer	Quaker passenger
Hannah Palmer	Quaker passenger, daughter of Caleb

HMS *Viper*

Duke	Captain of marines
Davis	1st Lieutenant of marines
Browning	2nd Lieutenant of marines

322

Tyler	2nd Lieutenant of marines
Dob	Purser
Cooke	Midshipman (volunteer)
Armfield	Midshipman (volunteer)
Ian Malcolm	Midshipman
Simon Williams	Midshipman
Edwards	Midshipman
John Balaam	Midshipman
Andrew Bewley	Loblolly boy

HMS *Caledonia*

Edward Pellew	Admiral and Commander-in-Chief (Mediterranean)
Edward Reynolds Sibly	Flag captain

The *Mary Anne*

Goodman	Master
White	First mate

and

Aimée Silva	Common-law wife of Thomas King
Millie	Aimée Silva's maidservant
Peter Palmer	Son of Caleb Palmer
Suzie Summers	Canadian married to Michael Summers
Hadj Ali Dey	Dey of Algiers
Ali bey ben Hamoudad	Bey of Mezmada
Mehmed	Advisor to the bey
Visser	Pirate captain

Selected Glossary

Able seaman	One who can hand, reef and steer and is well acquainted with the duties of a seaman.
Back	Wind change; anticlockwise.
Backed sail	One set in the direction for the opposite tack to slow a ship.
Backstays	Similar to shrouds in function, except they run from the hounds of the topmast, or topgallant, all the way to the deck. (Also a useful/spectacular way to return to deck for a topman.)
Backstays, running	A less permanent backstay, rigged with a tackle to allow it to be slacked to clear a gaff or boom.
Baltimore Clipper	A topsail schooner or brigantine traditionally built on the Mid-Atlantic seaboard of America.
Banyan Day	Monday, Wednesday and Fridays were normally considered such, when no meat would be issued.
Barky	*(Slang)* Seamen's affectionate name for their vessel.
Barrack Street	Area of Halifax known for tap houses and brothels.
Beaver	*(Slang)* A mid-morning snack – elevenses.
Bey	The governor of a district or province of the Barbary States.
Bilboes	Iron restraints placed about an offender's ankles, allowing him to be of some use, picking oakum, etc.

Binnacle	Cabinet on the quarterdeck that houses compasses, the deck log, traverse board, lead lines, telescope, speaking trumpet, etc.
Bird of passage	A passenger usually only present for one leg of a voyage.
Bitts	Stout horizontal pieces of timber, supported by strong verticals, that extend deep into the ship. These hold the anchor cable when the ship is at anchor.
Block	Article of rigging that allows pressure to be diverted or, when used with others, increased. Consists of a pulley wheel, made of *lignum vitae*, encased in a wooden shell. Blocks can be single, double (fiddle block), triple or quadruple. The main suppliers were Taylors, of Southampton.
Blücher	Gebhard Leberecht von Blücher, Prussian military officer.
Board	Before being promoted to lieutenant, midshipmen would be tested for competence by a board of post captains. Should they prove able they were then known as passed midshipmen, but could not assume the rank of lieutenant until appointed as such.
Boatswain	*(Pronounced Bo's'n)* The warrant officer superintending sails, rigging, canvas, colours, anchors, cables and cordage etc. committed to his charge.

Boom	Lower spar to which the bottom of a gaff sail is attached.
Bootneck	*(Slang)* Derogatory term for a Royal Marine. (American Marines are more usually referred to as leathernecks.)
Bower	A type of anchor.
Braces	Lines used to adjust the angle between the yards, and the fore and aft line of the ship. Mizzen braces and braces of a brig lead forward.
Brig	Two-masted vessel, square-rigged on both masts.
Bulkhead	A partition within the hull of a ship.
Bulwark	The planking or woodwork about a vessel above her deck.
Bumboat	A shore-based boat that supplies ships in harbour, usually unofficially. The name supposedly comes from the Dutch.
Burgoo	Meal (usually breakfast) made from oats, often served cold and occasionally sweetened with molasses.
Burthen	A measurement of a vessel's cubic capacity. (Originally based on the amount of wine that could be carried.)
Buzz	*(Slang)* Rumour or gossip.
Canister	Type of shot, also known as case. Small iron balls packed into a cylindrical case.

Carronade	Short cannon firing a heavy shot. Invented by Melville, Gascoigne and Miller in late 1770s and adopted from 1779. Often used on the upper deck of larger ships, or as the main armament of smaller.
Capel Court	Home of the London Stock Exchange since 1802.
Capstan	A man-powered device for raising anchors, or any heavy object. Capstans are horizontal, as opposed to the Windlass, which is vertical.
Cascabel	Part of the breech of a cannon.
Caulk	*(Slang)* To sleep. Also caulking, a process to seal the seams between strakes.
Channel	(When part of a ship) Projecting ledge that holds deadeyes from shrouds and backstays, originally chain-whales.
Clink	*(Slang)* Money.
Close-hauled	Sailing as near as possible into the wind.
Companionway	A staircase or passageway.
Conn/conning	The act of controlling or directing a vessel.
Course	A large square lower sail, hung from a yard, with sheets controlling and securing it.
Coup d'état	A rebellion.
Cove	*(Slang)* A man, occasionally a rogue.
Cull	*(Slang)* A man, usually a rogue.
Cutter	Fast, small, single-masted vessel with a sloop rig. Also a seaworthy ship's boat.

Dance the kipples	*(Slang)* Sexual intercourse.
Deadeyes	A round, flattish wooden block with three holes, through which a lanyard is reeved. Used to tension shrouds and backstays.
Dey	The overall ruler of (some) Barbary States – see also Pasha.
Driver	Large sail set on the mizzen. The foot is extended by means of a boom.
Dunnage	Officially the packaging around cargo. Also *(Slang)* baggage or possessions.
Dutch built	*(Slang)* Insult that insinuates something, or someone, is 'broad in the beam and buff bowed'.
Fall	The free end of a lifting tackle on which the men haul.
Fetch	To arrive at or reach a destination. Also the distance the wind blows across the water. The longer the fetch the bigger the waves.
Forereach	To gain upon or pass by another ship when sailing in a similar direction.
Forestay	Stay supporting the masts running forward, serving the opposite function of the backstay. Runs from each mast at an angle of about 45 degrees to meet another mast, the deck or the bowsprit.
Frumenty	A thick porridge sweetened with sugar or molasses and flavoured with cinnamon.

Futtock	A lower frame in the hull of a ship (similar to a rib). Futtock shrouds run down from the edge of a top to the mast.
Galliot	A small galley powered by sails or oars.
Gig	A ship's boat used mainly for carrying personnel.
Guineaman	A slaver.
Glass	Telescope. Also, hourglass: an instrument for measuring time (and hence, as slang, a period of time). Also a barometer.
Gingerbread	Common term for the ornate carvings common on larger ships' sterns.
Gunroom	In a third rate and above, a mess for junior officers. For lower rates, the gunroom is the equivalent of the wardroom.
Go about	To alter course, changing from one tack to the other.
Halyards	Lines which raise yards, sails, signals etc.
Hanger	A fighting sword, similar to a cutlass.
Hard tack	Ship's biscuit.
Hawse	Area in the bows where holes are cut to allow the anchor cables to pass through. Also used as a general term for bows.
Hawser	Heavy cable used for hauling, towing or mooring.

Headway	The amount a vessel is moved forward (rather than leeway: the amount a vessel is moved sideways) when the wind is not directly behind.
Heave to	Keeping a ship relatively stationary by backing certain sails in a seaway.
HEIC	Honourable East India Company.
Holder	One aboard ship who spends much of his time attending to stores in the hold.
Humours	Illness was thought to be caused by an imbalance of the four humours: Blood, Yellow Bile, Black Bile and Phlegm.
Idler	A man who, through his duty or position, does not stand a watch, but (usually) works during the day and can sleep throughout the night.
Interest	Backing from a superior officer or one in authority, useful when looking for promotion or a specific posting.
Jib-boom	Boom run out from the extremity of the bowsprit, braced by means of the martingale stay.
Jonathan	*(Slang)* An American.
John Company	*(Slang)* The East India Company.
Landsman	The rating of one who has no experience at sea.
Larboard	Left side of a ship when facing forward. Later replaced by 'port', which was previously used for helm orders.
Lascar	A seaman from India or South East Asia.

Leeward	The downwind side of a vessel.
Leeway	The amount a vessel is moved sideways by the wind (as opposed to headway, the forward movement, when the wind is directly behind).
Lighter	A large, open, flat-bottomed boat.
Liner	*(Slang)* Ship of the line (of battle). A third rate or above.
Lobscouse	A made dish, originally of fish but far more commonly preserved meat, onions and hard tack.
Lubber/lubberly	*(Slang)* Unseamanlike behaviour; as a landsman.
Martingale stay	Line that braces the jib-boom, passing from the end through the dolphin striker to the ship.
Mother Midnight	*(Slang)* A midwife.
Mothers' loll	*(Slang)* One overly protected.
Newky	*(Slang)* Newcastle.
Orlop	The lowest deck in a ship.
Packet/packet service	The HEIC maintained a number of fast sailing vessels to maintain communications and carry light cargo.
Pasha	The overall ruler of (some) Barbary States. See also Dey.
Paunch mat	A thick mat made from rope use to prevent the chaffing of masts and spars.
Plum pudding	The naval version was usually made with raisins.
Point blank	The range of a cannon when fired flat. (For a 32-pounder this would be roughly 1,000 feet.)
Polacre	A small vessel common to the Mediterranean.

Portable Soup	A boiled down mixture of beef and offal that could be reconstituted with water.
Pushing school	*(Slang)* A brothel.
Pusser	*(Slang)* Purser.
Pusser's dirk	*(Slang)* The traditional seaman's clasp knife consisting of an unpointed blade and a small marline spike (or fid). The tool remained unchanged for many years and even modern examples differ only slightly.
Quarterdeck	In larger ships the deck forward of the poop, but at a lower level. The preserve of officers.
Quoin	Triangular wooden block placed under the cascabel of a long gun to adjust the elevation.
Ratlines	Lighter lines, untarred and tied horizontally across the shrouds at regular intervals, to act as rungs and allow men to climb aloft.
Reef	A portion of sail that can be taken in to reduce the size of the whole.
Rigging	Tophamper; made up of standing (static) and running (moveable) rigging, blocks etc. Also *(slang)* clothes.
Rondy	*(Slang)* Rendezvous. A recruitment point and base for the press for men joining a ship.
Rosin	A naval store, its uses included waterproofing and reducing the harshness of lye soap.

Roundhouse	Private heads for the use of junior officers and the medical department.
Schooner	Small craft with two or three masts.
Scran	*(Slang)* Food.
Scupper	Waterway that allows deck drainage.
Scuttlebutt	A cask used for dispensing drinking water. Men would gather at it to talk.
Shambles	A slaughterhouse.
Sheet	A line that controls the foot of a sail.
Shellback	*(Slang)* An older seaman.
Shrouds	Lines supporting the masts athwartship (from side to side) which run from the hounds (just below the top) to the channels on the side of the hull.
Skylarking	Recreational exercise aloft, often including elaborate games of 'follow my leader' and the like. Skylarking was considered an excellent way to train topmen but would only be sanctioned during periods of calm weather.
Smoke	*(Slang)* To discover or reveal something hidden.
Spirketting	The interior lining or panelling of a ship.
Sprit sail	A square sail hung from the bowsprit yards, less used by 1793 as the function had been taken over by the jibs although the rigging of their yards helps to brace the bowsprit against sideways pressure.

Squarehead	*(Slang)* Derogatory term for a Dutchman.
Staysail	A quadrilateral or triangular sail with parallel lines hung from under a stay. Usually pronounced stays'l.
Steel's List	The forerunner to *The Navy List*. Founded by David Steel, a London publisher, it showed the seniority of every officer commissioned or otherwise in the Royal Navy, Royal Marines and Revenue Service. In addition, all commissioned ships were included together with their stations, the date of sailing for Post Office Packets and other information that must have proved invaluable to Britain's enemies.
Sternsheets	Part of a ship's boat between the stern and the first rowing thwart and used for passengers.
Stingo	*(Slang)* Beer.
Strake	A plank.
Suds (in the)	*(Slang)* To be in trouble or difficulties (occasionally drunk).
Tack	To turn a ship, moving her bows through the wind. Also a leg of a journey relating to the direction of the wind. If from starboard, a ship is on the starboard tack. Also the part of a fore and aft loose-footed sail where the sheet is attached, or a line leading forward on a square course to hold the lower part of the sail forward.
Taffrail	Rail around the stern of a vessel.

Tophamper	Literally any weight either on a ship's decks or about her tops and rigging, but often used loosely to refer to spars and rigging.
Toe link	Lower projection from a channel.
Traverse board	A small piece of wood that acted as a rough log during a watch.
Trick	*(Slang)* A period of duty.
Tye	Thick line or chain used when raising topsail and topgallant yards.
Veer	Wind change, clockwise.
Waist	Area of the main deck between the quarterdeck and forecastle.
Watch	Period of four (or in the case of a dogwatch, two) hours' duty. Also describes the two or three divisions of a crew.
Wearing	To change the direction of a square-rigged ship across the wind by putting its stern through the eye of the wind. Also, jibe – more common in a fore and aft rig.
Wherry	A small boat usually used for carrying passengers.
Whip	Light tackle usually consisting of a single block.
Windward	The side of a ship exposed to the wind.
Wiseacre	*(Slang)* A know-all; from the Dutch *wijsseggher*.

About the Author

Alaric Bond has written for various periodicals as well as television, radio and the stage but now focuses on historical nautical fiction with seventeen published novels, fourteen of which being in his acclaimed 'Fighting Sail' series.

He lives in Sussex, is married and has two far taller sons. Apart from researching nautical history he enjoys cycling (in gumboots, rather than lycra), sailing and carpentry as well as jazz, blues and dance band music from the thirties onwards. He also collects musical instruments and 78 rpm records.

www.alaricbond.com

About Old Salt Press

Old Salt Press is an independent press catering to those who love books about ships and the sea. We are an association of writers working together to produce the very best of nautical and maritime fiction and non-fiction. We invite you to join us as we go down to the sea in books. Visit the website for details of all Old Salt Press books:

www.oldsaltpress.com

The Latest Great Reading
from Old Salt Press

Rick Spilman
Evening Gray Morning Red

A young American sailor must escape his past and the clutches of the Royal Navy, in the turbulent years just before the American Revolutionary War. In the spring of 1768, Thom Larkin, a 17-year-old sailor newly arrived in Boston, is caught by Royal Navy press gang and dragged off to HMS *Romney*, where he runs afoul of the cruel and corrupt First Lieutenant. Years later, after escaping the Romney, Thom again crosses paths with his old foe, now in command HMS *Gaspee*, cruising in Narragansett Bay. Thom must finally face his nemesis and the guns of the *Gaspee*, armed only with his wits, an unarmed packet boat, and a sand bar.

V E Ulett
Blackwell's Homecoming

In a multigenerational saga of love, war and betrayal, Captain Blackwell and Mercedes continue their voyage in Volume III of Blackwell's Adventures. The Blackwell family's eventful journey from England to Hawaii, by way of the new and tempestuous nations of Brazil and Chile, provides an intimate portrait of family conflicts and loyalties in the late Georgian Age. Blackwell's Homecoming is an evocation of the dangers and rewards of desire.

Seymour Hamilton
Ellie: A Story from the World of The Astreya Trilogy

Ellie is a story about losing your way and finding it again. Ellie, the youngest navigator in the fleet, challenges the authority of her uncle Astreya, the Grand Commander. Only hours later, cannon shots cripple her boat, she falls overboard and is lost ashore. Ellie tries to return home to Matris, but unexpected friends and threatening foes intervene. As her uncle, sister, and cousins search for her, Ellie is forced to travel by foot, horseback, and land crawler to the Castle, where the Governor is fomenting war.

Ellie is the sixth book set in the world of The Astreya Trilogy..

337

Antoine Vanner
Britannia's Morass: The Dawlish Chronicles September - December 1884

1884: Florence Dawlish remains in Britain when her husband, Captain Nicholas Dawlish, leaves for service in the Sudan. She faces months of worry about him but she'll cope by immersing herself in welfare work for Royal Navy seamen's families at Portsmouth. It'll be a dull but worthy time . . .

. . . until the suicide of a middle-aged widow whom Florence respects. Left wealthy by her husband, this lady died a pauper, beggared within a few months, how and by whom, is not known. The widow's legal executor isn't interested and the police have other concerns. Lacking close family, she'll be soon forgotten. But not by Florence. Someone was responsible and there must be retribution. And getting justice will demand impersonation, guile and courage.

Alaric Bond
The Seeds of War
(The Fighting Sail Series)

1811 and the war with France continues although conflict of another kind is raging on America's Eastern Seaboard. For many years oppressive trade sanctions have soured Britain's relations with the newly formed United States; tensions rise further as seamen are illegally pressed and what had been a purely economic dispute soon turns into something far more deadly. Amid the conflict and confusion of fierce political debate, those aboard the frigate HMS Tenacious must also do battle with illegal slavery, powerful privateers, violent tropical storms and enemies that had once been the best of friends.

With vivid naval action and intense personal dynamics, The Seeds of War tells a gripping tale of loyalty, ambition and true camaraderie.

Linda Collison
Water Ghosts

Fifteen-year-old James McCafferty is an unwilling sailor aboard a traditional Chinese junk, operated as adventure-therapy for troubled teens. Once at sea, the ship is gradually taken over by the spirits of courtiers who fled the Imperial court during the Ming Dynasty, more than 600 years ago. One particular ghost wants what James has and is intent on trading places with him. But the teens themselves are their own worst enemies in the struggle for life in the middle of the Pacific Ocean. A psychological story set at sea, with historical and paranormal elements.

Joan Druett
Tupaia, Captain Cook's Polynesian Navigator

Tupaia sailed with Captain Cook from Tahiti, piloted the *Endeavour* about the South Pacific, and was the ship's translator. Lauded by Europeans as "an extraordinary genius", he was also a master navigator, a brilliant orator, an artist and mapmaker, and a devious politician. Winner of the New Zealand Post General Non-Fiction Prize.

Made in the USA
Middletown, DE
21 May 2022